Number

BLOOD EMPIRE

SELENA

Blood Empire

*Willow Heights Preparatory
Academy: The Exile*

Book Five

selena

Blood Empire
Copyright © 2021 Selena
Unabridged First Edition

All rights reserved. No part of this book may be reproduced or transmitted in any form or by any means, electronic or mechanical, including photocopying, recording, or by any information storage and retrieval system, without the express written permission of the publisher, except in cases of a reviewer quoting brief passages in a review.

This book is a work of fiction. Names, characters, places, and incidents are used fictitiously. Any resemblance to actual persons, living or dead, business establishments, and events are entirely coincidental. Use of any copyrighted, trademarked, or brand names in this work of fiction does not imply endorsement of that brand.

Published in the United States by Selena and Speak Now.

ISBN-13: 978-1-955913-05-8

Cover © Quirah Casey of Temptation Creations

BLOOD EMPIRE

"The past is not dead. In fact, it's not even past."

—William Faulkner

SELENA

one

Harper Apple

When I walk out of my house Monday morning, I'm zero percent surprised to see a black Range Rover parked in my driveway. It doesn't fill me with fear or dread this time, though. I'm not sure what I feel, and I don't want to think about it when I have to get to school and deal with the drama I inadvertently started last week.

I shake my head and make my way past my own car to where Royal's is parked. He rolls down his window and flashes me a smug grin. "Let's go, Cherry Pie."

"What are you doing here?"

"Taking you to school."

I sigh. "I thought we went over this. The party didn't change anything. The sex was a mistake. And you're supposed to be leaving me alone."

SELENA

"Yeah, we tried that, and it didn't work out so well," he says. "So now we're trying things my way. Get in."

"We also tried things your way," I point out. "How'd *that* work out?"

I fix him with a flat stare, forcing myself not to examine his face or show any emotion. In truth, I'm so proud I want to crow like a fucking rooster. A wide bandage covers the entire bridge of his nose and part of his cheeks, and he has stitches in his lower lip, which is swollen even more than the top one. Both his eyes are black, and the left side of his face is completely discolored. I've never seen him anywhere near that beat up, and I know he fights at the Slaughterpen every Saturday night.

I did that, and I'm not sorry.

"Get in the car," he says. "You know you're going to."

"I do?"

I roll my eyes and circle around the car, telling myself the smile on my face is solely a result of the evidence of how much I hurt him.

"See?" he says, shifting into gear when I climb into the passenger side. "That wasn't so hard, was it?"

He reaches over and lays a hand on my knee as we start down Mill Street, his fancy car looking even more out of place than mine does.

"Uh, what do you think you're doing?" I ask, plucking his hand off my leg and pushing it back at him. "I forgave you. That doesn't mean I want to be with you."

He gives me a look. "Okay."

"In fact, this forgiveness thing is more of an ongoing process than just saying it and it's magically done. Just because I'm forgiving you doesn't mean I'll forget or act like it never happened."

"I don't expect you to."

"Good," I say. "Because I still hate you, and I don't trust you for a second."

"Ditto."

SELENA

We drive in silence for a few minutes. What I said is true—I forgave him, but I'm not ready to act like nothing happened. But I've barely thought about *why* it happened, what I did to him. I've thought even less about how it hurt him, because on the surface, it didn't. Now I know why Mr. D never divulged his secrets, why he never wanted to help me take down the Dolces. Nothing came of me leaking Royal's secret, except now his brothers know.

But that doesn't mean it didn't hurt him in other ways. Just because his reputation didn't suffer and his family didn't pay, that doesn't mean Royal didn't. I hurt him. He trusted me in some way, even if he never trusted me enough to spill the secret himself. He trusted me with his heart, and I fucking sold it down the river to the highest bidder.

I turn to him before we reach the school. "Did you talk to Baron?" I ask.

After the party on Friday, we went to talk to Preston and get the DNA results. Afterwards, Royal barely said a word as he took me back to his car. Obviously, someone convinced him to go to the doctor between then and now, but we didn't talk all weekend. I figured he had family shit to work out, and it's not like we're dating. Still, I'd be lying if I said I didn't check my phone a time or two to see if he'd text after our hookup.

Royal glances at me. "No," he says, returning his attention to the road.

"Why not?"

"Because I haven't decided how I want to kill him."

"You don't kill people," I remind him. "You said death is easy. Life is suffering."

"Some people don't have the capacity to suffer."

"Are you serious?" I ask, watching him carefully. My heart starts pounding in my chest as I study his grim face while he stares straight ahead. I can't tell if he's really thinking about what he's saying. Not that I've never heard of someone our age murdering someone. There are gang shootings on my side of town on occasion, but it's so far outside my reality, outside what I associate with, that it's hard to comprehend an eighteen-year-old just going around murdering people who wronged him.

SELENA

"He did all that to you," Royal says quietly. "It's his fault."

"Part of it," I admit. "A lot of it, even. But he gave me the scholarship that got me here. I'd never even have met you if it weren't for him. He brought us both to the party on Friday, knowing we wouldn't talk otherwise. And… He was my friend, sort of."

I watch Royal's reaction from the corner of my eye. It makes me feel all kinds of pathetic to admit this, but Mr. D was the only friend I had at times. I remember last Christmas, when he was the only one who texted to say Merry Christmas. I imagined some lonely old guy at the time, someone thinking of me because he was just as lonely. When I thought it was Preston, that made sense. Now, I imagine Baron surrounded by family up in New York, stepping away from his brothers and taking the time to text me. I'm surprised he even thought of me. Royal didn't text, and we'd been fucking for months by then.

I don't know how to feel about all this. Baron is so much worse in person than he is online. Mr. D was a creepy pervert. Baron is… I'm not sure what he is. He's complicated as fuck, I know that much. But I can't sort out my feelings on one car ride to school.

The mind is a funny thing. Feelings don't just vanish the instant someone hurts you, like they should. They take as long to disappear as they do to be created—maybe longer. It's like realizing I still loved Royal, even after he destroyed me. My love didn't disappear. It just twisted into something else, something malformed and toxic and unpredictable, into hatred and betrayal and… Understanding.

Royal pulls into my parking spot, the one next to Colt's Ridgeline. I can see my friend sitting inside, but I turn to Royal.

"You can't just murder your own brother in cold blood. You don't want to live with that on your conscience. And I don't want you to. You shouldn't have to."

"Why not?" he asks flatly. "I murdered my sister."

My heart twists inside my chest. "Royal…"

"What?" he snaps.

SELENA

This time, I'm the one who reaches out. I lay a hand on his knee. "That's not true."

He snorts and brushes my hand away. "Fuck off, Harper. You don't know shit about my sister."

"I know plenty about her," I say, arching a brow. "You've told me."

"Guess I forgot to mention I killed her," he says. "Now you know."

"I know she drowned," I say. "You weren't even there."

"Get out of my car."

"Okay. If that's what you want."

"It is."

We sit there a minute, and then I climb out of the car. I've barely gotten the door closed when he roars out of the parking lot without a backwards glance.

I've been so busy dealing with my own fucked-upness that I forgot for a moment how fucked up he is. I've let myself be caught up in Dolce fever so many times—in the excitement and danger that surrounds him; in my own crushing desire for a pre-formed insta-family to have my back; in his insatiable, suffocating need for me; even in his single-minded pursuit of getting me back. It's intoxicating.

He's intoxicating.

But he's also a real person, one with his own shit going on that has nothing to do with me. Since he found out I was alive, he's moved worlds to prove himself to me. He bought me food, furniture, and a fucking car. He gave me power and let me use it the way I wanted, not deciding for me. He delivered my revenge on a silver platter. He gave me a scholarship so I can blow out of this town when this year is over. He opened up to me, and he sat beside the man he says assaulted him because I told him it was the only way to be with me.

Royal has done everything he could to take care of me and heal me these last few months. I don't know if I'll ever completely recover, but I've healed enough to recognize that he hasn't. That he's done all this for me but nothing for himself. He's helped me, but no one has helped him. He's still the same fucked up man who dragged me into that swamp and let his brothers punish me.

"Harper," someone calls, and I turn to see Gloria mincing toward me on her high heels. She gives me a little wave and a beaming smile, but I can see the wariness in her eyes.

"Hey, Lo," I say, waiting for her to join me. Maybe I should be pissed at her for blowing Royal at the party the other night, but I can't afford to make enemies. I need all the friends I can get, and even if she won't join me at our lunch table, if people see their Queen B seeking me out, it makes me seem more desirable. I'll take any edge I can get.

A car door slams behind me, and I turn to see Dixie standing outside Colt's truck, smoothing her skirt down. Her hair is mussed, and her lipstick is smeared. Colt circles the truck and slings an arm over her shoulders, grinning at us and not bothering to fix his untucked shirt.

"Hey, ladies," he says. "Or, should I say *lady*? From what I hear of the party on Friday night, Lo can't exactly call herself that."

Gloria stiffens, drawing herself up. "Who let this slathering beast out of his cage?"

"This animal can't be tamed," Colt says, squeezing Dixie. "Isn't that right, babe?"

Dixie's pale skin goes bright red when we catch her doing up a button she missed on her shirt. "Um, sure," she squeaks.

Gloria scoffs. "Get a room. The parking lot's not the place for your lewd behavior."

"Right," Colt drawls. "Should we save it for Gideon's next party?"

"You weren't even there," Gloria says, tossing her hair back. "And you should know better than to believe every rumor you hear."

With that, she turns and flounces away. I fall into step with Colt and Dixie as we head toward the building, a few steps behind.

"I just have one question," Colt calls ahead to Gloria. "When Royal finally pried your legs open with his crowbar, did an icicle fall out?"

SELENA

Lo pauses long enough for us to catch up before fixing Colt with a withering glare. "Your obsession with what's been inside me is getting old," she says. "Maybe you should worry less about me and more about the fact you can't even remember where your dick's been."

"Isn't it too early to start this?" I ask, shaking my head. "It's not even eight in the morning. Can't we have breakfast before you start sniping at each other?"

"And waste all my good ammunition?" Colt says with a grin. "Never. Besides, Dixie's already had her sausage and gravy this morning."

"Colt," Dixie squeals, turning even brighter red this time.

"I feel nauseous," Gloria says. "I'm going to go lie down in the nurse's office."

"See if she can sew your legs closed again while you're there," Colt calls after her as she veers off. I see her snag Quinn by the elbow and drag her into the bathroom, probably to hold her hair back—or more likely, to order her to tell Dixie to keep her man under control.

"What's your problem with each other, anyway?" I ask Colt as we head toward my locker.

"She's the Dolces' little lapdog," he says. "And she's a fucking hypocrite. Everyone knows she let all three of them run trains on her, and probably their dad, too. Then she goes around calling other girls sluts for less."

I narrow my eyes at Dixie. "She calls you a slut?"

"Oh, no," Dixie assures me. "We're friends. You know that."

"No," Colt says slowly. "She won't fuck with you because you could ruin her. You have more influence than her, and she can't do shit about it, so she doesn't bully you. That doesn't mean she's your friend."

"It's not like that," Dixie says. "We both have our place here. We're not in competition."

"Then who were you talking about?" I ask Colt. "Who did she call a slut?"

"She called *you* a slut all last year," he reminds me, leaning on the locker next to mine while I open it to get my books.

"Oh," I say, nodding slowly. "You don't like her because she helped bully your sister."

"The question is, why do *you* like her?" Colt asks. "She's a mean, spiteful bitch who hooked up with your man the other day."

"Whoa," I say, holding up a hand. "First off, Royal is in no way my man. He can hook up with whoever the fuck he wants, and so can I. And secondly, I'm getting tired of being the mediator between your family and everyone else. Lo is my friend. You're my friend. Can you just be civil?"

Colt gives a little grunt and pushes off the lockers. "Only for you, Appleteeny," he says, reaching out to ruffle my hair. "'Cause you'll kick my ass if I don't."

"Damn right," I say, closing my locker and grinning at him. "Now, who's hungry?"

Josie closes her locker and joins us as we make our way to the café.

"You really don't care that Gloria and Royal hooked up at the party?" Dixie asks.

I shrug. "Why would I care? I'm not with Royal."

That's not entirely true. I do care. I'm jealous as fuck.

But I can't be mad at either of them. I genuinely like Lo. Yeah, she's Royal's comfort fuck, but that's all it is. They're friends, and when I told him to hook up with someone else if he wanted my forgiveness, he did it. Not for her, but to prove to me he would do anything for me. Of course he'd go to Lo, the only girl he trusts, when he was hurting. He couldn't exactly come to me after I said that. And she'd just been dumped, not to mention her brother died, so she was hurting, too. That's what fuck buddies are there for. If Royal stuck his dick in her, that's on me, not either of them.

When we pass the mess of flowers and cards still in front of Dawson's old locker, I look away. I shiver when I think of the emotionless way Royal talked about killing his own brother this morning. I'm not sure if he could really do that, but when I remember Preston's words on the bridge, I can't help but wonder. Is Royal capable of murder?

After he told me I could have my revenge, did he decide it wasn't enough, and take it for me? Or was

Dawson wracked with guilt for what he'd done to me, and seeing me at the Slaughterpen that night pushed him over the edge?

Either way, I'm part of the reason he's dead.

I don't want to think about that, though. I didn't kill him. I'd barely spoken to him before that night in the swamp. And I didn't do anything but hit him and step on his balls afterwards. He deserved worse. Maybe he was just going along with the twins, but that was his choice. He chose to rape me.

If he felt too guilty about it to continue living, that proves he has a conscience and knew better.

I will not feel guilty for his guilt.

I can't stop thinking about it all morning, though. It's one thing to know someone who's taken their life and another to be one of the causes for it. I fucking hate that I can't just despise him the way I could if he were alive. I hate that I find myself wondering how he really died, if anyone could have stopped it, what he thought in his last moments. Did my words, my actions at the Slaughterpen, push him over the edge? Or did they push Royal over the edge?

By lunch time, I want to escape to the bleachers and smoke with Colt, but I know that's a luxury I can no longer afford. Claiming the crown means showing up, just like I did at the football game and the party last week. It means coming back to school right after your brother died so no one else can swoop in when you're vulnerable. One moment of weakness, and it could all be gone.

So I march into the café and take a seat at the protest table, where we sat last week. My stomach is tight and shaking as I sit there alone, waiting to see who will show up for me today. Gideon is the key, the one holding this all up from collapsing into a house of cards, and I turned him down at his party on Friday.

But it's not Gideon who has my stomach dropping out when I see him, so I have to grab the edge of the table to keep from crumpling to the floor in a heap. It's not Gideon who makes my head swim and my mind go completely blank when our eyes meet.

It's Baron.

SELENA

He strolls toward my table, a sucker tucked into his cheek, his little serving girl rushing behind him with his plate. And for one terrifying second, I forget what it's all for. I forget everything except that he's Mr. D.

I wasn't prepared for how it would hit me when I see him. It's worse than when I saw them at the Slaughterpen, when Royal prepared them for me.

Now, the shame of what I did slams into me with a force that takes my breath and leaves me gasping for air like a fish that flopped out of the tank and is drowning from the inside out. I told him everything. Not just Royal's secrets, but mine.

I told him my dreams, how I wanted to get out of this town, how I wanted to matter. I told him my childish fantasy of taking down his family. I imagine how funny he thought that was, how he must have laughed at my ridiculous bravado, how much he must have enjoyed toying with me, letting me think he was a Darling. I told him more than that, though. I told him intimate details of my sex life, about how good Royal fucked me, how I screamed and came for him.

I want to spontaneously combust and disappear in a blaze of fire when I think about all I've said to him, the details I've revealed. I remember him saying he had to live vicariously through my sex stories. I thought he was in prison or something, not that he was just picturing that it was him fucking me instead of Royal. And when he got tired of waiting, he made sure Royal dumped me so he could have his turn, so he could fuck me himself instead of imagining it.

He smirks at me as he walks by, but he doesn't speak to me. He sits at his new table, the new king with another table pushed up next to his, where the Dolce girls sit. I try to control my heart rate. I remind myself that a wrecking ball is not the only way to destroy a house. Royal didn't confront him. He's waiting. I can wait, too.

I take comfort in the knowledge that Baron doesn't know we found out his secret. He's still Mr. D, still has all the information I gave him. But he doesn't know that I'm aware of that, or that Royal is. He's just going to sit on the information I gave him last year and do nothing with it, because he doesn't want to take down anyone but me, and he already did that. It's over for him. He'll just gloat and enjoy the fact that he knows me better than probably anyone in the world except Royal.

But if it's over, what was he going to ask me when he contacted me the other day?

Before I can spiral too far, Dixie and Colt arrive with Josie. The café starts to buzz when they sit down with me. A minute later, Magnolia skips over in a frilly pink skirt, Doc Martens with pink hearts on them, and a tiny tee.

"Good thing I've practiced intermittent fasting," she says, edging into her chair.

I tense when I see Rylan and Amber heading our direction from the food line. She's staring at her plate, her face half hidden by her hair, but she doesn't look too happy about joining us. Rylan stops at our table and just stands there glaring daggers at the popular table. I turn to see Gloria, who's still sitting with the Dolce boys, studiously ignoring him and talking to Duke.

Rylan yanks out a chair at our table, banging the legs against the other chairs, and slams his plate down. I've never talked to the guy, but from what Gloria's told me, I'm not missing out on much. She said he'd be pissed if he found out she had a milkshake with Colt or if she joined the Swans. But hell, I'd be a hypocrite if I held that against him. Royal just about killed Colt for hanging out with me.

Plus, there's power in numbers. I was ready to let Cotton 'the Predator' Montgomery sit with us last week. Just because Rylan's a jealous bitch doesn't mean he can't advance for our cause.

"Welcome to the protest," Magnolia says, standing to grab two more chairs to round out the table at eight. Amber takes one and slips into it with the air of someone who wants to disappear. Clearly her brother convinced her to join when she's got zero interest in it.

"This is where people who hate Gloria sit, right?" Rylan asks.

"You're in the right place," Josie says, holding up a hand and leaning across the table to high-five him. I catch Lo's wounded look from the next table, and I know she saw it, too.

SELENA

"Actually, can we not make this about your breakup drama?" I interject. "Dixie and I are friends with Lo. This is more about disrupting the social order and protesting the power the Dolce boys have—and beyond that, the power the founding families have over the administration."

Rylan glowers at me and then jerks his chin at Colt. "Aren't you from a founding family?"

"Yep," Colt drawls, crossing his tattooed arms across his chest and leaning back in his chair. "But what've I got to lose? I'm a peon like the rest of y'all."

Amber glances at Magnolia.

"You are, too?" Rylan asks her.

"I'm a Darling," she says, pursing her pouty lips and looking down her nose at him. "What about it?"

"Oh, yeah," Josie says. "Why are you here? What's in it for you?"

Magnolia shrugs and raises her chin defiantly. "I believe in the cause."

Josie narrows her eyes. "But you'll be Queen B next year," she says, looking Magnolia up and down. "Look at you."

"She's right," Dixie says. "The Dolces are seniors, and that's the last of them. They only have that one family. You have cousins and a brother… Even if your family doesn't have the power it used to in this town, between your name and your looks, you'll still be the most popular girl in your grade."

Magnolia crosses her arms, but unlike Colt's relaxed position, she looks defiant. "A lot can happen in a year."

I watch their exchange, finding new admiration for the stubborn little freshman. Looking at her, it's hard to forget how young she is. She's got curves, but she's still small, the kind of small that girls are before they're done growing. Her cheeks are round, her eyelashes spidery and long, coated with black mascara that makes her big eyes stand out. She looks like a living doll, perfect and innocent, and I can't help but wonder if that's a Darling trait, if that's why people associate the word *Doll* with that family.

SELENA

But thinking about her age—she's only fourteen—makes me reconsider her joining us. I was so caught up in just filling the table on Friday that I didn't question why she'd put herself in this situation. If anything, she's made herself a target by openly defying the Dolces. *I've* made her a target by allowing her to join us.

Shit.

As if the Dolces need another reason to go after the Darlings. They already threatened Magnolia last year, and I've seen Duke talking to her multiple times since I came back to Willow Heights. I thought she was just some dumb, giggly freshman, flattered by his attention and flirting with him. Now I'm not so sure. Young or not, she's definitely not a dumb kid.

A hush falls over the room, and I turn my attention to follow everyone else's. Gideon Delacroix has just emerged from the food line with DeShaun, their serving girls behind them. It's just the two of them, so at least I know they're not in attack mode. Duke and Baron would be in for any mayhem like that. But it's just Quinn and some other girls behind them.

My heart sinks when Gideon laughs at something DeShaun says.

So, I guess that was it. He wasn't about our cause, after all. Not unless it came with a built-in girlfriend. Hell, for all I know, Baron put him up to it to discredit us, to make it look like it was about some petty high school dating drama.

But whatever. We may have lost him, but we gained two new members of the Dolce Defectors.

When they reach our table, DeShaun gives me a polite nod and keeps walking, heading for his seat next to Duke as usual. Gideon stops at our table, though. I stiffen, noticing then that he has a plate in his hands, too. My first thought is that he's going to dump it over one of us. Instead, he sets it down and pulls out the last chair. He motions for his serving girl, and that's when I see that Quinn and a handful of others are still with them. I look around in confusion. Quinn already told me she wouldn't join us.

She hurries over, sets a plate in front of Dixie, and scurries away. Gideon's server sets a plate in front of

SELENA

Colt, and I finally realize what's happening. I sit there frozen, suspended in some surreal world while my own serving girl, the one who carried my food for me when I was Royal's plaything, sets a plate in front of me, a plate with a little of everything, because she knows what I like after serving me for half of last year.

Two other girls I vaguely recognize as friends of Quinn's deliver plates to Josie and Magnolia, rushing away before we can ask what's going on.

"Thank you," I call after them, then turn to my friends. "What the fuck was that?"

"Can't fight the good fight on an empty stomach," Gideon says, giving me a quick wink before starting in on his chicken.

"You did this?" I ask, diving into my own food. I still get a panicky feeling about skipping meals, even though I no longer worry about whether I'll have dinner. Food hasn't been a guaranteed part of my days for long enough that I take it for granted.

"I can't take credit for the idea," he says, glancing at his old table. I wonder who's sitting there while secretly supporting us. Gloria, who I saw talking to Quinn this morning? DeShaun, who once told me he liked me but he'd put his boys first, who turned the tide at the Swans vote, who walked over here with Gideon? Or Cotton, who might be one of those secret Darling supporters Colt mentioned when I first came to Willow Heights?

All I know is that someone there is supporting us, which gives me hope. They're too scared to come out and join us now, but they're risking the Dolce boys' wrath if they're caught. And those girls who crossed the picket line to bring us food… They have a target on their backs now, too. How am I going to protect all of them, and Magnolia, when I couldn't even protect myself?

SELENA

two

Royal Dolce

"Get in the car," I say, throwing open the passenger door for Harper.

She sighs and gives me a look. "Are you going to do this every day?"

"I drove you this morning," I remind her. "How else are you going to get home?"

"I have friends, you know," she says, but she climbs in.

"Yeah, well, you're not going to want to miss this."

I thought about it, about how to do what I'm about to do. Whether to involve Harper. In a way, she's so fucking innocent. She may have lived a hard, poor life, but she's never been around the kind of men in my family—until now. Her life is so normal, so simple, so devoid of murder and mutilation. But letting her go again is not an option, so she's just going to have to learn to live with our kind.

I pull out of her parking spot and up to the front of the lot, right in the walkway, next to Baron's Tesla. Some kids give me dirty looks as they skirt around the Rover, making their way between cars in the lot now that their usual path is blocked.

Fuck them. They can go around.

"What are you doing?" Harper asks.

"We're taking a little drive," I answer.

"What?" she asks, grabbing for the door handle.

"Harper," I say, catching her other hand. I should have thought about her more and the twins less. I soften my voice, reaching for her face. I grip her chin between my thumb and finger and turn her face to me. "Hey. We're just going to talk to Baron. You want to be there, don't you?"

She swallows, her blue eyes searching mine. "That's it?"

SELENA

"That's it. I promise." I lean in, still holding her gaze, waiting for her to beat my fucking face in like she did last time, or at least tell me I'm full of shit and she'd never believe a promise from my lying lips.

Instead, she leans toward me, and I'm way too fucked by the knowledge that she's somehow allowing herself to trust me. After what I did, she can still make that decision. She must be a fucking saint. That, or she has the willpower of a god. There's no way in hell I'd trust a Darling. I don't trust her for a second, and she's not even a Darling.

But then, she did worse to me than any of the Darling girls.

I press my lips to hers anyway. I should have known she wasn't a Darling. Those girls are weak and plain. They're sheep, too worried about their reputations to put up a real fight. Harper, she's as manipulative as she is addictive, sly as a fox, poisonous as a snake. I thought it was because she wasn't raised in that toxic family, that she'd had to be smart to survive growing up like she did, but now I know the truth. It's in her nature, in her blood.

I can't help but admire that in her, the determination and strength, her willpower. It means she can feel something for a man she shouldn't, that she can forgive even me when she sets her mind to it. It's impressive as fuck.

More than that, I'm relieved I didn't fall for a Darling, that I can properly hate and destroy them with no remorse, that this is something separate from that.

Duke pulls open her door, and I register the way her whole body goes rigid, the little tremor that goes through her, and the way she instinctively shrinks toward me. It's that last one that about fucking kills me. I know it's not a conscious thought on her part, that it was an involuntary response to his nearness. If she had time to think about it, she'd remember that I didn't protect her, that I can't be counted on to keep her safe.

"Get in the back," I say, glaring past Harper at him.

Confusion crosses his face as he stands outside the passenger door, wondering why Harper's in his spot.

"It's okay," she says. "I can sit in the back."

"Don't move," I growl, still glaring at my brother.

He shrugs, still looking confused, and closes the door.

"I don't mind," Harper says quietly. "I don't want them behind me."

Duke opens the back door, tosses his bag in, and climbs in. "Where we going?"

"Taking a drive," I say, opening the glove box. "Where's Baron?"

I set my G19 in Harper's lap, and she tenses. "What the fuck, Royal? We're at a school."

"That's why I put it on your lap. Don't wave it around, and you'll be fine."

"Why are you giving me a gun?"

"I told you this morning."

"Uh, I wouldn't mind knowing the answer to that question, too," Duke says. "What the fuck, man?"

"If she wants to shoot you, you'll shut up and take it," I snap at him. "She has a right to feel safe."

"What the fuck is going on?" he asks. "Why are you keeping shit from us?"

"Because I don't know what you're keeping from me." I fucking hate that I can't trust my own brothers, but that's something I'll never do again after this summer. I am the only fucking person in the world I can trust. Not them, not the rest of my family, not Harper. That's something she had right all along, relying on only herself and never letting anyone else in.

Only Mr. D got to know the real Harper, got to hear her secrets and know what she really thought. I'd rather it had been a Darling than my own brother.

Duke doesn't say anything. He fucked up, and he knows better than to defend himself.

Baron approaches, tosses his bag into his car, and then climbs into the back of the Rover without a word. Duke likes to be up front, to be part of things, to have the attention. Baron likes to sit back and watch. I glance at him in the rearview as we pull out of the lot. He's taking in everything, putting the pieces together as he takes out a sucker and slowly begins to unwrap it.

Harper's holding the gun now, pointing it at the floor between her feet. So she doesn't trust me—not entirely.

Not when she's in the car with me and my brothers. She's ready to shoot, probably running through the different scenarios in her mind, deciding which one she'd take out first.

It's good to see her ready to defend herself instead of offering to let us kill her this time.

"What are we doing?" Baron asks when I turn onto the road to the bridge.

"Are you going to shoot us?" Duke asks.

"If you give me a reason," Harper says.

"We're going to talk first," I say. "Then we'll see."

"Talk about what?" Baron asks.

"That's a good question," I say. "Since you'll be doing the talking."

I pull onto the shoulder and shut off the car before turning to face my brothers in the back seat. Duke still looks lost, but Baron might be catching on. It's hard to tell with him.

"Why here, though?" Duke asks. "This place, man…"

"Get out of the car," I order.

Harper gets out first. My brothers hesitate, probably remembering the last time we came here with a friend. Just like that time, they know there's no use in fighting. After a pause, they glance at each other and then slowly climb out of the car. I get out, too.

I go around the front and stand next to Harper, facing my brothers. She holds the gun in both hands, pointed at the ground.

Baron takes the sucker out of his mouth. "What's this about?"

He's not one to waste time.

"Let's do this on the bridge," I say.

No one argues. We walk onto the bridge, my brothers in front of us. With the gun in Harper's hand, it strikes me that they're probably fucking terrified right now. If I don't know them, they don't know me. They don't know what the monster will do. Even I don't know that. He's under control right now, but they don't know that.

I give the order, and we stop in the middle of the bridge. Baron watches us, his eyes bright with curiosity. Maybe he's not scared. Nothing scares the psycho.

"We know you're Mr. D," I say.

Baron hesitates, his gaze moving back and forth between us. Then he nods slightly.

"Okay."

"What?" Duke demands, turning to him. "Those messages were from *you?* You're the old guy Harper was texting?"

Baron shrugs. "What about it?"

"Dude," Duke says, shaking his head. "Why didn't you tell me? You knew all that stuff about her and Royal?"

"Why didn't you tell *me?*" I ask. "She was trying to destroy our family."

"You weren't thinking straight," Baron says flatly. "I was looking out for you. For us. Our family."

"Then why didn't you tell us what she was planning?"

He shrugs one shoulder. "I had it under control."

"You had me under control," Harper says quietly. "If you knew what I was planning, you could keep an eye on me, make sure nothing ever came of it even when I found out about Royal and those women. You could redirect me when you didn't like what I was doing."

Baron raises his brows and rocks back on his heels. "Something like that."

"Did you know she wasn't a Darling?" I ask.

His gaze snaps to me. "What?"

"She's not a Darling. Did you know?"

His eyes narrow. "Bullshit. I found the letter from her mom to the grandfather Darling."

"Her mom's a junkie and a liar," I point out. "She was trying to get money out of him."

"Dad got a DNA test," Baron argues.

I shake my head, watching him wrestle with this. "It was forged."

"Or maybe the one she gave you was forged," Baron says, tossing the sucker over the edge with a disgusted look in my direction. "You know she's a liar. You know what she was planning. She's still probably planning it. We don't know anymore because I lost access to her. You should thank me for finding out all that stuff."

"You lied to me," I say flatly.

"And her?" he asks. "Just because she almost died, now you suddenly trust her?"

"She has no reason to lie," I say.

"How about, so we won't try to kill her?" he demands. "Or so she can take down our family, like she always wanted."

"I'm not lying," Harper says. "One look at me and you should have known. Aren't you supposed to be the smart science guy? You should know how genetics work."

"Where'd you get a DNA test?" he asks. "From the Dollar Store?"

"From Preston," she says flatly.

Baron chuckles. "You believe Preston Darling? And here I was starting to think you weren't so dumb after all."

"I believe him over you," she says. "He had no reason to lie. Your dad did."

Baron leans back against the side of the bridge and crosses his arms, turning his attention to me. "You believe this?"

"Yes," I say. "Dad wanted to keep us off the Delacroixs, including Lindsey and Preston, while he worked on the casino deal. We all started out thinking she was a Darling, but when he found out she wasn't, he kept it to himself. Harper was as good a means to distract us as any."

"She was keeping us pretty distracted," Duke admits, leaning back next to Baron. He probably doesn't even notice that he's mirroring his twin exactly. It's one of those things they do unconsciously, like the twin telepathy looks they exchange, that show they're still part of the same whole. Maybe that's what went wrong with the twins in this family. Maybe there's only one soul to go around.

"I want an explanation," Harper says, glaring at my brothers and lifting the gun a bit, pointing at their feet instead of the ground.

"A man has a right to protect his family," Baron says. "You were scheming on us."

"Did you know?" she asks, turning to Duke.

He grits his teeth and glances at Baron.

SELENA

"No," Baron says. "He didn't know. Someone who works for Dad saw the letters from your mom before we knew who you were. We tracked her down, and then found out who you were, and I hacked into the FHS computers to talk to you. As soon as you made an account on *OnlyWords*, I hacked into it and turned your location on so we could follow you."

"I know all that," she says.

"Then what do you want to know?" he asks.

"I don't know," she admits. "I guess… Why?"

"Why what?" Baron asks, like he genuinely doesn't know. The guy is smart—criminally so—but sometimes he misses the obvious things.

"Why me?" she asks. "Why take it so far? Why give me a scholarship? And why pretend it was someone else when you told Royal?"

Baron braces his hands on the railing beside him. "Why not? At first, we were just going to fuck with you a little. We got that video, and we figured we'd release it at FHS, ruin your reputation, and move on to the next

Darling. Dad was the one who said we should give you a scholarship."

"So it wasn't just you," Harper says, nodding.

"I was Mr. D," Baron says. "Dad just pulled some strings, got them to add an extra scholarship. He's the one who brought you to our school."

"To keep us off Lindsey," I say.

He shrugs. "Sure."

"But you were the one talking to me all that time?" Harper asks.

"Yeah. I figured I'd fuck with you a little more, probably let my brothers in on it, since you were at our school. It was never supposed to go past the video leaking. We figured we'd just leak it at Willow Heights and ruin your reputation there instead of at your old school. It's not like we murder the Darlings. We just wanted to ruin you, and that seemed like enough. It could have just ended there, with you being a social pariah like Colt."

"But?" she asks.

SELENA

"But Royal got some idea in his head about you being his." He turns to me. "You're the one who cut us out. We never cut you out. You were there all along with Mabel."

"I didn't give a fuck about Mabel," I snap.

"We let you in on it," he says, glaring back at me. "And you kept us from going after her."

"She left," I say bluntly. "She didn't want to be here. I pulled her out of the river for you."

"You wouldn't let us follow her."

We stare at each other a long minute. "You're in school," I say finally. "Yeah, you weren't going to drop out to chase some Darling snake across the country. You can go find her as soon as you graduate. I don't give a fuck about her."

"If we couldn't have her, why should you have Harper?" he asks. "Why did you get to keep her when we couldn't keep Mabel?"

"So that's it?" I ask. "You're fucking petty, you know that?"

"I kept track of your bitch when you didn't," Baron says. "She was pulling shady shit all along, and you were too blinded by your dick to notice. So don't give me shit. I'm not the bad guy here. I was doing your job all along—looking out for our family. Looking out for you."

"I didn't ask you to keep tabs on my girl."

"Someone had to."

I'm so pissed I want to put the asshole in the river, but I won't. I've already killed one sibling, and I won't lose more of my family than I have. Especially when I know that he's speaking the truth. I got wrapped up in her, lost my head. I lost sight of the goal. Baron never did.

"You lied to us," Harper says. "You would have gotten me killed."

He shrugs. "We thought you were a Darling. We don't normally kill them, but it's not like we care if they die. And after what you did? You got off easy."

"But why pretend to be someone else? A Darling, no less. You let me think you were helping me."

SELENA

"I did help you," he says. "You went to Willow Heights, didn't you? And of course I wasn't going to help you take down my own family. You're the one who made assumptions. I never said I was a Darling. I never said I wanted to take down the Dolces. You wanted it to be true, so you believed it."

She stands there for a minute and then nods. "You're right. I thought we were friends in some sick way, because that's what I needed."

"I really don't see what you're so upset about," he says. "Unless you're just pissed that you didn't fool us all. You may have pulled one over on Royal, but you should know we always have his back. I stayed sharp because I had to, just like he did with Mabel when things went down with her. That's the way it works. We're a family. We look out for each other. And it's not like I did anything to you. Yeah, I sent you into some situations to test you, like telling you to go after the Swans. I never told you to go after Royal. I never even told you to fuck him. You did that on your own."

"You told me to fuck you," she says. "You and Duke."

"He did?" I ask, turning to her.

"Yeah, so what?" Baron says. "I knew you were getting in too deep with her, and I knew you'd be done with her if she fucked us. But she didn't. She just lied about it. If anyone's the liar here, Harper, it's you. You lied and told Mr. D you'd fucked us, that you were a Swan. I never lied, not even as Mr. D. I just let you believe the stories you made up in your own head."

"And what about when you told Royal that I'd told all his secrets to a stranger, probably a Darling?" Harper asks, looking annoyed now. "When you made him turn against me and give me to you and Duke to punish. How are you justifying that to yourself, Baron? It was just a joke, you never meant him to take it seriously?"

"You told a stranger about our business," Baron says, frowning at her. "It doesn't matter that it was me. You didn't know that. You could have been telling anyone, and you didn't care. You were trying to tell our enemy. You deserved what you had coming."

SELENA

"No," she says, shaking her head. "No one deserves that."

"No one deserves what you did to Royal," Baron says. "To tell something like that… It does something to a man. To imagine that being any of us, and having you tell someone something like that about us…"

Rage and shame swell inside me, and I feel the monster stirring, pushing toward the surface, knowing he's needed the way he is every time I think about what Harper did to me. I can never undo what I let happen to her. She's right about no one deserving that. But Baron's right, too.

"What do you mean, our business?" I ask.

Baron turns to me. "What?"

"You said she told someone our business. Has Dad been asking you to meet with…clients?" I can barely get the words out past the swell of the monster inside. If I did all that for nothing, I'll fucking kill Dad. He manipulated me into doing his bidding to protect first my sister and then my brothers. If all along he was using them, too…

Baron shakes his head. "No. I have my own shit with him."

Of course. He and Dad run the business under the candy business, the one that's bringing Dad closer to the powerful families in New York, the way he always wanted. He may be in Arkansas, but his influence with Al Valenti has grown this year despite the distance. After all, he's got more to offer now than he ever did before.

This isn't about that, though.

I hate that Baron knows what I've done for Dad. I hate that it's because of Harper. I don't want anyone, not even my brothers, to know. I've kept other things from them, and I don't regret it. I only regret telling King and Dad what happened when the Darlings took me. Now Harper knows that, too. Will she use that as ammunition the first chance she gets, the first time I piss her off?

I've spent months trying to make things right with her, and I know our crimes against each other are not equal, but she hasn't even acknowledged hers. I just swallow it down every day like bitter poison, and know I fucking deserve worse. But it didn't go away. It never goes away.

"Are we done with the inquisition?" Duke asks. "Because it doesn't sound like Baron really did anything wrong, so maybe you could put the gun away and we can go home. I'm starving, and I could really use a beer."

"Yeah," Baron says levelly. "It's over. I don't see the point in this, anyway. You could have just told me you knew I was Mr. D. The worst thing I did was get a few jerk-off fantasies out of you. Hell, I got more from Preston with those videos he sent this summer. You got a fucking scholarship, Harper."

He turns to me. "And just because you're pissed about what we did to her, or you regret what you did, don't forget what she did to you. She almost died this summer, and suddenly you forget everything? Come on, Royal. Death doesn't erase her crime. Sure, I can believe she's not a Darling if you saw a DNA test. That changes who she is, though, not what she did. Even if she's not a Darling, she deserved punishment. We punished her accordingly. It's over. Move on or not, but it has shit to do with me talking to her online for a few months."

"And hey, if she's not a Darling, you could be together," Duke says. "Now that everyone's done stabbing everyone else in the back, and we're all on the same page. We've all paid, right? So we can go back to being friends?"

"You say that like we were friends to begin with," Harper says.

"Aw, come on, don't be like that," Duke says, slinging an arm around her neck and kissing the top of her head. "We were friends. And if you're with Royal, you're still our friend. What do you say we go light some shit on fire down by the tracks tonight?"

Harper lets the gun hang by her side and rubs her temple with the other hand. "I have one more question for Baron. Why'd you tell us both to go to the party?"

He shrugs and starts back toward the car. "I wanted to see what would happen."

Of course he did. Life is just one big fucking experiment to him, and one big game to Duke. I return

SELENA

to the Rover with them, but it all sits wrong in my gut. It didn't go the way I wanted, the way I thought it would. I was supposed to deal with Baron, but now he's reminded me where my loyalties should always lie—with our family. His never wavered. I'm the one who fucked up.

Yeah, maybe I want to make things right with Harper, but she's not blameless. She was being shady all that time. Every minute we were together was a lie.

Baron was being shady, too, but not to me. He may not have told me he was talking to her all along, but he never touched her, never hurt her. He didn't hurt me. When I was off the deep end for her, he was watching my back, watching out for our family. And he did it without touching a hair on her head, out of respect for me and my claim on her.

He's not the one who betrayed me. She is.

Now I don't know what to do with her, with this, with my fucking addiction to her. It was easy when I knew it couldn't last, that I'd get rid of her when I was done. When I thought she was a Darling, I knew the end. Now we've passed that ending, and there's no map for what comes next. She's still wrapped around me like her spider's web, and I have no clear direction, no way out. I destroyed her. She was supposed to die, to disappear like Crystal, to never come back. Instead, she rose from the grave, another ghost to haunt me, this one in the flesh.

I don't know how our story ends, and it pisses me the fuck off. But I know I have to have her, that I can't let her go. I know that her life is mine, and it always will be. I won't let her take the easy way out, like she tried to do before. She's in this with me, whether she likes it or not, until one of us draws our last breath. I just don't know when that ending comes, what it looks like if she's not a Darling, where destruction is the only option.

If I tell myself she was just doing a job in exchange for a scholarship, that it wasn't personal, I can stop myself from wanting to destroy her all over again every time I think about what she did. So that's what I'll keep doing until I know where it's going, what inevitable end is in store for us both.

SELENA

three

Harper Apple

The rest of the week passes in a tense tightrope walk. I'm on edge, not sure how to feel about Baron's blasé attitude about being Mr. D. He acted like it was no big deal, but I know better. It was a big deal.

Wasn't it?

He's so good at manipulating the situation that even I left the bridge second-guessing myself, trying to remember what he did that was so bad. I was so set on taking down the Dolces last year, on having Mr. D help me do it. I was the one who spun the fantasy that we were friends, that he was some powerful man who was on my side. I needed that powerful ally, so I turned him into that, even though he never gave me any indication he was looking out for my best interest—if anything, the opposite.

But if he's the enemy, he needs to be taken down more than ever. Because he might not have done anything bad when he was acting as Mr. D, but he did plenty when he was being Baron Dolce—not just to me, but to other girls and the Darling men, too.

But how can I take down the Dolces without taking down Royal? He's the center of it all.

I know I don't have that power, anyway. Not alone.

Still, they need to be stopped from what they're doing to this town, and I'm the only one who seems to realize it. Or at least the only one who can admit it. I don't know how to heal the town, how to make it better, with the Dolces still running it—especially without sinking to their level.

I've done that before, and the price is too high. I barely survived it. Some part of me didn't. Some part of me is gone and will never be replaced. I couldn't live through it again, and I sure as hell won't put anyone else in that position.

SELENA

And if I can't do it alone, and I can't risk anyone else, how am I supposed to do it at all?

I keep mulling over it for the next few days. Royal doesn't come to pick me up before school the next day or the next or the next. I know I should be happy about that, since he's giving me space, but I can't help but wonder how much Baron's confession got to him, too.

I shouldn't care. I shouldn't want Royal to want me. But after we hooked up at the party, I crave him, crave his texts on my phone, his touch, the way he needed me. When he doesn't show up every day to insist on taking me to school, my dumb bitch heart cries for his familiar hovering. Some masochistic part of me enjoys his crazy stalker tendencies. Without them, how do I know if he's losing interest? Instead of being excited at the prospect, a sick terror grips me. I don't think I could stand losing him again.

But fuck if I'm going to show my cards. I remember Gloria telling me not to stalk him last year on New Years, to let him want me. So, I do. I don't text him, don't tell him I miss his stupid car in my driveway and his controlling insistence on driving me places.

At school, Baron and I avoid each other, but we never stop watching the other, like we're both waiting for the other to make the first move. It's an uneasy truce. He lets me have my table at lunch, and everyone knows the new table where he sits as king is the center now. But his allowing me to exist, to claim their table with my rebel crew, to challenge him, takes the Dolce boys' power down a notch. Everyone expected him to put me in my place, but he didn't.

They watch me warily in the halls, unsure if they should worship me as the queen I proclaimed myself to be. They can see I have power, since Baron hasn't cut me down, but I don't exactly fit the princess mold they're used to. The tension amps up every day at lunch, but the D-boys don't try to take back our table or stop the handful of girls from delivering our food each day before scurrying back to their own tables and pretending they're not part of this. Even I'm waiting to see what Baron has up his sleeve, if he's really going to let me keep openly rebelling against the order that benefits him and his dude bros.

The rest of the school is too wrapped up in Homecoming preparations to notice aside from lunchtime. The girls are campaigning for queen while the guys worry about their tuxes matching the girls' dresses. PTO moms fill the school, fussing about mums. Student council and other clubs plaster the halls with posters for the game and the dance the next day. There are pep rallies and spirit week activities, all leading up to the big Faulkner/Willow Heights showdown on Friday.

Last year, I didn't go to the game. I was an outsider.

Now, I'm inside, but no one quite believes I'm queen. I'm more of an interloper, a usurper that the king has somehow allowed to remain instead of beheading me.

On Friday morning, I walk out of my house to see Royal's Range Rover sitting in the driveway behind my car, and my chest inflates like a fucking balloon. Guess I really am just another dumb bitch who let the Dolce boys do whatever they wanted to her, and she still wants them.

I still want him. I hate my decimated heart for filling with hope when I see his car, but I can't stop it from happening.

I climb in like it makes no difference to me and give him a cool nod. "What's up?"

He shakes his head and doesn't say anything as he backs out of the drive.

"What?" I ask.

"At least you've stopped acting like a brat when I come get you."

"So you can just show up whenever the fuck you feel like it, and I can't have anything to say about that?"

"What do you have to say about it?"

"Nothing."

"Go on," he insists. "Say it."

"It's bullshit," I say. "And things don't work like that anymore."

"I said I wouldn't show up every day unless something happened." He glances at me sideways and then gives me a knowing smirk. "Are you feeling neglected?"

SELENA

I cross my arms over my chest and glare out the windshield. "No."

"I can pick you up every day if that's what you want."

"I don't."

"It's okay to admit you want me," he says. "After the way I blew your back out last Friday, no one could blame you."

"Who says that was even about you?" I ask, smirking back at him. "Making out with Gloria that got me all worked up. She's not into girls, so she wouldn't go through with it. You just came along and finished me off for her."

Royal's hand lands on my thigh, and it's all I can do not to squeeze my knees together. I force myself not to react. "Then I guess I owe her a thank-you card," he says, sliding his hand slowly upwards. "She did all the work, but I'm the one who got to feel this sweet cunt milking my cock. Why don't you invite her to join us again tonight?"

He slides his hand between my thighs, and I tense and draw a deep breath as his fingers skim the seam of my jeans. One touch and I'm just about panting and begging for more like a pathetic, dick-whipped idiot. But his warm hand electrifies me, sends hot tingles racing through my veins.

"So now you're not jealous?" I ask, refusing to let him know the effect he has on me. "What happened to the 'there will be no threesomes when you're with me' policy?"

"What's there to be jealous of?" he asks. "It was my name on your tongue when you were gushing on my cock."

"That's because it turned me on to beat the shit out of you," I say, fighting the urge to unzip my jeans and let him sink those long, beautiful fingers into me. I can feel myself getting wet at his touch, but I cling to my dignity with all I have. "I like seeing your face beaten to a pulp. Seeing you get what you had coming… That was hot."

"Keep pretending if it helps you sleep at night," he says, stroking the seam of my jeans until he must feel how damp they are.

SELENA

I'm torn between slapping his hand away and knocking the smug grin off his face, and opening my legs and riding his hand until I cum. After so long without good sex, my body is screaming to let him remind me all over again. I can't decide if I hate myself more for reacting or him for teasing. He tickles his little finger along my crease. "Did you shave for me, Cherry Pie? If you didn't, go home and do it after school. I want you bare when I eat you out later."

I jerk my knees away and push him back. "Who says you'll be eating me out again? I told you, that was a mistake. It should never have happened, and just because I'm working on forgiveness, that doesn't mean I've forgotten what you did. Just because we fucked, that doesn't mean we're together."

"Okay, Jailbird," he says, pulling into my parking spot. "Whatever you say."

"Ugh, I hate you," I say, jumping down from the Range Rover and tugging at the knees of my jeans.

"I hate you, too," he calls after me.

I slam the door in his face and walk away fuming.

I'm halfway across the lot when Gloria catches up to me, grabbing my elbow and linking her arm with mine. "What was that about?" she asks. "Are you back with Royal?"

"No," I say. "Definitely not."

"Hm, too bad," she says. "I'm still rooting for y'all."

"Even though Rylan dumped you?" I ask. "I'd think you'd be going after Royal yourself now. Seemed like it last Friday."

"I told you, we're just friends. And yes, sometimes we're friends with benefits, but we don't catch feelings. Y'all, though…"

"Are just friends, too," I say firmly.

"Well, I'm still sorry I let that happen. I was drunk and dumb and upset about Rylan. But I don't have feelings for Royal, and now that I know you two might get back together, I can guarantee it'll never happen again. Promise-swear, cross my heart." She makes an X over her heart and gives me a hopeful smile.

"I'm not mad at you about it," I say. "I told him to go hook up with someone. I'd rather it was you than some rando. Besides, I hooked up with you, too."

"For what it's worth, I'm not mad at you about last year anymore, either," she says. "I'm glad we're friends. I need a friend like you."

"Me, too."

"Then, as your friend, let me give you some advice. If you want to be queen here, you should really think about getting back together with him. I mean, if there's one thing that'll give you more status than dating Baron Dolce, it's dating a college guy who used to be the king here."

"You're shameless."

"I just want my two besties back together," she says. "I'm still working on getting him to forgive me, as a friend of course. But I'd really like it if we could all hang out again, like we did last year."

"Me too," I admit.

"Hey, want to ride to the game with us?" she asks, brightening. "It'll be like old times. The court walks tonight at the game, and tomorrow, I'll be crowned at the dance."

"Sure," I say. "Are you going with Baron?"

"Yeah, but I'm riding with Dixie to the game tonight. We'll have a limo for the dance. Now that Rylan's not speaking to me…" She drops her gaze, and for a moment, I catch a glimpse of the real Gloria Walton, the one who's not a bitch at all, the one who cried when she told me about Royal's secret and told me she just loved him the only way she knew how.

"You're really upset about that, huh?" I ask, stopping at my locker with her.

"Well, yeah," she says. "He was my boyfriend… Before. Y'know. Back in Georgia."

"He was?" I ask, drawing back. "I didn't know that."

"Yeah," she says, nodding and holding her books to her chest. "I think… It sounds crazy, but he moved here for me. And now…"

"Now he found out about you and the Dolce boys."

She nods, her nose going red as she sniffs up her tears. "Just Royal. But he's so pissed."

SELENA

"Lo… I'm sorry. I had no idea. I thought you'd only been with him a few months."

"It's fine," she says, lifting her head and running her finger along the bottom of her lashes, wiping the tears before they can fall and ruin her makeup. "I'm fine, really. I'm going to the dance with Baron, and I'm going to be queen, and he'll be king, and everything's going to work out perfect."

"Hey, Appletini," Colt say, swaggering up with Dixie clinging to his side. He sticks a black-and-gold sticker to my shirt. "Vote for Dixie. Powell in Power. Pussy Power. Something like that."

Gloria lets out an annoyed huff and rolls her eyes. "Do you ever stop?"

"Stop campaigning for my girl? Nope. Vote for Dixie, or she'll put you in the blog and ruin your rep."

"I'm literally on the court with her," Gloria says.

"Right," he says. "Of course the self-obsessed witch is voting for herself."

Gloria shakes her head. "I'd rather be obsessed with myself than your dick. That's all you seem to think about."

"And yet, you're the one bringing it up," he says, giving her a lazy grin. "I admit, it's hard not to be obsessed with dick this good. Right, babe?"

Dixie giggles, looking like she's ready to bust out a happy dance in the hall. Good for her. I'm glad they sorted out whatever was wrong between them, even if it sort of seems like his lost memory might be the cause of that. It's none of my business, though. I have enough shit on my plate, especially when I notice a few girls squealing and pulling jerseys out of their lockers, holding them up and buckling necklaces on each other. I don't remember Baron's number, so I'm not sure if he's 17, but I'm guessing he is. He must be up to something and is handing them out for a reason. My stomach knots at the thought of impending drama.

"I've gotta run," Gloria says to me, studiously ignoring Colt and Dixie, who are now wrapped in each other's arms. "See you after school?"

I agree, and Colt breaks away from Dixie to yell down the hall after Gloria. "Don't worry, one day you'll get good dick, too!"

I make it through the morning without incident, though it's hard to focus when I'm sure that the other shoe is about to drop at any moment. I can feel it, a tide of energy rising, an undercurrent of unrest. I don't try to talk myself out of it, to tell myself I'm being paranoid and that it's just excitement about the game and the dance. I know better than to ignore my instincts.

I stash my books in my locker before lunch, check to make sure my knife is within easy reach in my boot, and flex my fingers inside the brass knuckles Preston had custom made to fit my hand. Then I start for the café.

When I step inside, I take a quick sweep of the room with my eyes. Baron and Duke are holding court at their usual spot to the left of the door. At the table slightly to the right, where we normally sit, Dixie and Colt are waiting. I slide into my seat, my stomach tight. Girls have been bringing our lunch all week, but I'm not hungry today, anyway.

"What's going on?" I ask Dixie. "Something's weird today."

"You'll see," she says, just about bouncing in her seat. Her face is flushed, her eyes glowing with excitement. She's wearing one of the jerseys I saw girls pulling out of their lockers this morning, with the number 17 on the front. Dixie tied hers up at one side and combined it with a black skirt and fishnets, along with a black lace bow that's trying to contain her unruly curls.

"You know?" I ask, narrowing my eyes at her.

"Just wait," she says. "Here he comes."

I look up to see Gideon Delacroix heading our way, a plate in his hand as usual. He doesn't buy into the whole serving girl thing. Behind him are a couple pretty girls I remember from last year, friends of Gloria's, wearing the same jerseys as Dixie. Behind those girls is a group of half a dozen more, all wearing the number 17, Quinn among them.

I look from them, to the same number on the front of Gideon's chest, and then to Dixie.

SELENA

"What is this?" I ask, gesturing at the fucking parade of Gideon's fangirls leaving the food line. There must be two dozen girls wearing his jersey. That might not seem like many at a school like Faulkner, but the entire student population of Willow Heights is under four hundred. That's quarter of one entire grade at this school.

And they're not rebel girls, either. They're pretty girls, popular even. Girls I remember from parties last year, girls I sat in the bleachers with. A couple are even cheerleaders and majorettes. I spot the captain of the dance team among them. They all set their plates down and start pushing tables up to ours, forming a big cluster of five or six tables.

Gideon sits down across from me at his usual spot. "Here's your army, Apple," he says, flashing me a grin. "They're all yours."

"What is this?" I ask. "Some of these girls are… Dolce girls."

"They *were* Dolce girls," he says over the racket of scooting tables and everyone else in the café gossiping as they turn to watch. "But the Dolce boys didn't want them anymore. They said I could have them. So here they are."

"We're Apple girls now," Quinn says, pulling a chain bead necklace out of the front of her jersey. I stare at the little red apple charm on it. It's cheap, something a first grader would give a teacher, nothing like the *D* necklaces the Dolce girls wear. But it makes my throat nearly close.

I turn back to Gideon, barely able to speak. "You did this?"

"Now will you go to Homecoming with me?" he asks, the smile on his face nearly breaking my heart. I wish he hadn't done this in public, where the whole room is watching. I don't want to hurt his pride, but leading him on is even crueler.

For a minute, I can't answer. If I shoot him down in front of all these girls, after what he did for me, they'll think I'm a heartless bitch. But I can't let him think I'm interested, either.

"As friends," I say finally.

"Friends," he agrees, beaming at me.

SELENA

I give him a hard look. "But you have this all wrong. I'm not the leader here. I didn't do anything."

"I think you did," he says quietly, and I'm glad he's keeping his voice down, too. I know this will be all over the school by the end of the day, but I'd rather it take its time getting there. "I was fucking terrified to go to this school because I heard what the boys here have to do, and I knew I couldn't do it. You're the one making it so I don't have to. You started something, Harper, whether you know it or not. You didn't just stand up for what's right. You gave other people the courage to do it."

"No," I say, shaking my head as Magnolia slides into a seat next to Gideon. She's wearing his jersey over a gold tulle skirt with black velvet polka dots, along with a pair of enormously long fake lashes with gold glitter in them. I've always felt this protective instinct when it comes to this girl, maybe because I sacrificed my relationship with Royal when I stood up for her and Lindsey last year or maybe because I thought I might be her cousin at one point. Or maybe it's because in some weird way, I sensed that she was someone I could respect, despite her immaturity.

"Magnolia's the one who gave me the courage to stand up," I tell Gideon. "She's the one you should be asking to the dance. She's your age, and she's not fucked up like me. Listen, I'll go as your friend, if you want, and I think you're cool as hell. But your admiration is misplaced."

"Maggie's great," he says, awkwardly glancing at Colt and Dixie. "But I've known her all my life. And... I like older girls."

Before I can answer, a chair scrapes back at the Dolce boys table, and the room falls from a low roar of excitement to dead silent in seconds.

"Hey," Duke says, jerking his chin at us. "What the fuck, man?"

A look of pure dread settles over Gideon's face as the color drains from it. I have to admire his dogged determination to win a date to Homecoming with me, even if he's not the kind of guy I'd ever date. But I know he can't face the Dolces on his own, which means I'm going to have to take one for the team this time.

"Gideon, bro," Duke says, gesturing at our huge group of tables that dwarfs their exclusive two-table setup. "You can't just steal our girls. That's not how this works."

"He didn't steal anyone," I say, pushing back my chair and standing. "These are girls who chose to sit with us after *you* rejected them."

"We didn't reject them," Duke says. "We passed them on when we were done. That's how it works. Me and Baron get them first, then DeShaun and Cotton, and then Gideon and the rest of the team."

"And what if they don't want to be run through by a bunch of assholes who probably don't even remember their names afterwards? We're people, Duke, hard as that may be for you to understand. You can't *steal* a person's loyalty. These girls chose to be loyal to me. They have minds of their own. Believe it or not, some people have goals in high school that don't involve being passed around by the football team."

"Yeah, but not those girls," Duke says, flashing a huge grin. He drops into his chair and scoots back, slouching down so it's just about impossible not to stare at his crotch. Then he pats his knee and gives us an inviting smile. "Isn't that right, girls?"

A few of the girls who haven't sat down hesitate, crowding together and tucking their hair behind their ears, looking all bashful.

"Aww, did we neglect our Dolce girls?" Duke croons, stroking his fingers lightly up his thigh. "Come on over, *bellissima*. We'll take good care of you from now on. Remember how good I took care of you before?"

He wiggles his brows, and a few girls lean in to whisper to each other, probably wondering which one he's talking to. I know he's not talking to any of them—he's talking to *all* of them. I can't believe that works, but then, I guess I sort of can. Duke's hot, and he's got a pair of puppy dog eyes that could melt the hardest heart.

I'm no different, after all. Just because I chose Royal instead of Duke, I'm no better than any of them.

"I've got a spot for you right here," Duke goes on, tapping his knee with two fingers. "Come on over. You can sit at our table."

"Every day?" asks the dance team captain.

Duke slides his hand up the front of his pants, palming his crotch. "Every night," he says.

"Everyone in this school knows you can't keep a girl longer than a few weeks," I cut in. "Your dick's not going to change anyone's mind."

A bunch of people start whispering and tittering.

"It might," he calls over the noise. "Maybe you need a reminder of how persuasive my dick can be."

He slips his hand into his pants, and suddenly, I have to brace my hand on the table to keep myself anchored. I know how persuasive his dick can be—in the most horrifying way.

A roar goes through the room, girls giggling and grabbing each other, craning their necks to see, asking what's going on as Duke pulls out his penis. It's still shocking to see a dick in the middle of the school cafeteria, even if I know he has no problem whipping is dick out in public. He slapped me in the face with it my first week here, after all.

"You want a seat at our table, Ginger Snap?" Duke taunts. "Come bounce on this."

Everyone at their table is rolling with laughter. Suddenly, Baron shoots to his feet, dropping a half-eaten sucker onto the table. "She has a phone," he bellows, pointing in our direction.

Chaos explodes through the room. The Dolce boys and their squad lunge for us. In a split second, I see Magnolia holding up her phone, and then a football player shoves me back in my chair as he passes. Magnolia shrieks and ducks around the table when Baron grabs for her. Someone else grabs my chair from behind, slinging it aside to get by. I spill out, my ass hitting the floor. Magnolia dives behind Colt, who's next to me. Dixie shoves back her chair, too, and the next second, she hits the floor beside me, rolling into me. Our heads collide, and I curse savagely, trying to untangle myself from her and our chairs as several football players run over us. Colt is up and swinging, but I've lost sight of Magnolia.

SELENA

I finally roll free and jump up. Rylan, who was also at our table, gets in one swing before a beefy football player named George decks him. He pinwheels his arms and crashes back into the table of cast-off Dolce girls beside us. Plates and cups are upended, drinks splashing across the table and rolling to the floor. More bodies join them as people dive out of chairs and are knocked over in the fight.

I hear a shriek and whip around to see Baron holding Magnolia from behind, one arm wrapped around her middle while he swipes for her phone, which she's waving wildly. I jump toward them, making a swipe for it, but he wrenches it out of her hand. He drops it on the floor and stomps on it, his heel crushing the glass.

"You're too fucking late," she yells over the noise. "You're too late!"

I try to pull her free of Baron, but before I can, Gloria steps in my way. Her eyes widen as she tries to convey some unspoken message, but she shoves me in the shoulders without giving me a chance to figure it out. I throw a punch, but she ducks, then rams her shoulder into my solar plexus, making me see stars. I grab her hair as we topple backwards.

"Not my face," she says through panting breaths. "It's Homecoming weekend!"

"Are you fucking kidding me?" I growl, sinking a fist into her side as my ass hits the floor.

She grabs my hair and yanks my head down to the floor, so I'm flat on my back instead of sitting. "Just keep fighting," she says, smacking my cheek with her palm. "I'm not going to hurt you, either. This is just for show."

I buck my hips and roll her over, straddling her hips with my knees and drawing back a fist. She grabs my arm with both hands, barely twisting her head out of the way as I go in for the punch.

"Harper," she shrieks. "Don't hurt me!"

I pull back, wrestling with the adrenaline and the rush of fighting, registering her words. She's not some tough chick at Femme Fight Friday. She's not even really fighting. A real fighter doesn't slap your cheek so softly it barely stings. She slugs the shit out of you.

SELENA

All around us, the brawl rages. This isn't a fake fight. Chairs are scattered and tables shoved out of the way. A crowd is gathered near the door and along the wall, gaping at the mayhem unfolding. A couple football players pound on a few hapless guys who got involved while DeShaun and Duke are throwing down with Colt and Gideon. Another football player is whaling on Rylan, who's curled up on the floor with his arms over his head.

But the guys on the team won't fight girls, which means they're in the minority. Most of the fighters are of the female persuasion. A dozen former Dolce girls are duking it out with the current members. I spot one the Walton twins shrieking as Amber holds her by the hair, yanking her head down into some spilled food on the table. The girl who told me about being branded like it was a good thing is rolling around with Josie, who was at our table.

"You fucking bitch," screams the other Walton twin, throwing a handful of mashed potatoes at a former Dolce girl. Her face is red with rage and streaked with tears. The girl ducks, and the Walton flies after her, screaming in fury. She slams into her back, and they crash into a chair and then into some bystanders, finally hitting the floor.

I grab Gloria's hair so no one will notice we've stopped fighting. "What the fuck is going on?" I demand, slapping her cheek hard enough to send tingles of pain and pleasure searing across my skin and down my arm.

"Ow," she yelps. "You fucking hit me!"

"Yeah, I fucking hit you," I say. "We're fighting."

She reaches up and grabs a handful of my hair, yanking my head down toward hers. "I didn't want you to get hurt," she says. "But you couldn't just skip out on the fight. It'll all fall apart without you."

"What will?" I ask, letting her get in a good slap from her position under me.

"Your little rebellion," she says.

"You're not part of the rebellion, though."

"Yeah, but that doesn't mean I don't agree," she says. "Who do you think sent Quinn and the former serving girls to your table to bring you food every day?"

SELENA

So it was her. I remember seeing her drag Quinn into the bathroom on Monday morning, but I was quick to dismiss Gloria and think she was doing something bitchy.

"You're helping us?" I ask, wrapping my hand around her throat.

"Babe, I'm always on your side," she says. "Even when I can't risk doing it publicly."

I slam a fist into her gut, and her eyes widen with shock, her body curling in on itself. "What the fuck?" she gasps through the pain.

"That's for fucking Royal over spring break," I say. "Don't ever touch him again."

"Y-you said you didn't care," she groans, wrapping her arms around her middle, her eyes filling with tears.

"That free pass was for last Friday only," I say, leaning down and pressing my lips to hers. "Now we're even."

I sit back and see some teachers heading our way, so I hold out a hand to Lo. She slaps it away and stands, smoothing her skirt.

"If you pulled out any of my hair, I'll have my daddy sue the pants off you and your no-account mother, too," she screams at me, dialing it up to a ten. "I just got a blowout!"

I have to hold back a laugh at her antics. Now that I know the girl a little, I can't help but admire the whole Jekyll and Hyde vibe she's got going. She's like two completely different people, and she can switch it off and on in two seconds flat.

The teachers rush over and shush her, separating us while she continues to hurl insults and threats my way. I remember when she did that last year, what a bitch she was when we fought. But her parents didn't press charges—was that because she told them not to? That line of thought brings me back to my own situation then. They called someone they said was my dad, who was actually the anonymous donor of my scholarship. Baron or maybe Mr. Dolce talked to them and said I wouldn't press charges against Gloria. Of course they did. They love the Waltons.

SELENA

At least, they did last year. Royal kept his dad from renewing Lo's scholarship this year, though. Preston's the one who gave her one.

"That was crazy," Dixie gushes, interrupting my thoughts and pulling me over to the crowd of onlookers. "Want to give me a quote for the blog?"

"I'm good," I say, shaking out my hands and bouncing on my toes, trying to dispel the unspent adrenaline. I wish Gloria had let me really fight someone. Now I'm all itchy and unfulfilled, like when you get close to a really good orgasm and then lose it at the last moment.

I spot Magnolia sprawled in a chair, looking dazed. She's got mashed potatoes in her hair, which is sticking up in weird tufts, and ketchup on her cheek. I circle the table and crouch next to her. "You okay?"

She turns her baby blue eyes my way and blinks a couple times. Her false lashes have come askew on one side, and they flutter at me as she tries to focus. "I… My phone," she mumbles.

"Come on," I say, taking her hand. "We're going to go to the bathroom and get you cleaned up. Okay?"

She nods mutely, letting me pull her up and into the bathroom off the café. The nurse is tending to Rylan, who seems to be the only one who got seriously hurt, though a couple other teachers are talking to kids on the floor and handing out gauze for split lips and ice packs for bruises.

At least a dozen girls are crowded into the bathroom. Ignoring their stares and whispers, I grab a handful of paper towels, wet them in the sink, and start cleaning Magnolia's face. She has a red mark on one cheekbone, but otherwise doesn't look banged up, just messy.

She doesn't say anything while I dab away the ketchup and order her to lean over the sink so I can get the potato glue out of her hair. The bell rings, and half the girls leave. A teacher sticks her head in and orders us to class, and everyone else leaves. I crouch in front of Magnolia. "Did Baron hurt you?" I ask. "Or touch you?"

She shakes her head, her eyes welling with tears. "No," she whispers. "But he said—he said—" She breaks off, a sob stealing her words, and throws her arms around my neck. I try to keep my balance but eventually give in and just sit on the bathroom floor holding her while she sobs into my shirt.

I can imagine what sick things Baron said to her.

Rage simmers in my veins.

Fuck Baron Dolce. Just because he gave me a scholarship, that doesn't mean he gets away with murder. He may not have done anything as Mr. D, but he sure as fuck manipulated that situation to get what he wanted in the end. He got Royal to dump me when his little trick in the basement didn't work. He told Royal how they could punish me. Now he's threatening and traumatizing poor little freshmen. Even if I didn't already feel a kinship with Magnolia, I'd be pissed. This town will never heal as long as he's in it, wreaking havoc on the future generations.

At last, Magnolia sits up and wipes her eyes. One set of her lashes comes off entirely, and she gives a shaky laugh and peels off the other side. "Did you get my phone?"

"I didn't see it. It was a mess out there."

"Do you think we'll be in trouble?"

"Maybe," I admit. "But I don't think they'll suspend us. There were too many football players involved. They need them for the Faulkner game tonight, and they can't suspend the rest of us and let them off. Not to mention all the cheer and dance girls involved."

Magnolia nods and stands to splash water on her face. "What about me?" she asks. "Will I get in trouble for having my phone out?"

I give her a funny look. "Everyone has their phones at lunch."

"I was filming, though," she says. "On school property."

"You won't get in trouble," I assure her. "But they'll probably make you erase it, especially if Duke's dick is in it. They won't want it getting out that those kinds of things happen here."

"I can't erase it," she says, gulping and turning big, guilty eyes my way. "I was livestreaming on the *OnlyPics* app."

SELENA

four

Harper Apple

"So, the good news is that no one paid to see the video she was streaming," Dixie says from the back seat of Gloria's Mustang. We're on our way to the game, and I just filled them in on what happened with the freshman after lunch.

"Can you erase it?" I ask, twisting around in the passenger seat. I passed along the login information that Magnolia gave me, since I've never used that app. Dixie and Lo both seem to know their way around it, though.

"There's no video to erase," Gloria explains, glancing at me with a funny look on her face. "It doesn't save the livestreams to watch later like some other platforms."

"What?" I ask, noticing her guarded expression.

"Nothing."

"Don't fuck with me," I say. "Didn't you learn your lesson at lunch?"

"My stomach is still bruised, so yes," she says. "Anyway, I just... Well, this summer, someone was sending Royal videos, like, porn clips. Of you. I watched Baron try to figure out who it was, so... That's how I know you can't rewatch the lives."

"Fuck," I say, laying my head back on the seat. Preston took dozens of shots of us fucking, and I pretty much knew what he was doing, but I didn't care enough to stop him. I also didn't think anyone else would have seen them. "So Baron watched them, too?"

"Yes," she admits. "And Duke. But that's it. Oh, and my brother."

I swallow hard, trying not to be sick. I imagine all those guys standing around watching a porno of me getting fucked with a pillow over my face. Not like they hadn't already fucked me themselves, but... I wish Gloria hadn't seen it, too. And I really, really wish she hadn't said anything in front of the school gossip columnist.

SELENA

"You have an *OnlyPics* account?" Dixie squeaks behind us. "You were doing porn?"

"Um, no," I say. "And you should probably be more concerned that your fourteen-year-old future cousin-in-law has an account than me. I'm eighteen."

"I'm going to need details about your porn clips," she says. "Or I'll put it on the rumor mill."

"You're the devil," I say. "Tell me about Magnolia's video. It's gone? There's no views?"

"Unfortunately, she did activate the optional fifteen-second preview clip," she says. "That's the only part of the video that was saved and posted, and it's still up. That's the bad news."

"Has anyone viewed it?"

"Over a thousand people," she says. "And it has a pretty clear shot of Duke's dick."

"Can you erase it?" I ask, my heart pounding. "He's eighteen, thank fuck, but he didn't consent to be filmed. I'm pretty sure they could sue the shit out of the Darlings for that."

"Yeah," she says. "I'm deleting it now. But if anyone screen-recorded it…"

"Then it's too late," I finish, dropping my head back again. "Fucking Magnolia. What was she thinking?"

"She was probably thinking she'd get something she could use to sue the Dolces," Dixie says. "Do you realize the extent of what they've done to her family? Her uncles have been killed, mutilated, and driven out of town. Her aunts have been committed to mental institutions and attempted suicide. Her cousins have been disfigured and tortured and beaten. Her brother left town before they could get to him, but she probably hasn't seen him more than once or twice a year because of them. You can't blame the girl for trying."

I swallow and press my nails into my palms. I know what the Dolces have done. They've done it to me, too. But hearing it all laid out like that makes me feel sick. It has to stop. Someone has to stop them. But I always come back to the same question.

How?

"Oh my god," Dixie shrieks suddenly, sitting forward between the seats. "Turn it up!"

"What?" I ask.

"The radio," she squeals, lunging forward to twist the dial.

"Shit, you almost ran me off the road," Gloria says over the music, covering her heart with one hand. "Don't scream like that while I'm driving."

"Shhh," Dixie says. "This is Dolly's new song."

"Who?" Lo asks.

"Dolly Beckett," Dixie says. "My cousin. Now listen."

"The mayor's daughter?" I ask. I vaguely remember hearing a song from her a few years ago, and everyone in town made a big deal of it, like they thought she was going to be the next Taylor Swift or something. Instead, the song faded away and people forgot all about it, like they do after a one mini-hit wonder or any other small town's lame attempt at a claim to fame. Sadly, the only real celebrities that come through Faulkner are the ones who detox at Cedar Crest, the fancy rehabilitation center on the outskirts of town.

"Yes," Dixie says. "She's been in LA since she graduated, but she's only ever had one song out. This is off her second album."

We dutifully listen to the song with Dixie, since it's her cousin, even though I'm not really into pop-country bops. Though I've never met her, it's still cool to hear someone from your hometown on the radio. When the song is over, Gloria turns it back down. Dixie chatters on about her cousin until we get to school, and we get swept up in the Homecoming madness. The court lines up at halftime, all of them wearing mums that drape to the ground and must weigh half as much as the smaller girls on the court. They walk a red carpet and wave to everyone, and I cheer for Gloria and Dixie. The Walton twins and another Dolce girl round out the court.

The girls leave the field, and the halftime show continues, and then the football team comes back on. I watch Duke clowning when he gets a touchdown, watch the town loving him. Am I the only one who knows these boys are monsters? The only one who cares?

If I took them down, would I be the town's enemy instead of their savior because I took away their golden boys? Maybe they don't want to be saved. Maybe they don't deserve it. What has this town ever done for me?

There's no party after the game, since the dance is the next day. When Gloria drops me off, I go inside my small, smoky house. The big sectional Royal bought is gone, leaving one side of the living room bare except for a few beer bottles and cigarette butts that had rolled under the couch, some dust bunnies, and the dents in the threadbare carpet where the legs of the couch rested.

"Mom?" I call, shrugging out of my jacket.

"Oh, thank god you're home," she says, rushing out of my room and down the hall toward me. I stiffen, instantly on alert. I know this Mom. It's not the one who sat on her bed and told me she was proud of me for getting a sugar daddy. This is the Mom who talks too fast, walks too fast, her movements jerky and almost robotic but also exaggeratedly quick. The one who stayed out all night partying and didn't sleep it off before crawling home, spaced out and jittery and coming down. This Mom is still up.

"What do you need?" I ask carefully, watching her for sudden movements. It's been a while since she came home tweaked out, but that doesn't mean I've forgotten her sudden rages.

"The keys," she says. "Where are the keys?"

"What keys?" I ask, tucking my jacket under my arm instead of tossing it on a chair. The key she wants is in the pocket of my jacket. I know better than to leave something like that at home when I'm out with friends.

"The car keys," Mom says impatiently, holding out a hand. "Where are they?"

"You don't have a car, Mom," I remind her.

"Baby, I know that," she says. "But I got a little behind on my payments, you know, to Bobby Dale, you remember him? He's been around here before, came to my retirement party. You remember? He was wearing a trucker hat, I think it was black, had the little figure of a woman on it, what's that called? You know, just the shape? What's it called?"

She snaps her fingers fast, fast, fast.

"A silhouette," I say, staring at this woman, willing her to look like a stranger and not so bone-tired familiar. "And yes, I remember Billy Bob, but he's not getting my car."

"No, no, no, it's just to borrow," she says. "Like collateral. He's just needing me to pay him back, and see, I don't have the money right now, baby. But I'm gonna get it, and real soon, too, you'll see. I'm fixing to get a job tomorrow, I just need to hold him off a little."

"No, Mom," I say, taking a step back.

"Baby, please," she says, seizing my arm. "You gotta help your mama out. I know I ain't always been the best, but I tried, baby, I'm trying so hard. I just need a little more time, and he's coming by tonight with his boys, and I don't have the money, so I told him he could have the car until I get it. I'm going out first thing tomorrow, I'm going to go talk to Scarlet. She's hiring, you know. I saw a sign up at the diner the other day. Not the one out by the truck stop, the one right in town, by the square. Did I ever tell you she went to Faulkner with me? She was a regular slut, let me tell you. Legendary for it, too. She helped found the Slut Club."

"Mom." I grip her shoulder, trying to slow her down, because she's talking a mile a minute, waving her hands around like a crazy person.

"Come on, baby girl, I just need it for one night, maybe a little more, until I get my first paycheck. Bobby Dale just needs to know I can pay him back, and I ain't got a car right now, but you do, and he'll know I'm good for a lot if I can let him borrow an Escalade."

"But you can't let him," I say. "I'm not giving him my car. You know perfectly well I'll never get it back."

"You will," she cries, clutching my arm. "I promise, baby. You don't know him like I do, he's real honest, I swear it. He'll give it back. He's going to hurt me if I don't deliver what I promised. You've got to help me, baby. You don't want your mama to get hurt, do you?"

I stare at her a long moment, my throat tight. "No, Mom."

SELENA

"I knew it," she says, throwing her arms around me. "Now come on, give me the keys. He's on his way over now. He'll be here any minute."

"No," I say, stepping away. "I'm not giving you my car. It's literally all I have."

"Just tell your man you wrecked it, he'll get you a new one," she says, grabbing for me again, clinging desperately to my arm. "The insurance, they'll pay."

"No, they won't, Mom. Unless it's stolen. And I don't think Billy Bob Joe will like it if we report a car stolen after we let him borrow it."

"Yes, let's do that!" she says, clapping her hands. "Then you can get a new one, and he can keep that one."

"Mom, that's a terrible idea," I point out. "He's going to get arrested and his 'boys' will come murder you."

"He's going to do that anyway if I don't pay," she says frantically. "I been getting Alice from him for a month. Now hurry up, baby, you gotta get me those keys. Just help me out here, just this one time. I promise, I wouldn't ask if I wasn't desperate, and you got money now, you can just ask that Darling man for some more.

They got lots. He helped us out before, he won't mind helping me out one more time."

I close my eyes, pressing my lips together. Fucking Preston had to buy me all those clothes, and Royal with the fancy car… Before now, I was invisible to my mother. I filled the cabinets with food, and she pretended she didn't notice so she didn't have to ask where I got the money. But buying groceries is one thing.

Having a flashy car makes me a target.

Now I've made it. And people who've made it attract leeches like my mother.

"I'll take you somewhere," I say. "So you won't be home when he gets here. But that's all I'm willing to do, Mom. You can't have my car."

She stares at me a minute, her tiny pupils fixed on me like she's trying to drill a hole through my forehead and dig out the location of the keys. Then they go hard, glinting with fury. "You ungrateful little—"

She lifts a hand, but I take a step back, raising my fists. "You really don't want to hit me, Mom," I say, moving my hand enough to make her gaze fall on the weapon blanketing my knuckles in its protective embrace. "It will not end well for you."

"I brought you into this world," she snaps. "I can take you out. Now give me the fucking keys."

"You're going to have to find your own way out of this mess," I say. "You've got about two minutes to get in the car, or your ride's leaving without you."

I turn and walk out, unlocking the car as I go. Glancing up and down the street, I hurry to the driver's side, my heart skipping when I see a pair of headlights turn onto Mill. I scramble into the Escalade and start the engine, my fingers shaking. I have zero interest in being here when Mom's dealer and his tweaker gang shows up.

I wait for her to run out and climb into the car, but she doesn't, and I'm not risking going back in for her. I'm way too fucking vulnerable, even with a pair of brass knuckles on my hand. Only the car makes me feel safe, the big steel body of it, the heaviness, the size.

I back out of the drive so no one can block me in, then honk a few times. A light goes on in Blue's house, and I hope she comes out so I can have someone to talk to, someone who understands. But no one comes out. After a few more minutes, a truck turns onto the street, and I decide it's time to go. Mom will have to pay the way she usually does.

Like her, though, I have nowhere to go. As I wind through the empty streets of Faulkner, I find myself wishing she'd come along. Yeah, she's tweaked out on Baron's designer drug and high as fuck, but once she wasn't freaked out and asking me for money, she'd probably be good for a laugh at least. After all, she manages to snag lots of guys for a few days or weeks. She's probably more fun high than she is the next day, and I've dealt with that plenty.

Even if she's annoying, she's predictable enough that I could handle her. And she's family, all the family I have. At least I wouldn't be alone.

I spent so much of my life wanting to survive on my own, pushing everyone away who got close, keeping my distance. Now, it's the last place I want to be. It makes me feel weak to know how much I've come to rely on others, to crave them. But it also makes me feel weak and vulnerable to be alone.

I know I could call Royal, but I'm too raw after that encounter with my mother. I can't be with him right now, can't deal with more than I've already got in my head right now. So I pull up at a stoplight, and while I'm waiting for it to turn green, I text the other man in my life, the one who carved a safe space for me and guarded it while I hid inside until I had healed enough to step back out into the world. The one who makes my life easier, not harder.

BadApple: Can I come over?
SilverSwan: yes

The light changes, and I turn that way, heading north of town on the interstate. I haven't driven this way in weeks, and my pulse quickens when I pass the cotton fields on the drive, then the rice paddies. I turn off at his exit, my heart still beating erratically in my chest. I pull up to his building and punch in the code to his garage, since

I don't have the opener anymore. It doesn't work, so I have to go back to my car and text him. I'm unaccountably hurt that he changed his garage code.

Preston's no saint, but he's the reason I'm alive right now. Not just because he pulled me off that tree, though he did save my life that day. There's no doubt in my mind that I would have ended it if it weren't for him, though—more than once. With him, everything was always simple, as simple as I needed it to be. He allowed for that, for whatever I needed, and didn't ask for more.

He didn't have to. He took what he needed, too.

A minute later, the garage door slides up. Preston is standing in the doorway that leads from the garage into the building, his mask over the top half of his face and a gun in his hand. Only when I park the car and climb out does he lower the gun a few inches. "Are you alone?" he asks, jerking his chin toward the car.

"Yes, I'm fucking alone, now stop pointing a gun at me."

"Last time you showed up with a Dolce," he says. "You can't blame me for bringing a gun to a gun fight."

"This isn't a gun fight," I say. "I was lonely, and my mom's spun out, and I couldn't be at home."

He looks me over. "Royal dump you again?"

"Can we not do this?" I ask. "I just needed somewhere to go, okay?"

He must hear something in my voice, because he puts the safety on and tucks his gun in the back of his pants. Then, he pulls me into his arms and hugs me hard, pressing his pointy chin into the top of my head. It hurts, but I don't mind. I want the ache that anchors me, the smell of his soap, the familiarity of his arms. He's the closest thing to family I have besides my mother.

"Can you spend the night?" he asks after a while.

I turn my face into his chest, pressing my forehead to his sternum. "Preston…"

"Am I not supposed to want you anymore?" he asks. "You're not a Darling."

"That's not why I'm here."

"Okay." He squeezes me tight and then pulls away, holding me at arm's length. "You okay?"

"Not really."

"I'd invite you up, but there's nothing left but a couple pieces of furniture."

My heart stumbles in my chest when I remember what they did to his fancy house last year, the way there was nothing left but a shell when they were done bombing it with their hatred. "What happened?" I ask, looking up at him, my arms still around his strong, slender body.

"I sold the loft," he says.

"Because of me," I say, feeling like a complete asshole.

"Because the Dolces know where I live."

"I'm sorry."

"Want to go somewhere?" he asks.

"Sure," I say, drawing away at last. "Want to show me the new place?"

"Do you still associate with the Dolces?"

"I'm not sure," I admit. "Probably."

"Then no." He pulls his keys from his pocket and hands them to me. "Start the truck. I'm going to load the kayaks. I have an idea."

SELENA

I want to ask what the fuck we're doing with kayaks, but he's already gone to take them down from where they hang on the wall. He loads them into the truck bed while I start the truck and then sit there watching him, admiring the beauty in the way he moves. I noticed toward the end of my time with him, when I'd started to come back to myself, how he's as graceful and strong as some kind of big cat, like a panther or a leopard. But I'm more myself now, more able to appreciate him without needing him.

Part of me wishes I did need him, that I could love him the way I love Royal, that I could feel something for him that I don't. Whatever love my heart is capable of giving, it does. I love Preston, I suppose, in some way. But I'm not capable of loving someone else the way I love Royal, the way I could have loved before he destroyed me. Now, the only person I'll ever love that way is the boy who shattered me.

And Preston deserves more than my tentative, pieced-together kind of love.

As I study him, I try to remember what he looked like before, in the family picture I saw at Lindsey's house. Was his face as beautiful as the rest of him? I can't recall. The scarred face and mask I've known for so long replace the image when I try. He's not that boy anymore, anyway. He's the man in the mask, the Phantom.

He climbs in the passenger side, startling me back to reality, reminding me I never moved out of his seat after starting the car. I was too busy watching him.

"Want to drive?" I ask.

"No," he says. "You need to drive tonight."

"Okay," I say, giving him a funny look. He doesn't explain, though, so I back out of the garage. "Where to?"

"Get on the highway," he says.

I obey, and a few minutes later, we're heading back toward Faulkner. He tells me to get off on the exit before that, though, and then get right back on, heading north this time. "Are you just taking me in a circle?" I ask. "Where are we going?"

"Do you trust me?"

"Umm… Right now?"

"Yes."

"Less than I did a few minutes ago."

"We're going back to where I found you."

"What?" I ask, shooting a startled glance his way. "You better be kidding."

"I'm not."

"You're insane," I say. "There's no fucking way I'm going back there. Ever."

"Pull off right here," he says. "This is where I tracked Duke's Hummer."

"Nope," I say, keeping the truck at a steady speed as we pass the rice paddies. "I don't even like looking over there. No way in hell am I voluntarily going in."

"I'm not going to force you to go," he says. "Which means you're going voluntarily."

"Never gonna happen."

"I'm going in with you," he says. "You know I'm not going hurt you."

"I realize that," I say. "But I'm not Royal. I'm not that masochistic. I'm not going to go back to the place where I was destroyed. No matter what happens for the entire rest of my life, it will never be worse than that night. Nothing can be worse. I could get hit by a car, and then shot in the face, and hung from a bridge, and it would still be better than what happened in that swamp. Don't you get it, Preston? Dying would have been better."

"Are you pissed that I saved your life?"

"No," I say. "But it still would have been easier to die."

"Try again," he says, reaching over and laying a reassuring hand on the back of my seat. "Just keep driving until you're ready to stop."

I pull off at his exit, then swing around and go south again. I don't know why. I could drive in circles all night, and I'll never be ready to go back there.

"This is pointless," I say as we pass the rice paddies again.

"Places only have as much power over you as you let them," he says.

"Try telling that to Royal."

SELENA

"That bridge has power over Royal because he lets it, because he isn't willing to let go. That's where his sister disappeared, and that's his way of holding on."

"And yours is refusing to believe they're dead?" I ask. I'm not even surprised he knows what I'm talking about. Hell, he probably knows Royal's habits better than I do. He tracks his car, so of course he knows how much time Royal spends there. I always suspected that's where his sister died, but this is the first time someone's confirmed it.

"They aren't dead," Preston says with complete confidence. "And I don't hang out there hoping they'll show up again."

"Uh huh," I say. "So why are you trying to make me go back, if you don't?"

"Because I already let go."

I bite my lip, checking his reaction as I ease off the gas. It's my third time past, but my heart lurches crazily inside me at the thought of stopping.

"Just pull over," he says. "We can sit in the truck this time if you want. Next time, maybe we'll go further."

I pull over on the side of the highway and stop the truck. Then I just press my fist to my chest, trying to keep it from blowing open and spilling the contents of my heart when it explodes from beating too hard. Preston rubs my shoulder and neck, like a little back massage is all it'll take to fix this tension.

"What about people?" I ask, turning toward him and leaning my arm along the top of the steering wheel. "You let the Dolces have power over you."

He shakes his head. "I'm the only one they haven't been able to control, the only one they don't have power over. That's why they hate me most."

"And yet, you're moving out of your house because of them."

"There's a fine line between keeping your dignity and losing your life for foolish pride. I may bend when that's what it takes to survive, but I don't break."

"Funny, I'm pretty sure your cousin said something like that."

"Colt has no pride," he says. "He sucked their dicks and crawled in the dirt for them a long time ago."

"He's also still going to Willow Heights while you had to drop out."

He shrugs. "I guess we all do what we think is right. I wasn't willing to compromise what he has, but I'm practical enough to know when self-preservation comes above pride. I'd rather move to a new apartment than fucking bend over and take it up the ass from them every day just to keep living there."

"Interesting choice of words," I mutter.

"How so?" He cocks his head to one side, watching me with his good eye in a way that reminds me too much of the way Baron studies people, that intent curiosity that lights up his eyes.

"Never mind," I mutter, opening the door and climbing out. "Let's go."

"You sure?" Preston asks, climbing out, too.

"Yeah, come on," I say, because I don't want to lose my nerve, and thinking about someone else is the only thing keeping me going.

Preston doesn't say anything, but I feel him studying me as he fits a headlamp onto my head and takes down the kayaks. He puts one on my back and shows me how to carry it, and I start across the rice paddy without waiting for him. My feet squelch into the mud, and water begins to seep into my boots. It's been rainy, so the aisles are filled with water, just like they were last year. It's cool like it was when they brought me here last spring, too, so the snakes will be moving slow if they're out at all.

The kayak is unwieldy on my back, and focusing on it keeps me from having to think about what I'm doing as I pick my way across the open area toward the dark woods on the far side. This is totally different. I'm not scared. I'm not vulnerable. And beyond my justifications, he's right. I do trust him, just as I love him—to the best of my ability.

By the time I reach the far side of the rice field, Preston has caught up to me. My heart is beating erratically, and I can tell I've slipped into my shell a little, like I do every time I go over the reasons I don't have to be afraid. Yes, I'm alone out here with a man with a gun, but what's he going to do to me? He's already fucked me every way he wants, and he's not into hurting people. If he wanted to kill me, he could just do it.

"How you holding up?" he asks, setting down his kayak and taking mine.

"Fine," I say, digging my nails into my palms until I feel the skin break, the pain easing my racing thoughts.

"We could wade through," he says. "The water's shallow for a kayak, but it'll be faster. Plus, no snakes this way. If you get stuck, just holler, and I'll get you going again."

"Okay."

He sets the kayak into the water, wading in and holding it while I climb in. I've never been in a kayak in my life, but he shows me how to use the paddle and then just lets me go. I start paddling, moving off into the trees. It strikes me again how odd it is that he trusts me so much, just like all those times he gave me his truck. Maybe he's the one who should be afraid, but he's not. Men are so fucking fearless.

I get the hang of paddling pretty easily, gliding through the shallow water and pushing myself off tree root clusters with the paddle. I don't know if I'm damaging his gear by doing that, but it's easier than steering, and he doesn't say anything. I only know he's behind me because I can see the beam of his headlamp along with mine. Every now and then, he tells me to steer right, but otherwise, the only sound is our paddles dipping into the murky water. It's eerie in the swamp, but I don't feel the terror I expected. There are no memories closing in, no lightning strikes of *déjà vu* that take my breath away. It's as if I've never been here at all.

I was too terrified on the way into the swamp last year to take note of my surroundings, too deep in shock on the way out, when Preston carried me wrapped in a blanket all this way. Even in a kayak, moving without the resistance of wading through thigh-deep water, I can tell it's a long way. I remember playing chase with the twins, their taunting words as they pursued me through the swamp like prey. It felt like they caught me in no time.

But I don't remember much of that. My mind was blank with terror.

SELENA

Instead of reliving it, I find myself imagining Preston's journey in. I picture him coming out here alone at night, not knowing if he'd find a body or a stash of stolen goods, if he'd find anything. Not knowing if he was walking into a trap.

I wonder how long he waded through the water before he found me. I remember hearing his voice, how it woke me. I picture him casting the light of his headlamp around, how creepy this would be if I were alone, without his reassuring presence at my back. He must have been determined as hell to come all this way.

I imagine what he thought when his light finally hit me. When he saw me tied up, hanging against that tree, my body bound and gagged with the hood covering my head. I see that picture in my mind, the one he sent me to show to the twins, the blood running down my arms from my bound wrists to my shoulders, down my legs to the ground.

"Here," Preston says. I twist around and see him looking at his phone. He puts it up and pulls the kayak up to the base of a tree. There's a little island of dirt around the swollen root base. It looks so small, I'm not sure more than two of the boys could have stood on it at a time.

"Are you sure?" I ask. "Can you find something that precise with your phone?"

"Yeah," he says, pulling my kayak up to the tree, too. "It's like geocaching."

Like geocaching.

The ridiculousness of his statement strikes me as hilarious, and I have to force myself not to laugh. He takes my hand and helps me out, and we stand on the little hillock, inches apart. I could reach out and touch the tree where they tied me.

"What now?" I ask.

"It's up to you," he says. "It's your exorcism."

It strikes me again how fitting his choice of words. Royal is my demon, but he can't be exorcised. Like an addiction, people say you have to really want to quit before it will work. I don't think I ever really wanted to quit Royal, even when I hated him. I still hate him half the time, but his demon has invaded me, put in roots. It is part of me. When I went into the darkness, it became a part of me. I can never truly leave. It became my own, melded with mine. Trying to exorcise Royal would be like trying to separate two tendrils of smoke once they've combined into one.

When I went into his darkness, it went into me. And I don't want it to leave.

"I brought stuff," Preston says, snagging a backpack. "I have a hatchet. Gasoline and matches. I can leave you alone and go over there for a minute if you want to be alone. Hell, I've got food if you want to sit here and have a fucking picnic."

"I don't understand you," I say, shaking my head. "I'll never understand why you're so nice to me."

"Nice?" he asks, a ghost of a smile on his lips. "Didn't you just accuse me of taking advantage of you and not giving a fuck whether you wanted me to fuck you all those times?"

"That's still true, too," I say. "But you don't have to be nice to me anymore. You don't even have to talk to me. You could have told me to fuck off when I texted.

I'm not a Darling. You're not responsible for me just because you rescued me out here, Preston. I still love Royal. You should hate me."

"We've all got demons," he says. "We just deal with them in different ways."

I nod slowly. "So I'm not your sun. I'm your demon."

He shrugs. "Some people try to atone for their sins. Some people repeat them. One way or another, this town fucks everyone up. But it's still my town, and I failed it. If I see a way I can help even one person, isn't it my job to at least try?"

"Shut up and feed me," I say. "You're going to make me cry."

Preston shakes his head and opens his backpack, but I see the smile he's hiding, and it makes my heart break for him. He deserves so much more than I can give him, so much more than this town. I will never do for him what he's doing for me right now. This town will never do for him what he's doing for it.

SELENA

"Maybe the real place that has power over us isn't a swamp or a bridge," I say. "Maybe it's a town."

five

Harper Apple

Preston spreads out a blanket, and I sit with my back against the tree and my heels right at the edge of the water. He sets out two kinds of fancy crackers, olives, cheeses, sliced meat with coarse black pepper coating the edges, thin sheets of smoked salmon that come apart in flaky layers, and a bottle of wine.

"Rich people," I say, rolling my eyes.

"You don't eat cheese and crackers?"

"How much did that wine cost?"

He shrugs. "I don't know. Not much. Probably fifty bucks. I didn't know if you'd want it, so I didn't bring the good stuff."

I just shake my head. "A bottle of cheap wine is like five bucks, not fifty. You could have brought Post,

Saltines, and a can of spray cheese, and I wouldn't know the difference."

"What's spray cheese?" he asks, looking taken aback.

I can't help but laugh. I snag a few crackers and make a tiny sandwich with them.

"You're taking this really well," he says, watching me as he twists a corkscrew into the wine cork. "You okay?"

"Totally repressing the shit out of some memories right now," I say. "Wine me up, pardner."

He brought actual wine glasses, which tells me he's probably never had a picnic before in his life. Not that I have, either, but even I know people don't usually bring glassware. After handing me a generous amount of wine, he sits down beside me.

"To letting go," he says, tapping the glass against mine. "Whenever you're ready."

"I'm getting there," I say. "Or getting drunk. I haven't decided yet."

I drink the wine too fast, but I don't care. There's a reckless, careening feeling inside me, like I'm teetering on some edge. I'm not ready to face what's on one side, but

I know I'll have to if I fall that way. I'm not sure I can handle it without a little alcohol to pad the landing.

"Can I ask you something," I say, holding out my glass for a refill.

"You can ask."

Suddenly, I remember him saying that when I asked him a question online, when he was the Silver Swan. I don't know why that sets me more on edge. I've known that's who he is for a week. He was never Mr. D. We'd barely talked before he found me.

"You were stalking me before you came out here," I say. "You were at my house. I saw your footprints, and you talked to my neighbor. Why?"

"You saved my sister," he says. "You told me when she was in trouble. I wanted to pay you back, but as you know, I don't like to be seen. I was there when your electricity was shut off one day, so I paid the bill."

"You didn't know you were looking for me when you came out here?"

"No," he admits. "I didn't know what I'd find. I just knew there was something sketchy going on when

Duke's Hummer came out here and then left, and then came back. I waited it out, and then I waited until I was pretty sure they weren't coming back, and then I started looking for whatever they'd left."

"Wow," I say, a shiver curling through my body when I realize how very close I came to death. It's a miracle he looked as long as he did, that he found me way out here. It's a testament to his hatred for the Dolces, his determination to take them down. If he had been Mr. D, he would have helped me do it last year, before they ever got to me.

"You're like my avenging, guardian angel," I say after a while.

He lets out a little scoff of breath. "Definitely not any kind of angel."

"You still have the blanket, right?" I ask. "And those pictures. Do you think it would be enough, if we wanted to use them?"

"You want to get Royal arrested?"

I shake my head. "Royal didn't do it."

"Really?" he asks, drawing back.

"And as much as I want to get the twins thrown in jail for life, I don't think that will help much. Monsters make monsters make monsters."

"Then you want to go to the root cause."

"Mr. Dolce brought them here. He made them who they are. He's the one poisoning this town, isn't he?"

"Since the day he moved back," Preston agrees. "Faulkner won't ever be the way it was, though. They've ruined it with their blood money. Even if we went to the police, half of them are in Tony Dolce's pocket. He got the judges elected, and he'd probably find a way to buy off or intimidate the jurors if it even went to trial."

"So, what can we do?"

"What they did to us," Preston says.

"What?"

"Drive them out of town," he says. "That's the only way it can begin to heal."

"Okay," I say, slowly chewing an olive. He doesn't get the little black kind that comes on pizza, or even the green ones with a red center. No, his are fancy purple and brown ones coated in oil. "If we wanted to make them leave, we need to know what makes them stay."

"Revenge," he says immediately.

"Right," I say. "Revenge on you, on your family, because they blame you for their sister's death."

"Disappearance."

"Okay, her disappearance," I say. "Which means they need closure, and I'm guessing if all your millions and their millions can't find them, then I can't, either."

Preston sips his wine and doesn't answer.

I slosh some more into my glass and go on. "What if we got rid of everything here that reminds them of her, everything that ties them to Faulkner."

"You want to burn the bridge to my grandpa's house? That's the only way in or out."

"Would that be a bad thing?"

He clears some food from the side of his mouth with his tongue before answering. "No."

"What if… What if getting revenge on him is the only way to give the Dolces closure?" I ask. "He's the patriarch of your family, like Tony is theirs. If getting rid of him is the only way to get rid of Tony…"

"Then I'd do it," Preston says.

"Really?"

"In a heartbeat."

"You don't like your grandfather very much, do you?"

He shrugs. "You're right. He's as much at fault as Tony Dolce. They may have started this, but he deepened it. He made it worse, and he wouldn't let it go when the rest of our family was willing to walk away."

I nod, finishing off my wine. I'm definitely feeling it now. I wish I hadn't drunk so much, but it's been a long time since I was drunk, since I trusted someone enough to let myself drop my guard and not have to be the one on alert, looking out for myself. Tonight, Preston's looking out for me.

"Would you help me if I wanted to get him to Royal somehow, so Royal could get revenge?"

"Trust me, Royal's gotten revenge," Preston says. "If he wanted to kill Grandpa Darling, he would have. But he'd rather see him cut down to nothing so he can gloat. He literally castrated the old man."

"What?"

"Oh, your boyfriend didn't tell you that?" Preston says, shaking his head. "Yeah. That's their M.O. Grandpa Darling isn't the only one to face that particular dismemberment, either."

"Shit," I say, leaning my head back and closing my eyes. "No wonder you don't want them knowing where you live."

I believe him, though. Royal doesn't kill—not usually. He likes to let people live to suffer. Even if I brought him Preston's grandfather, he wouldn't kill him. He's already gotten revenge, and it didn't help.

"They destroyed or drove away everyone in my family," Preston says. "And it's still not enough. Look at my face, Harper. You'd think that would be enough for them, but their thirst for revenge only grows the more they try to quench it. The only way it will ever end is if we end them."

"Or make peace with them," I mutter aloud. There has to be some way, something that can bring these families together. Maybe there's too much bad blood to ever have friendship between them, but peace must be possible. An end to the feud, a truce between them.

"There's no making peace," Preston says. "We were willing—at least some of us. We tried to reason with them after the disappearance, but they just went apeshit. It's been three years, Harper. They're not going to let it go. And now Tony wants to build this casino. Seems like it's out of spite alone, to ruin the town as we know it."

"So he's the problem," I say, nodding. "There has to be a way to make him leave, or at least make him call off his sons."

"I don't think he controls Royal," Preston says. "Royal's the one looking for revenge. Tony's just looking for an opportunity to exploit the place."

"Do you know what Royal wants revenge for?" I ask, my heart suddenly hammering when I think of what Royal told me on Gideon's back porch.

SELENA

"His sister," Preston says, splitting the last of the wine between our glasses.

"Don't you think part of it is because your family kidnapped him?" I ask, watching him for a reaction. Preston doesn't scare me, but he's a slippery snake, deceptive when it suits him.

"We didn't kidnap him," he says. "He and his family tried to set us up to look that way."

"So it's his fault you assaulted him?"

"I didn't do shit to him," Preston says. "They left him tied up in my grandfather's house. What did they fucking expect to happen? I wouldn't leave my own sister alone in a room with that man."

"Still sounds like you're blaming Royal for what happened to him."

"He helped set it up," Preston says. "I don't blame him, though. He was a kid. He probably didn't know shit about it. But his father should have known. And now… It's hard to feel bad when something bad happens to someone like that. It's like feeling bad when you find out a serial killer was abused as a child."

"What happened to him then doesn't excuse what he's doing now," I say, mostly to myself. I said something similar when Royal told me what happened when he was kidnapped.

Preston finishes his wine and begins to wrap his glass back up, so it won't break in his bag.

"Do you know what happened to him when your grandfather found him?" I ask Preston. "When he took him to the Swans' lair?"

Preston hands falter, and then he carefully starts picking up the crackers. "Do you know?" he asks, his words measured.

"Yes."

He tucks the crackers back into his bag. "I'm surprised he'd tell you that."

"So, you do know," I say, my heart hammering. I wanted him to say it wasn't true, to tell me Royal was wrong, and he didn't know anything about it. He told me Preston knew what happened to him the same way the twins knew what happened to me when I was tied to this tree. Because they did it.

"Yeah," Preston says quietly. "I know."

Suddenly, it gives me a jumpy feeling to know this is where I was attacked, where I almost died. I shrink away from the tree, hugging my knees.

"Did you do it?" I ask, because I've never been one to leave a question unasked, to shy away from hearing the truth, even when it hurts the most. Preston is my friend. I love him. But I know he's not above using someone who's not in a state to protest.

"What the fuck, Harper," he says, turning toward me. "How can you ask me that?"

"Because Royal said you did."

"And you got him to sit in my truck and not murder me?" he asks. "Damn, Miss A. I'm impressed."

"Did you?" I press. "I need an actual answer."

I made way too many stupid mistakes over the past year by assuming things based on people's words or reactions. Apparently, I'm not so good at reading people, even if I like watching them. Between him and Mr. D, I don't trust anyone who won't just say what they mean.

Preston pulls his mask off and rakes his hand through his hair. His fingers tangle in his headlamp strap, and he pulls it off, shaking his head. "No," he says. "I wasn't there. I found out later."

"I'm sorry," I say, touching his shoulder. "I didn't mean to offend you—"

"You didn't mean to offend me," he says flatly. "By asking if I raped your boyfriend."

"Look, I know you'd never hurt me because you have some weird, transference thing going on with your guilt about their sister, but you've told me yourself that you have things to atone for," I point out. "Including some pretty blurred lines when it comes to consent."

"Because I care about you."

"What?"

"I'd never hurt you because I care about you," he says, turning toward me. "It has nothing to do with her. Maybe at first, yeah. But I barely knew her. I know you, Harper Apple." He leans in, pressing his shoulder to mine, his eyes hooded as his gaze dips to my lips.

SELENA

For a second, I don't move. I wait for his mouth to find mine, for him to take what he wants like he always does. My heart is beating double-time, and I'm not sure if I'm scared or excited that he'll kiss me.

When he starts to angle his face toward mine, I lean away, though. "I care about you, too," I say, my heart hammering in my ears. "But… I don't know if it's that way or not. It's too complicated. I got attached to you when I was all fucked up. I felt safe. *You* felt safe. But it's not the same…"

"Not the same way you feel about Royal," he says, bitterness curling the edges of his words like frost.

"I don't think you care about me that way, either," I say. "You deserve more, Preston. You deserve to love someone in a big way, not just because you got attached or they're comfortable. And you deserve someone who loves you back that way. I just don't think it's me."

He scoffs and picks up his mask, pulling it back over the top half of his face. "Of course it's not," he says. "Look at me. And look at you."

"Preston…" I reach out and touch his arm. "It's not about how you look."

"Right," he says. "Well, I didn't fuck your boyfriend, so I guess we can still be friends."

"I'm sorry I had to ask you that," I say. "I know you're not into hurting people, but… Well, maybe he's the exception. And in my defense, three years is a long time. I know I'm not the same person I was three years ago, and I bet you aren't, either."

"You could say that."

I finish my wine and hand him the glass. "I don't know what kind of person you were. To be honest, I've heard things that weren't exactly complimentary."

"Whatever you've heard, I'm sure it's true," he says. "Groomed in my grandfather's image to take over the practice, just like Dad, because we were the most like him out of each generation."

"If it makes any difference, I don't think you're like him," I say. "And if you are, then he's a damn good person."

SELENA

"He's not a good person," Preston says, picking up the rest of the food. "And neither am I. I've run your boyfriend off the road, vandalized his house to remind the neighborhood he's corrupt, and fucked with their candy business. Want honesty? I wouldn't give a fuck if he died. Hell, I'd throw a party. But I'm not his kind of monster."

He finishes shoving the stuff roughly back into the bag and glares at me, like he's pissed that I love that kind of monster instead of him.

"Maybe he wasn't that kind of monster before your family did that to him," I say quietly.

"Maybe you're right," he says, pulling out the rest of the contents of his bag. "I don't know. I wasn't there when Grandpa found Royal. I just know he took him to the Swans for the incoming pledges to beat up as part of their initiation, and it went too far. I don't know who participated except one of my cousins."

"Colt?" I ask, my throat going so dry I can't swallow.

"No," he says. "Colt was already a Swan. Sullivan was in the upcoming class who would have been freshmen the next year, though."

"The one you said was obsessed with Royal's dick."

"I said he was fucked up enough to ask that kind of thing," Preston corrects. "He was a fucking kid, and our grandfather isn't a person who takes no for an answer. So yeah, he participated, but it completely screwed him up. He's been in and out of psych wards ever since. As for the others, I assume my grandfather, maybe my father, and possibly a couple other Swan pledges or alumni. Any of the current members who are juniors or seniors could have been there. But they'll never tell you. It's not something you talk about, even if there wasn't an oath."

"Bound together by a shameful act," I say, remembering the words from the Midnight Swans book. I don't want to think about the Swan members who could have been there—the Dolce boys' friends are seniors.

Preston tugs on the blanket, and I stand. I've avoided thinking about where we are, but now I stare at the bark of the tree, and it's like I can still feel it. I can feel the unforgiving hardness, the roughness against my bare chest when they shoved me against it. I thought I'd die here.

I reach out and run my fingertips over the rough, cool surface of the trunk. I look for blood in the crevices in the bark, but there's nothing, no sign marking this tree as different from the others. When I look up, though, I can see a line where some of the bark is rubbed away, where the rope was wrapped around. I dragged and yanked on it until pieces of bark came away, and it didn't grow back. It's just the outer layer, not noticeable if you aren't looking. But it's there.

Another shiver rolls through me, and I'm grateful for Preston's company. I step against the tree, lifting my hands to touch the damage I caused, so minimal it's almost invisible. I remember how insignificant I felt, the raw fury of helplessness as I hung here. And I remember the moment I realized I couldn't get free, that I would die there.

Something in me did die.

I squeeze my eyes closed and press my forehead to the tree's trunk. I remember the burn deep into my skin when Duke fucking branded me, proud of the notch he was adding to his belt. I was desperate, panicking, terrified for my life to be over, and he didn't even worry about repercussions. He was so arrogant he didn't even consider there would be consequences if I was found with a new brand burned into me. He was proud of what they'd done to me, and he wanted to show it, like he secretly wanted someone to find me so he could boast about it. Maybe that's the real reason they brought Dawson. So someone could admire their cleverness, their savagery.

And Baron… Baron didn't worry, either. He didn't want me to be found, and he knew I wouldn't be. He made sure to tie good knots, like a Boy Scout. He made sure I couldn't scream, knowing no one would come here for years. They even talked about it at the end of the night.

"Are we supposed to kill her now?" Duke asked when they were packing up to go. His voice was slurred and quiet. I heard a

click, and I thought it must be a gun, that they were going to finish me off after all the torture. I always said they'd kill me if they found out about Mr. D. And yet, it didn't feel real. I didn't truly believe it until that moment. I'd endured it all for nothing.

"Royal said to leave her," Baron said. "She'll die out here in a couple days. No one would hear her even if she could scream, and she can't."

He'd made sure of that. I could barely breathe through the thick, wet hood he'd tied into my mouth. I'd tried to scream, at the end, when they both used me at the same time. I could barely croak out a sound now.

"What if someone working smells her once she's dead?" asked another guy, a stranger at the time. Now I know it was Dawson. "I came in her. Our DNA is all over her."

"They'll think it's a dead animal," Baron said. "After what she did to our boy, she deserves to suffer for more than one night. He'll be feeling that for a long time."

I'm shaking now, gripping the tree to keep myself upright. My fingers dig into the rough bark, gripping the texture as I sway on my feet.

I remember their laughter. The clink of beer bottles as they raised a toast to each other for how thoroughly they destroyed me. I remember their hands on me, their bodies against my bare skin, the revulsion I felt. I remember when they stopped taking turns at the end, turned me sideways, and both went at once, assaulting me from both sides. I remember the shame that built in me like a volcano that could never erupt, the violation as they came inside me.

I think I'll be sick. I press my fist to my stomach, but it's not vomit that comes.

It's a scream.

I open my mouth and let it out, let it spew out of me like the lava from that volcano they put inside me. The memories swirl up, but it's not fear I feel. It's rage. Rage at how beaten I felt because I couldn't even scream, couldn't let out the horror they were stuffing into me with each violation. I was forced to contain it, not even express the pain, the betrayal and shame and defeat. I press both fists into my stomach, and I double over with the force of it, and I scream again, and again, and again.

Finally, my voice is gone, but this time, it's not from being silenced.

It's from using it.

My throat hurts more than when Royal choked me out until I almost passed out. More than after that, when it was clogged with tears. More than when I tried to scream behind the gag, and barely a sound came out, only loud enough for my own attackers to hear and mock.

I'm vaguely aware of Preston's hands on me, that he's holding me up from behind, so I don't pitch headfirst into the murky swamp water. That my face is wet and cold. That inside me is a hollow pit of raw exhaustion.

I straighten, allowing him to pull me into his arms and hold me with all the fierceness of his misplaced love for me. After a while, I pull away.

"I'm tired."

"Do you feel better?" he asks.

"No," I say. "But thank you for this."

"Do you want to chop at the tree for a while?" he asks. "I brought a hatchet. You probably can't cut it down with that, but it might feel good to hit it."

"No," I say. "Burn it."

It's too wet to worry about it catching the surrounding trees on fire, but I take the small can of gasoline from Preston, just a gallon, and slosh it over the tree. He helps me back into the kayak, climbs into the other one, and hands me the matches. I throw one onto the tree, watching a blossom of fire consume the trunk. I know it'll go out, that it won't burn the whole tree. But somehow, knowing that the bark will burn off, that anything I touched will be gone, brings me a shadow of relief. And I know if I ever want to come back, I can find the tree, the one blackened by my hand the way I was scarred by theirs.

As we slide silently through the swamp, I can't help but feel that it's all somehow hollow and inadequate. The Dolces should be the ones burning for their crimes.

SELENA

six

Harper Apple

Mom's asleep when I get home in the morning, and I hear her leave in the afternoon while I'm doing homework. I go outside a few minutes later just to check on my car. Mom doesn't have a key, but I'm still paranoid. It's ridiculous how much that car means to me, and not just because it's the nicest thing anyone's ever done for me, or the nicest thing I've ever owned a thousand times over. Having a car of my own means I can escape this town. Even if it only represents my dream right now—I don't have enough in my stash to live on for more than a few months—it gives me hope that maybe I'll really make it out.

"Hey," Blue calls, raising a hand in a little wave. She's standing out by the street watching Olive race up and down on a tricycle meant for kids half her age. Her skinny knees jut out to either side as she pedals, and she whoops and circles her arm over her head like she's swinging an invisible lasso. I smile and walk over, tucking my hands into the front pocket of my black hoodie.

"What's up?"

"Just watching Olive," Blue says. "Want a smoke?"

"Sure," I say with a shrug. "I probably owe you a whole pack by now."

"Get me back later," Blue says, pulling a pack out of the pocket of her faded jean jacket. I notice bruises around her wrist when the sleeve rides up as she lights up before handing me the pack.

"You know, I have a punching bag in my basement," I say after a minute, blowing smoke out the corner of my mouth. "I could show you a few moves sometime, if you want to come over and hang out there instead of always having me over."

"Could I bring Olive?" she asks, blowing a strand of lank hair out of her mouth.

"Sure," I say. "Never hurts to know how to throw a few punches, no matter what age you are."

She nods, watching her sister tear down the road, her long hair streaming out behind her, a big grin on her face. I wonder when I stopped playing. It seems like such an odd thing now, so far removed from reality, that I can't really remember when I outgrew it.

"You remember what I asked you this summer?" Blue asks, scuffing her toe along a crack in the sidewalk.

"About finding you a rich guy?"

"No," she says. "About watching Olive if… You know. If I ever needed you to."

"Yeah, sure. I remember. Why?"

"You'd keep her safe?"

"Of course," I say, frowning at her. "I promise. What's up?"

"I just… Worry about her. When I'm at work. Would you watch her while I'm gone, if I needed you to? I mean, if you're home and you're not busy and stuff. I don't really know anyone else around here. I'd ask my aunt, but she lives in Oregon…"

"You know I would," I say. "Just don't leave her with my mom if I'm not around. She's got all kinds of sketchy guys in and out of there."

Blue nods. "Thanks, Harper."

I want to ask her more, but I know she doesn't need me prying on top of whatever else she has going on, so I finish the cigarette in silence before heading in to get ready. The Homecoming dance is tonight, so I take a shower and lay out a little black dress Preston bought me this summer. I wasn't planning on going until yesterday, but I wouldn't buy a dress to wear for one day even if I had known. This is fine for a friend-date with Gideon. Just to make extra sure it doesn't seem too much like a date, I text him letting him know I want to meet him there. I don't want to leave my car at home in case Mom comes back, anyway.

I've just pulled on my dress when I hear a knock at the front door. I still get a little burst of fear any time someone knocks, so I grab my knife before going to the door. I open it to find Royal Dolce standing on my doorstep in a tux. He looks so fucking good I'd melt if I didn't know better.

"What are you doing?" I ask.

"I'm taking you to Homecoming."

I cross my arms and glare up at him, not moving from the doorway. "I'm going with Gideon."

"Like hell you are."

I sigh. "We're going as friends, but I already told him I'd go. Besides, I told you before, just because we slept together once, it was a mistake. We're not together. You and me are not a thing."

Royal just looks at me and holds up the tall bag he's holding with a hanger at the top. "Go put this on."

"Royal. I already have plans."

"Cancel them."

I glare at him, refusing to move. But I know he won't back down if I fight him, so I try a different tactic. "I didn't think you were the type to want to go to a lame high school dance even when you were in high school," I say with a smirk. "Do you really want to go dance with a bunch of kids? Not to mention you told me you don't dance."

"If I want to dance, I'll dance," he says. "And I have no interest in lame high school anything. I have an interest in keeping a bunch of assholes' hands off you. So if you're going, then I'm going. Now, go get dressed."

I look him up and down, trying not to fucking drool. His tux looks like it was custom made for him, hugging his huge, broad shoulders to perfection and practically screaming money. "Where'd you get a tux last minute?"

He smirks down at me. "You think this is the first lame function I've had to attend? I told you before, just because I have money, that doesn't mean I do whatever the fuck I want. I've been going to shit like this since I was old enough to walk. I own a tux. Now go put this on."

I hesitate before accepting the bag. "How do you know it'll fit?"

"It'll fit," he says with a cocky little smile.

"Why do I get the feeling you're going to make me look like a two-dollar hooker?"

SELENA

"Because you underestimate me."

I sigh and reach for my phone. "I need to text Gideon."

"I'll do it."

I give him a hard look. "Be nice."

He holds up both hands and gives me a look of feigned innocence. "What else would I be to the little boy who thinks he can ask out my girl?"

"Royal," I warn. "He's a nice guy."

"If he was a nice guy, he wouldn't have asked you out again after you told him to fuck off last week. Now go get ready before I change my mind and just stay here and fuck you all night to remind you who you belong to."

I roll my eyes, but I turn and head down the hall to put on the dress. In truth, staying here and fucking Royal sounds way too fucking tempting, especially when a high school dance is the alternative. Which means I need to get out of the house before I lose my head and do something I'll regret.

The dress does not, in fact, make me look like a streetwalker. It's the softest, most buttery smooth fabric

I've ever felt, in a shade of red so deep it's almost black. When I pull on the rich garment, I just about melt. It hugs my curves and cinches at the waist like it was custom made for me. The bodice is fitted but not too tight, with a high, halter neck that shows off my toned shoulders instead of attempting to make me look like I have cleavage. After the tapered waist that highlights my tiny middle, the cut loosens, opening up at the hips, the luxurious fabric falling in silky folds to my feet. I don't even have to look at myself in the mirror to fall in love. It feels so good I want to moan just standing in the middle of my room in it.

When I look in the mirror, though, I'm dumbstruck all over again. I turn a minute later and see Royal standing in the door to my bedroom, leaning on the doorframe with his arms crossed. I have no idea how long he's been standing there, but I'm too awed to care.

"Royal," I say, trying to put into words how incredibly, amazingly beautiful he made me feel. "It's… How did you know my size so well?"

SELENA

"It's made for you," he says, his eyes heated as he takes me in.

"I can tell," I say, turning and watching the skirt flow out slightly around my ankles. "But… How?"

"Once in a while, a Darling makes himself useful," he says. "Now come here and put your shoes on."

I remember Preston measuring me over the summer, and it feels like a different lifetime.

Royal holds onto my hips to help me balance while I step into the heels he brought, which are also the correct size, although that's less impressive than a dress that actually fits my bottom-heavy figure. When I straighten, he pulls me closer, his hands circling my waist possessively. I slide my arms around his neck with no hesitation. I don't know when I stopped thinking he'd hurt me, but there's no fear in me as I stand on tiptoes and pull him down for a kiss.

He presses his lips to mine, a little growl of pleasure catching in his throat as his hands tighten, pulling me flush against him.

"Thank you," I say, pulling away at last. "This is so beautiful, Royal. I didn't know it was possible for clothes to make someone feel so good."

"You sure you want to go to this conformist nightmare, Jailbird?" he asks, tucking a strand of hair behind my ear. "Because I could take this right back off and make you feel a hell of a lot better than this dress can."

"That's what I'm afraid of," I say. "So, stop tempting me."

"You're tempted?" he asks, smirking down at me and flattening his huge hand against the small of my back. "Then let's get this over with so I can spend the rest of the night with my head between your thighs."

I roll my eyes. "I told you, we're not together, and you're not changing my mind."

"Okay, Cherry Pie," he says, shaking his head.

"And I'm driving my car," I say.

"Not happening."

SELENA

"Fine, then *you* can drive my car," I say. "But I'm not responsible for what happens to yours if you leave it parked here."

He just smirks at me. "I have insurance."

"I thought you were afraid my neighbors would dismantle it for parts," I say, repeating something he once said when he dropped me off.

"I'm not afraid of your neighbors," he says, holding out a hand. I sigh and hand over my keys. I've accepted the fact that I will never drive anywhere when Royal's involved. He's way too much of a control freak to let anyone else behind the wheel.

At school, I make my way inside with Royal, ignoring the whispers and stares in our direction when people see last year's king returning. Royal puts on an air of complete boredom, but I know he's watching. In a weird way, his presence allows me to let my guard down. I can take out my phone and text my friends, find out where they are, without worrying about watching out for myself.

"Harper!" someone calls.

"Great," Royal grumbles.

Dixie rushes over in a black satin dress that shows all her curves, a pair of red lace-up boots, and red clutch to match, Colt trailing behind her.

"Damn, girl," I say, looking her over. "That dress is criminal."

"I know, right?" she says, giggling and fanning her very ample cleavage.

"She's a walking titty fuck," Colt says cheerfully before glancing at Royal. "Didn't expect to see you here. Or anywhere with Harper."

Royal gives him a cool look. "Get used to it."

Colt shrugs and flashes me a smile. "Looking fine as usual, Teeny."

"You too," I say, returning his smile. "Are our other friends here?"

"Josie doesn't believe in school dances," Dixie says. "But everyone else is here. Come on, let's go in."

We head into the café, which shows no signs that it was the site of a brawl yesterday. It's decorated with streamers and posters, little twinkling lights winding along the rafters of the high ceiling and mirror balls twirling from the giant fans.

"Harper," Gloria squeals, rushing over in what looks like a wedding dress. "You came! And look what you brought." She wiggles her brows at me and leans over the full skirt to give me air kisses.

"What did you bring?" I ask, glancing behind her to where two guys stand watching. "Baron or Rylan?"

"I came with Baron, and we'll be crowned for sure." She gives an excited little grin and grabs my hand. "But Rylan wanted to talk, so maybe I'll leave with him."

"Well, good luck," I say. "If that's what you want, you should have it."

"You look so gorgeous," she says. "Especially with Royal. You should have come over to my house to get ready. I could have done your hair."

I shrug, since I didn't really do myself up too much. I did my hair and makeup, but no more than usual, since I didn't think I'd be on a real date.

"We'll do it before prom," she says, taking my hand and giving it a quick squeeze.

"Sure," I agree.

"Hey, maybe you can campaign and win prom queen," she says. "When everyone sees Royal here with you… You're going to knock me right off the top girl spot."

"Do I need to watch my back?" I ask, quirking a brow.

"Not from me," she says. "I won last year, and they don't let the same person win two years in a row. So I'm just here to watch your back for you."

I thank her, and then Dixie drags me over to where Susanna and Quinn are sipping punch near a table. I spot Gideon with them and stiffen, ready for him to tell me what an asshole I am. But he smiles and comes over.

"Hey," he says, holding out a hand to Royal. "I didn't know you and Harper were a thing, but we were just going as friends, anyway."

Royal gives him a cool look, and Gideon shifts from one foot to the other. I elbow Royal, and he grudgingly gives Gideon's hand a quick pump.

SELENA

"Who are you here with?" I ask just as the music starts and the lights go down.

"Those girls," he says, raising his voice over the music and nodding to Dixie's group. "None of us have dates, so it worked out."

"Sorry to cancel on you last minute," I say, leaning in so he can hear me. "I'm not with Royal. But until he knows that, it's probably best if you don't ask me to things like this, even as friends."

He shakes his head and looks at me like I'm nuts, and I realize how crazy it is that I've gotten used to this, that I don't even question Royal's behavior. But he is who he is, and I've accepted it. I think I've finally accepted that I'm his, even if I'm not willing to admit it to him just yet.

"Harper," a voice shrieks over the music. I turn to see Magnolia and her two freshman friends. She races over and throws herself into my arms, her friends tottering after her, looking like they've never worn heels before. Magnolia's wearing a pink chiffon nightmare of a dress and a pair of black Converse sneakers. She clings to my neck, pressing her mouth against my ear. "My cousin told me he told you about my brother. If you get him killed, I swear on my Brody Villines poster I'll climb in your window and smother you in your sleep. I'm not kidding. I have a gun."

"Good to know," I say, fighting through the cloud of her dress to push her off me.

"Oh my god, it's my favorite song," she squeals. "Come dance!"

She bounds off like a hyper puppy, her friends trailing after her. I shake my head and turn back to Royal, who's staring at me, some unreadable expression on his face.

"What?" I ask. "You know I'm friends with the Darlings now."

"Nothing," he says, shaking his head. "Want to get a drink?"

He nods to the table, but Cotton Montgomery cuts us off, three drinks in his hand. They do the usual guy greeting, and Cotton hands Royal a cup of punch. "Duke's already dumped the flask, so don't drink too much," he says. Then he acknowledges me for the first

SELENA

time, jerking his chin in a quick nod at me and handing me a can of soda. "Figured you'd appreciate a sealed one."

He turns and walks off, and I stare after him. For some reason, I never thought about him hearing those rumors. I've never heard anything going around on the gossip circuit, but it's common knowledge in his own group that girls don't take drinks from him, and Dixie's said something, too. I wonder if there was something on the blog the year before I came, or if this is more of an open secret. Either way, it must suck to know your own friends call you a predator behind your back.

"You're friends with Cotton?" Royal asks as I open the soda.

"Not really," I say, shrugging. "But I think we have a mutual respect since I joined the Swans."

It's a little more than that—Cotton respects me because I'm helping the Darlings, and I respect him for giving me a heads up about putting Colt in danger. Even a creeper can do something decent on occasion, and he risked himself and went out of his way to warn us. I'm not going to tell Royal that and get him booted from his friend group… Or worse.

I still haven't asked Royal exactly what happened to Dawson.

He's watching me in that weird way again, so I bug my eyes at him. "What?" I ask.

"You didn't tell me you were popular this year."

I cover my mouth so I don't snort out soda. "I don't think that's the word for it."

"Baron said you started shit with him and got a bunch of pissed off chicks they ghosted to help, not that you had friends."

"Yeah, well, I guess I do," I say. "Funny how that happens when there's not someone there chasing away every guy you talk to and telling all the girls you're a trashy whore."

"You had friends last year," Royal points out, obviously unmoved by my dig.

"Yeah, *your* friends," I say.

He looks at me blankly, and I realize he doesn't see the difference. Maybe there isn't one to him. I didn't really see the difference until I said it aloud. But it matters.

They're not here because I'm with Royal. They won't disappear if things don't work out between us. They're not my friends because I have the best boyfriend or because I'm in with the populars. Most of them aren't even popular themselves. I don't have a clique, but somehow, I've managed to gain the respect and friendship of people from a bunch of different groups. And they're not here to ingratiate themselves or gain status, like they were when I was with Royal.

They're here for *me*.

People have my back. I remember how excited I was last year when Gloria invited me to the mall, because as pathetic as it sounds, no one had ever sought out my company like they wanted to spend time with me. Now, people call my name when I walk into a place like this. People come say hi. Even Cotton, who's on the enemy team, brought me a drink and made sure it was one I'd be comfortable drinking.

BLOOD EMPIRE

Last year, I wanted so badly what Royal had. I wanted the tight-knit group he had, the family, the brotherhood. So I tried to get in with them, and when I got Royal, I told myself they cared about me, too. I let myself get caught up in the fever of longing, of wanting to belong, to be a part of something. Now I realize I didn't want to be *with* them. I wanted to *be* them. I wanted to be Royal, to have brothers who were loyal and had my back no matter what.

But Baron doesn't have his back. Baron's never had anyone's back but his own. And besides all that, I could never have that because I'm not part of that family.

Now, I have something better, something I built on my own, this group of friends who've come together from all different paths, groups, and families. It reminds me of Faulkner—a little microcosm of the mostly rich, mostly white side of town, anyway.

I like that somehow, I brought together this group who reflects more than just the most elite. There's also the fallen elite. There's the tatted up bad boy who smokes under the bleachers and is missing a finger. There's the plus-sized goth girl who runs a gossip column. There's the elite queen bee who's really poor, a sassy little girl from the next generation to take over WHPA, and the girl who isn't here because she's too cool. And by extension of my friendship with Dixie, there's the blue-haired wannabe rebel girl, and the chick who likes to stay home and bake on a Saturday night. And because of my Midnight Swans status, I can call the elite friends, too.

When Magnolia gestures for me to join them on the dance floor, I find that I have a place now, a niche I've carved out here. I have Royal, who's older and doesn't even go to school here, and Colt, who's also older but still goes to Willow Heights. They're enemies, and yet, they manage to coexist in our little circle on the dance floor. The gossip girls are goofing around, dabbing and doing the sprinkler and other cheesy dance moves, and the Walton girls are grinding on their dates, the Swan guys. But they don't call me a skank like they did last year, and they don't chase off Magnolia and her freshman friends who join us.

Gloria and Baron leave to receive their crowns, and then they play a slow song, and I wrap my arms around Royal's neck and sway against him. Somehow, I've come back around to myself, back to a place where I can have fun for a moment, where I can carve away a sliver of happiness just for myself. "Do you think we could have this for the whole town?" I ask, looking up at Royal.

"Homecoming is for the whole town," he says with a tiny smile tugging at the corner of his lips.

"Not just Homecoming," I say, nodding at the dancefloor. "This. Everyone getting along, having fun together. Do you think Faulkner could ever have that?"

"I managed not to murder Preston Darling when I had the chance, so I guess hell's already frozen over," Royal says. "Anything's possible now, Cherry Pie."

"Would you help me?" I ask.

He narrows his eyes. "Help you do what?"

"Make it happen," I say. "At least try. Or start the process."

"I thought you didn't need my help."

"I do," I admit, my pulse fluttering in my throat. "I need you more than anyone."

Royal slides his arms all the way around me, pulling me flush against him. He nuzzles into my neck, and I slide my hands over his broad shoulders and close my eyes, laying my head on his strong chest. I do need him, and not just to heal the town. But that's true, too. More than anyone, this town needs him to make things right. The only question is, how can I get him to want to heal this town rather than destroy it?

Preston gave me the answer to that question last night. If I want him to stop destroying this town, I need to figure out how to heal *him*. That's what people do for the people they love. Maybe I don't love Preston enough to do the same for him in return when he does those things for me, but my job isn't to heal Preston. My job is to heal myself. And maybe, if I love him enough, I can heal Royal, too.

After all, he's the one who helped me heal when I was broken beyond repair. He didn't just give me a safe place to heal. He actively made it happen. He said he moved the world for me, and it's true. And I haven't done anything in return.

I'm not the one who broke him, but that doesn't mean I can't help him heal. It doesn't matter who inflicted those wounds. I don't want to see him suffer anymore. Not from what happened in his past, and not from the consequences of his own retaliations. The revenge he keeps raining down on this town adds to his own suffering as much as those he's hurt. I need to find a way to end it, to make him stop. I don't want anyone to hurt the man I love, not even himself.

"Royal," I say, pulling back and looking up at him. "I need to tell you something."

He watches me, his dark eyes searching mine as we sway to the music around us.

"I asked Preston if he knew what happened when you were kidnapped, and he said he found out later," I say. "He wasn't there. He didn't do anything to you. Neither did Colt. It was the older Swans and some of the new recruits that year. That was their… Gauntlet."

SELENA

Royal's lips press together, and for a second, I wonder if he already knew. DeShaun said Royal made the Midnight Swans into a joke. It used to be an organization that tried to keep order but also do good, but obviously it was corrupted at some point, maybe by Grandpa Darling himself. The school officially disbanded it after Royal's kidnapping, but Royal brought it back. And then he destroyed the Midnight Swans image by making it into a giant frat party.

"Why are you talking about me to Preston Darling?" Royal asks, his hands tightening on my waist.

"Because we're friends," I say, refusing to flinch as I look into his eyes. "And he's helping me heal."

"*I'm* helping you heal," Royal growls.

"You're right," I say. "But he's my friend, and I just wanted you to know that, in case it helps you stop wanting to murder him."

"I want to murder him more for being your friend," Royal says. "Do you really think I give a shit what he says he did or didn't do? I don't trust a word that comes out of his mouth."

"Then trust me," I say, laying a palm on his cheek. The bruises on his face are mostly gone, leaving only the ones around his nose, now faded green and yellow.

"I don't trust you, either," he says, turning his face away.

His words steal my breath. I didn't know how much he could still hurt me until he said them. That's the problem with feeling again, with letting myself go back to who I am instead of being Preston's doll. When you can feel, things don't just feel good. They fucking hurt.

"Royal," I say, trying to turn his face back to me. "If I can trust you again after what you did, you can trust me."

He steps back, dropping his hands from around me. My body cries out in protest, instantly cold at being abandoned by his touch. When I see the look in his eyes, I'm gripped in the heaviness of anguish that radiates from him. "I fucked up, and I admitted it," he says quietly. "I can't erase what happened, but I did everything I could to make it right. I'm not saying you're to blame for what I did, and I won't pretend there's any comparison between what you did and what I did. But you fucked me over, too, Harper, and you haven't done one fucking thing to make it right, or apologize, or even admit it."

"I did apologize," I say, my throat suddenly tight and my eyes aching. "I'm sorry, Royal."

He holds up a hand. "I don't care. I'm not asking for anything from you because I don't need anything. I already have you. You're mine, and you always will be. Nothing will ever change that. It doesn't matter what you did. But don't fucking stand here and ask me to trust you, and then fake hurt when I don't."

"I'm not faking," I say, my eyes filling with tears.

"I'm done with your lame-ass dance," Royal says, and he pushes past me and through the crowd, disappearing toward the door.

seven

Harper Apple

I look around, blinking back the tears and hoping no one noticed our fight. My friends are still dancing around me, the DJ having gone back to something with a dance beat. The Dolce twins are dancing with the Walton twins. I don't see Gloria, the girl most likely to care about drama between me and Royal. She's probably off reconciling with Rylan and fussing over his arm, which is in a sling after the fight. Magnolia's friends are doing the fourteen-year-old white girl version of twerking, though Magnolia herself has wandered off somewhere. Dixie and Gideon are grinding on each other but making funny faces at each other to keep it from getting awkward.

I turn and slip out through the crowd, heading for the exit. My car is still in the lot, so at least he didn't leave me stranded. I stand there in the cold for about five seconds, wondering if he walked somewhere, forgetting that I'm still stranded even if I have my car, since he has the key. Then I realize I'm being stupid, thinking with my heart and not my head.

I know Royal Dolce, and I know exactly where he'd go.

I turn and step back inside, head past the café and down the hall. When I reach the library, I can see a sliver of light from under the door to the basement, and I know I was right. I pull away the section of bookshelf and start down the stairs.

I'm halfway down, still blocked from view of the main room by the stone wall on the side of the stairs, when a voice that is definitely not Royal's calls up.

"Who is it?" demands the sassy, girlish little voice I recognize way too well by now. "I can't keep an eye on you both, so I *will* shoot one of you if you try anything."

"Magnolia?" I ask, hurrying down the rest of the steps and turning the corner into the main room. Royal's standing with his back to me, his hands raised, his whole body tense. Magnolia is standing across the room, her back to the bookshelf, with a gun pointed straight at us.

"Are you with him?" she asks, waving the gun back and forth between us.

"Whoa, what the fuck, Magnolia," I say as I slowly raise my hands, too. "Put that thing down."

"Oh no," she says, gripping it in both hands. Her eyes are wide, her hair a little messed up, and her hands are visibly shaking, but she clearly knows how to hold a gun. "I know what the Dolces do to girls down here—especially Darling girls. Do you really think I'd come down here unprepared?"

"I don't know why you're down here at all," I say, glancing at Royal from the corner of my eye. I've finally found the limit to my curiosity, a question I'm too much of a coward to ask. The answer could break me in a way even he can't heal, and I may be a masochist, but I'm no longer suicidal.

"I'm here for Sully," she says, raising her chin defiantly. "I told you I had a gun."

SELENA

"I didn't think you meant you had it on you right now," I say. "We're at school. You do know you'll be expelled, right?"

"Not if you don't make me shoot," she says. "Now turn around and leave, both of you."

"Gladly," I say. "I was just looking for Royal."

"Your brother's not down here," Royal says, speaking for the first time since I came down. I won't think about what happened before I got here.

"I know that," Magnolia snaps. "I'm not looking for him. I'm looking for information. And anyway, I've been through all the tunnels, even the one to your school, a million times. We used to play here as kids."

"I thought your brother was in a mental institution," I say, confused.

"He got out," Magnolia says. "And I'm going to make sure he never goes back."

"But he's not here," I say slowly.

"Of course not," she says. "The tunnels only go in three directions. One goes to another door, one dead ends at another room, and one goes to the Thorncrown underbelly."

"It does?" I ask, turning to Royal.

"It was the men's college when Willow Heights was founded," he says. "They have... Connections."

I shake my head, focusing on the girl with the gun in her hand. "Then what are you looking for?"

"Something to help him," she says, her chin quivering. "It all comes back to the Midnight Swans. He was being initiated, and something happened, and... And that's why I stole Grandpa's key, to come down here and see what I could find."

Her breath hitches, and I hold out a hand toward her. "Put the gun down, Magnolia. Royal's not going to hurt you. The person you need to talk to is your grandfather, okay? He's the one who did the initiation. And if you want the book with the Swans' information, it's behind you on that shelf."

She sniffs and squares her shoulders. "Why should I believe you?"

SELENA

"The theme of tonight's Homecoming," Royal mutters beside me.

"You can trust me because I'm your friend," I say to Magnolia. "I'm not going to rat you out about having a gun here if you don't use it for anything stupid. So just put it away. And I'm a member of the Midnight Swans, so I know where the book is. I'll show you once you put that down."

"Put your weapons down first," she says, poking the gun toward me. I drop my bag that has my knife in it, but she gestures at me again. "And the brass knuckles."

If I wasn't having a deadly weapon pointed at my face, I'd be impressed. I slip off the weapon and drop it near my purse.

"Now get it off the shelf," she says, creeping backwards toward the other side of the room as I approach the bookshelf.

"Stop pointing the fucking gun at her," Royal growls.

"Fine, I'll point it at you," she says, swinging back toward him. "You're the one who deserves to be shot, anyway."

"You don't know what you're talking about," I say, pulling the book off the shelf. "Royal's not the bad guy here, Magnolia. I know you think so, and you have a good reason for that, but this started way before us. Your grandfather and Royal's father are the ones who set all this in motion."

"Yeah?" she says. "Did they kill my uncle? Did they kill my cousin?"

"I don't know," I admit. "I don't have all the answers. I wasn't there. But I can say with confidence they were more at fault than anyone in this room."

"You know who *was* there?" she asks. "The Dolces."

"So were your cousins," I point out. "Why don't you ask them?"

"Haven't you heard?" she says. "Dead men tell no tales."

"Preston's still here," I say, setting the book on the table. "And Colt's upstairs… I think." I glance at Royal, since I'm not actually sure where Colt went. Last time I saw Dixie, she was dancing with Gideon. Maybe Colt went out for a smoke, but Royal's not above taking out his rage on the guy when there's no one else to take it, and I'm not sure how badly I pissed him off on the dance floor.

"I haven't seen him," Royal says.

Magnolia starts toward the table, her gaze dropping to the book. I back toward Royal.

From the corner of my eye, I catch a blur of movement as he leaps past me.

"Royal, no!" I yell as he lunges for Magnolia.

She jerks her attention back to us, her gun rising, her finger squeezing the trigger. The sound is deafening in the small, windowless room. The next second, Royal tackles her. They slam to the dirt floor, and all I can see in the dim light is the gash in the shoulder of his tuxedo, the furrow in his skin, and blood. I jump at him, but he's already on top of her, holding her between his knees the way he held Colt when he beat the life out of him.

He rips the gun out of her hand and grabs her jaw. She cries out, her eyes wide with shock as he squeezes, forcing her mouth open. Then he shoves the muzzle of the gun into her mouth.

"Royal, stop," I yell, my voice sharp even though my whole body has turned to pure, liquid fear. It's one thing to know he's killed someone and another to see him do it.

"If you ever point a gun at Harper again, I will fucking end your life," Royal growls, his fingers biting into Magnolia's soft cheeks. "*Capisce?*"

She nods frantically, tears pouring from the corners of her round eyes.

"Don't," I say, my voice quiet but firm. "Let her go, Royal."

"I'm going to let you walk away this time," Royal says, his voice so cold I barely recognize it. "Because for some unexplainable reason, Harper takes pity on pathetic little bitches like you. But if you ever so much as breathe a threat in her direction… Next time, your brains will be on the floor."

Magnolia makes a high, hiccupping sound of terror as Royal tenses, gripping her face harder and shoving the gun deeper into her mouth, until she retches. Then he pulls it out and stands.

SELENA

"I'll take this," he says, tucking the gun into the waistband of his tuxedo pants, under the jacket. His arm is freely bleeding, soaking the sleeve. "Come on, Harper. Let's go."

"We can't just leave her here," I say, though I know Royal needs to take care of his wounded shoulder. But I can't abandon Magnolia, not when he just terrorized her for my sake.

"Don't take the gun," Magnolia cries, sitting up and reaching for him. "What if someone else comes down here and finds me?"

He steps aside, out of reach of her clutching hands. "Then you better run, little rabbit."

He grabs my hand and drags me toward the stairs, and I know he's not going to let me stay even if I want to. I barely bend to grab my purse from the floor on the way past. When we get outside, I wrench my hand free at last.

"What the fuck was that, Royal?" I ask.

"That was me defending you," he snaps, striding ahead to the Escalade. "Now get in the car."

"I didn't ask you to traumatize children for me," I say. "I didn't ask you for anything."

"She's not a child," he says. "She's fourteen."

"That's a child," I snap back, trying to keep myself under control. My whole body is shaking, careening back toward a place I never want to go again. "You can't just show up and take over whenever you feel like it. You're not my boyfriend. I didn't ask you to defend me from Magnolia. I didn't ask you to take over this night when I could have just come with my friends."

Royal turns back to me, something predatory and hungry in his eyes when they take me in. "So you could have come with fucking Gideon? That kid's a joke and you know it, Harper. You know he can't give you what I can."

"What exactly are you giving me, Royal?"

He smirks down at me, stepping closer. "Let me show you, since you seem to have forgotten."

"Get away," I say, shoving him back when he gets in my space. "Yes, we fucked, but that doesn't mean everything is okay. It was a mistake, and I told you that as soon as we did it."

"I don't think so."

"You're wrong," I say. "I don't know what I was thinking, letting you even touch me after what you did. Call it temporary insanity, like when I let my guard down for one second on the dance floor, thinking you might think of someone else for one second. But you can't and we can't be together. We're poison. I'll keep telling you until you get it through your head—it won't happen again. *We* won't happen."

Royal slides his hand down over my hip, still smiling at me like this is all a game. "I'm happy to drive you out of your mind any time, Cherry Pie. Now get in the car or I'll fuck you up against the side of it."

"I'm not playing," I say, shoving his chest.

Instead of stepping back, he prowls closer, swaying against me, and brushes my cheek with his knuckles. "Neither am I."

Suddenly, it's not just adrenaline making me shake. I don't know how I ever felt safe with him, let alone just earlier tonight. I'm not safe. No matter how many weapons I have, how big my car, I'll never be safe again.

"Just because we fucked once, that doesn't mean I can do it again," I say, my voice shaking. "I'm fucked up, Royal. You fucked me up. It doesn't go away just because I got caught up once."

"Then get caught up again," he says, sliding his hand behind my head and stepping in, leaning down to press his lips to mine. The kiss is warm and possessive, comforting and dominating at once. It's a kiss that commands me to let him take over, make me feel good again. For a second, I let it carry me on its current.

But I know what happens when that current turns, when it pulls me under.

I shove him back, tearing myself away, my breathing ragged. "You can't just kiss me and undo what you did. You can't unbreak something once you've broken it. I'll always be shattered, Royal. Because of you."

"I don't care," he says. "I don't care if you're shattered. I'll put you back together. And if you break again, I'll put you back together again. As many times as it takes, Jailbird. That's how many times I'll be there to pick up the pieces."

"I don't *want* you to put me back together," I say, shoving his chest again, despair welling back up inside me, threatening to fill me like it did for so long. I just want to be normal again, not to feel like I'll blow to bits every time I get upset. "Don't you get it, Royal? I don't want to have to be fixed. I want to be unbroken. But I can't. I'll always be broken. I'll never be the same."

"You'll be better," he says, his voice quiet but firm with conviction.

"Better than what?" I ask incredulously, tears coating my lashes as I blink up at him, my throat tight as a fist.

"Better than before I broke you," he says, grabbing my face between his big hands again. He steps to me, backing me against the car, his body heat shimmering in the air between us, making me lightheaded. He strokes his thumb across my cheek, smearing wetness over my skin. "Every scar makes you more beautiful. Every tear makes you more mine."

"How am I better?" I demand, the unbearable ache in my throat threatening to choke off my words. "I'm not better than anything. I'm ruined. You ruined me, and no matter how hard you try to give me what I need, it can't undo what already happened. I'll never be that girl you wanted again, Royal. I'll never be yours the way I was before. This doesn't go away. I'll never recover."

"You will."

"No," I say, shaking my head. "We're a sickness, Royal. And once you get it, you never get better."

"You want to know how sick I am?" he asks, bending to touch his forehead to mine. "I don't care. I don't care if you're broken in a million pieces. I will find every single one of them, and I'll put them back together. And I'll want you even more when I see those cracks in you and know I made them. I'll want you more when I see the lines of glue that I put there to fix you, because I'm that glue. I'm a part of you now, Harper. I want you more now than I did before, because I didn't just mark your body, I marked your soul."

SELENA

I thought I was cried out, that I was getting better, getting stronger, but the hurt just keeps hitting me again, breaking me again. My whole body is shaking uncontrollably, and I can't stop the tears from forcing themselves between my lashes and streaming down my cheeks.

Royal leans in closer. He grips my throat, pushing my head back until it meets the car. He pushes his thigh between mine, holding me in place while he opens his mouth and runs his tongue up my face from my jawline to my eye, licking up my tears in one hungry stroke. "I love that these tears are for me," he murmurs, burying his other hand in my hair and tightening his grip, pulling my head back further. "I love knowing you can't undo what I did to you. I'm part of you, and you can't get rid of me no matter how much you want to. I'm inside you, and I'll never go away. I'll always be there. Every break is mine. Every healing is mine. Every scar is mine."

"I hate you," I whisper, gripping his wrist with shaking fingers and squeezing my eyes closed, rage swelling inside me like a tsunami when I realize that no matter what he does for me now, he'll never be sorry for what he did before.

He licks my other cheek, grinding his thigh between mine, his fingers tightening around my throat. "I hate you more."

"No, you don't."

"Don't fucking tell me how much a Dolce can hate."

He takes my mouth, slamming me back up against the car, devouring me with violent possession. One hand is so tight in my hair that tears blur my eyes again, the other wrapped tight around my throat, so I can hardly breathe. I reach up, my other hand finding his shoulder. My palm meets slick, warm blood, and I grope around, finding the tear in his sleeve and sliding my fingers in, digging into his torn flesh.

He sucks in a sharp breath and releases my throat, reaching past me to open the back door. He yanks his mouth from mine, breathing hard. "Get on your back and show me what's mine."

SELENA

"I have nothing of yours," I say, digging my nails into his broken skin, relishing the swell of power inside me, that I can give him pain, too.

Royal lifts me and plows onto the seat with me, wrestling my dress up while I kick and fight, scratching at his shoulder, slapping at his other arm.

"You said the wrong fucking words there, Cherry Pie," he says, sliding down the seat until he's between my thighs. He throws my legs over his shoulders and leans down, pressing his nose to my panties and inhaling deeply. I shove at his forehead, but he only moans low in his throat in response, rubbing his nose back and forth against me, the heat of his breath warming my center.

"Royal, don't," I gasp, struggling to get my legs together.

He grips them with both hands, burying his face deeper. Suddenly, he bites me, sinking his teeth into me through my underwear. I yelp and struggle harder, slapping at his head.

He chuckles and reaches down, pulling my panties aside and flicking his tongue against my clit. I gasp, the slippery warmth of his tongue making a shudder of pleasure ripple through me.

"Stop," I gasp, my thighs shaking as he spreads me open with his fingers and slowly strokes me with his tongue.

"When you admit this is mine," he says. He slides his tongue along my slit, tasting the wetness inside. Moaning, he presses in deeper, licking and sucking his way from my clit to my entrance, as if making sure to claim every part of me, to remind me how well he knows me and owns me.

I drop back on the seat, shivers of pleasure coiling through me, melting me from the inside out. "Royal," I whisper, burying my fingers in his thick, dark hair.

"Mmm?" he answers, the vibration of his murmur making me quake under him. I give in, letting him spread my thighs wide and sink his tongue into my opening. He moans again, rhythmically pumping his tongue into me while he strokes my clit with his thumb, fucking me with his mouth, his fingers, until I think I'll explode.

"Royal," I cry out again, gripping his hair between my fingers and rocking against him, riding his tongue.

He draws back, making his way from my opening to my clit with wide, sure strokes. He moans with pleasure, tugging the bud between his lips. My hips jerk involuntarily, and he tightens his grip on my thighs, holding me still as he moves the tip of his tongue in slow, sensuous circles around my swollen clit.

"Oh god," I gasp. "Royal, stop, I can't—"

He rips my panties off, dropping the torn fabric on the floor, and spreads my knees wide.

"Tell me who you belong to," he commands, his voice rough with lust. "Tell me you're mine."

"Never," I breathe, sinking back on the seat. He growls and pushes his face back into me, sucking and licking and stroking, commanding my pleasure as he takes me over, takes what's mine, what's his. I try to hold back, but he pushes me until I'm almost sobbing with pleasure, and finally, I break.

I buck my hips under him, and he keeps up the strokes of his tongue while he works a finger into me, pulsing against my walls as they clench rhythmically around it. I gasp and stifle a cry, heat rushing to my face when I feel the gush of cum flood his mouth. He groans and pushes his finger deeper, sucking at my swollen flesh to draw out all of it.

Then he moves over me, settling his huge body between my legs. Shudders are still wracking my body, and I'm gasping for breath. He grips my chin between his thumb and finger and leans down over me, spitting a stream of warm liquid between my panting lips. I almost choke when the salty fluid washes over my tongue and I realize it's me, that he spit my own cum back in my mouth.

"What the fuck," I manage, gagging as it runs down the back of my throat.

"You taste so fucking good it drives me insane," he says, his voice wild and hoarse. "Don't you want to taste of that sweet cunt that brought your king to his knees, my dirty little slut?"

He raises up just enough to pull out his cock, pressing the bare head of it against my slick entrance.

"Are you ready for me?" he asks, slowly rubbing it through my wetness and sinking just the tip inside me.

"Yes," I breathe, grinding up against him, wanting more even now, when I just came. "God, yes. Fuck me, Royal. Show me."

With a groan, he pushes forward, slowly sinking into me. "Oh fuck, Harper," he says, dropping his forehead to mine. "I hate that you do this to me."

"I hate you, too," I whisper, stroking his hair, his neck. I pull him in, seeking his mouth, and he rewards me with a kiss, his lips finding mine. He tastes like salt and pussy, like me. His tongue slides over mine, coaxing me to him as he begins to move inside me, his thick cock stretching me and filling me with delicious torment as he forces it to my depths and grinds slowly against my clit.

It's never enough. There's never too much of him, and I know I want him, need him, as much as he wants me, and shamelessly, even more. Even when it hurts, when he's so deep inside me I can hardly breathe, I crave it. I crave his roughness, his violence, his demon that possesses me, that drowns me in its insatiable hunger for me, swallows me whole.

I let it, let go, let him have me, let him thrust his bare cock so deep inside me I can't help but cry out.

"You're mine, Harper," he says, thrusting into me slow and hard, winding the coils of pleasure inside me tighter and tighter each time he pushes into my core, filling me until I ache. "Whether you admit it or not. You've always been mine, and you'll always be mine. Your body is mine, your pleasure is mine, your soul is mine. Now say it."

"I can't."

"Then I'll keep going until you can."

He kisses me again, steals my cries of pleasure and torment, my moans, my fury. He fucks me until I can't stop myself even if I wanted to, and I don't. I finally break, opening myself, giving in, submitting to the dominant rhythm of his strong body claiming mine, taking every part of me.

Suddenly he pulls out, his hot, slick cock landing on the cool skin of my abdomen, exposed where he has my dress pushed up. He's still hard, his rigid length throbbing against me.

"What are you doing?" I gasp, my fingers clutching his shoulders. "I was almost there."

"Say it, and I'll let you cum," he growls.

"What?"

"Tell me what I want to hear."

I pause a second, and then I give in.

"I'm yours," I whisper, my thighs shaking around his hips.

"That's right, my little slut. Your body is mine. Your cunt is mine. Your orgasm is mine. Even your black cherry soul is mine. And I'm going to fuck you until you scream it for the whole world to hear."

He takes my mouth again, his tongue claiming mine while he slides back into me, filling me with one powerful, dizzying thrust. I swear I see fucking stars, and I never want to come down. He pumps into me in an addicting rhythm, one that makes my toes curl and my hands fist in his jacket, gripping him like he's the only thing anchoring me to this world when he pushes me over the edge and I spin out, consumed with pleasure as the climax washes over me.

I hear myself telling him what he wants to hear, crying his name, telling him I'm his, that I've always been his, that I always will be.

And I tell myself what I want to hear, too, that it's just the orgasm talking.

SELENA

eight

Harper Apple

After we fuck, we drive to the river. It's chilly for October, so we climb into the back seat of the Escalade. I don't have a blanket, but Royal takes off his jacket, and we lie together on the seat.

I turn toward him, circling my finger around the back of his ear. "Do you need to go to the hospital?" I ask. "You probably need stitches."

"I'm fine," he says. "It's just a scratch."

"I'm sorry," I say, leaning in to press my lips to his.

"You didn't shoot me."

"I'm sorry I freaked out."

"I think you've earned the right," he says, flattening his hand on my lower back and holding me tight against him.

"I'm sorry… For what I did, too," I say. "For telling Mr. D… Everything I did. Especially about the Hockington. Did Baron already know?"

"No," Royal says quietly. "Only Dad knows. Knew."

"So, I did expose you to someone," I say, swallowing hard. "I'm sorry. I was scared, Royal. I didn't have anyone else, and I was scared of what you were doing to the Darlings. Not just because it hurts them, either. It hurts you. I wish you'd stop. That there's some way you could at least move on, even if you don't forgive."

"You thought you were telling one of them," he says. "You knew how I felt about them."

"You thought I was one of them," I say. "I just… I wanted to get out of this town, Royal. It's been my dream since I knew what dreams were. I've never even left the state. I just wanted to go to college. It's the same reason I was blowing Mr. Behr. Not just because I wanted a good grade so he'd be proud of me or some shit. I wanted the grades to get into college. That's why I took the scholarship from Mr. D… From your dad. I would have done anything to get out of Faulkner."

"You still can."

"I know," I say. "It's just not the same now. I want to help people here, too. Not just leave them on their own."

"Why?" he says, pressing his lips to my forehead. "They never did anything for you."

"I just do," I say, thinking that I said something similar to Preston. "And I know my reasons aren't an excuse for what I did. But that's my explanation. I knew I was going too far when I told him your secret. I just didn't have anything else. I was desperate, and I thought maybe it would get rid of your dad. I hate that you do that for him."

"I don't," he says. "I told you, I stopped."

"But you did it," I say. "He made you do it for… How long?"

"He used to make King do it, but when he moved, it fell to me or my brothers. I didn't want them to have to deal with that. I wanted them to be able to be kids, do their thing. I know they're fucked up. It's not that I think they're innocent. But I didn't want one more thing fucking them up. I don't want to find out where the line is, what will make them finally snap."

"They don't deserve you," I say, sliding a hand behind his neck. "You're too good to them."

"They're my brothers," he says simply. "They're all I have."

I wind a small curl behind his ear around my finger. "Royal... Can I ask you something?"

"Anything," he says, his breath warm against my face as we lie there, inches apart.

"Do you forgive them?" I ask. "For what they did to me?"

"I don't have the right to take offense to what they did," he says. "Does that make sense?"

"No," I admit, folding my arm under my head and searching his face in the dim moonlight filtering in from outside.

"I want to fucking kill them when I think about it," he says. "But all I could do was bring them to you and let you get your revenge. I would have let you do anything, Harper. I hoped you'd do more than what you did. I wouldn't have stopped you. But that was your revenge because they wronged you."

"They didn't wrong you?"

He pauses a long moment before answering. "No," he says quietly. "I gave them permission to wrong us both. You are mine. They understand that. You belong to me—every part of you. I chose to share that with them. That's on me. I can regret it, but I can't punish them because I changed my mind after the fact. I gave you to them, gave them permission to do what they wanted to you. I gave them your consent because it belongs to me."

"I don't agree to that," I say. "I never agreed to that."

"You don't have a choice," he says. "I don't, either. You're mine. That's just the way it is."

"That's bullshit."

"Bullshit or not, they took what I gave them. I don't have the right to punish them for my mistake."

"And what about Dawson?" I ask, swallowing hard, thinking he has the most fucked up moral code in the world, but he sure as fuck has one.

"Dawson didn't have my permission."

We lay there for a minute, my heart beating so hard I can hear it. "You killed him?" I whisper.

"I let you punish him for what he did to you," Royal says. "And I punished him for what he did to me. I didn't share you with him. He took what was mine, and he paid the price."

Some sick part of me is glad Royal did it, so I don't have to feel the guilt of knowing someone took their life in part because of me. Instead, Royal took Dawson's life because of me. Maybe it makes me sick, but that's somehow easier to swallow. I suspected Royal played a part in the death of at least one Darling, but knowing I love an actual murderer sends a chill down my spine.

I swallow past the tremor in my voice. "And the twins?"

"I helped them understand the severity of what they did," he says. "He was their friend, and now they live with what they caused. And they know what happens to people who wrong me."

I nod, toying with the top button his shirt. "And what if you get mad at me again, Royal? What happens then? How can I trust you when I know what you do to girls who wrong you?"

"You don't have to trust me," he says. "But you'll see. Now that I understand, now that I know you're mine whether I want it or not, whether *you* want it or not… I'll never let anyone touch you again, Harper. I promise."

"But if I'm yours, if my consent belongs to you, then you could share me again."

"I won't," he says. "You might not trust me now, but you will. And you're still mine, whether or not you trust me or I trust you."

"Do you?" I ask. "Do you trust me?"

"I haven't hunted down your hero for being with you last night," he says. "I haven't torn his dick off with my bare hands and made him eat it while he slowly bleeds out from the hole left where it used to be, have I?"

"Nothing happened," I say. "I don't think of him that way."

Royal's quiet for a minute, his thumb stroking my hair as he cradles my head in his hand. "I don't trust you, either," he says. "But it doesn't change anything."

"Because I'm still yours, even if you don't want me."

"I didn't say I didn't want you," he says. "I said I didn't want it to be true. But it is. We're part of each other now, Harper. There's no out."

"And if I agree to that, to being yours, no matter what you do to me, can you forgive me?" I ask, gripping the front of his shirt. "If I stop fighting it, will you try to understand why I betrayed you and forgive me for it?"

He stares at me in the near darkness, so I can only see a glimmer of light reflected in his eyes, the sculpted shape of his jawline that makes me want to cry it's so perfect. "Yes," he says at last.

He leans in and presses his lips to mine, and this time, he doesn't make me speak. He moves on top of me, inside me, and I hold onto him, and I feel tears leaking out the corner of my eyes, but I don't know why I'm crying.

Maybe it's relief, that I can finally let go, let someone else take charge, be responsible for me. Or maybe it's because I know it's not enough, just like his apology wouldn't have been enough for me. I needed him to show it, not say it. I needed him to do the things he did, even when I didn't know I needed them. He loved me enough to do everything he could to heal me until I was able to forgive even without him saying he was sorry.

He needed me to say I was sorry, to apologize, before he could forgive. But even now, when things are right between us, I know that he hasn't healed. Maybe he never will.

nine

Crystal Dolce

"She's down," Devlin says, stepping into our bedroom and pulling the door closed. "Though I still don't think it's fair for you to make me put another man's child to bed."

I lay my tablet in my lap and give him a half-hearted smile. "It was your turn."

"You're not even going to pretend you didn't cheat on me with Satan to produce that one?" he asks, padding over to the bed and lifting the blankets to slide in next to me. "Or remind me that I'm the one who wanted a girl?"

"I have to show you something," I say, watching him carefully. "But you have to promise not to get mad."

He leans over and nuzzles my cheek before wrapping an arm around my waist and pulling me off the mountain

SELENA

of pillows until I'm flat on my back. He smiles down at me. "Were you picking out houses without me again, Sugar?"

"No," I say. "I was just wasting time online until you came to bed, and I saw this video. I wasn't looking for it, I swear. It's going viral. More than 4.3 million people have already seen it, so don't worry, no one will notice one more hit from California."

"What are you talking about?" Devlin asks, his face turning guarded.

I swallow and press the button on tablet, turning on the screen. I lean up on my elbow, and we watch the video together. Fifteen seconds of cafeteria chaos. I can hardly hear anything but the roar of voices, a shriek, and a deeper voice. I can't tell exactly what my brother is saying, but he's sitting in a chair, pointing at his lap, taunting someone while he pulls his dick out. Someone blurred out the video footage across his lap before posting, but it's clear what just happened.

Then Baron shoots up, yells that there's a phone, and dives for whoever is holding the camera. There's about ten seconds of shaky, careening footage that makes me seasick as the camera jerks around, but I can see my brothers pulling chairs from under people, throwing them to the floor, and then the blur of someone's shirt. Then the camera falls, and there's flashes of movement above it, unidentifiable clothes and limbs moving over it, and then the screen goes black.

I look up at Devlin, my heart pounding.

"Where did you see this?" he asks quietly.

"It's all over every social media right now," I say. "I was just scrolling on *The Tea*, and it came up. I saw the name of the school, and I clicked on it. That's my brother, right? I'm not hallucinating?"

"It definitely looks like them," Devlin confirms.

"I searched afterwards to see if there was anything else, but I didn't click on anything local to Faulkner, just in case…"

"In case they're still looking for you," he says, setting the tablet on the bedside table and pulling me into his arms. He holds onto me like he's still afraid they'll find us, tear us apart. I'm just as scared, too scared to even hope that they've stopped looking.

"It's already spawning articles about how private schools let kids get away with murder, and how they cover up stuff like this," I say, laying my head on his chest. "And the posts on social media are about sexual assault and why girls don't report stuff, because apparently the school didn't do anything. They still played in the Homecoming game that night."

"Sounds even worse than when we were there," Devlin says. "But I'm not surprised. You remember how it was. That town worships football."

"And it's not like he touched anyone," I say, feeling suddenly defensive of the little brother I haven't seen in three years. "He was just flashing someone."

"Yeah, but… Still. We might have done shit, but not like that, right out in the open. They had to know someone could film it. Everyone's got their phones out at lunch."

"Preston gave me a milk shower in the middle of the café."

"Yeah," he says with a cocky grin. "But that's hot."

"Maybe they changed the policy," I say, ignoring his comment. "Baron sounded pretty upset that someone had a phone out."

It's hard to imagine that school, how much it must have changed by now. The twins and Dixie are the only people I knew who are still in high school. King graduated years ago. Royal graduated last May. I would have graduated if I'd stayed. Devlin would be playing football at some university. I'd be a freshman in college.

I wonder how different they are, everyone we left behind. I wonder where Royal is. Thinking of my twin sends a knife of pain twisting through me, so I turn my thoughts away from him.

I want to watch the video again, but I resist. The twins are bigger, but they look exactly the same. Their antics aren't anything shocking, either. They were always like that, pushing boundaries, getting in trouble, having to be bailed out for lighting fires, breaking windows, DUIs, or whatever mischief the night brought. Even before we left New York, when they were overgrown preteens with overgrown bank accounts, they were little hellions. In eighth grade, the year before we moved to Arkansas, they were already six feet tall and known for partying hard, having threesomes, and getting into scrapes with the law.

At the time, I was too busy feeling resentful that they were allowed to drive and go to parties with Royal and King, who barely let me out of their sight even though I was a year and half older. Now, as a mother, I shudder at the thought of my own kids growing up that way. Thirteen seems like the right age to have your first kiss, not already have a reputation for sleeping around. If all the twins are doing four years later is flashing someone in the cafeteria, Arkansas was definitely the right move on my father's part.

I wonder if Mom knows about this, if she ever moved to Arkansas. Not that she'd do anything. When they got in trouble in New York, she'd just say "boys will be boys," take another Valium, and tell Dad to take care of it. After all, she grew up in a mafia family, where the boys didn't just break windows, they broke kneecaps. My brothers' antics are hardly on the same level with murder.

"Do you still miss it?" I ask after a few minutes of letting my thoughts wander to the past.

"What?" Devlin asks. "Home? Football? The South?"

"All of the above," I say, wrapping my arms around him and snuggling closer.

"All the time," he admits, kissing my forehead. "My family more than anything."

"Me too."

"But if I could go back three years, I wouldn't change a single thing," he says, running his fingers through my caramel hair.

"I might change something," I say. "Royal was kidnapped this weekend, three years ago. Remember, it was the night of Homecoming."

"I remember that night for different reasons," Devlin says, pulling my knee up over his hip and pushing against me. "That was the night some sweet little virgin ended up in my bed."

I pull him closer with my leg. "Not such a sweet little virgin anymore, am I, *Steve?*"

SELENA

He chuckles and kisses me on the nose. "See, we don't need them. Y'all are my family now."

"I just wish…" I trail off and lay back on the bed. "I'm glad I could see them. Even if it's just for fifteen seconds."

"We agreed after I got Dolly's demo to the producers at work," Devlin reminds me. "It's too risky."

"I'm so glad she didn't recognize you," I say, shivering even though our bed is warm. "I wouldn't give this up for anything."

"Need me to remind you how worth it we are?" he asks, rolling back to me and pushing his erection against my hip.

"I'm all milky," I protest.

"Mm, I love it," he murmurs into my neck, his big hand covering my swollen breast. He strokes my nipple through my shirt until it stiffens, bringing a blossom of wetness with it. "I'm going to get myself wet with it before I fuck you."

"Devlin," I scold.

"You can't pretend to be uptight after putting period blood in my coffee."

"Sounds like the name of a bad country song," I say, a game we play since he works for a record label.

He sings the line with a country twang, strumming on my ribs until I'm giggling. Then he leans down and closes his mouth over my nipple, sucking it through the wet fabric of my T-shirt.

"You're getting milk in your mouth," I protest, still laughing.

"You think a little milk is going to scare me off?" he asks, pulling up my shirt and lathing his tongue across my leaking nipple. "I eat you out when you're on your period."

"Okay, but…"

He pulls my shirt over my head and tosses it into the laundry hamper in the corner. Then he turns back to me, grips my torso, and rolls us over so I'm on top of him. "Get my dick wet, Sugar. I'm gonna fuck you tonight."

I pull my hair to one side and lean down, tugging at the top of his boxer briefs. He groans and lifts up, pushing his cock toward my face. I draw him out and run my tongue over his tip. He reaches down, fondling my breasts until they're slick with milk.

"Now who's getting a milk shower," he teases.

"Let me get a towel," I say, sitting back, flushing with embarrassment.

Devlin pushes himself up on one elbow, his other hand reaching out. His fingers close gently around my throat. "Wet me with your tits," he growls.

I swallow my embarrassment and lean down, squeezing my swollen breasts together around his shaft. He groans and lifts his hips, slowly gliding in and out between my tits for a minute. When I look down and see drops of creamy milk clinging to his thick tip, heat pulses between my thighs.

"You're so fucking sexy," he growls. He grabs me under the arms and lifts me up, pulling me onto his lap. Burying a hand in my hair, he pulls me in for a rough kiss before flipping us over. He reaches down to line himself up before thrusting his bare, milk-slick cock deep inside me. I gasp and arch up, clinging to him while he pumps into my hot center, already slippery with my own arousal.

He leans down to kiss me, his fingers closing around my throat again.

"Until you get your period again, this is my favorite lube," he says, driving into me with a smooth, powerful rhythm until I'm begging for more, for him to let me finish. He grasps both my wrists in one hand, pulling them above my head while his other hand remains around my throat.

"Your cunt is a fucking miracle," he growls, nipping at my lip. "Now let me feel it sucking the milk from my cock, my sweet sugar crystal."

He drives into me hard, dominating me with each thrust until I obey, my back arching as climax grips me. A strangled cry escapes before he slams a hand over my mouth and his fingers tighten around my throat, squeezing until I choke. My walls clamp down around him, and he curses and drives into me savagely before stilling, his cock pulsing thick before liquid heat pours into my throbbing core.

SELENA

I gasp for breath, gripping his shoulders until my nails break the skin, grinding up against him. He holds me pinned, one hand over my mouth to silence me, his other hand cutting off the blood to my brain until I think I'll pass out. Gasping for breath, I cum again even harder, bucking wildly, scratching and biting, stars dotting my vision through the blackness until he relaxes his grip and lets me suck in a breath.

He presses his lips to my gasping mouth, chuckling and stroking his fingers down my neck. "Sweet little virgin, my ass," he says, sinking down on top of me. "I may be the first man who ever fucked you, but you were always a freak."

"Says the man obsessed with bodily fluids," I manage, still panting for breath.

"You started it," he reminds me, nuzzling my neck. "With the coffee."

"Guess my grandma's trick worked," I say. And even though I'm happier than I have any right to be, even though I have a beautiful family and a husband I love more than life itself, the familiar pain twists in my chest at the mention of the beloved grandmother I will never see again.

"It surely did," he agrees. "Nothing on this earth could take you away from me, Brooklyn Tate."

"Nothing will," I promise, my arms tightening around him, as if holding on hard enough will make the empty places in my heart disappear, the ones that a husband can't fill no matter how much he loves me and gives me everything I could ever ask of him. He's worth every sacrifice I've made, but that doesn't mean I don't still miss the things I've lost, the people I've left.

My mischievous grandmother, my selfish mother, my controlling father, my protective big brother, my rambunctious little brothers, and my twin, the better half of me.

Most of all, I wish I could see Royal, if only for fifteen seconds of a viral video. Just to know that he's okay, that he recovered from whatever happened when he was kidnapped, that he's moved out and is free of our father, who he always hated.

SELENA

I just want to know he's happy, but I can't risk it. Baron would probably find it somehow if I looked them up. He'd see my IP address and track me down, and I didn't sacrifice all that only to end up with a dead husband. So I focus on Devlin as he gets a cloth and cleans me up, telling myself I'm the luckiest girl in the world. When he comes back to bed, I curl into him, and I think of all I've gained so I don't have to think about all I've lost.

ten

Harper Apple

Royal drops me off around dawn. His car is still across the street, apparently unharmed. Maybe Mom didn't tell her boyfriends it belongs to someone I know.

"Meet at the river on Tuesday?" Royal asks after parking the Escalade in my driveway.

I shake my head. "Royal. We fucked. That's all. It doesn't mean we're together."

"Okay," he says. "But if you want to *not* get together on Tuesday, meet me at our usual spot."

"You're okay with this being just sex?"

"Sure, sweetheart."

I narrow my eyes. "Why?"

"That's what you said you wanted," he says. "Why are you questioning it?"

SELENA

"Because you're not fighting me," I say. "You always fight."

"There's no point in arguing," he says with a smirk. "We both know you're full of shit."

I grit my teeth and glare. "Because you know me so well?"

"I know this isn't just fucking," he says, leaning across the seat and sliding his big hand behind my head. He pulls me in and kisses me hard on the mouth before drawing back. "And so do you."

He climbs out, and I shake my head at his fucking nerve. But in truth, I wouldn't mind meeting up. The sex is too good to ignore, and I miss the other parts, too. I miss talking to him, having him talk to me. I miss feeling needed by him, feeling like I was the only one he showed that part of himself to.

But I don't want to make promises when I'm not sure I can keep them. I don't know where it will lead, when I'll freak out again and decide I can't be around him. And I don't want to hurt him more than he's been hurt, not just by me, but by everyone in his life—not just the Darlings, but every single person in his family. His mother left them and from what he's told me, doesn't give a fuck about anyone but herself. His sister disappeared and he blames himself for it. His older brother left him to do his father's disgusting bidding. He can't even trust Baron and Duke anymore.

So I just head inside without making a fuss about it. I'm still working on forgiving him, but I'm also coming back to the person who wanted to know people, to study and understand them. I'm starting to understand Royal again, in the old ways and new ways, too. I'm beginning to understand why he can't let me go, even after I betrayed him. He has no one else, no one he can be real with, no one he can trust. And even if he doesn't trust me, he's already told me so much that it's easier to forgive me and keep me close than start all over, especially for someone like Royal, who doesn't open up easily.

I always envied his family so much, especially him and his brothers. They had everything—money and power and status and family. And most of all, they seemed to have this bond. They were always together. But I know now that it's not the brotherhood I imagined. They have each other's backs when the world is watching, but they have secrets from each other. Baron was Mr. D. Royal was turning tricks. And Duke… I still don't know Duke's secrets.

Maybe it's just the open secret, the thing everyone knows but no one says—that he's obviously an alcoholic or well on his way. I remember him falling off the porch at Preston's house. Everyone laughed because it was just classic Duke with his drunken antics. He's seventeen, what do people expect? They'll laugh it off, and he'll go off to college and binge-drink his way through four years in a frat, and then be the drunk uncle at every family gathering. And that's the best-case scenario.

Even though it's already getting light out, I can't sleep. I lie there thinking about Royal, wanting to text him like some dumb bitch who can't wait five seconds after a guy leaves before I miss him. I should be getting my own shit together. I should be looking into getting back into the fight scene, into the poker games. I haven't spent much from my stash, but I haven't added anything either.

I remember saying money solved everything, but it really only solves one thing. It can get me out of town. But it doesn't fix the town's problems. It doesn't get rid of Mr. Dolce. It doesn't make Duke stop drinking or cure Baron of being a psychopath. It didn't make their mom stay, and it doesn't bring their sister back. At the end of the day, despite Royal's money and power and status and family, he's as alone as I am.

*

On Monday morning, I'm walking into school when Baron comes storming out of the office.

"Fucking cunt," he growls at me.

"Good morning to you, too," I say, giving him my most cheerful smile.

"You're going to pay for this," he says, glowering at me.

SELENA

I quirk a brow. "It's early to start shit, even for you. I haven't had my caffeine yet, so just enlighten me. What'd I do this time?"

"You went after the wrong Dolce," he says, his eyes narrowing. "Trust me, Dad won't let you off with a slap on the wrist like Royal did."

I hook my thumbs through my backpack straps in an outwardly casual pose, though my stomach is clenched with dread. "That's what you call what you did to me last spring? A slap on the wrist?"

"By the time this is over, you're going to wish you'd never walked out of that swamp."

Baron turns on his heel and shoves out the front door, leaving me standing there blindsided and still in the dark, my least favorite place to be.

At least I know where to go for information. I sigh and head down the hall, keeping an eye out for Dixie. I've been at this school long enough to pick up a vibe that something weird is going on. The clusters of people whispering and gossiping, a few too many glances in my direction… It's all a little too reminiscent of last year.

I stop at my locker, relieved when Josie appears at hers a minute later. She flashes me a grin, the first one she's ever given me, before propping her bag on her knee as she spins the dial on her combination. "The admin's definitely feeling the pressure now," she says, sounding downright gleeful.

"What's going on?" I ask.

"Too early to know what'll come of it, but we definitely stirred things up," she says, finally looking like she respects me instead of thinking I'm some rich bitch who's going to make her life hell.

"How, exactly?" I ask, closing my locker.

"Oh my god, Harper," Gloria says, sweeping up beside me, looking all flustered. She links her arm through mine, squeezing it so tight against hers it's almost painful. "You're famous!"

I glance around, the knot of dread in my belly hardening as I see people turning to look, alerted by her volume.

"We better get your makeup on in case anyone wants a photo op," she says, dragging me down the hall.

SELENA

"Please don't tell me there's another video," I murmur, gripping her arm as tight as she is mine. "I don't think I'll survive one more hit."

"Just watch your back," she says, keeping her smile in place as she marches me into the bathroom.

"For what?"

"Out," she commands, pointing to the door and glaring at the handful of girls already in the bathroom. They grumble and roll their eyes, but they obey. She is the Queen B, after all.

"What the fuck is going on?" I demand.

Gloria starts checking the stalls, so I join to make it go faster, since I know she won't talk before she knows it's safe. Finally, she relaxes, her shoulders sinking and her whole face changing from intimidating bitch to concerned friend.

"Don't you ever look at your phone on the weekend?" she asks.

"I thought we were all too busy with Homecoming to do anything scandalous," I point out. Sunday, Royal didn't drop me off until morning, so I slept half the day and then did homework.

She sighs and pulls her phone out of her purse. "Do you have *The Tea* app?"

"No," I say, frowning at her. "Why?"

"No wonder you're always the last to know," she says, rolling her eyes. "It's like Twitter and TikTok rolled into one. How do you even know what's going on without it?"

"Somehow I've managed for eighteen years," I say, rolling my eyes.

She shoves her phone at me, and I stare at the screen for a second. Or fifteen seconds, to be more exact. Then I shake my head. "Is that the *OnlyPics* video?" I ask. "Or was someone else filming, too?"

Besides Duke's dick being blurred out, it looks like the same one from Friday. The one Magnolia took and then couldn't delete because her phone was broken.

Wasn't it?

SELENA

"Now it's the private school scandal video," Gloria says, pointing to a number in the top corner of the video. "Eighteen million people have watched this."

I can't even comprehend a number that big. "What?" I ask, gripping the sink so I don't keel the fuck over at that number. "How is that possible? Are there even that many people on *OnlyPics*?"

"Probably not, and they don't have the capacity to blow things up like this," Gloria says, watching the video replay. "But there are probably billions on *The Tea*, and that's where it went viral. You can share and repost on here. And then it got picked up by media. Mom said it was on *Local News with Jackie* last night."

"Then I think Duke's the one who's famous, not me," I say. "All I do in that video is fall on my ass."

"Yeah, well, eighteen million people saw you and Dixie fall on your asses and knock your heads together," she says, stifling a giggle as she watches it.

"It's not funny," I say, snatching the phone.

I can see why it went viral. Despite the shaky footage and the blurs of people stepping in front of the shot, it's hard to stop watching. I let it loop again. It's captivating, in the way a train wreck is captivating.

Duke pulling his dick out. Baron shooting to his feet and pointing with such urgency. The dive for the camera. Magnolia dodging him. The guys yanking our chairs back, sending us rolling, and our comical collision. Magnolia's little shriek before the camera is yanked away. It's raunchy and funny and exciting, priceless entertainment that they got for free.

Watching it again, I decide it's definitely Magnolia's video, not someone else's. The shirt Colt was wearing on Friday takes over the screen when she steps behind him, and the screen goes black when Baron steps on her phone.

The bell chimes, but Gloria and I both ignore it.

"That little bitch," I say, handing the phone back to Gloria. "Was she streaming there at the same time? Or did she put this up before we erased it off *OnlyPics*?"

Gloria shakes her head. "Magnolia didn't post it. *Rumor Has It* put it up. Pretty sure no one outside Willow

SELENA

Heights was following her before that. Now she's got like ten million followers."

I look at her blankly. "Who is *Rumor Has It?*"

"Seriously, Harper? My grandmother has more of a social media presence than you."

"Who put it up?" I demand.

"Dixie," she says, widening her eyes at me like it's the most obvious thing in the world.

"But… She has the blog."

"Yeah, but that's like big news. *Rumor Has It* posts little tidbits all throughout the day, any scrap of gossip."

"She said she'd erase it," I say, feeling unaccountably wounded. We share gossip, and she cried to me when Colt was beaten. But more than that, she joined the protest.

"And then she posted it," Gloria confirms.

"Why would she do that?" If I'm honest, though, Colt's about the only thing we have in common.

"Probably because you handed her Magnolia's log in, and she saw viral gold?" Gloria guesses, turning to the mirror. "I mean, can you blame her for not wanting to erase this from existence? All that girl wants is to be popular, and there she was, listening to her cousin on the radio while she held a damn lottery ticket in her hand. Of course she cashed in."

"So, *she's* the one getting famous."

"Hell, yeah," Gloria says, adjusting her hair over her shoulders. "At least she's getting her fifteen minutes. She tried before, with that picture of Preston's house when we ruined it. She posted it on the blog, but that wasn't sensational enough. But a video… She was on *Local New with Jackie* last night, and I heard the school board already asked her to speak at the next meeting."

"Why is she going to the school board?"

"Almost twenty million people saw a freaking brawl in our café and some pretty graphic sexual harassment," she reminds me. "Willow Heights is not looking so good in the media right now."

"Fuck," I say. "So that's what Baron was pissed about. I bet they got suspended."

"Hey, you got what you wanted," Gloria says. "The admin's definitely going to be making some changes after they get done fielding questions from pissed off parents."

"That's not what I wanted."

"Well, they're going to have to hold those boys accountable. Isn't that what you were after?"

"Maybe that's why Dixie did it," I say, nodding. "Not to get attention, but to get the Dolces in trouble. She's definitely Team Darling."

"It's probably a bit of both," Gloria says. "But yeah. All y'all are going to get called down to give statements. And the Dolces will be out for blood."

"Shit," I say, pushing off the sink, my heart skipping a beat. "Magnolia."

"Oh, shit," Gloria says, her eyes widening. "That could get ugly real fast."

"I've got to warn her," I say. "She hasn't had a phone all weekend."

"I'm sure she knows," Gloria says, rolling her eyes. "Just because you live under a rock…"

"I better check," I say. "Since she lost her phone. Thanks for the heads up."

"Of course, girl. I got your back. Any time."

I lean in and kiss her cheek before pushing out of the bathroom. I text Magnolia and then hurry down the hall and peek through the door of her classroom. Her seat it empty, and class started a few minutes ago. I think about interrupting to ask if anyone has seen her, but that seems crazy even for me. Instead, I head for the office, where I might be able to wheedle the information from the assistant.

I'm just passing the library when it hits me. That's where she'd hide out. She has Grandpa Darling's key to the basement, and if she got to school and found out the Dolce boys were coming for her…

It's the last place they'd look, in their own lair.

I'm about to open the shelf when someone clears his throat behind me. "Can I help you?"

I turn to see a fairly hot, twentyish guy with brown hair and a vaguely familiar face watching me with something between curiosity and expectation.

SELENA

"I'm… Just looking for someone," I say, though there's nothing in the corner where I'm headed except a window and the bookshelves.

He keeps watching me, like he's waiting for me to come up with a better excuse. When I don't, he taps a plastic nametag hanging from the belt loop of his dress pants, which he's wearing with a button shirt with the sleeves rolled, a grey vest, and a tie. "I'm Mr. Delacroix," he says. "The new librarian. I can help you find a book, but there's no one else in here."

My brain bounces through about five thoughts in the next five seconds.

He looks about as far from a stuffy old bespectacled librarian as humanly possible.

Judging from the family resemblance, he's Gideon's older brother, hence the reason he seemed familiar.

A school library is an odd place for a Delacroix to work.

As a member of said founding family, he was probably a Swan, which means he must at least suspect where I was going.

He looks young enough that he might even have been a Swan when Royal was kidnapped…

I swallow hard, my hand curling into a fist around the key. "There's no one else in here?" I ask.

"No," he says, watching me expectantly.

I hold up the old-fashioned key. "Do you know what this opens?"

He quirks a brow and slips his hands into his pockets. "Do you?"

It strikes me then that he doesn't just look like Gideon. He looks like a dark-haired version of Preston. I find myself studying his face, wondering if this is what his cousin would look like without the burn scars.

"Once a Swan, always a Swan," I say lightly.

"Where'd you get that?" he asks, reaching for the key.

I close my fingers around it. "I'm the key master."

"You're a girl."

"And?"

His eyes narrow. "You're not a Swan."

"I'm not?"

"Prove it."

SELENA

I raise my brows and give him some side-eye. "Mr. Delacroix," I say. "Are you asking me to show you a tattoo that's under my clothes, while we're alone in the library together? I really don't think that's going to help Willow Heights wake up from its current publicity nightmare."

He jerks his hand back, his eyes widening. "No! That's not—I wasn't—"

I raise a brow and hold up the key. "I'm going downstairs. Are any classes coming in this morning?"

He shakes his head, still looking freaked out. I step past him, unlock the door, and slip behind the bookcase.

When I reach the bottom of the steps, I turn the corner with my hands up, in case Magnolia brought another one of Daddy's guns to school. But Magnolia's not the one sitting slumped over in the chair against the wall, the one where I tried to curl up and sleep last year when I was trapped down here with the twins.

"Duke," I say, coming to a stop.

He jumps up from the chair and scrambles backwards, holding up a hand as if I'm the one wielding a gun. He doesn't have a gun, either, but he's holding a beer bottle. The light filtering through the dark glass shows it's already half empty.

"Seriously?" I ask. "It's eight in the morning."

"You shouldn't be down here," he says, sounding as freaked as he looks.

"Is Baron down here?" I ask. "Or are you pissed and somehow blaming me for that video, too, even though I had nothing to do with it?"

"Baron's not here," he says, glancing over his shoulder at the open door to the other room. "But I can't be alone with you."

"Why?" I ask, planting my hands on my hips and narrowing my eyes. I'm on alert, though. I don't like being alone with him, either. I glance around at the floor, hoping Magnolia didn't grab the brass knuckles that I dropped down here. I don't see them anywhere. Damn it. I can still take Duke if he tries anything, maybe even Baron, too, if he shows up. But I'd feel safer with a weapon.

SELENA

Duke just stares at me, then drops his hands to his sides. "You could say something happened."

"Oh, how the tables have turned," I say, shaking my head. "Remember when you and Baron brought me down here, and you tried to coerce me into having sex with you by saying you could tell Royal it happened anyway, and he'd believe you?"

Duke swallows, looking like a puppy that's been kicked. "I know," he says. "I'm shit when I'm drunk."

"Is that why you're always drunk?" I ask. "So you don't have to take responsibility for your shittiness?"

He takes a drink of his beer and gives me a baleful look. "Are you going to tell Royal I tried something?"

"Are you going to try something?"

"No," he says, scowling. "I would never do that."

"Of course not," I say, rolling my eyes. "Now that you're the one in danger."

"I promise I won't," he says. "But please don't lie about it to Royal."

"See, that's the thing," I say. "You have to worry about me saying something happened when it didn't, ruining your reputation, or worst case, taking you to court. I have to worry about it actually happening. And it's not something that just goes away, Duke. It changes who you are. I'll never be the same person I was before. Even if you went to jail for the rest of your life, it wouldn't help me. The damage is done, and it can never be undone."

"Royal will literally kill me," he says quietly. "Not that it matters. After that video, I'm done at this school." He lifts the bottle, finishing it off in a few long gulps, then throws himself back into the chair and reaches into his backpack, pulling out another. "Want one?"

I have no interest in drinking before noon, but I pull over a chair and sit a few feet away from him while he opens two beers with a lighter and hands me one. What I said is true—I'll never be without scars from their assault—but some things remain or return. I haven't forgiven him, but I don't exactly hate him, either. I want to understand this boy, this monster.

Like Dixie, he's one of the biggest mysteries at this school. She is a mirror, reflecting back everyone else,

SELENA

their dramas and rumors, so you can never see what's behind the glass. Duke is a clown, a jester, deflecting truth with crude humor. But today, his paint is off, and I'm just fascinated enough to stay. I'm not scared of him, not even when we're alone together. I don't need a weapon. I have the armor of power.

"They're saying someone wants to press charges," he says glumly, slumping forward with his elbows on his knees, the beer hanging between.

"For what?"

"For… Pulling out my dick," he says. "Because some of the freshmen are only fourteen, and their fucking parents think they've never seen a dick before."

"Some of them probably haven't."

"They're saying I should be labeled a sex offender."

A laugh bubbles up inside me, but it comes out as a snort of disbelief. "Am I supposed to feel sorry for you?" I ask. "You literally raped me, Duke."

"I'm sorry," he says miserably. "You know how fucking sorry I am, Harper."

If he hadn't said it until now, when he's finally in trouble, I wouldn't believe him. If Baron said it, I wouldn't believe it. But Duke apologized from the start, and even though I don't forgive him, I think he's sincere.

"Actually, I don't know," I say, taking a swig of the beer. "I don't know why you do that shit. I mean, I sort of get it for Royal, after what happened to him. I even think I understand Baron in some fucked up way. But you have a conscience, Duke. I know you do, even if you pretend you're like Baron. So what is it? You want your brothers to think you're as psycho as them? Or is it something else?"

For a minute, Duke doesn't answer. He just sits there drinking and staring at the wall. He finishes his second beer and cracks open another before I've taken more than a few sips of mine.

"Have you ever seen someone die?" he asks at last.

I shrug. "Yeah."

"Really?" he asks, turning to me. "Who?"

"No one I really knew," I say, sipping the beer. "One of the old Crosses got hit by a car on our street one time, a hit and run. They said it was the Disciples, but it seemed more random. And when I lived in the trailer park, a dog got out and bit a kid's neck, and she died. Oh, and one time, I was walking with my friend Blue, and we found a dead body. But we didn't see him die. We just called the cops and left. I don't even know how he died. Probably an overdose or gang related."

Body found near tracks…

He nods thoughtfully, picking at the label on his bottle and leaning forward to rest his elbows on his knees again. "I was a kid the first time I saw someone die, too. I think I was five. Mom was at some party, and we were supposed to be sleeping. I guess my uncle came over and needed Dad to go along for something. They must have been in a hurry because Dad didn't call our nanny. They just carried us out and put us all in the back seat of the car and told us to go back to sleep."

"He took you to kill someone?"

"We went out to this pier. He told us to stay in the car, they'd be right back," Duke goes on. "There was another car, one of my other uncles. We saw them dragging this guy out and beating him up. Then they took him down to the water."

I take another drink. I've seen some fucked up shit in my life, but none of it included murder. That's by design. Any violent urges I have are expelled at the Slaughterpen. I stay away from the gangs and all the shit that goes along with it. I know how much a life is worth, even a life like mine.

"We were supposed to stay there, but Baron really wanted to go see what they were doing. We were a bunch of kids, so disobeying our parents was exciting. We snuck over to this cement barricade thing and hid behind it. They took the guy down to the river, and they threw him in the water. My uncle held him down until he stopped struggling. Then they just… Let him float away."

"Damn," I say, shaking my head.

"I started crying," Duke says, though I'm not sure he's really talking to me anymore. "They told me to shut up because Dad would hear and we'd get in trouble. We ran back to the car, and we were supposed to pretend we'd never left. Dad and Uncle Donnie got back in the car, but I couldn't stop crying. Dad asked what was wrong, and Baron said he'd hit me.

"Dad turned around in the seat, and he said, 'Well, son, what are you going to do?' I didn't want to hurt my brother, so I wasn't going to do anything. Dad got all quiet, and then he said, 'If someone hits you, you hit them back.' But for some reason I just couldn't, even when he said it again. 'Hit him back.' I just sat there crying like a fucking pussy. After a minute, Royal reached across me and punched Baron for me. Then we left, but I knew… I could tell Dad was disappointed, that I made him look bad in front of my uncle. I should have hit him. I shouldn't have needed Royal to do my dirty work."

"Or maybe your dad shouldn't have taken you along for a murder when you were five years old," I say, the old anger at the Dolce patriarch rising inside me. Sure, it's nice to take the D-boys down a notch, especially Baron. I didn't release that video, but I can see why he'd think it was my doing, that I put Dixie up to it. I've been gunning for him since I started back. But even if she ruined their untouchable reputation at this school, it doesn't really solve the bigger problem. It's alleviating the symptoms without eliminating the root cause.

"By the time we got back, Mom was home," Duke says, his eyes glazing over. "She'd lit some of her candles and passed out drunk, and one of them had fallen over. The couch was completely engulfed in flame. King ran and got the fire extinguisher. I wished he'd let it burn, though. The couch was already ruined, and the fire was so… Alive. I wanted to watch it forever."

He's speaking in a faraway tone, like he's back there now. It gives me a creeped out feeling, like when Royal gets all hollow-eyed. I shiver and take another drink. "Good thing you got home when you did, though. Right?"

For a long minute, Duke doesn't speak.

"The next time, it was Dawson," he says at last, his voice so quiet I'm not sure I heard him right. He finishes his beer and then hangs his head down, his shoulders jerking when a hiccup erupts. At first, I think it's a beer hiccup, but after a few more, I realize he's… Crying.

"You did that?" I ask.

SELENA

"It's my fault," he says, his voice rough with tears. "It was my idea to bring him. I don't know what's wrong with me, Harper. I don't *think*."

I know I should be disgusted, should despise him, because he was the one who said they'd bring friends when they were leaving me in that swamp. I should take this moment when he's broken, and I should use it against him, use it to ruin him. But I don't know if he'd survive it, if he'd ever be vulnerable again.

When I found the one spot where Royal was most vulnerable, I exploited it, and even if he said he'd forgive me, I don't know if he'll ever truly let me in again. I won't make that mistake with Duke. I won't give him one more piece of evidence proving the world is cruel, that everyone exploits everyone else at their most vulnerable. I will give him more than he deserves, be better than he was to me.

So I get up, and set down my beer, and go to Duke.

"Don't come near me," he says, scrambling out of his chair and landing on his ass on the floor, like I'm toxic to the touch. "Please, Harper. He'll kill me."

It strikes me then that he's truly afraid of me. Not physically, but afraid of my power. He knows I have Royal's unwavering support, that I can do anything I want, that if I say something happened, Royal will believe me, not him. And why wouldn't he be afraid? All he's ever known is monsters making monsters making monsters. That's what the people around him have always done. It's his world, and he's a product of that world.

But it's not mine.

I make my own world. I choose to step out of line. Not to forgive, but to give. Even though I owe him nothing, even though he doesn't deserve it, even though I should take a video of him crying and begging and pass it around school the way he did with my video, I don't. I sit down next to him, and I pull him into my arms, and I hold him the way he held me once, the way not enough people have done for either of us.

"I'm sorry," he chokes out. "I'm so fucking sorry, Harper."

SELENA

He clings to me, his sobs loud and ugly, echoing through the underground room. When they finally stop, I keep holding him, waiting for him to put himself back together. I think he might have fallen asleep or passed out from drinking so fast and then exhausting himself with tears.

I look around, trying to see if I can find somewhere more comfortable to sit, or at least rest my back on the chair. That's when I see a shadow in the open doorway to the other room. I tense, my heart lurching as I look up to see Baron standing there, a sucker tucked in his cheek, watching.

Fuck.

Duke said he wasn't down here, but he looked that way, like he was expecting him. Baron must have come through the tunnel from the parking lot after leaving.

I don't move, don't react. Duke's arms are around my middle, his head pressed to my chest. My eyes meet Baron's, and I wish I could read him, wish I knew if he was going to start shit about this, tell Royal it's something it's not. Or maybe he'll just watch, the way he watches from the back seat when they ride together. I once thought Duke was the favorite brother, but now I know better. Baron's not resentful about it. He prefers to stay halfway in the shadows, watching.

But he doesn't just watch. He gathers information—ammunition. I know better than to trust him. Whatever he sees, it will be used later.

He steps back into the other room, swallowed by shadows so completely I wonder if I imagined his presence. Before I can decide what to do, Duke finally sits up, turning away and pulling the hem of his shirt up to wipe his face.

"Fuck," he says with an awkward little laugh. "I haven't cried like that since I was a kid. Probably since that time I told you about."

"Not even with Mabel?" I ask.

He gives me a funny look. "No way."

"When your sister died?"

He shakes his head, his eyes sober for once. I know then that I did the right thing, that whatever he's done, he's also experienced pain, and adding to it would only make him worse. It might feel good, but it would do more damage to him, and through him, this town. Anyway, I'm not like Royal, like the Dolces, ruled by a thirst for revenge.

I reach out, take Duke's hand, and squeeze. "Why me?"

He shrugs and pulls his hand away, reaching into his bag and pulling out another beer. "You saw me at my worst, what I'm capable of, and somehow you don't hate me."

"It's hard to hate what you understand so well," I say, watching him open the beer and tip it back, letting it slide down his throat. I know the relief that the bottle offers all too well. I've watched it pull my mother back in time and again, after every breakup, every attempt to be better, do better, get better. It always starts with drinking.

Duke finishes his beer and picks up his bag, shaking it before pointing to my beer. "You gonna finish that?"

I hand it to him with the same hollow, sad feeling I used to get when Mom would ask me for a drink. He's on a binge, and I know how those work. He'll leave and find it somewhere, so there's no use in dumping it out to try to stop it.

"I better get back to school," I say, standing and glancing at the door to the second room. "You'll be okay?"

"I don't know," Duke says, his voice toneless. "If Dad can't fix this with another donation…"

"Then you'll go to Faulkner for the rest of the year," I say, thinking how funny that twist of fate would be. "You never know. Maybe the change would be good for you."

Duke just nods, staring morosely at his beer.

I don't like the feeling of being watched, knowing Baron is in the other room, so I give the room one last sweep for my brass knuckles and then head upstairs. I don't want to show up with ten minutes left in class, so I wait it out in the bathroom. At least the Dolces are suspended, so they won't be here to mess with Magnolia at school. And she has a weapon now, one she can carry at school without being expelled. I might just let her keep the DOLL rings. She probably needs them more than I do.

As I sit there, I realize I had it all wrong. I thought if I could become queen, I could make a difference here. The social order isn't just at this school, though. It's something that happens at every school, in every state and country. I'm never going to change the fact that athletes and blondes are the standard, the most desirable and therefore in the highest positions.

And I don't care to. That's not my fight.

I took it easy on the twins, in part because I knew Royal wouldn't survive losing another sibling. And even when I hated him, I still loved him. I saw a way I could get more out of his gift, make it last longer, so I took it. And then I tried to use that power to take them down in a different way, a way I thought was my own.

But it was never my way at all. I tried to show the twins their place, to show them they were no better than me. I wanted them to call me the queen, equal to their king status, so they could see that I was strong, that they couldn't defeat me. I wanted them to see that I wasn't ruined by what they did to me.

Now I see clearly, though. It wasn't for me at all. It was all for them. I was trying to prove myself worthy to them and their people. To show *them* I was strong by beating them at their own game.

But that's bullshit.

I don't need to prove anything to them. I am already worthy, a better person than they'll ever be. I'm done playing Baron's games, playing into his manipulations.

I want something for myself, something bigger than what I can do at this school.

In truth, I only wanted to be queen so that Baron wouldn't be king, not because I have any interest in the position. Now that he's suspended, gone for the time being, I realize I don't give a single fuck about ruling the school. Gloria has that spot locked in, and she's good at it in ways I have no interest in learning or imitating. If I wanted it, she'd show me how, even knowing it would mean losing her own spot. That alone—her support and friendship—means more than any spot at the lunch table or on a proverbial throne. She can have her title, her crown and all.

Hell, I'll give her my fucking blessing. In the Dolce boys' absence, she can run this place like she always has. She earned it, endured the Dolces in ways I couldn't and don't want to. If being their queen means being at their beck and call, I have no interest.

I disrupted the complacent obedience of the student population by showing them they had other options, and I brought attention to the school's corruption with the little earthquake of my protest. The uprising of the cast-off Dolce girls and servers let people know that there is power in numbers, that they didn't have to accept the way things were. Dixie and Magnolia's video debacle showed that the Dolce boys are only human, that they're not immune to all consequence. My job in that movement is done. I'll leave the peasant revolt at Willow Heights to them.

I have bigger goals.

I need to use the power that both Royal and Preston gave me for something bigger than high school drama.

That's just a reflection of a bigger problem in Faulkner, an evil that's run unchecked for too long. It's the reason for Royal's unquenchable thirst for revenge, the mold that formed the twins into the psychos they are. If I'm going to solve this problem in Faulkner once and for all, I have to go back to the root cause—their father.

SELENA

eleven

Royal Dolce

"You going to tell me where we're going?" Harper asks, locking her Escalade and climbing into my car.

"No," I say. "Buckle your seatbelt."

She does as I order without protest, and tightness twists around my sternum like it does every time she doesn't fight something she would have before. She once told me that after what happened to her, a person would think she wouldn't get in a car without knowing where I was taking her, but that she didn't care. I don't know if she'll ever fight that way again, the way she used to.

But I'll keep trying until it happens. I fix what I break, clean up my own messes. Especially when that mess is her, and she's mine. I'm the only one who can fix her, and I fucking love it, even if it makes me more of a monster than anything else. I love her brokenness, want to run my fingers tenderly along every jagged edge of her shattered soul, secure in the knowledge that I've been here. I did this to her. I broke her, and she will never forget it.

She'll never forget me.

I'll always be a part of her, even when she hates me with every fragment of her decimated being. Even if she walks away, if she runs to the edge of the earth to escape me, she can't leave me behind. I'm inside every molecule of her body. She can never truly escape me, never truly be gone. I'll always be with her—not a piece of her of the puzzle that makes up Harper Apple, but every break, every cut. It's all mine. She's mine. Nothing on earth can change that, no matter how hard she fights.

Maybe she's realized that, and that's why she doesn't protest. When I pull into the parking lot and find a spot, though, she turns to me, her eyes wide. "What is this?"

"It's the airport."

"I can see that, smartass," she says. "Why are we here?"

SELENA

"We're going to New York," I say.

"It's Tuesday," she says, blinking at me with disbelief.

"New York is open on Tuesday, too, sweetheart," I say, smirking as I unbuckle her seatbelt.

"I didn't bring any clothes," she protests.

"I'll get you some when we're there," I say, climbing out and looking her over. "I'm done looking at my girlfriend and seeing Preston Darling fetishizing my dead sister, anyway."

"Girlfriend?" she asks, drawing back and crossing her arms. "I thought we agreed this was just fucking."

"Okay," I say slowly. "Then I'm tired of seeing the girl I'm fucking dressed up as my dead sister. I should gut the bastard just for that."

"I'm not picking a side," she warns. "I already told you we're friends, and that's not going to change. Don't make me choose between you and him."

"I'm not."

"Good," she says. "Because you already lost a sister that way."

No one but Harper would dare say something like that to me, hit me with the truth like it's just another fact, as if it doesn't make me want to go to my knees like she took a battering ram to my balls.

"Fine," I grit out. "I won't talk shit about your other boyfriend."

"I appreciate that," she says lightly. "And this. But I can't just flit off to New York on a Tuesday. I have school tomorrow. You have school. Not to mention I don't have the money."

I capture her hand and pull her toward the building. "Don't worry about it. Your school allows absences for college visits, and mine is a joke."

"You arranged for me to take off school without telling me?"

"Get used to it," I say. "I take care of what's mine, and you are mine. Got it?"

"I didn't bring any money," she protests. "I don't have a ticket."

"Did you not hear what I just said?"

SELENA

She doesn't say anything as we make our way inside. She starts to get in line, but I smile and shake my head. "Dolces don't wait in line," I say, pulling her aside. "We're first class all the way, sweetheart."

"Why are we going to New York?" she asks as we bypass the line for customs and step through the scanner. "Are you going to introduce me to your mom now that I'm your *girlfriend?*"

I know she's teasing, but I just smile and shrug. "I told you," I say. "It's a college visit."

"Wait, we're really going to visit a school?" she asks, looking more excited than the old Harper would have at the prospect of meeting my mother.

"That's right," I say as we head for our gate. "Syracuse. You'll be going there next year."

"I will?" she asks, her baby blues round as she stares at me.

"You will," I say, taking her hand and squeezing it.

"What about you?" she asks.

"I'll be there, too," I say, sitting down in the waiting area.

She just stares at me a second, and then she sits down across my lap. "Royal… This is way too much."

"It's college," I say. "Everyone goes. It's not even an Ivy League school."

She links her hands behind my neck and stares into my eyes, looking like she might cry. Instead, she leans in and presses her lips to mine, hard. "Thank you."

"Duke told me what happened yesterday," I say, resting my hands on her little waist.

"I figured Baron would tell you we fucked or something," she says. "Since you don't trust me."

"I know you wouldn't fuck my brothers," I say. "If you wanted them dead, you'd have killed them yourself."

"Ah," she says. "So Baron wouldn't say I fucked Duke because he doesn't want you killing him."

"There's too much drama here for my family right now, anyway," I say, squeezing her to me. My brothers and Dad are all pissed about the shit she started at school, and I'd rather get her out of their way while they calm down, just in case they get any ideas about going after her behind my back. "It'll be good to get away for a week."

She lays her head on my chest and snuggles against me, and I cradle her small body in my arms, holding her in silence until they call for first-class boarding. When we're settled into our seats, Harper turns to me with a nervous smile. "I've never been on a plane before."

"I know."

I don't say the other part, that I'm proud I made it happen, that I can be here for her first time on a plane. I can't fucking stand how happy it makes me to see her smiling and looking around with so much excitement.

"I'm surprised you don't have your own private plane," she teases.

"Just wait," I say, capturing her knee and pulling it against mine. I can't keep my hands off her, and I don't plan to let her out of my sight for the entire trip. "When I take over the business from Dad, it's not just going to be a few candies. Dolce Sweet is going to be an empire. I'll get you a private jet then, Cherry Pie."

"And when will that be?" she asks carefully. I can tell she's got something up her sleeve, that it has nothing to do with my offer to get her a private jet. For a while, I thought she was just another gold digger. But it was never about money for her. It was about escape. I know her well enough to know that now, well enough to know this is the gift she'll treasure more than anything else I could offer, more than all the private jets in the world.

"Whenever I can get the board of directors to replace him," I say. "You anxious for me to run my own company?"

"Who would run it if your dad got fired right now?" she asks.

"I would," I say, watching her from the corner of my eye. "I'm eighteen. Everything's set for me to take over when he's out."

"Would you want to do that before you graduate college?"

I know her scheming look by now, can almost see the wheels turning inside her head. "What are you thinking?" I ask.

SELENA

"I'm not sure yet," she says. "I'm not trying to take down your family anymore, but… I'm not going to lie to you, Royal. I think we need to get him out of Faulkner."

"How about we get you out of Faulkner?" I say, squeezing her knee. "Who cares what happens to that shitty little town? We'll be in Syracuse for the next four years."

She shrugs. "I care. It's still my hometown, even if I move. And I haven't agreed to this, you know. You can't just pick where I go to school."

"Okay," I say with a smirk.

"You're infuriating," she says, glowering at me.

"You're cute," I answer, reaching across her and pulling her seatbelt over her lap before buckling her in. "Now shut up and let me take care of you."

We fly into Syracuse a few hours later. Harper tries to play it cool, but she can't keep the smile off her face for most of the trip. Everything impresses her—the flight, the service, the landing. I pick up our luxury rental and take her straight to the hotel. Seeing her this happy has me horny as hell.

"So, this is what it's like being rich," she marvels as I hand the keys to the valet and lead her to the glass elevator inside. "You better watch out or I'll get spoiled like you."

I wrap my arm around her waist and pull her in. "You have no idea," I say. "I'm just getting started."

In our room, we shower the travel off separately before we fall onto the soft bed next to the windows overlooking the city. "So, when is this college tour?" she asks, stretching her little body on top of mine. I put on a t-shirt and boxers, but she's naked and sexy as fuck.

"Tomorrow," I growl, palming the backs of her thick thighs. "Tonight, I'm going to fuck every hole in your body until you beg for mercy, and then I'll fuck you one more time, just to make sure you remember who all this belongs to. I'll give you a hint. It's not you."

"You're a pig."

"And you're a collection of tight little holes begging to be wrecked."

I roll us over, sliding a hand between her legs, stroking her clit until she's wet and panting for me. When

SELENA

I push into her tight, bare cunt, I just about lose my mind. I savor her cries of pleasure and pain with each slow, deep thrust. Fucking her raw is like nothing I've ever felt, and I have to make it last, hold myself back. I make her cum before I let myself go, forcing my cock so deep into her that tears pour from her eyes when I fill her core with my own release.

Afterwards, she dozes while I order room service. We eat and then fuck again before drifting off. Being away is a relief, like we've left everything behind. Maybe there's a chance for us, away from my family but close enough to go into the city to visit every few months. Away from her family and the ghosts of mine that haunt Faulkner. For the first time in three years, it seems like a possibility. Like maybe I really can start over somewhere else, without Crystal.

Like maybe the girl who's still here, still alive, could be more important than the one who's not.

Over the next few days, we tour the campus and get everything lined up for her admission. Since I've already graduated, I'm all set to transfer as soon as she's able to join me.

I was going to bring her to meet Ma while we were up here, but at the last minute, I decide not to. It'll happen eventually, since I'm never letting her go. I still don't trust her, though, and I don't want her near something as complicated and fucked up as my relationship with my mother.

Instead, we fly into the city, where we have dinner with King and Eliza. The next day, Eliza's all too happy to leave the baby for a few hours and take Harper shopping. Thanks to her stylist, Harper comes back with some decent clothes that make her look like herself and not like she's playing dress-up as my sister. I tell her she looks hot because I remember how much I'm supposed to care. Once, I wouldn't have given a girl like her a second glance. But now I don't give a fuck what she wears. I'll just be taking them off later.

King offers to take us to the Hamptons, where he has free rein of Uncle Al's house, but I don't want to involve Harper in that world. Even though Al won't be there, I'd

SELENA

rather take her somewhere else. One day, she'll have to dip her toes into the Life, but not yet. I'll keep her far from that for as long as I'm able. So, instead of going out there, we hop on a plane and fly into Hyannis, get another car, and drive out to the Cape.

"It's pretty cold for the beach," Harper says, craning her neck to see the ocean as we wind along Route 6 toward Chaos Cove.

"You've never seen the ocean," I point out. "I'm not waiting until next summer."

It's late October, so the traffic is basically nonexistent, unlike the gridlock of summer traffic. I pull up to the little rental, which, after a little convincing, they opened for us despite it being the off season.

"How many times have you been to the ocean?" Harper asks as we climb out of the car. I can hear the surf pounding the beach from here, and even though I've been here plenty, excitement rises in me at the thought of bringing her here for the first time.

"I don't know," I say, shaking my head. "Enough to lose count."

"Then how many times have you been *here*?"

"Every summer," I say, handing her the down jacket she got in the city. "Until three years ago."

I take her hand and lead her around the house, down the boardwalk, and onto the beach. I watch Harper's face from the corner of my eye as she takes it in, her gaze rapt. The cold, salt air dampens our faces as we cross the sand to the water. Harper drops my hand and crouches to touch the icy water when a wave rolls in. Then she stands, just watching the ocean while I watch her.

We're the only people on the beach, and I'm suddenly glad we didn't come in summer. I don't want to share this moment with anyone. I step back and let her have it for herself. The roar of the waves fills the air, but all I see is her. Her hair ripples out in the wind, and she pulls her jacket closed around her. Her little body is dwarfed by the sea, the sand, the sky. She looks so insignificant for a girl who's endured the brutality she has, so inconsequential for someone who's the center of the whole fucking universe.

SELENA

My chest aches for both of us. She's not just my curse. I'm hers. I'll never be done with her, no matter how much she deserves freedom. She deserves so much more, a man who can treat her like the fucking queen she is, not some asshole who takes what he wants and doesn't know the meaning of the word love.

But she's not going to get it. She's going to get me because I can't let go. She's my weakness, and she's cursed with that as much as I am.

After a while, she turns and walks up the beach to where I'm standing in the dry sand.

"I should make your brothers cry more often," she says, flashing me a grin that's like an ice pick to my sternum. She looks so fucking happy, so free, as if the past doesn't exist.

"What?" I ask.

She sits down on the cold beach, patting the sand until I take my place next to her. "You said this was to thank me for being with Duke last week," she reminds me.

I shift around, then pull her into my lap, setting her between my legs and wrapping my arms around her from behind. I rest my chin on top of her head, and we watch the waves for a while.

"I worry about him," I admit at last.

"The drinking?" she asks.

"Yeah," I say. "And the fire."

"The fire?" she asks. "Like when he burned your neighbor's house?"

"When he burns anything," I say. "Or anyone. One of these days…"

"There will be someone in the house?" she asks. "You're afraid he'll kill someone?"

"Or himself."

"Some people like playing with fire," she says slowly, nodding.

"And people who like playing with fire get burned," I say, tightening my arms around her. I curse myself for reminding her of home, for taking away her smile like the bastard I am. But just because I will never find peace, that doesn't mean she can't. She submitted to me, accepted my claim. In return, I'll make sure she gets what she wants, too, that she finds her own happiness, even if I never find mine.

twelve

Harper Apple

As the plane angles down toward the Little Rock airport, I can't shake the Wonderland feeling that's clung to me all week. Girls like me don't fly on airplanes, never mind first class. Girls like me don't get whisked off to colleges or on whirlwind vacations that include sight-seeing in New York City and cozying up at a private cottage on Cape Cod. They don't dip their toes in the ocean. They don't go on shopping trips to designer boutiques with personal stylists. They don't step inside Chanel stores, let alone leave with anything.

And yet, in some world, Royal's world, a girl like me just did all those things. But I'm not sure if that girl is actually me. All my life, I've wanted nothing more than to get the hell out of Faulkner, but now I don't know.

SELENA

Something doesn't feel right. I'm so incredibly grateful for what Royal just did for me, and it's not that it isn't enough. It's that I don't know if I'm still a girl like me.

I'm being handed my dream on a silver platter, but something in me makes me draw back, makes me hesitate. Maybe all I really wanted was the option, a way out of the trap of my life. Now that I can come and go as I please, do I still want to leave Faulkner?

This town is fucked up, and I don't know if I'm the kind of girl who walks away from a mess, even if it's not one of her making. Faulkner is my home. Can I turn my back on it now, when it's falling apart, and leave it to its fate in Mr. Dolce's hands? Can I move to New York and live my own life and never think of it again, never wonder about those I've left behind? It seems selfish to flit off and live my best life, knowing people here are still suffering.

I think about it all the way back to Royal's house, where I left my car. When we turn into his neighborhood, I find myself humming "Back to life, back to reality." In what feels like another lifetime, I remember

Colt singing that song as we pulled up to the school after spending the afternoon at his house. That was the day Royal almost killed him. The day he claimed me at the river, told me I was his.

I barely knew him then.

Now I know every secret this terrible, brutal boy contains, and somehow, I still love him.

"Thank you," I say, turning to him as he shuts off the car. "I don't know how to thank you enough. This whole week felt like a fairytale."

"You can thank me on your back later, Cherry Pie," he says, pulling me across the console and kissing me roughly on the mouth. "I'm not sure I can make it more than a day without fucking you now that I've had you to myself every day."

"Somehow I think you'll manage," I say, smiling through our kiss.

"I think you'll manage to be here tomorrow," he says, gripping my shirt when I try to pull back. "Unless you want me to fuck some Thorncrown bitch while I'm thinking about you."

SELENA

"Fuck you, Royal," I say, jerking back.

"That's the plan," he says with that asshole smirk that infuriates me so much I want to scream.

"If I mean that little to you, that you'd go fuck someone else if I won't come over, then go right ahead," I say. "See what happens."

I climb out of the Rover and slam the door as hard as I can. Royal's laughing when he gets out, transferring the two suitcases of clothes into my car. When he tries to pull me in for a goodbye kiss, I shove him away. "Touch me and I'll break your nose again," I threaten, holding up my fists.

"Do it," he says, grinning down at me and backing me into my door. "I'll use the blood as lube and fuck you up against your car again."

He grabs my head between both hands and kisses me hard, so hard I feel the bruises already forming on my lips. I twist against him, but he kisses me harder, forcing his tongue into my mouth. Struggling against him, I bite down hard, tasting his blood before letting go. I pull back with a smile on my face.

Royal grabs my hair and drags me back against the car, thrusting his tongue back into my mouth, slicking mine with salty blood. When he finally pulls back, his eyes are heated, his breath ragged.

"If my father wasn't home, I'd throw you down on the garage floor and fuck you until you screamed for me," he growls.

"I fucking hate you," I say, opening my door and climbing in.

"I hate you too, Jailbird," he says before I slam the door and back out of the garage.

By the time I get home, I'm a little calmer, but still pissed. I pull into my drive and see Blue and Olive sitting outside on the steps of their house. The afternoon is cool but muggy, and Blue's wearing her usual shabby jean jacket. I think of the bruises I saw under it, the ones she hides, and again I wonder how I can just leave Faulkner and go live the high life with Royal and his fancy family. Those are not my people.

These are my people.

SELENA

When she sees me, Blue gives a little wave and a smile without expectation. I can go in the house without the burden of guilt for blowing her off, or I can go talk to her, and she'll be fine either way. It's things like this, the little ways we understand other girls like us, that make it hard to imagine a life in Royal's world, where so much is expected… And faked.

I've never been anything but a girl like me, and everyone knows it. There's no pressure to be better, to be *on* all the time, my life a constant performance like Gloria Walton's. It feels exhausting, trying to meet expectations and be what everyone wants at all times. I've never been anyone but myself.

I lock the car and cross the scraggly grass of the yard to Blue's front steps.

"Look what I can do," Olive says in lieu of a greeting. She proceeds to link her hands and legs around the railing on their tiny porch and hang over the side. She lets go with one hand and waves, grinning big. "I'm a sloth."

"You okay?" Blue asks, cocking her head and watching me. "I haven't seen you around."

"Yeah," I say. "I was with Royal."

"The rich guy?"

"One of them," I say, feeling suddenly defensive. Besides the three guys who were there, she's the one person who knows the truth about what happened last spring. She's not going to understand how I could take Royal back.

"I was hoping you were over there," she says. "It's been a little crazy at your house."

Dread knots in my stomach.

"Yeah," Olive says, flipping over and landing on her feet on the ground beside the porch. She stumbles back, windmilling her arms, and then tosses her long hair back. "The ambulance came and everything."

"What?" I ask, the heaviness inside me going cold. "Was it my mom?"

"No," Blue says quickly. "Some guy was tweaked out in your front yard, rolling around on the ground and all that. They took him off on a stretcher."

"Shit," I say, sinking onto the steps beside her. "Got a smoke?"

"Just one," she says. "We can share."

"Cool," I say. "I seriously owe you."

"Consider it my insurance payment," she says, cracking a little smile before turning to Olive. "Grab my cigarettes?"

Olive groans and then runs up the steps between us and into the house.

"My mom's had a lot of guys over?" I ask.

"People have been coming in and out for a few days," Blue says, glancing at me from the corner of her eye.

"I guess she's paying off her dealer." I sigh and lean back on my elbows on the concrete steps. Olive comes back with the pack of cigarettes, hands it over, and picks up a big Folgers can. She heads down to the walkway, where she dumps out all her toy cars and starts lining them up.

Blue pulls out a cigarette and drops the empty pack in the coffee can still on the steps. "So you're back with the Range Rover guy?" she asks, lighting up. "I saw his car around a couple times before you took off."

I nod, waiting for her to cast judgment. She doesn't react, though. I should have given her more credit. If anyone in the world would understand, it's her.

"He took me to New York," I admit. "And Cape Cod."

"Wow," she says, her eyes widening. "It's that serious?"

"Oh, we're not together," I say. "I told him I can't, you know. Not after what happened. But Blue… He took me to see a college up there. He wants me to go to Syracuse with him next year."

I can't keep the smile from bursting onto my face, no matter how much of a dick he was when he dropped me off. And really, he was just being Royal. He didn't do anything except be his asshole self, and I've accepted that he never will be. In truth, I'm fine with it, even if he does still irritate the fuck out of me sometimes.

"Wow," Blue says. "That's crazy."

"I know," I say, laughing. "He's basically taking care of everything except the application. He said it's really just a formality, because if I want to go, I'm in. They must have made a big donation. Can you imagine, me in New York?"

"Yeah," she says, dragging on her cigarette and looking at me funny. "You've wanted to get out of this town since the day we met. Remember when we tried to hop the train?"

I nod, taking the cigarette when she offers. I inhale and twist the cherry against the step beside me, knocking the ash off. "I don't know, though," I say, reality sinking back in. "I mean, I want to travel, but my roots are here. I don't know if I want to pull them up and put down roots somewhere else. This is my town. My home."

"You sound like Maverick," she says. "Except he's got a point. He's a legacy. His whole family is Crossbones. And he's got the tattoo parlor all lined up. He'll work there with his brother forever. What are you going to do if you stay?"

"I don't know," I admit. "Maybe it wasn't Faulkner I wanted to escape. It was my life here."

I look at my drab house, the dirt on the bricks, the tiny windows. Poverty was always my cage, not the town itself.

"And he's giving you a chance to escape it," Blue points out. "Why wouldn't you take it?"

"It's too much," I say. "I could never make it up to him. I don't want to owe him all my life."

"If you go to school there, you'll probably get a good job," she says. "You can pay him off from that, if he wants it back."

"I know," I say. "But I don't want to take that much money from him, and more than that, from his family. It's... Blood money."

She gives me a funny look. That term always sounds so reasonable when Preston says it, but coming from my mouth, it sounds like an excuse.

"It's money," Blue says. "What does it matter where it comes from, if it gets you out of here?"

"I'll come back," I say, feeling guilty as I watch her drag on her last cigarette. She's not going anywhere anytime soon.

"Why?" she asks incredulously.

"Because," I say. "This town is fucked up. I want to fix it."

"You're going to fix Faulkner?" she asks, grinning.

"Maybe I am."

She doesn't have to believe in me. I know what I'm capable of.

"You don't have to save everyone," she says. "Just save yourself. You can't take the town with you. All you can do is escape. I'd do it in a heartbeat if I didn't have Olive."

"You're right," I say. "But I'm not leaving yet. I have until graduation. Maybe I'll feel differently then, but now... I don't know. It doesn't feel complete. My work here isn't done. Maybe it's stupid, but I do want to fix Faulkner. At least as much as I can before I go."

"And how are you going to do that?" Blue asks.

I want to say that I'm going to get her out, but I don't know how to do that. Even if I could convince Royal to pay tens of thousands of dollars to a complete stranger, she wouldn't go. She'll never leave Olive. She's a part of

Faulkner, like Maverick. Some people don't get a chance to get out. Which makes me think she's right—I should take the chance while I have it.

I know she won't care. She's not someone who will pull me back down, try to trap me here because she's trapped, and if she can't get out, no one can. No, Blue's the opposite. She's the kind of person who would boost me up, stand there and let me climb onto her shoulders and scramble up, even knowing she'd be left behind.

Right now, though, I still have six months to smooth things over between the Dolces and the Darlings. That's the only way they'll stop ruining my town. It might not be my fight, but I'm the one in a position to stop the never-ending feud between them. I'm the only one with a bit of power over someone in both families, the only one with a connection to both. If I want to have anything to come back to in four years, if I want to go away for college and not feel like a selfish bitch who turned her back on everyone, I need to fix what I can before I go. Which means I need to fix the Dolces.

SELENA

I sit with Blue a little longer before waving goodbye to her and Olive, who's lying on her stomach in the dirt, driving her cars along the sidewalk cracks in the fading twilight. I head inside, on guard thanks to Blue's heads up about my mom's latest binge. The lights are off, the house dark, but I can hear Mom moving around in her bedroom, which means she's still on a binge. I sigh and step into my room.

I stop dead in my tracks. It looks like my whole room's been tossed. Drawers are pulled out, clothes strewn across the floor. The mattress lays halfway off the bedframe, the box spring propped up against the wall. The closet door is open, shoe boxes tossed haphazardly around the door. Inside, most of the clothes are gone, only a few old shirts sagging halfway off the hangers.

My heart stops, and I have to swallow the wave of terror rising inside me like a tsunami. No, no, no. This isn't happening. I don't dare think about the possibilities.

I plow through the clothes on the floor, falling on my knees in the scattered shoe boxes. Panic roils up my throat like sickness as I throw the boxes aside, scrambling on all fours to the back of my closet, crawling like an animal, a scream building in the pit of my stomach.

Please don't let her have found it, I pray silently, crazily, to nothing in particular.

Gods don't exist for girls like me.

No higher power takes care of us.

No one watches over us except, if we're lucky, other girls like us.

I find the corner of the carpet that I tuck down so neatly each time, now folded back, left sloppily open. I still reach inside, my brain refusing to accept what my eyes are telling it. My fingers touch nothing but the raw, cheap particleboard under the carpet.

Something rises inside me, a wall of despair so thick no amount of hope or healing, making my own family or healing someone else's, can withstand it.

Hope is a curse.

Healing won't get me out of this town.

Friends are temporary, a distraction from what's real, what's important.

SELENA

Determination to heal Faulkner can get me through another semester at Willow Heights, but not this.

I shoot to my feet, stumbling out of the closet like a drunken person, barreling across the hall and into my mother's room.

"Mom," I scream. "Where's my money?"

She whirls from where she's been pacing. "Your money?" she demands, a cruel smile twisting her lips. "You little thief. You've been hiding that money all this time while I fed you and kept a roof over your head!"

"It's my money, Mom," I say, my volume rising in desperation. "I earned that money. I fed you. My friend kept a roof over both our heads for the past six months."

"You ungrateful little brat," she says. "I busted my ass working to keep you taken care of for eighteen years, and all you can say is that your boyfriend paid the bills for six months? While you stole and hid money from me, your own mother?"

"Mom," I say, wrestling to control myself. "I never stole a penny from you. Now give me back my stash."

"You didn't?" she asks with an incredulous snort. "It's stealing to hold out on me, keeping all that for yourself, while I could barely pay the bills. It's stealing to let me buy all the shit we need while you had the money all along!"

"It's *my* money," I say again. "You have no right to take it without asking. I've paid plenty of bills in the past few years."

"What about before that?" she demands. "What about for the fourteen or fifteen years when I worked myself to death for you, and you didn't contribute a dime? You think that shit was free? You think the bills just magically appeared when you started making money?"

"I was a *child*."

"I never asked for a child," she snaps, wheeling around to pace the room, her gait unsteady and frenetic.

I take a breath, trying to calm down and keep my voice from shaking. "I didn't ask for you to be my mom," I say. "But here we are."

SELENA

"I didn't ask for you to come along and ruin my life," she fumes, wheeling on me. "I didn't ask for a kid to get in the way, to keep me from doing what I wanted with my own life. Hell, if it weren't for you, I could have made it good with a Darling, too. You think you're all that because some rich guy paid attention to you, but you're nothing special. I could have done it, too, if you hadn't come along and fucked it all up."

"You did plenty of fucking up, too," I snap back at her. "Now give me back my money, Mom."

I'm too mad, too broken, to think of any other argument. It's mine. The unfairness makes me want to scream. The injustice of it all hits me, of her taking what I worked for years to save, just to have something, anything, while paying for food and bills and living on nothing but hope some weeks, the dream of getting out of this town the only thing keeping me going when she was out bingeing away her paycheck.

"You ain't stopped screwing me over since the day you were born," she says, stopping to light a half-smoked cigarette from the ashtray on her dresser. "You was always a selfish little bitch. I shouldn't even be surprised that you'd be happy to watch me work myself to death while you sucked me dry and kept your own good-time fund right under my nose."

"I worked for that," I hurl back at her. "It's not my fault you have a drug problem. It's not my fault you spent all your money. Your good-time fund is your regular fucking paycheck. Why do you think I pay the bills? I busted my ass for that, and you can't just take it."

"Just ask your Darling to bail you out," she says. "Or that other one, the football player. I'm sure he's good for a few thousand."

"That money wasn't from them."

The desperation welling inside me almost brings tears to my eyes. I can't explain to her that having something of my own matters, that the fact that I earned that money and didn't take it like some charity case matters. It matters to me. I've been saving that for years, forgoing a social life to work every Friday and Saturday night to put something into my fund to get out of this town on my own two feet.

SELENA

Maybe that's why I don't want to accept what Royal's offering. I want to be strong enough on my own.

"Who cares?" she says, coughing out a cloud of smoke. "They got plenty where that came from."

"That's not the point," I say. "I need that money, Mom. Please give it back."

"What do you need it for?" she demands, sucking quick on the filter and planting her other hand on her hip. I see the jumpiness in her tensed body as she waits for an answer, but I stopped being scared of her a long time ago.

"To get out of here," I say quietly.

She stares back at me, and in that moment, something passes between us, some unspoken truth. I've watched her all my life. I know her.

The realization sinks in slowly.

She knows me, too. She knows what that money was for.

That's why she took it.

She doesn't want me to get out. She's not like Blue. She wants me to be stuck here just like her, to *be* like her.

She doesn't just hate me for screwing up her life. She hates me because she can't screw up mine. She can't break me, can't make me have a life as bad as the one she blames me for making her live, and she can't fucking stand it.

"You want to get out, then go," she snaps at last. "I never wanted you, anyway."

I face her squarely. "Give me the money, and I'll go."

She stands there a minute, her hard eyes calculating as she watches me. "It's gone," she says at last. "I ain't got it."

My hands ball into fists, my limbs shaking with rage. "You spent all my money on drugs?" I ask. "The money I worked for since I was fourteen, that I got beaten up for, that I gave up homework time to earn, so I could get out of this town on something besides grades alone… You spent it on crystal?"

"I don't do that shit anymore," she says, stubbing out her cigarette butt with the others in her ash tray. "Just Alice. It's not even addictive. If you tried it, you'd understand."

"I fucking understand," I snap.

"Yeah, well, I paid off my debt," she says, raising her chin and glaring at me with a self-righteous expression. "What do you want, not everyone can be Mother Teresa. I do my best, but I'm not getting myself killed because you can't stop thinking about yourself for one minute and think about the mother who raised you."

"I raised myself," I say quietly.

"I gave you everything," she says. "The one time I got desperate and asked you for help, you turned your back on me. I was just going to sell those fancy clothes your sugar daddy bought you. Imagine my surprise when I found that lump in your carpet. I thought I'd hit the jackpot, and your spare key would be under there. But no. I pulled it up to see you had a hell of a lot more than fancy shoes in your closet."

"No," I say, feeling the fight drain out of me, the hope, everything. I want to sink onto her bed and sleep for the next decade. I don't even want to cry. There's nothing inside me, not even sadness.

"I threw a hell of a rager, thanks to you," she says, grinning. "You should've been here for it. Not like you were much fun at my retirement party, but Bobby Dale sure took a shine to you."

"Gross."

"Don't worry, you took care of your mama, whether you meant to or not. That'll keep Bobby Dale off me for weeks. But don't think you're keeping that car, Harper. He got his sights set on it, and he won't give up. Plus, I still owe him some for this weekend…"

"You've got to be fucking kidding me, Mom."

She turns to me, a pleading expression taking over her face. "It's so good, baby, you don't understand. If you tried it, you'd see. I thought it was just something the kids were doing, but once I got my hands on some…"

"I'm going to fucking kill Baron," I mutter.

"Who's Baron?" she asks, her gaze locking in on me with eagerness. "He got some Alice?"

"He's… Selling in this neighborhood," I say, not about to tell her I know the asshole responsible for putting this stuff on the streets.

SELENA

"Can you get some from him?" she asks, seizing my arm. "I need more, and I'm all out. Bobby Dale won't sell me more until I pay off what I used this weekend. I can't go on for long like this. I'm already itching for it, see?" She holds out her arms, where she's scratched red lines into her white skin. I can see the glaze of hunger in her eyes, the need already clawing its way back up. That's her demon, like Royal is mine.

"Mom," I say. "I'm sorry you're on this stuff and you can't kick it. But I won't buy you drugs. I couldn't even if I wanted to. You took my fucking money and gave it to your dealer."

"You have to," she wails, her nails biting into my skin. "If you knew what it was like, Harper…"

"I don't," I say, peeling her fingers off. "For the last time, I'm not interested in finding out. I'm sorry, Mom. But you're going to have to get it through your head and stop taking shit from him if you don't want to owe him. You took everything else I have, Mom. I'm not giving you my car, too."

"He's coming back for it," she says. "It won't be enough, what I gave him. Not after this weekend. I had friends over. I don't even know how much I owe. But he said if I didn't have it next time I owed him, he'd take…" She breaks off, her jittery gaze bouncing around the room.

"What, Mom?" I ask. "He's going to cut off your nose? I'm sure you already fucked him. He'll just stop giving you drugs."

She shakes her head. "You have to give him the car."

"I'm not giving him my car," I say, exasperated that we're back to this. "So what is he going to take?"

"My daughter," she says, finally meeting my eyes. "He said if I didn't have money next time, he'd take you."

SELENA

thirteen

Harper Apple

I stare at my mother a long minute, my heart thudding in my chest. "What did you say, Mom?" I ask quietly.

"I didn't have nothing else to offer," she says, dropping my arm. "I said I'd get him the car, of course. What do you take me for? Always acting like I'm the bad guy. Have I ever let any man touch you?"

"But you told him you'd give him my car," I say. "Knowing that if I wouldn't give him that, he'd take me? And you still took drugs from him? You still fucked him, knowing he's that kind of man?"

"I needed them," she wails.

"And I needed my mom to protect me," I say, my throat aching as I turn away. I walk out of her room, hating that I still love her somehow, because she's my mother and I can't help it, even though I know her fucked up version of love did more harm than good. I grab a handful of t-shirts from my bedroom floor, not paying attention to what I'm picking up. I need to get out, need to leave, but my brain feels numb, stunned with shock. I don't have anywhere to go.

I grab a small switchblade Maverick gave me one night when I left his house after dark, then give up on finding anything else in the mess and leave my room. I stop in Mom's door. "I need my birth certificate," I say. "And any other papers you have of mine."

"What for?" she demands, turning on her heel from where she's been pacing.

"I'm moving out, Mom," I say.

"You can't move out," she says with a sneer. "You don't have nowhere to go."

I snort and shake my head. "That might have worked three years ago, but you know it's bullshit now. I lived with Preston all summer. I'm eighteen. I don't have to stay here anymore."

SELENA

She stares at me a long minute. I don't drop her gaze even though I'm lying through my teeth. I don't have anywhere to go. Blue's not an option. Preston moved and won't give me his new address. I've already taken way too much from Royal. And I can't just crash into Gloria's life, besides the fact that they don't want to feed an extra mouth, either. I have friends, but not the kind I need in this moment.

"Fine, whatever," Mom snaps at last, turning away. "I don't want you here anyway."

"You should get some help."

"I don't need help," she snaps. "I just need one more pearl, just to help me come down."

I sigh. "Where's my birth certificate?"

"In the drawer," she says, turning and pacing, her thumb tapping at her screen as she tries to find another supply. I pull out the drawer where she keeps important stuff, sorting through until I find a folder with my birth certificate, social security card, and shot record. Along with the important stuff, there's a diploma from middle school graduation and an honor roll award from the same year.

She saved them. She was proud of me.

I swallow hard, looking up at Mom. But she's busy snapping at someone on the phone, too lost in her own craving to notice anything else, even her daughter.

I sigh and turn away, calling goodbye as I head down the hall. I climb into the Escalade and just sit there. My suitcases are still in the back, two big ones full of brand-new clothes that cost thousands of dollars. I could give them to Mom to get her dealer off her back.

But I don't have anything else.

I pull out of the driveway and drive aimlessly through Faulkner, quiet on a Sunday evening. At last, I pull up to Willow Heights, using the side parking lot. I get out the jacket that Royal's sister-in-law pointed out when I said I needed a warm jacket while we were up there. It's not cold here—a hoodie would be plenty. But it's always chilly where I'm going.

I walk around the back of the building to the door that's inset at the bottom of the slope. It's nondescript, painted the same color as the wall, but I know where it goes. I could sleep in the rooms under Willow Heights, where I've slept before, but too many people use that room. Obviously, my key is not the only one, but there's nothing interesting in this room.

I unlock the door and step into the musty darkness that smells of dirt and cobwebs. I take a few breaths, letting myself adjust to the close feeling of being underground. I know it's not actually a tight space—three tunnels open into the large room—but being underground still activates my claustrophobia a little. I turn on my phone's flashlight and do a lap around the space, making sure there's nothing creepy down here. After I've calmed my racing heart, I go back and pull the door closed. Then, I curl up on the dirt floor, wadding up the down jacket for a pillow.

It takes a while to fall asleep in the cold, strange space. I'm not sure how long I've been asleep when something wakes me. I sit up with a start, sure there's a scream echoing in my ears. From somewhere in the tunnels, the sound of a droning chant echoes.

Goosebumps rise on my arms, and I grope for my phone, scooting back until I'm pressed to the wall. I reach into my boot, pulling out the small switchblade and turning on my phone's light. I'm still alone, but the creepy chanting makes my skin crawl, especially because I can't tell which direction it's coming from as it echoes through the underground tunnels.

Suddenly, I'm sure I hear running footsteps.

I shoot to my feet, scrambling to shove the key into the lock and turn. My knife slips from my hand, but I don't bother retrieving it. If someone catches me, my fists will do as much damage. I bash my shoulder against the door, my heart racing. It flies open, and I just about tumble out, barely keeping my feet under me. I slam it shut, pressing my back to it for a second. Then I turn and lock it, my fingers still shaking.

Back in my car, I lock the doors and turn on the heat, rubbing my arms until the goosebumps disappear. It's after midnight, so I must have slept a while, but I'm wide awake now. I crawl onto the back seat and lie there for a while, jumping every time a leaf falls on the car and skitters across the roof. Finally, when the light is starting to creep into the sky, I fall asleep.

I wake to the sound of someone tapping on the window. I startle awake and sit up, instantly reaching for my boot, only to remember I dropped my knife in the cave room. Outside, Gideon and the librarian are standing next to my car, talking. I run my fingers through my hair before opening the door.

"Harper," Gideon says. "I thought that was you. What are you doing?"

"I *was* sleeping," I say before I can think better of it. No matter how nice they are, there's no way in hell I'm going to explain to two preppy rich guys that my mother's an addict whose dealer is going to take me or my car the next time he comes over, and I'm not willing to give either of those things for some fucked up street-drug version of Viagra mixed with crystal.

"Why are you sleeping in your car?" Gideon asks, a troubled frown on his brow.

"I got here early," I say. "I was waiting for school to open, and I fell asleep."

"Oh," he says, looking confused. "Why are you so early?"

Mr. Delacroix looks less than convinced by my excuse, and he frowns at me as I stumble through a nonsensical explanation about going for a run and thinking it would take longer than it did. I avoid their eyes, grab my backpack, and head in with them, though. There's not much they can do about it. I'll have to remember to move my car to the student lot if I sleep here again.

There are obvious problems with that, too, though. Now that Gideon's seen my car here, he'll probably notice it in the student lot by itself, even if I park at the back. Plus, I'm going to need a shower and a place to freshen up every morning. I'm too groggy to think it all through, but I go to my locker and then sit on the floor at Gloria's locker doing homework until she shows up. Of course she has breath mints, and even better, a travel sized bottle of mouthwash in her purse.

"Everything okay?" she asks in the bathroom as I rinse my mouth.

SELENA

I spit and turn on the sink, more awake now than when the Delacroixs roused me. "I just got in a fight with my mom," I say. "I left without brushing my teeth."

"Ew," she says, wrinkling her cute, freckled nose.

"I know, right?" I say, forcing a little laugh.

"Well, at least you got dressed," she says, looking me over. "Is that a Gucci belt?"

"Uh, yeah," I say, looking down. "It was worth it to break dress code and wear jeans on Monday just to show it off. I mean, what's one more write-up at this point?"

"I can't believe you skipped a whole week of school to run off to New York with Royal," she says, digging through her purse. "That's so romantic."

"Well, it was a college visit," I say. "We're not together."

"Sure," she says, rolling her eyes and leaning into the mirror to check her mascara.

I relax, relieved that I got off without more questions. Gloria might be on scholarship, but her family is obsessed with looking perfect. She wouldn't understand sleeping in my car any more than Gideon would.

"I'm just saying," she says. "If you wanted to be queen, last week was your chance, while the D-boys were suspended. You could have claimed the throne once and for all, put in the new world order or whatever."

"You know, I've been thinking, and that's not really me," I say. "You have my blessing to be the queen you are. I'll be the rebel I was meant to be."

She gives me a skeptical look. "You don't want to be queen anymore?"

"Nope," I say. "It's all yours. I've got too much on my mind to focus on school politics."

"If you say so," she says, dropping her lipstick back into her bag after freshening up. "Hey, you don't think that's why Royal took you away, do you? To make sure you didn't displace his brothers?"

"No," I say, giving her a funny look. "Royal doesn't care about high school drama."

It never crossed my mind, and even when she says it, I don't have to think about it. I have complete confidence in Royal, fucked up as that is. It's weird how much I trust a man who hurt me more than I knew was possible. But I know he's not scheming on me anymore. I wouldn't put it past Baron to have put the idea in his head, but if that's the case, he was playing Royal as much as me.

"I mean, I'd have gone to New York, too," she says. "Even without Royal. The shopping there is to die for you, am I right? We used to go up for New Years Eve every year."

"You are a mystery to me," I say, shaking my head.

"That's the milkshake that really brings all the boys to the yard," she says, flashing me a grin. "If I'd gone, though, I'd still be dying of FOMO from missing all the drama here."

"What's the drama?" I ask.

"It's Willow Heights," she says, widening her eyes. "There's always drama."

"Even without the twins?" I ask. "I'm surprised the school survived an entire week without them. How did it not crumble to dust in their absence?"

She laughs and closes her purse. As we leave the bathroom and make our way down the hall, she fills me in. "They're back today, so I'm sure there will be more drama. Most of last week, we were just watching social media to see what happened with that video. A bunch of parents are throwing a hissy fit because they were suspended from the team for a week, but it just happened to be Bye Week, so they didn't actually miss any games, just practice. A bunch of others are saying that's just good luck, because we're undefeated this year, and they know we'd have lost a game if the twins weren't on the field."

"Is Magnolia okay?" I ask. I was more worried about that when I was out of town than anything. The Dolce boys may not have been here, but that doesn't mean they weren't out causing trouble. In fact, they're probably more dangerous on the loose than when they're at school all day.

"Yeah," Gloria says. "She was here all last week. Why?"

"You know why," I say. "She's a Darling."

SELENA

"Right," Gloria says, shuddering. "Sometimes I forget how bad they were my first year here. It was so much better last year, when the Darlings were all gone."

"Better for you," says a voice behind us. I turn to see Colt walking behind us, a cool expression on his face.

"Exactly," Gloria says, smoothing her hair over her shoulders. "I didn't have to look at your hideous face for a whole year. The Dolces blessed this school with peace at last."

"And I'm sure you got down on your knees and worshipped them like the gods you think they are," Colt says.

While they argue, I can't help but think of how badly they beat Colt last year to get rid of the last Darling at Willow Heights. The year and a half before that, when the twins were only fourteen or fifteen, they and Royal burned his hand and cut off his finger, burned Preston's face, and permanently disfigured who knows how many other Darlings. Baron said one of the Darling men died in an accident, which was probably not an accident at all.

They probably killed him. And then there's Mabel, who tried to kill herself because of what they put her through.

Now, when they're seniors, bigger and more dangerous than ever, poor little Magnolia is the lone Darling besides Colt, who won't fight them anymore. She's a girl, and a freshman, and in no way prepared for their barbaric tortures. The fact that she dared to walk through the doors of this school at all makes her about the bravest little badass in history, to say nothing of her taking a stand against them by publicly opposing them when I did, and then taking that video…

"Remind me why you're here again?" Gloria says to Colt as we reach our class. "Shouldn't you be trolling the rooftops of Notre Dame or something?"

"Since the bleach seems to have hit your brain more than your hair, I'll walk you through it again," Colt says with a grin.

Gloria's mouth falls open in indignation. "I do not bleach my hair," she hisses. "I'm a natural blonde."

SELENA

Colt quirks a brow and gives her a lazy once over. "I'd ask for proof that the carpet matches the drapes, but you seem like the kind of girl who prefers hardwood."

"Like I'd show you," she huffs.

"Well, I'm here because I'm repeating senior year," he says. "At least I have an excuse for forgetting."

"Right," she says. "The brain damage. Are you petitioning Willow Heights to add a short bus?"

"I need to find Magnolia," I interrupt. "The Dolces will be on the warpath now that they're back."

"She's not here," Colt says, leveling me with that cool look.

"Where is she?" I demand, my heart skipping. "Is she okay?"

"She's fine, and she's safe," Colt says. "You think we don't know how the Dolces operate by now? Come on, Teeny. We're not going to send the baby of the family into a pit of demons."

"She… Left school?" I ask.

"She's taking her classes online," he says. "From a safe location."

"Your grandfather's house," I say, swallowing hard. I remember what Preston said about him. "Is someone there with her?"

"She's safe," Colt assures me again. "I'm surprised you care so much. I hear you're back to being Royal's bitch."

"I'm my own bitch," I say. "And just because I've made peace with Royal, that doesn't mean I don't still care about Magnolia, or Preston, or you. I'm trying to make peace between your families, but none of you are making it easy."

"Yeah, well, good luck with that," he says. "Unless you can raise people from the dead, that's never going to happen."

SELENA

fourteen

Harper Apple

Colt turns and walks away, and Gloria pulls me into our class. I try to focus and forget all the drama. Magnolia is safe, and that was my main concern with the Dolce situation. I have too much shit going on in my own life to be worrying about anyone else right now. I'll have to put saving Faulkner on the back burner, because I sure as fuck can't save anyone while I'm living in a car.

I plan for that as I make my way through the day. There are showers in the gym, so if I get here early, I can use them as soon as they open the doors. I can eat breakfast and lunch at school, and if I stuff myself, I won't miss dinner too much. I have enough clothes to get me through the week. The main problem is cash. I only have a few dollars, which means choosing between a few trips to the laundromat or toiletries.

I decide I can wear my clothes a few times before I need to wash them. As long as I rotate them each week and make sure not to spill anything on them, I'll be okay. So I head to the drugstore after school and grab a toothbrush, toothpaste, and deodorant. I have to choose between soap and shampoo, but since I can wash everything with either one, I choose the cheapest bar of soap. I toss in a disposable razor and head to the counter, praying I have enough to cover everything.

I don't, so I have to take the razor back. At the last second, I think of how much Royal likes me shaved, and how much shit he'll give me if I'm not. I'd normally just tell him to go fuck himself, but I don't want to give him any reason to be suspicious about what's really going on, so I slide the razor up my sleeve and go back to the checkout. I've just taken my bag and turned away when a manager steps in front of the door.

"I'd like to see you back in our office," he says, his voice hard.

SELENA

Shit. I think about dashing past him and out the door, but I really don't want a warrant out for my arrest for stealing a ninety-nice cent razor. I can probably talk my way out of it.

I follow him back to the office, thinking how fucked up it is that they waited until I checked out, making sure they got my money before they confronted me. I give the razor back and plead my case, and the manager gives me a long lecture about shoplifting and how much money they'd lose if they let every petty thief get away with stealing.

I know he'll never understand a girl like me. He doesn't understand that I already know everything he's telling me, but I was too desperate to care. I want to fucking cry when he gets on the phone to call my mother. Once, when I was dating Lauren, we got nabbed by the mall cops for shoplifting. Her dad came down and made a big fuss and said all the right things, apologizing and joking around until the security guy was laughing with him. We returned the stuff and apologized, and he let us both go with nothing more than a warning, even though he couldn't get my mom on the phone.

If she answers this time, she won't come down and get me. She's not the kind of person that security will joke with and forgive, anyway. She's not a handsome rich guy making excuses for his wild daughter. She's a girl like me. They take one look at her and see where I got it, see that we're both trash, and they figure we've done it a dozen times for every one time they've caught us.

When the manager comes back, he sits behind his desk and stares at me. "Is there anyone else you can call?"

"No."

"Then I'm afraid I'll have to turn this over to the police," he says. "I'd hate to do that for such a small item, but we take these matters very seriously. If you can't pay for this, we'll have to prosecute."

I close my eyes and lean my head back on the white cinderblock behind me. I think of Syracuse, about writing my application essay and trying to convince the admissions board that I'm not a delinquent.

SELENA

"I can try to call my friend," I say at last. My pride can only get me so far. If I have to beg for money to get out of having a record, I'll do it.

Fifteen minutes later, Royal storms in. I could have called another friend, but in some weird way, Royal understands my relationship with my mother better than anyone else.

"What the fuck are you holding my girlfriend for?" he demands of the manager.

The poor guy turns white as a sheet. "I didn't know," he cries, holding up both hands and cowering away from Royal.

Royal snatches the razor off the desk and grabs the guy by the front of his shirt, pulling him up from his chair. "I should saw your fucking balls off with this," he growls in the guy's face. "And with this puny razor, it'll take a while."

"Please," the guy blubbers. "She didn't say anything. I didn't know she was with your family. Just take it and go, please."

"Royal," I say. "He's fine. He's just doing his job. Can we not make a scene? Let's just go."

"You better count yourself fucking lucky," Royal says, dropping the manager back into his chair. "She's a hell of a lot nicer than I would be."

"T-thank you," the guy whimpers.

Royal grabs his face, forcing his mouth open and shoving the razor inside. The guy retches, his eyes widening, and all I can see is Magnolia when he shoved that gun in her mouth.

"Royal," I say quietly. "Come on. I'm fine. You don't have to do this."

He shoves the guy's chair against the wall and turns to me. "Why the fuck are you shoplifting? I just took you to Fifth Avenue and gave you my credit card."

"Can we not do this here?" I ask, cutting my eyes at the manager.

Royal's nostrils flare, and I can tell he's still pissed, but he presses his lips together and nods. He grabs my elbow and marches me out of the store like I'm… Well, a

SELENA

kid who just got caught shoplifting a ninety-nine-cent razor. He doesn't let go until we're at his car.

"Care to explain why I had to bail you out for stealing when not one week ago I bought you everything you could ask for?"

"Because I don't need fucking Gucci," I explode, throwing my hands up. "I need a toothbrush, Royal. I need a razor."

"Why didn't you just ask?"

"Because I don't want to have to ask," I say. "You've given me way too much already. I don't want you to have to take care of me."

"I don't have to," he says quietly. "I want to."

"You don't get it," I say, my voice quiet now, too. "You've never had to ask for anything in your life. How would you feel if you had to ask me every time you wanted to buy a pack of gum? It's humiliating."

"Being caught shoplifting is better?"

I shake my head, swallowing past the lump in my throat. "A trip to New York is a dream. This is reality. I'm fucking poor, Royal. I don't belong in your world.

You can put me in a fancy car and drape me with diamonds, but I'm still trailer trash, like you always said."

He doesn't say anything for a minute, and I try to blink away the ache behind my eyes.

"Harper," he says at last.

"What?" I snap. "Face it, Royal. This is my reality. I don't have any money. I do shit like this because it's better than begging on the corner or turning tricks at the truck stop."

"What about the Slaughterpen?"

"It's not until Friday," I say, pulling my hands into my sleeves and looking up at the lamp post, away from him.

Royal reaches out, taking my chin gently between his fingers and pulling my face to his, forcing me to meet his gaze. "Harper Apple," he says, a smile tugging at the corner of his perfect lips. "You don't just belong in my world. You *are* my world. Understand? That's your reality now."

I shake my head, tears blurring my vision, and he leans in, pressing his lips firmly to mine. When he pulls

SELENA

back, he wipes a tear off my cheek with his thumb and presses a kiss to my forehead. "Come on," he says. "I'm guessing you haven't eaten, so why don't we go get a burger and you can tell me why I had to bail you out of jail for the second time in as many years."

I laugh with embarrassment and nod, wiping my cheeks and climbing into the passenger seat of his car. We don't speak until we're sitting outside Boehner Burgers at a picnic table with our food between us.

"I'm sorry," I say, ashamed for my earlier outburst and for the stupid thing I did. "Thank you for this. And for bailing me out. I swear I'm not as much of a criminal as I look."

He arches a brow. "You're practically a serial killer."

"Shut up," I say, throwing a fry at him. "It's embarrassing."

"I'd think it would add to your badass reputation, Jailbird."

I roll my eyes. "I don't have a badass reputation. I don't even do anything illegal anymore. I quit fighting and gambling months ago, and I haven't painted since the last time I was arrested."

"So you thought you'd get back into a life of crime by stealing a razor? You could have at least gone for a five blade. You shouldn't even take a single blade if they give it to you for free, let alone risk yourself for it."

"I was going to buy it," I protest. "But I ran out of money. If you think about it, it's really your fault. I was only buying a razor because you like me shaved."

He shakes his head, looking at me like I'm insane. "I like eating you out," he says. "I don't give a single fuck what you do with your hair. I'd fight my way through the Amazon jungle to eat your pussy."

"It would've been nice if you told me that before I shoplifted."

"Harper," he says, his face turning serious as he lays a hand on mine. "If you need a new razor, or money, or anything, you know you can just tell me."

I shake my head, pushing my fries away. "Like you tell me when you need something. Besides, you're not my boyfriend. We agreed we were just fucking."

SELENA

"You agreed for both of us that we were just fucking," he says. "And then you agreed that you were mine. So, how much do you need?" He reaches for his wallet, but I hold up a hand.

"You don't owe me anything. I already forgave you, which means at this point, I'm just racking up debt. Stop trying to buy me shit."

"Stop trying to stop me," he says, pulling out a hundred-dollar bill. "Is that enough?"

"Royal, no," I say, pushing it back. "I'm not taking money from you. Then I really would be a whore."

"I didn't say anything about fucking you," he says. "You agreed to my terms. You're mine, and I'll keep saying it until you get it through your head that I'm damn sure going to take care of you, whether you like it or not. Now, how much do you need?"

I close my eyes and take a breath. This letting go thing is harder than I expected.

I talk myself through it one step at a time. I no longer want to be on my own. I want friends, want to let people in, even want to let them help me. He didn't get where he is without help. No one does. The rich people all take care of each other.

But I still hate letting someone take over and take care of me. I've done it so long, it's part of who I am. And after what I did to Royal, and considering what everyone else wants from him, I can't let him think that I'm after his money.

"If you really want to help me, you can come by my house with me and help me get my stuff," I say. "I'll be fine until Friday, and I'll book a fight then."

"Why are you getting your stuff out?" he asks. "Going somewhere?"

"Just my toothbrush and tampons and stuff," I say. "I'm not moving. Or hey, you could just give me Magnolia's gun. I can give it back to her when I'm done."

"Why do you need a gun to go home?" Royal asks, his voice going quiet in that intense way it does when he's mad and lowers his voice instead of raising it.

"My mom's hooked on that fucking Alice in Wonderland shit your brother's cooking," I say. "And who knows what she mixed with it."

SELENA

My heart starts hammering, and the next thing I know, I've spilled the whole story. Royal's quiet while I talk, and then he gets up to throw away the trash and use the restroom. By the time he comes back, I've pulled myself together.

"Get in the car," he says. "We'll go get your stuff."

When we pull up at my house, a huge Mercedes van sits in the driveway. I'm instantly on alert, but Royal gets out and walks up the driveway with complete confidence. I open his glove box and get out his Glock, tucking it into my waistband before following. Two men have gotten out of the van and are talking to Royal when I walk up.

Olive stands on her porch, her hands braced on the railing as she jumps up and swings her feet between the bars before dropping back down onto her heels. I'm sure she's more interested in the van than she is in us, but I still keep my voice low when I ask Royal what's going on.

"Come on," he says, taking my hand and pulling me toward our front door.

"You brought bodyguards?" I ask when the two men follow us inside.

"Is that you, Harper?" Mom calls from her bedroom. "It's about time you got your ass home. I was about to—"

She breaks off when she steps into the hallway and sees me with three big men at my back. Recovering, she runs a hand through her fried blonde hair and gives a little giggle. "I didn't know you brought company. I was about to call the authorities, I was so worried about you."

"Harper's here to get her things," Royal says, his voice cold and hard. "And these men are here to take you to Cedar Crest."

"What?" she asks, her eyes widening and her mouth dropping open. "Oh, I don't need all that. I'm doing fine, just fine. Aren't I, baby?"

Her eyes are full of warning, the kind of look she'd give me when I was in elementary school, and she told me not to take off my hoodie at school because a teacher might see the bruises on my arms from where I fought too hard when she dragged me down the hall.

SELENA

"Royal," I mutter. "You know we can't afford that."

"For the last time, shut up and accept that this is happening," he says. "Your mom is your family, and she needs help. So, we're going to get her the help she needs."

"This is a bad idea," I warn. "She doesn't want help."

"Nobody better lay a hand on me," Mom calls, backing toward her room.

"We're not going to touch you," says one of the men. "We only take voluntary admissions."

"Then get the hell out of my house," she says. "I ain't going nowhere with your asses."

Royal takes one step forward, and she stops dead in her tracks. "You're going to get sober, or you're never seeing your daughter again," he says, his quiet voice full of command. "No one's going to force you to go, but I'd take a minute to think about that before you decide."

"Mom," I say, my throat tight. "I've heard it's really nice there. Celebrities go and everything. Maybe you'll meet—Jace Wilder or Amy Bedgood or…"

"You're trying to lock me up?" she asks incredulously. "After all I sacrificed for you, you think I'm no better than your no-good daddy who never even wanted to see your face. Now you're going to make me rot in jail just like him?"

"It's better than you deserve after what you asked her to do," Royal growls. "This is the best offer you're ever going to get, Ms. Apple. So either take it, or say goodbye to your daughter and get the fuck out of my sight."

Mom's eyes widen, and she looks back and forth between us and the two men from Cedar Crest. She licks her lips and meets my gaze, her eyes desperate, like the trapped animal she is. "I… I did hear it was real nice," she says at last.

"It will be," I say, my chest tight with the pressure of all the words inside me that want to explode out, to fill the house and the world with my fury and hurt and love for my mother.

"We can help you pack some things to make your stay more comfortable," says one of the Cedar Crest guys. "Whatever you need, ma'am."

SELENA

Mom nods, biting her lip. She holds my gaze one more second before turning and going into her room. The men squeeze past us and follow her, and I turn and press my face into Royal's chest, holding onto him and willing back the tears until the urge passes. Then we get my toiletries and a bag of clothes. I stop in the door to Mom's room on the way out.

"I'll come visit," I say. "I really hope it help, Mom."

"My own daughter, getting rid of me like trash," she says to one of the men, shaking her head. "You'd think after eighteen years of giving up everything for her and getting kicked in the teeth at every turn, I'd be used to it."

I wait, part of me clinging to the hope that she'll come over and hug me, even though she doesn't deserve a hug. Still, she's my mom.

She's too busy telling them how ungrateful I am, though. After a minute, I swallow down the ache in my throat and turn away. Royal takes my hand and leads me out of the house I've hated for so many years. I'm not sure why a pang of sadness goes through me at leaving now.

"Where are we going?" I ask.

"My house," he says.

"I don't even know where you live," I say, a little laugh escaping at the ridiculousness of that statement. I know Royal down to his deepest traumas, better even than his own brothers do. He's bruised my cervix, cum down my throat, in my ass, even on my eyeballs. And somehow, I don't even know if he lives in a dorm this year.

"You know where I live," he says, giving me a funny look.

Olive waves to me from her porch, and I tell Royal to wait while I jog over. "Where's your sister?" I ask.

"Working," Olive says. "She told me to stay out here until she's done, but I'm not supposed to leave the porch."

"Can you tell her I'm moving in with Royal?" I ask.

"His name is Royal?" she asks, her eyes going wide with awe.

SELENA

"Yeah," I say, smiling up at her. "Tell Blue where I went, and I'll come by and take you for a ride in the Escalade next week. Okay?"

"Can we go get burgers and go to the quarry again?"

"Sure, Olive. It's a date."

I spare one more glance at the only real house I've ever lived in, and then I climb into Royal's Range Rover, and I tell him I'm ready. I don't look back as he drives away.

fifteen

Harper Apple

"I made it abundantly clear that no one in this family is to touch a hair on your head, or there will be consequences," Royal says, stepping into his bedroom and pulling the door closed behind him.

"Because I'm yours?" I ask.

"I'm glad we're on the same page about that," he says.

"Ugh, you're infuriating."

"Only when I don't get my way," he says with a haughty smirk.

"Has anyone told you lately that you're an arrogant asshole?"

"And you're a stubborn bitch," he says, sitting down on the edge of the bed. "Now get on your knees and show me how much you hate me."

"By the way, I stole your gun," I say, pulling it from my waistband. "I may just keep this, though. In case you piss me off."

He snorts. "You couldn't shoot someone if your life depended on it."

"You sure about that?" I ask, raising the gun. My heart is hammering in my chest as I aim it at him. I don't like guns. I prefer fists. But he taught me that my fists aren't enough when the person is as crazy as everyone in his family.

He leans back on his hands and gives me a challenging look. "So, shoot me."

"I could," I say. "But I have no reason to."

"Don't threaten to shoot someone if you don't mean it," he says. "It makes you look weak. Now stop waving that thing around and come here."

He pulls me onto his lap, scooting back so I'm resting on the edge of the bed between his thighs. "Once you take the safety off, you're committed," he says, putting his hand over mine and pulling the safety off. "Then you aim for his torso if you want to cause real damage or kill. Don't aim for his head unless he's standing still and you're a good shot. It's too small. He'll go down if you hit a major organ, and you can get close enough to shoot again, get that kill shot."

He skims his lips over my ear. "You hold onto this as long as you're in this house. But don't ever point it at me again unless you plan to pull the trigger."

"You want me to shoot you?"

"I'd rather you shoot me than make empty threats," he says, putting the safety on before taking the gun and setting it on the bedside table. "I'll get you lessons at the gun range so you know what you're doing and can hit a target. I have a feeling you'll be a natural."

I don't have much experience with guns, but I grew up in a trailer park where all the little white trash kids shot beer cans with bb guns for hours on end, so hopefully my aim isn't too shabby.

"I'll do my best to make you proud," I tell him, twisting around to kiss him.

His hand slides around to my belly, pressing me back against him. "I'm going to shower off," he says. "But first, tell me who you belong to?"

"You," I say, kissing his nose lightly. "Of course."

"Good," he says. "Just making sure we're past your little rebellions. Now, my little slut, you'll do as I say. So get on your hands and knees and play with your pussy until I get out of the shower. I want you dripping wet when I come out. Understand?"

I swallow, my knees squeezing together involuntarily at his dirty command. "You don't want to play with my pussy?" I ask, smiling up at him and biting my lip.

"No," he says, gripping my hair and pulling my head back. "I want to use your pussy like a cum dumpster. Tonight, all the pleasure you're getting is what you give yourself. So get started if you want to cum before I'm done with you."

He slides me off his lap and stands, turning to grab my hair and pull my head back again. He kisses me hard on the mouth. "Now open wide for me, my pretty plaything," he murmurs, pulling back, his dark gaze heated as it locks on my mouth.

I open my lips, wincing as he tightens his grip in my hair.

"Wider," he commands.

I open my mouth, and he leans down, working his tongue around before spitting into the back of my throat. I swallow reflexively, gagging a little, tears blurring my eyes. He smiles, stroking my throat with his free hand. My cheeks heat with shame and arousal at once.

"That's my little whore," he says. "Are you wet already?"

"A little," I admit.

"I want you soaking," he says, releasing me and striding into the bathroom, shutting the door behind him.

I don't know if I should be pissed or turned on, but I'm pretty sure I shouldn't be both. But he's always done this to me. We're both fucked up, and we're even more fucked up together. Maybe that's why it works.

SELENA

I make sure the door is locked before I strip off my clothes, thankful for the moment alone to clear my head of the lust fever he puts me in when he calls me those things. I climb onto the bed and slide my hand between my legs, touching myself. Suddenly, all I can think about is how many times I've done this before—gotten on the bed and waited for a man to use me for his own pleasure, caring nothing for mine.

Hands and knees... Good girl.

Preston's voice is in my head as if he's in the room with me, and suddenly I can't breathe. I don't feel safe in his clean world. I feel suffocated. I bury my face in the pillow and scream. I don't want him in my head, invading the bed I share with Royal. My limbs start to shake, and I roll over onto my side, breathing through the spiraling thoughts, the panicking pulse rate. After a few minutes, I hear the water shut off.

Fuck Preston Darling.

He doesn't get to take this away from me. He took what he wanted from me, but I never consented to it. I consent to what Royal does to me. Sometimes I burn with shame while he does it, but I always enjoy it. I always cum—he makes sure of it.

I roll back over, pressing my face to the pillow and shoving my ass into the air almost defiantly. I grip my feet and pull them up to add extra spite to the position.

"Holy hell," Royal says, emerging from the bathroom in a pair of sweats and a t-shirt.

"Was this not what you wanted?" I ask innocently.

"Shut up and don't move," he says. "I'm getting a picture."

I open my mouth to protest, then close it again when I realize how ridiculous that is. Once, I refused to send Royal nudes. But we're different people now. He's watched videos of Preston coming in my ass and then sticking it back in my cunt. One more picture isn't going to make a difference. If he wants to ruin my life, he will. I've accepted that, accepted that I'm his to do with as he pleases. If he destroys me, then I'll live through it or I won't. But there is no out, and I've stopped looking for one.

SELENA

In truth, I want his claim, his need, his obsession. I love that he can't let me go, that he moves worlds for me. No one else would go to half the trouble he did for a girl like me, even if they'd done to me what he has. Even if they felt sorry, they'd walk away after the fifth or tenth time I told them to, told them I hated them and they didn't deserve forgiveness. They would accept that as the truth. Royal knows it's true, but he doesn't care. Nothing will stop him from taking what he wants, even when he knows he's unworthy.

And for reasons I still don't fully understand, he wants me. I'm not going to throw that away because he hurt me before. Not just because I won't find it again, but because I want it. I know how lucky I am to be the object of his obsession. I've found my way back to myself, and now, I'm finding my way past that, to the person I am with him.

The mattress sinks under his knees as Royal climbs onto the bed behind me. He pushes my knees further apart and lowers the front of his pants just enough to free his cock. Gripping the base, he rubs the hot head up and down my wet slit, coating his tip with my slickness.

I moan and push back, but he grabs my hip, keeping me still from impaling myself on his thick shaft. "I know, Cherry," he says, his voice thick with desire. "Hold still, just like that."

I try not to squirm as he slowly drags his bare cock up and down until it's soaked. Then he pushes forward, sinking just the tip into me.

I bite my lip and sigh with pleasure, gripping my ankles tighter.

"That's right, my dirty little whore," he says, pulling out and pressing the slippery head of his cock to my rear entrance. "Tell me who you belong to."

"You." I gasp in a breath as he pushes inside the knotted ring of muscle. The stretch stings enough to bring tears to my eyes when he doesn't prep me, but I don't move from my position. "I'm yours, Royal," I say. "Use me however you want."

He pulls out, pushing into my cunt this time, deeper than before. He grips my hip and slowly slides in until he's buried to the hilt inside me. His cock is so thick and full inside me I can hardly breathe.

"Oh, I'm going to use you," he growls. "I'm going to use you like the whore you are. Now show your owner how you can finger that cunt while I pound your ass."

He strokes my ass, spreading my cheeks wide and pushing his fingers inside while his hips remain motionless, his bare cock still stretching me open to my depths. My walls clench around him, thirsty for more, but he responds by giving me a hard smack on the ass. I yelp and tense up, and he groans, grinding his fingers to their knuckles inside my ass and his cock balls deep inside me at the same time. I wait for him to finish, wincing as he fucks my ass with his fingers, which feels somehow dirtier and more humiliating than when he uses his cock, even if it doesn't hurt as much.

When I've adjusted to his fingers, he pulls back, positioning his cock between my cheeks. I force myself to stay relaxed, not to tense up again. He gives a quick little thrust, breaching my rear entrance and making me cry out. Tears drip from my eyes again, and I bite my lip as he pulls out and then enters me again, groaning as he forces his cock deeper.

"Royal," I choke out. "It's too much."

"Shut up and finger your pussy and take it like a slut."

He begins to move, working himself deeper while I drop my ankles and obey his commands, sliding a hand under myself. I stroke my clit while he pumps into me until he's buried to the hilt. Then he shoves me roughly into the bed, bracing one hand on my shoulder blade to hold me pinned as he thrusts into my ass with rough, punishing strokes.

The pain and pleasure spiral through my body, coiling tighter and tighter until I can barely hold myself back. Royal's hand fists my hair, shoving my cheek into the pillow as he slams into me harder.

"Cum, my little whore," he growls at me. "Show me how you obey your owner."

I squeeze my eyes closed and let myself go. My core clenches, and I slide my fingers inside, keeping pressure on my clit as waves of bliss and agony alternate inside me. The orgasm grips me from head to toe as he drives deeper and stills, his hips crushing my ass as his cock pulses, spilling wet heat deep inside me. My brain shuts off, and all I can think is *yes*.

There's something freeing in the simplicity of it, in knowing something with such certainty. There's no fear, no doubt, no room for insecurity. This is forever, so there's nothing to do but accept it and admit to ourselves it's what we both want. Being wanted by him, owned by him, even at his worst, is as addictive as it ever was. I might have gotten clean for a while, but the moment I gave in and fucked him, it was like I'd never stopped. I was off the wagon, and there's no getting back on. I will revel in this addiction until it kills me. I won't exorcise my demon. I'll open my heart and body and invite it to possess me, to fuck me, to decimate my soul until there's nothing left of it but his claim.

I'm still reeling from the orgasm when a sharp pain slices into my hip from behind. I cry out and try to turn over, but Royal's hips pin me to the bed. He leans up, dragging a sharp blade through my skin.

"What the fuck?" I cry, starting to struggle. He places his huge palm on my back, holding me flat while he turns the knife, slicing through my skin.

"If anyone's initials are going on you, they better be mine," he says, his breathing still labored.

"Royal, no," I cry, twisting around to see him finish slicing the letter into my skin, an R carved into me in front of the D that Duke burned into me.

"You said you were mine," he says. "To do with as I please."

He pulls out of me and slides down the bed, his hands cradling my hips as his mouth meets my skin. I gasp at the stinging sensation when his tongue strokes over the cut. He moans, running his tongue slowly over the sliced skin. He gives a little suck, and I cry out in pain. He moans again, sucking harder.

"Royal, stop," I gasp, tears of pain stinging my eyes.

He leans up on his elbows, wiping away the fresh blood with his fingers. Then he sinks his hand between my legs, pushing his bloody fingers into me.

"I thought you were tough," he says, a taunt in his voice. "You can handle a little cut, can't you?"

I bite my lip and nod, and he lowers his mouth to the wound again, sucking at it while his bloody fingers pump into me. I don't know why it hurts so much, but I have to bite down on the pillow to keep from sobbing aloud. After a while, he slides back up the bed, lying on my back.

"Even your blood tastes sweet, my little Cherry Pie," he says, kissing my shoulder blade.

He's hard again, and he pulls his fingers out and wipes more blood on them, then strokes it over his shaft to get it wet before pushing inside me, in the front this time.

"Fuck," he breathes. "I'm going to like having you in my bed every night."

A tear leaks from the corner of my eye, but I lie still and give myself over to him, let him use me like his plaything. The sensation on his bare, slick cock pumping into me while I lie still is so familiar I don't even know

I'm slipping away until he pulls out and flips me over, throwing me roughly onto my back.

"Harper," he says, grabbing my chin in his hand. His eyes are blazing, heating my frozen soul.

"Royal," I say, touching his cheek softly.

"Cum with me," he whispers. He pushes back into me, gently this time, and coaxes another climax from me before he finishes. Then he wraps his arms around me and rolls us onto our sides, arranging the pillows for both of us.

"You okay?" he asks, smoothing my hair back from my cheek.

"Yeah," I say. "I'm fine."

And I am. He's rough with me, but that's just who he is, how he is. I like it, maybe even need it.

"You can stay here as long as you need," he says. "Until you graduate, if you want."

I nod, my mind already racing with possibilities. "Thank you," I say. "And for what you did for my mom… You're giving me too much, Royal."

"She's family."

"Does that excuse everything?" I ask.

"No," he says, scowling. "It doesn't excuse anything. But that doesn't mean we can't get her help when she needs it."

"And what about your family?" I ask carefully. I'm already thinking how I can leverage this into something big, get something on his dad that will ruin him once and for all.

"I don't make excuses for them, either."

"So, you'll protect your brothers from your dad, even though you don't excuse what they've done?"

"Yes."

"What about your dad?" I ask. "Why should you have to protect his own children from him? Especially because you're one of those kids."

"Who else is going to do it?" he asks, glowering at the wall.

"What if you didn't have to protect them?" I ask, tracing my fingers down the front of his white t-shirt. "What if you didn't have to worry about him or live with him even though you're eighteen?"

"Nineteen."

"What if you didn't have to live here?"

"You want to get our own place with my brothers?" he asks, frowning at me.

"No," I say slowly. "I want to know if your life would be worse in any way if your dad was… Out of the picture, like my mom."

Royal shakes his head and rolls onto his back. "Dad's not an addict, and even if he was, he'd never agree to go. They only take voluntary commitments."

"My mom went."

"Because she was afraid of losing you," he says. "She had nothing else going for her, and her dealers are after her. Dad has a company to run and status in this town. It could ruin his reputation."

"He also has you," I say. "Isn't he afraid of losing you?"

Royal scoffs. "He'd give us up without even blinking rather than go the swankiest rehab center. It's always about the bottom line for him. The board of directors would see a stint in rehab and question his authority."

SELENA

"Then maybe rehab's not the right place," I say.

Royal doesn't answer, and I wonder if I'm going too far. But he must know things that could send his father to jail. He's the one who could take down the Dolces, not Preston. The answer has been right here all along.

But would he want to?

"I never really understood why you needed that scholarship so bad until tonight," he says at last. "I knew you wanted to leave Faulkner, but I thought it was just because it's a shitty town and you wanted to go to college and travel. I think I get it now. Why you were blowing that teacher, and talking to Mr. D, and everything you did."

Now it's my turn to be silent. I've told him about my mom, but it's not like seeing her tweaked out. It's easy to let him believe that we're the same. His mom is the Upper East Side kind of addict who drowns her troubles in martinis and prescription pills instead of crystal meth and street drugs, after all. It's easy to say it's the same demon that possesses them both. It's harder to admit the full truth of it, to admit something that shameful—that your mother would rather trade her daughter to her dealer than cut him off.

"Let's shower off before we go to sleep," Royal says after a bit. "Hold still. You're bleeding again."

He sits up and peels off his T-shirt, pressing it to my hip. I gape at him, at the familiar face staring back at me from one of his massive pecs.

"Royal…" I whisper, reaching out and skimming my fingertips over the new tattoo. On one side, where it's always been, is his sister's face. On the other, is… *me*.

I try to remember the last time I saw him without a shirt. I thought it was a little weird that he didn't want to shower together in New York, and that he always wore clothes to bed. I didn't push it, though, because I thought maybe the shower thing had to do with him being held captive in that dirt room, and that the clothes might be some kind of control thing from that same trauma.

"When did you do this?" I ask, swallowing hard and raising my gaze to his.

SELENA

"When it was all I had of you," he says quietly. He covers my hand with his, pressing it to the solid wall of muscle of his chest.

After a minute, he picks me up and carries me into the bathroom, and we take our first shower together, washing off all the sex and blood. He covers the cuts with a bandage, and we fall into bed together, with nothing between us this time. I snuggle into his bare chest, and he wraps his arms around me.

"Royal," I say, sliding my arm under his hugely muscled one. "I can't thank you enough for everything you've done. But you know I can't repay you. My mom took my money."

"For the last fucking time, you don't have to repay me," he says. "That's what you do for someone you… Own."

"Okay," I say, my heart feeling all swollen and feverish with love for him. He's given me exactly what I needed so many times—the car, college, and now going beyond that to help my mother and give me a safe place to stay. He's shown me that he knows me, knows my hopes and dreams and the deepest desires of my heart. He's made them all come true to show me how much he loves me, how much he wants my forgiveness, and to make up for what he's done.

I haven't given him anything but an explanation.

And though I'm glad he finally understands why I betrayed him, that maybe now he can truly forgive me, I haven't done the same for him. I haven't made up for my betrayal. I can't repay him with money, but he doesn't need that.

I know him as well as he knows me, though. I know exactly what he needs, too.

And I'm going to give it to him.

If he truly understands my need to escape this town, well, I've understood him for a lot longer. I know he thinks no one can love him for who he is, as he is. That if anyone truly knows him and sees him, the monster and the boy, they'll leave. That's why he didn't care that he hadn't forgiven me. He didn't care if I was just here for the money, for what he can buy me. He still wanted me, even if I didn't prove I loved him. He doesn't think I do,

SELENA

that I can. That's why he has to own me—because he doesn't believe I'll choose to stay otherwise.

But I do love him, even after all he's done. I never really stopped. I couldn't.

I lift my head to say something, to tell him, but his breathing is deep, and his face completely relaxed in sleep. I watch him a moment before dropping my head and squeezing his body to mine.

While he's proven his love and regret in a million huge and tiny ways, I've never atoned for what I did to him. Sure, I apologized even though he hadn't. But I understand now that it wasn't about what I did so much as what it meant. It doesn't matter that only Baron and Duke learned his secret. It doesn't matter that they never told anyone else, that there were no consequences for him in terms of his reputation or status. The betrayal itself is what hurt him, broke the last bits of his soul, when he dared to believe I genuinely cared. How can he believe I do when he thinks I faked the whole thing?

I haven't shown him love in the way he's shown me. I haven't said it, and I haven't moved worlds for him, not even after he gave me exactly what I needed to heal without me having to say a word. Every step of the way, he's been there for me. In return, I made less than a halfhearted attempt and then moved on.

I thought I'd find out who assaulted him, and that it would help him. But he's already gotten revenge on the Darlings. I could bring him Grandpa Darling and tell him what Preston told me, but his revenge has never helped anyone, least of all him. He could have killed Grandpa Darling, but he chose to let him live to suffer longer. He doesn't need me to deliver his revenge to him. And revenge won't fix what's wrong. Not with Royal, not with the Dolces, not with this town.

More bloodshed, more revenge isn't the answer. It only makes things worse. Royal's destroyed the entire Darling family, but it hasn't quenched his thirst for revenge. It only grows. Nothing will ever or can ever be enough because nothing has brought him the one thing he wants—not revenge, but his sister.

He doesn't need to find his attackers. He needs to find himself.

SELENA

He doesn't need more violence. He needs the antidote. He needs healing.

Just as I found myself again when we came back together, I have to help him do the same. I found my strength, not away from him, but with him. Not alone, but with friends who let me be vulnerable, who back me up so I no longer have to do it alone. Letting them in didn't make me lose myself or make me weak. It helped me find myself and see the power and strength in having people to support me and have my back. And he's the one who made it all happen, who gave me his strength when I had none until I was strong enough to go on, to raise myself from the dead and rebuild my life, not as it was, but better.

Now it's time I used that strength to do the same for him. Forgiving him didn't make me weak. It's the hardest thing I've ever done, and it required more strength than I knew I had, made me stronger than I've ever been. Now, I will heal him and make him better, just as he did me. Because he might not believe it, but I love him as much as he loves me.

I will give him what he needs just as he's done for me. I'll let him know I truly see him and love him for exactly who he is. I'm not here for the money or anything else. I just want him, monster and all.

And I won't show him by helping him find more Darlings to complete his revenge. That's never helped before, so why would it make things better now?

I could try to heal this town by killing his father or even Baron, but I know Royal would never recover from losing another sibling. He gave me chances, and I know he wouldn't have stopped me from killing his brother. I could have done it, destroyed him even more thoroughly than he destroyed me. I finally know how to break him completely, how to bring him down, and it's too late.

I don't want to hurt Royal more. The hurt he's already suffered has been raining down on this town for three years. In some fucked up way, I still have hope for him. I have to. I will never give up on him, just as he never gave up on me. And hurting his family will only make things worse, not just for him, or me, but for this town. He's a monster rampaging through the land in his pain, searching endlessly for the one thing he's lost that can never be returned—the other half of himself. When he doesn't find it, he lays waste to everything in his wake. There's no way to stop him because he can never find peace.

What if he could, though?

sixteen

Harper Apple

When we walk into the kitchen the next morning, the twins are already up and sitting at the breakfast nook. A sense of *déjà vu* sweeps over me, and the morning after I first fucked Royal rises in my memory.

Duke shoves a chair out with his foot and grins at me. "If you're living here, does that make you our stepsister?"

"Gross, no," I say, scooting in at the table and surveying the spread of bagels, fresh fruit, and orange juice.

Baron watches me while he spreads cream cheese from a little crystal dish onto half a bagel.

"I'm not opposed," Duke says. "Some of my favorite porn has dudes nailing their stepsisters."

SELENA

"Shut up," Royal snaps at his brother.

"It's fine," I say, nudging the chair next to me. He pulls it out and sits, glaring across the table at the twins. I think again how much it must suck for Royal to live here, protecting these heathens by sacrificing himself when they don't deserve it.

"Too bad," Duke says. "That would be pretty hot, since we've all banged you."

Royal starts to stand, but I lay a hand on his thigh. He won't always be here to get between us, so I need to establish myself now. He must understand that, because he frowns but doesn't go over the table at his brother.

"You didn't *bang* me," I say. "You raped me. Making jokes about it doesn't change what happened."

"What makes you think that was a joke?" Baron asks, cocking his head and watching me intently.

"Based on the lack of actual funniness, I guess it wasn't much of a joke at all," I agree.

"I thought it was funny," Baron says.

"I'd expect nothing less of you," I say, raising my chin and refusing to drop his gaze. "But your brother was sobbing like a bitch about it the other day, so I know he doesn't think it's funny. He just doesn't want you to call him a pussy."

Duke's eyes widen, and a panicked look crosses his face.

"What, you didn't tell them that part?" I ask. "Sorry, I thought you shared everything with your brothers. Don't worry, I won't tell anyone at school."

"I don't know what you're talking about," he finally mutters, sounding miles short of convincing.

"I have a video, if you need reminding," I say, reaching for my phone in my pocket.

"What?" he asks incredulously. "You took a video?" He stares at me like he's never seen me before, probably because he's yet to realize I'm an actual person and not just someone to serve him in whatever way he needs at any given moment. I start to rethink my decision not to off anyone in Royal's family. The twins are scum.

I shrug at Duke and bite into my bagel. I'm bluffing, but he doesn't know it, and I'm not about to change that. I wish I'd taken the video. In the moment, my sympathy

SELENA

for him was greater than my urge for self-preservation, but I should have known he couldn't leave his guard down for long. He has to look cool in front of his brothers, after all. Can't have Daddy Dolce thinking he's weak, like when he was a kid.

"I took a page from your book," I say after I finish chewing. "Isn't that your M.O? Receipts or it didn't happen? Maybe promise not to show anyone, and then send it around to the whole school?"

"I thought that was your game," Baron says. "You sure got that video of Duke out fast."

"I learned from the best," I say, quirking a brow at him. If he thinks I did that, let him. I'd rather take the blame than let them go after a freshman who's relatively unscathed by their wrath so far. Magnolia's no shrinking violet, but I can handle them better than she can.

"Damn right, we're the best," Duke says, giving me a sloppy grin that's almost convincing. But I know him now. I know when he's faking it.

"Tell you what," I say, putting my phone back in my pocket. "I'll just hold onto this one. I won't tell anyone you're human and shatter the illusion that you're a complete sociopath like your brother. It'll be our little secret."

"If…?" he asks.

I can't help but smile and shake my head. "See, you might pretend to be a clown, but you're just as smart as your brothers," I say. "But since you asked, I'll be straight with you. Here's what I want. I want you to stop treating girls like shit. Like, no whispers, no rumors. I don't even want to hear a girl crying in the bathroom that you ghosted her after hooking up. That's the price of your secret."

"I can't have sex?" he asks, gaping at me.

"That sounds like a *you* problem," I say. "If you can't have sex without treating someone like shit, maybe that's something you should work on. I never said you couldn't hook up. I said don't make girls cry about it."

I stand and grab the other half of my bagel.

"Wait," Duke says, holding up a hand. "How do I do that? That's not fair. I can't help it if girls cry over me."

SELENA

"Figure it out," I say. "You're a smart boy, Duke. I believe in you."

Royal stands with me, grabbing a handful of grapes. "I'll take you to your car."

"Thanks," I say, taking his hand and smiling up at him. "We'll figure out how to be a big happy family one of these days."

He just shakes his head and starts for the back door. Just as we pass the office, Mr. Dolce steps out, knocking into me. I distinctly feel his hand on my ass, and I shove myself away from him as hard as I can. He looks amused as I glower up at him.

"Harper Apple," he says coolly. "I heard you'd be staying under our roof for a while."

"Then you must have also heard I belong to Royal," I say, reaching for Royal's hand again.

"I did hear that," Mr. Dolce says, watching as Royal grips my hand possessively, his other hand on my shoulder as he stands behind me.

"Then don't fucking touch her," Royal says, his voice a growl of warning. "In fact, don't even speak to her."

"We're bound to bump into each other on occasion, living in the same house," Mr. Dolce says with a shrug. I didn't imagine his hand on my ass, but I have no proof that it was intentional. I don't like Mr. Dolce, don't like how powerless and naïve I feel around him, how fucking intimidating he is, and the way he uses his sons. But that doesn't mean he groped me. In fact, knowing him, he'd never do something so bold in front of his sons.

I decide to let it go and just get out of there. I don't want to be in the house with three men I hate, with only Royal on my side, but my options are running a little low right now, and I don't want to screw it up on the first day. It's Mr. Dolce's house, after all. He's letting me live here, feeding me fancy breakfasts. Hell, he paid for my scholarship last year, and even if Baron was reporting back to him, all he ever learned from me is something he already knew.

Royal drops me off at my car, and I head back to Willow Heights, wondering what bullshit drama will be happening today. Like Gloria said, there's always something. I can't wait to graduate and get out of this

SELENA

cesspool of rumors and petty squabbles. Since visiting Syracuse campus, I care less and less about high school. All I want is to get my diploma, bust out of here, and never look back.

But as soon as I walk into lunch that day, I see Dixie holding court at the table I claimed. There are extra chairs pulled up, ten crammed around the table that's made for eight max. Gideon is still there, but everyone else at the table is female. The girls are watching Dixie with awe and admiration as she stands with one foot in her chair, telling some story. She's wearing fishnets, black combat boots, and a schoolgirl skirt, along with a cat-ear headband. She looks positively radiant as she performs for her audience.

Gloria guessed she did it for the fame, and it looks like she was right. I head for the food line, not bothering to stop and talk to her. There are no empty seats for me at that table, anyway. The café is divided now, with the Dolce boys and their followers on the left side of the door and all the disgraced Dolce girls on the right. Like Gloria said, I missed my chance to really step up when I skipped the week the D-boys were suspended. Now, the queen of the dissent seems to be Dixie.

I sit at a table with a bunch of girls I don't know. I get a few smiles, and a few nervous glances from the ones who probably think I'll start shit and put them in the spotlight, but no one says anything to me. It feels weird to realize I've become irrelevant to my own rebellion, but then, I was never aiming to start something so big. I just wanted to show Baron he couldn't control me, that I could take the best table. At the time, I guess I did want to be queen, but I was never cut out for that role.

Gloria is still at Baron's table, now with Rylan back at her side. She can lead the populars, as always, and Dixie can lead the rest of the school. She's a better representative than I ever was. She's a normal kid, not on scholarship. She's involved in all the activities, from student council to dance team. And she has her finger on the pulse of the school, is part of everything. I've always been an outsider, even when I was a Dolce girl.

SELENA

Still, as I watch her being adored by all the other girls, I can't help but think about Magnolia, hidden away somewhere on the Darling estate, doing her classes online. I was just proving a point until the pretty little freshman came along and told me I needed a speech, that I needed to stand for something. She's the one who made it a rebellion. She's the one who took the video that catapulted Dixie from gossip girl to rebel queen.

Now she can't even show her face here for fear she'll be attacked over a video that she never wanted released. Dixie's the one who released it. Dixie's the one who should be hiding out, but she's in the spotlight now. She was on the news. She's the face of the fight for the administration to hold the boys accountable. They can't touch her without the whole world knowing about it. And yet, Magnolia's the one who's paying.

Suddenly, I'm not hungry. I return my plate and head outside, only realizing when I'm halfway to the bleachers and catch a whiff of smoke that I didn't see Colt at Dixie's table.

I step into the shadows under the bleachers, letting my eyes adjust after the walk through the bright, fall sun. Colt is leaning against one of the supports, his left hand in his pocket, a cigarette dangling from his right.

"Trouble in paradise?" I ask, joining him in the shadows.

"I'm not really into all that," he says, tapping his cigarette with his ring finger before taking a drag.

"Don't tell me you don't like the attention," I tease. "Pretty sure I remember you waxing nostalgic about your glory days as a football god and womanizer on more than one occasion."

"Yeah, but that was when *I* was the center of attention," he says, a lazy grin playing over his lips.

"So you don't want to play a supporting role to your leading lady?" I ask. "And here I thought you were one of the good guys."

He snorts. "What made you think that?"

"I don't know," I say with a shrug. "The fact that you're generally pretty decent to me."

"Because you can kick my ass," he points out.

SELENA

"Okay, so what's the real reason?" I ask. "Or do you not trust me because I'm back with Royal?"

"Are you?" he asks, holding out the pack to me.

I take a cigarette out, finding a lighter in the pack as well. I light up before answering. "Yeah," I admit at last. "I guess I am."

I haven't said it out loud to anyone, even Royal. Somehow, it seems fitting that Colt's the first to know.

"See," Colt says, quirking a brow and gesturing to himself. "Always the bridesmaid, never the bride."

I shake my head at that. "At least you didn't say nice guys finish last."

"Nah," he says. "That's bullshit. I'm not a nice guy, and yet, here I am."

"Come on," I say. "You're not interested in me."

"I might have been once," he says.

"But not anymore," I say. "You're with Dixie, and I'm with Royal, and he's agreed to leave you alone because we're friends."

"Really?" Colt asks, raising his brows in surprise. "He said that?"

"Yep," I say. "All my friends are off limits."

"That's a pretty big promise if it includes Darlings."

"Three of you, actually," I say. "Preston, Magnolia, and you."

"Huh," he says. "Thanks, I guess. Be a lot better if you could get the same promise from the demon twins."

"Yeah, they're a bit of a problem," I admit. "Duke would get on board if Baron did, but I don't think I'd believe Baron even if he said he'd leave you alone."

"Ah, so you figured out who was the psychoest of them all."

"I figured you'd pick Duke," I say. "Wasn't he the one who burned you and Preston?"

Colt makes a noncommittal sound and drags on his cigarette before leaning his head back and blowing a few smoke rings toward the bottom of the metal seats above.

I picture Duke holding a blowtorch to his arm, and I'm glad I didn't eat lunch. Just thinking about the way it must have smelled makes me gag. Every time I think Duke might be somehow human, I'm reminded that he's just as barbaric as his brother.

SELENA

"Seriously, though," I say. "They'll be gone next year. You know they won't stay in this town once they graduate."

"I heard they're getting scouted pretty heavily for college ball next year," Colt agrees.

"And Royal's leaving, too," I confirm. "Which means the only Dolce left will be their dad."

"I'm sure he'll pay off some thugs to keep us in line after they're gone," Colt says. "He won't stop until our family is in his pocket, too."

"You think he'll stop then?"

"Of course," Colt says. "Once they beat us, they don't care about destroying us. Why do you think I'm still here?"

"Then I guess you must be pretty pissed at me for getting Magnolia involved."

"I didn't want her to go along with their rules," he says, giving me a funny look. "They'd rape her and shit. We didn't figure she'd make it through the year, but we wanted to try, now that Royal's gone. I was supposed to be protecting her. I'm the one who fucked up."

"It's not your fault," I say. "I never should've called her to our table."

"I was sitting right there," he says. "I could have stopped her, but I thought it might be helpful, that I could keep an eye on her. Maggie's our cousin, but she's kind of everyone's kid sister—in the good ways and the bad. The minute she knew I was watching over her, she'd have rebelled like a brat and done everything to escape my sight."

"She does seem to have a mind of her own," I concede.

We smoke in silence for a minute.

Colt finishes his cigarette and tosses the butt in the bare, packed red dirt with the rest of them before pulling out a joint. "She's a good kid," he says. "I'd worry about her even if the Dolces weren't around. She's too pretty for her own good."

"Is that why you're really out here?" I ask. "Are you mad at Dixie for releasing that video?"

He takes a drag on the joint and coughs a few times before answering. "It's nice to see the demon twins taken

SELENA

down a peg," he says when he recovers. "But I'd rather it hadn't been my cousin with the phone in her hand."

"Is she grounded from her phone?" I ask. "Or am I allowed to text her?"

"Why would you want to?" he asks. "She's fourteen."

"She's my friend," I say with a shrug. "Would you be mad if I texted?"

"Are you going to fuck her?"

I laugh at that. "Uh, no."

"Then you can text her," he says. "Thanks for asking me first, though."

"Gotta respect the southern, overprotective older brother tradition."

He grins and hands me the joint. "Don't get her in any trouble."

"No promises," I say. "But I can promise I'll involve you first when said trouble arises."

"Why do I get the feeling you're plotting something?" he asks.

"I've got a few ideas marinating," I admit with a grin. I take a drag and hand back the joint. "So, which of the Darlings are in Tony Dolce's pocket?"

"None of us," he says, giving me a funny look. "He tried to get to us through the Delacroixs, but they told him to fuck off when he wanted to buy the land over by the mall, and now they're on his shit list, too."

"Really?" I ask, straightening. "This is huge, Colt."

"Why?" he asks, narrowing his eyes.

"Because," I say. "That's two founding families."

"So?" he asks. "My mom was a Montgomery, and the other Montgomerys joined the Dolces in taking us down. She married a Darling, so she was fair game to them."

"Yeah, but their family didn't stand up to the Dolces," I point out. "If we can get your family and the Delacroixs…"

I wonder if Gideon was aware of that when he broke ranks. Maybe he knew it was coming and got a jump start on building his own support system in advance. After all, he saw what the Dolces did to his cousin's family, to this

SELENA

town. He must have known he'd need all the help he could get if things went south with the casino land deal.

Maybe I should be mad that he was scheming all along, using the rebellion as a cover for what he was doing so the D-boys wouldn't suspect it. Maybe he even asked me out so they'd think he only joined us to get a date, and all along, he had a lot more going on behind the scenes. But I'm not mad about it. I actually respect the fuck out of the kid for it. If that's what he was doing, he's more cunning than I gave him credit for, and I'm here for that level of deception.

"Whoa there, Teeny," Colt says, holding up a hand. "There's no *we* here. I'm done with that fight."

"Well, I'm not," I say. "If Tony's the only Dolce left, surely two powerful families combined can stop him."

He just shakes his head. "You don't know anything about him if you think it's that easy. It's not just Mr. Dolce. He's got the mayor, the judges, everyone in his pocket. He plays golf with the fucking governor. He's not one man. He's an empire."

"Maybe," I say. "But empires fall every day."

seventeen

Harper Apple

When we step inside, the Dolce boys and their friends are standing in the short hallway between us and the café, blocking our way.

"Well, well, well," Duke says. "Look what we have here."

"What, you're going to try to keep me from having friends again?" I ask, rolling my eyes. "Been there, done that. Can't you find something new to have a mantrum about?"

"I don't think my brother would be very happy to see you fucking around on him with a Darling," Baron says, crossing his arms and planting his feet wide. A little crowd starts to form behind them, ready for a show. I spot Dixie among them, looking as excited as everyone

SELENA

else, probably ready to capitalize on her new fame with even more drama.

"Try again," I say to Baron. "Royal knows I'm friends with Colt, and he's fine with it."

"Yeah, and I'm not interested in Harper," Colt says. "I learned my lesson last year."

"If you'd learned your lesson, then you'd know that if you fuck with her, I'll rip the metal plate out of your head and skull fuck your brains out your ears," Baron says. "Do you really want to risk that?"

"I'm not fucking with him," I say. "We were having a smoke."

"You got proof?" Baron asks, pulling a sucker from his pocket and beginning to unwrap it.

I'm about to ask if he wants me to go get my cigarette butt, since Colt doesn't fight back, but he speaks from behind me before I can. "What, you want to see if my dick is wet? Maybe give it a lick, make sure it doesn't taste like pussy?"

"Colt," I hiss. "Know when to shut up."

"Nah, let him keep talking," Duke says, cracking his knuckles and giving us that unhinged, psychotic smile of his. "I hear you lost your memory, Colt. We'll take you to the basement later and remind you what that mouth is for."

"Leave him alone," Gloria says from beside them, giving us an imperious once-over. "You can't pick on the sped kids. That's like, a rule."

"You're defending Colt?" Baron asks, turning to her, his voice even but ice cold.

"What? No," she cries, her eyes going wide and the color draining from her cheeks. "I hate Colt!"

Baron must see what I do, the realization dawning in her eyes that she just made an unforgiveable mistake in the eyes of the Dolces—defending a Darling from their wrath. I did it once, and Royal dumped me on the spot. Now Gloria's about to find out the price of the one cardinal sin in their eyes. She's been their queen for two years, but it only takes one word to undo everything she's gained. Breaking rank, showing any form of dissent or disapproval, the slightest whisper of disloyalty, and she's done.

She's apologizing profusely, trying to backpedal already, but Baron's face remains hard. His eyes light up with something vicious and predatory as he takes a step toward her.

"I shouldn't be surprised," he says, his voice almost cajoling, an edge of taunting in it that doesn't match the malicious gleam in his eye. He prowls forward as he speaks, the hallway dead silent except for his words. "You've already been run through by all the guys on our side. Guess you had to go pretty far to find someone desperate enough to fuck you now that you're so loose a guy can't feel a thing when he sticks it in you."

"I would *never*," she huffs, looking scandalized. "Colt is disgusting!"

"He must be, if he'd fuck a pussy that's so used it looks like a worn-out old baseball glove," Baron says, grabbing her shoulder. He spins her toward us and gives her a shove in our direction.

"You're not even hot," Duke says as Gloria stumbles on her heels and lurches forward from Baron's shove. "Without makeup, you look busted. And everyone knows that scar on your stomach isn't from a hernia."

Colt catches her before she can fall, but she wrenches away, throwing back her hair that flew into her face. "Don't touch me, you freak," she snarls.

"He's the only guy in school who'll ever touch you again," Duke says, throwing an arm around Rylan. "I guarantee that. Isn't that right, Rye-Rye?"

Rylan stands frozen, looking shocked and horrified. Guess he's not used to the savagery of Willow Heights yet, the way the tides can turn with a snap of the right fingers. Gloria's sacrificed herself for over two years, given everything to maintain her spot, but all it takes is one misstep, one offhand comment, to topple her from her throne.

"Rylan, he's lying," Gloria cries, stepping toward her boyfriend.

"Did you fuck them?" Rylan asks, his voice quiet in the silence of the hall.

SELENA

Gloria gulps, tears filling her eyes. "I didn't have a choice," she says quietly, a tear spilling down her cheek.

Duke throws his head back and laughs. "Dude, we've been running trains on your girl since the first day of sophomore year. She's just like every other pathetic bitch with no self-respect. They can't help themselves. Once they get the twin double-stuff, they just keep crawling back for more."

"It wasn't like that," Gloria insists. "You know I'm not like that!"

"You lying whore," Rylan says quietly. "I don't know you at all anymore."

"You can't believe them," Gloria says, her words choked.

"We speak the truth," Duke hollers, looking so damn proud of the discord he's reaping. "The whole truth, and nothing but the truth."

Rylan turns away, shoving through the crowd. Gloria starts to follow, but I grab her arm and pull her back.

"Don't fucking chase that asshole," I say, yanking her around to face me. "You're better than that."

"I'm not," she says, then collapses in on herself with a sob, her shoulders shaking as she hides her face with both hands, her hair falling to curtain her from view. I wrap my arms around her and glare over her head at the Dolces. Rylan storms past Amber, who gives us one glance before turning to follow her brother as he's swallowed by the crowd.

"No one is immune," Baron says quietly, dropping his sucker wrapper and popping the candy into his cheek. "Remember that, Jailbird."

He turns and flicks a hand at the crowd, and they all step back, jostling to get out of his way even though he's calm. They part like the fucking Red Sea, letting him and Duke pass. DeShaun and Cotton follow, and then there's an awkward pause while the Walton twins look at Gloria across the empty space in the hallway, like they can't decide if they should cross the picket line and give up their spot at the top.

"Go," I say, waving them away as Gloria sobs into my shoulder. "If they'll have you."

SELENA

They glance at each other, shrug, and turn to follow their guys.

"Come on," I say. "Let's go back out."

I start for the door, and Colt holds it open, since my arms are busy holding Lo. He steps out with us, and I stop. "You should go to class," I say. "I don't want to give the twins any reason to hurt you again."

He just laughs. "They don't need a reason. They'll do what they do. And something tells me your friend might need something to help her chill out."

I'm too busy worrying about Gloria to argue with Colt. I wrestle her out through the door, though I'm half carrying her, since she's basically gone limp in my arms. Colt lets the door fall closed behind us, then scoops Gloria up and starts across the lawn. When we reach the bleachers, he circles around to sit on them instead of retreating to the shadows underneath. He sets Lo down on the metal seats, and she doubles over, holding her legs and crying. I sit beside her in the sun, and Colt takes the spot on her other side and fishes out his pack of cigarettes.

For a while, the only sound is the sobs echoing along the metal seats. Colt reaches over and rubs her back absently while he smokes.

"I fucking hate them," Gloria says at last, her voice thick with tears, her body still folded in two over her knees.

"You think they'll cut you out for good?" I ask.

"That's how it works," she says miserably, straightening at last. "Once they're done with a Dolce girl, they're done, except maybe a super degrading booty call every once in a while to keep you in the queue. They don't respect them once they're done."

"I hate to break it to you, but I don't think they respect anyone," I say.

"You're probably right," she says, sighing and slumping down on the bench seat. "What am I going to do now? I'm done at this school, and it's not even Thanksgiving. How am I going to get through the rest of the year?"

"I'm sorry," I say, putting my arm around her. "You know I'm here, though, whatever that's worth. And you

SELENA

know what? Fuck them. They're all dicks, Rylan included. Who cares if you fucked the twins?"

"He cares," she says, sniffling and wiping her eyes. "Obviously."

"Yeah, but it's not like he can really blame you for something you did before you were together," I point out. "It's none of his business."

"But it is," she whispers. "We promised we'd wait for each other, and I didn't wait. I knew this was coming. Cotton warned me and everything. I should have just told him."

"Yeah, maybe," I say. "But you weren't together then. Besides the night Rylan dumped you, have you been with anyone else?"

"No," she admits. "And I never would have done anything with Royal *or* you if I'd known he'd want me back."

"He gave up the right to care about you hooking up with other people when he dumped you," I say. "And fuck all that bullshit, anyway. Your worth is not determined by the amount of dick that's been in you."

"Hold up," Colt says, leaning back and looking from one of us to the other. "You two hooked up?"

"Just for a minute," I say. "And please don't make a big deal of it and be gross right now. That's the last thing Lo needs."

"Damn," he says, shaking his head and pulling out a joint. He lights up and then blows smoke out the corner of his mouth, a little smile on his lips. "Can I be gross about it later?"

"If you must," I say. "But only when it's just us. Lo does not need this getting out."

"What does it matter?" Gloria asks glumly. "Everyone already thinks I'm a whore. I might as well tell them I fucked the whole football team."

I swallow hard, gripped by the reminder of the cruelty the twins put me through.

"So, you're saying karma's catching up with you?" Colt asks, handing her the joint. "For all the shit you called Harper last year?"

I frown at him. "I forgave her for that."

SELENA

"No, he's right," she says, taking the joint. "I was a bitch. I totally deserve this."

"You were, but no one deserves this," I say.

Gloria drags on the joint and then hands it back, thumbing on her phone. Her eyes well with tears again. "It's already on the blog," she says with a groan. "I'm done at this school forever now."

"Wow, Dixie didn't waste any time on that one," I say, glancing sideways at Colt. "Almost like she was waiting for it."

"For a chance to take down the untouchable Gloria Walton?" he asks with a smirk. "You can bet she already had that one queued up and ready to post the second shit went down."

"That's harsh, considering how many times she's told me Lo is her friend."

"We're not that kind of friends," Gloria says, wiping her eyes. "It's fine."

"It's not fine," I insist.

"It is," she says, taking a deep breath to collect herself. "We're friends because we understand each other. We both look out for ourselves first. And it's not like she's telling some big secret. It'll be all over the school by the end of the day. I've been cancelled."

"The Dolce boys need to be taken down," I say. "They shouldn't be able to wield power like that if they're going to hurt people. But I can't seem to find the way to do it without, you know, actually murdering them."

"Maybe that's the problem," Colt says. "You need to have all options on the table."

"I'm not a murderer," I say. "Tempting as it is."

"I have a gun," Gloria says, handing me the joint. "And I live down the street. I could stage an accident."

"I think their dad's the one pulling the strings," I say. "We need a way to take him out. I'm living there now, but I'm still not sure how to find what I need."

"Wisteria," Gloria says. "If you can wait until spring."

"The flower?" Colt asks.

"Girls best friend," she says lightly. "In lethal doses."

"You're terrifying," Colt says, leaning around her to retrieve the joint from me. "So, Teeny, what exactly do you need?"

SELENA

"Information," I say. "Something to prove he's doing something illegal."

"Right," Colt says, nodding. "We all know he's not just selling 'candy.' Or making it. But the closest we ever got was when Preston put glass in a batch of Dolce Crystals."

"That's fucked up," I say, but my mind is only halfway present. I'm remembering something Baron said on the bridge—that he and Mr. Dolce had their own thing going, so he wasn't doing what Royal did at the Hockington. He had to mean drugs.

"So Baron's making Blue Pearl, and you think Mr. Dolce's selling it?"

"He wouldn't get his hands dirty," Gloria says. "Even the twins don't sell. Dawson had exclusive dealing rights at Willow Heights last spring, when it first hit the scene."

I fight the urge to shudder. I know why. Dawson was their best friend, bonded by their shameful act, just like a Midnight Swans ritual.

"So, one of their friends will be selling now," I say. "Maybe I can find out through the Swans."

Gloria takes a dainty little puff on the joint. "Rylan's the dealer this year," she says. "That's why they let him in even though he's not like their other friends. Outside here, though, they've got a bunch of lowlifes selling. Never their own family."

"Of course," I say, shaking my head. "Colin was the main hookup at FHS, but he graduated. I'm sure they've got lots of people there on the roster, though."

"What we need is proof," Colt says. "That they're cooking it and distributing it."

"Baron told me," I say. "But it's my word against his. Unless Royal will testify against him…"

"He'd never turn against his family," Gloria says.

"He hates his dad more than anyone in the world," I say. "And with good reason."

We sit in silence for a while, finishing the joint. Gloria takes out her compact and fixes her makeup, and for once, she and Colt don't snipe at each other. When she's all made up again, she stands and smooths her hands over her skirt. "Well, I'm ready to help," she says. "But how are you going to take down Daddy Dolce?"

"If we want to get to him, we need to get Royal on board," I say again.

"The hard part will be getting the twins on board," she says. "Royal won't go against him if it'll hurt his brothers, and his brothers still like their dad, from what I can tell."

"So now you're going to be working with the twins?" Colt asks. "I thought this was all to get rid of them."

"Mr. Dolce is the head," I say. "If we cut off the head…"

"And boil it in oil for a thousand years," he says with a grin.

"If you can't beat 'em, join 'em," Gloria says. "Except I've been doing that for two years, and they dropped me like a bad habit the second they decided I wasn't worth it."

"I think I know a way to get them on our side," I say. "Just give me a few weeks."

eighteen

Harper Apple

The Friday before Thanksgiving break, I head back to Royal's after school, thinking how fucking weird it is that I live in the same neighborhood as Gloria Walton and Cotton Montgomery now. I live in the Dolce boys' house. I have the gate code.

I pull into their garage and let myself in the back door. The twins and Royal are all at football practice, and Mr. Dolce's Porsche SUV isn't in the garage, which means it's just me and their staff. Helga comes to take my bag upstairs and give me a glass of water and ask if I want a snack. I tell her I'm fine, and after she's gone off to do whatever she does, I go back down the hallway toward the back door. Glancing up and down to make sure I'm alone, I try the door to Mr. Dolce's office.

SELENA

Locked.

I check that I'm still alone, then pull out my pocketknife and make quick work of the lock, silently thanking my ex as I always do when I pick a lock. I step inside and pull the door closed as quietly as I can. Then I tiptoe to the big wooden desk, my heart hammering. What if someone hears me? Are they loyal enough to Mr. Dolce to tell him, or do they hate their boss? Would they sympathize with a poor upstart like me or be disgusted that I'd betray him after all he's done for me?

I crouch in front of his desk and check the drawers. Two of them are unlocked. There's a wide, short one above the chair, so I start there, rifling through quickly and finding nothing of note. To the right, there are two more drawers, one relatively shallow and the other deep. I pull open the top one and stop when I see a Glock. My heart hammers harder as I pull my sleeve over my hand and pick it up. I don't know if he's shot anyone with this gun or where it'll be used next. I'm sure as fuck not leaving fingerprints on it.

I check it and find it loaded. I put it back where I found it and check the last drawer, the deep bottom one. It's locked.

I drop to my knees and work the lock open after a few minutes. Pulling it open, I see a bunch of hanging files. I go through the tabs quickly—taxes, property, vehicles, receipts. My heart skips when I see a tab with my name on it. I pull it out, feeling the weight of the thick file before I flip it open.

Last year's school picture is stapled to the top corner of the paper, along with a few more pages. When I flip through, I see that it's receipts and terms for the scholarship he gave me. I start to breathe again. Royal said he gives a handful of scholarships, so maybe he keeps a file on all of them. I scan the pages. It wasn't a one semester scholarship, like Mr. D said. He said for spring semester he was paying my tuition monthly, that he'd take my scholarship if I didn't get him the info he wanted. But the scholarship is for a whole year, and the terms say it can't be revoked by the donor and is non-refundable. Student behavior, attendance, and grades

SELENA

could have put me on probation, had me expelled, or kept my scholarship from being renewed, but it was already paid.

That fucking bastard. I was never in danger of losing it. He was just making me jump through hoops for the fun of it.

I flip to the next page. It's a printout of an email, and when I manage to decipher it despite the atrocious grammar, spelling, and lack of punctuation, I realize it's the letter they found from my mother to Grandpa Darling. So, at least that part was true. She says she's pregnant and that it's his and he "better take care of it or else."

Sounds like Mommy Dearest.

Obviously she didn't have the resources to follow up on her threat, and since it wasn't actually his, she couldn't do shit about it. But there's proof of why they targeted me.

The next page is a very convincing DNA test result saying that the samples are a match. I flip to the next page and stop. It's a printout of my first conversation with Mr. D. At the top of the page, scrawled in adult handwriting, is the username and password for his account. I take a quick picture on my phone in case I ever need it, though I'm not sure what I'd do with it. Then I sink down on the floor and fan through the pages and pages and pages of conversations. So, their dad knows all of it. Maybe he wasn't the one behind the keyboard, but he must have read all of these, the jerkoff fantasies, what I was doing with his son, what I was telling his other son I was doing. It makes me feel sick and humiliated.

The sound of footsteps in the hall sends me into panic mode. I shove everything back in my file, slide it back into the drawer with shaking fingers, and push it closed. I don't have time to lock it before the office doorknob rattles. I slide under the desk, my heart banging so loud I'm sure he'll hear it when he walks in. I pray it'll be like when I hid under the desk in the school library last year, that he'll walk by and not notice me.

SELENA

Footsteps cross the room, and I hear his heavy breathing. It makes the hair stand up on the back of my neck. He has a loaded gun a few feet from my head.

I have one in my belt, though. Royal told me to keep it, and I did.

I focus on breathing as quietly as I can while he goes to the liquor cart and pours himself a drink. When he lets out a fart and a satisfied sigh, I have to hold back laughter. He moves closer to the desk, and I slide my hand behind me, cursing myself when I feel that I'm sitting on the edge of my shirt, so the gun is trapped. If I move enough to get it out, he'll hear me. I squeeze my eyes closed, praying so hard it hurts that he'll go in the other room.

As if in answer, he stops walking. My heart thuds in my chest and I hold my breath, wondering if he heard me.

"Mr. Dolce," says a perky, accented voice I recognize as Helga's. "Do you require a beverage?"

"I've got it, sweetheart," he says in that Tony Soprano voice of his.

"A snack then?" she asks. "You've been working all day."

Go away, go away... I will them silently.

"Bring me something, would you?" he says. "Surprise me."

Then he steps around the desk, moving his chair back further before pausing.

Fuck.

I'm caught.

He leans down, his eyes fixing on me. "Well, what do we have here?"

I don't have a single smartass comment. He caught me in his locked office, going through his locked drawer. He grabs my wrist and drags me out, his grip unbreakably strong. My heart is hammering in my chest so hard I think I might pass out. My mind is flashing back to that day when Royal grabbed my wrist, when he broke my hand and dropped my knife in the swamp, when the world spun so far out of my reach that I was lost for six fucking months.

SELENA

Tony sits down in his ergonomic leather chair, pulling me down on his lap. "You're not dressed up like my daughter anymore," he says, holding me on his knee while I squirm to free myself. "That's too bad. She was prettier than you."

"Let me go," I grit out, straining to break free of his strong arms that are wrapped tight around me, pinning my own arms at my sides.

"But you have one thing going for you that she didn't," he says against the back of my neck. "You're not my daughter."

I lean my head forward and then slam it back against his face. He curses and grabs the back of my head, forcing it forward again. My neck aches with the strain of how hard he's pushing, but now only one of his arms pins mine, which gives me a little more leverage, even if my body is crushed against his. I struggle harder, twisting my shoulders to try to break free.

"If you're trying to steal from me while you're living under my roof, it's not going to end well for you," he says, squeezing me harder.

"I wasn't fucking stealing from you," I snap.

"Then what are you doing in here?" he asks. "There's nothing in this office of value. But then, a girl like you wouldn't know that, would she? That's why you lost everything. You kept it in your house. A smart girl would have used a bank, or at least a safety deposit box."

Of course he'd keep anything confidential in a safe. Whatever's in his drawer is probably just throwaway stuff, things he doesn't care about. With all the people who work here and have access to this room, he's going to have more than one little drawer lock between him and his most confidential and dangerous secrets.

I'm too fucking removed from this world to outsmart anyone in it. I've never experienced things like this, so things that are obvious to his kind never occur to me.

Curling his fingers into my hair, he stands suddenly, shoving me forward over the desk. My hipbones smash into the unforgiving edge of the heavy desk. It doesn't even budge, and I have to bite down on my lip not to cry out. Tightening his grip, he yanks my head down on the desk. My breath fogs on the polished wooden surface, and tears of pain blur my eyes, but through the shroud of pain and tears and blind panic, I see a figure standing in the open door.

Before I can call out, Mr. Dolce shoves his hips against mine, pinning me with his body while his other hand yanks up the back of my shirt. I thrash against the desk, shoving as hard as I can with both hands. A second later, my gun clatters across the wooden surface. He lays his full weight on me, yanking my head back. I can't fucking breathe, but I'm still fighting, kicking at his shins, reaching up to sink my nails into the side of his neck.

He snatches the gun and shoves it to my temple. He straightens some, letting air into my lungs, and I suck in an ugly breath. His fist is still tight in my hair, making tears of pain sting my eyes, and his hips hold me pinned from behind. Terror and revulsion ream into me when I realize he's hard. I can feel the ridge of his erection biting into my ass.

"Get the fuck off me," I yell, just in case there's someone in this house who isn't too terrified to intervene. The figure in the door is gone, leaving me to wonder if I imagined it.

"Tell me what you're doing in here, or I'll fuck the answer out of you," Mr. Dolce snarls, breathing hard as he presses the gun to my temple with bruising force.

"I was looking for the casino plans," I blurt out, my mind racing through the next steps, trying to find an out, a way to get him to let me go.

"Why?" he demands.

"For Royal."

He pauses, and I'm not sure if I epically fucked up or if I said the one thing that might get him to loosen his grip enough for me to free myself. I just know that Royal's the only person in this town stronger than him, the only one who might be able to defeat him, and one of the only people he won't kill. He uses his children, but I believe he honestly loves them in whatever capacity he's able. If nothing else, it might remind him that Royal said I was his and no one is allowed to touch me.

I'm not about to throw anyone weak under the bus, that's for damn sure. Royal is all I've got.

SELENA

"Why does Royal want the casino plans?" Mr. Dolce asks.

"I don't know," I say. "He said he'd tell me after I got them."

Tony lets out a little breath of a laugh and straightens fully, but he keeps his cock pressed firmly to my ass.

"Sounds like my boy," he says, and I think he's actually proud of his son even as he grinds his cock against his girlfriend's ass.

I try not to vomit across his desk, focusing on relaxing my muscles so I'll stop shaking. "Can I go now?" I ask.

"Well, if you're doing his bidding, I'll let you in on a little secret," Mr. Dolce says, setting the gun down and sitting back down. His hand in my hair never loosens, and I'm dragged backwards off the desk, every inch of my scalp burning as he lifts almost my entire weight by my hair. He pulls me back onto his lap. "Just sit here, and I'll show you what I have. Deal?"

"Deal," I grit out, hating myself with a loathing that goes almost as deep as the one I feel for him even though I don't have much choice in the matter.

He sets the gun down out of my reach and leans over, pulling open the bottom drawer. He slides out a folder and set it on the desk.

"Go on," he says. "Open it. You're part of the family now, aren't you? You thought you'd break us by getting my sons in trouble at school, but now that you're on our side, you're far less dangerous, aren't you? So go on. Once you're involved in our business, you'll see how it benefits all of us. Even you—especially you. But if my son insists on having you on the inside, you might as well know it all."

I flip open the folder, pretending I give a fuck about his land deal when his dick is shoved up against my ass. He grinds it against me, rubbing his chin on the back of my neck.

"You won't find anything about a casino," he says. "They didn't sell me the land. But they will. And our plans for Faulkner are so much bigger than a casino."

SELENA

"If we're spilling all our secrets, what's bigger than a casino?" I ask, ignoring his heavy breathing on the back of my neck.

"I hear through the grapevine that someone's using the abandoned mall for some very profitable purposes. Ones the authorities might not approve of. Just like some people wouldn't approve of us."

He slides his hand between my legs, grabbing my pussy and groaning.

"If you want to know the real secrets, if you want to get inside the Dolce family, first you have to let me inside you," he says. "Once I have this on you, I can trust you to be compliant. You'll obey me, or I'll expose you to Royal, let him know what you did to become a real Dolce girl."

Revulsion slams into me as his fingers knead my flesh. I dive forward, lunging across the desk and making a grab for the gun. Mr. Dolce curses and snatches me back, but not before my fingers close around the Glock. I twist around and slam the butt into the side of his head.

I may not know how to fight with anything but my fists, but that means I sure as fuck know where to land a blow for a knockout.

He crumples like a ragdoll, smacking his head on the desk and bouncing off the chair before tumbling to the floor. I get some satisfaction out of the knowledge that he'll have to explain the bruises to Royal.

"Fucker," I mutter, tucking the gun back into the back of my skirt. I smooth my shirt and step over him, deliberately placing a foot on his crotch and making sure it takes all my weight before I take the next step. When I get to the door, I see Baron lurking in the hall like a creeper. I shove past him, not even surprised to see him there.

"You better hope he's not hurt," he says.

"Were you just going to watch while your father fucking raped me?" I snap at him.

He shrugs, his eyes cool. "I like watching."

"What happened to you?" I ask. "Or were you born like that?"

SELENA

"I've seen him do worse," he says with a shrug. "You're eighteen, and you owe him a hell of a lot more than a turn in your busted ass."

"I don't owe him shit," I snap. "I don't owe any of you shit."

"He gave you a scholarship."

"I paid for that," I grit out, glaring at him.

He smirks, letting his dark gaze roam over my body. "Yeah, I guess letting the three of us raw-dog you all night might be worth a scholarship. What's the going rate for fucking a whore without a condom? A thousand? Between the three of us, I bet we fucked you twenty-five times that night. That's what your scholarship cost, so I guess you're paid up for last year."

"I didn't *let* you do anything."

"What about this year?" he asks. "You took a scholarship from my family this year. Ready for a repeat, with a little extra punishment for trying to ruin us at the school after you took the money?"

"Touch me, and you'll see how much I've improved at the shooting range this month."

"Nah," he says, jangling his keys in his pocket. "I'm just fucking with you. You're used goods. I don't do repeats with girls like you unless I'm bored, and I've got shit to do."

"Sorry to hold you up," I say sarcastically. "I guess now that your dad's not trying to rape me, the show's over."

"Guess so," he says coolly.

I edge past him and hurry down the hall, resisting the urge to pull out my gun and back down the hall, keeping him in my sights. When he doesn't follow, I continue upstairs and throw my stuff back into the two suitcases I brought with me, filled with clothes from our trip to New York. I throw in one of Royal's dirty t-shirts because I'm a dick-whipped bitch and I want to smell him while I fall asleep, and then I head out. At the bottom of the stairs I run into Duke, who's emerging from the kitchen.

"Want one?" he asks, holding up a six-pack of some expensive beer in glass bottles and offering a sloppy smile along with it.

"Is Baron joining us?"

SELENA

"He left," Duke says with a shrug.

"You mean he's doing something without you?" I ask, feigning horror.

"We do stuff without each other all the time."

"But how will he know you're worthy of the Dolce name if you aren't there to do his psychotic bidding?"

"I don't do his bidding," Duke says, scowling. "Now, you want to go have a beer on the front steps with me or not?"

"Not," I say. "But go wait at the front door like his loyal doggie."

I turn and drag my suitcases down the hall to the back door. I'm not scared of Duke, so I don't even worry that my hands are full, and I can't reach for my gun. I climb into my car and head back the way I came. Guess my time of living the high life is over. I used to think Royal had everything, but now I know the truth.

He has everything, but it's not worth it.

I pull up at my house and go inside. The familiar scent of stale smoke and mold almost makes me gag after living in a clean, light, beautiful house for a few weeks.

The inside is dim and depressing, and my room is still tossed. It doesn't matter, though. It's still better than Royal's house with his cooks and maids and butlers.

I sigh and get to work. About five minutes later, a tap at the window disturbs me. I look up to see Blue's face staring in from the twilight.

I slide open the glass. "Hey, Blue."

"I thought you left," she says. "I haven't seen you in weeks, and Olive said you were moving."

"Yeah," I said. "I'm back."

"Oh," she says, her eyes rounding as she takes in my room. "What happened? Did someone break in while you were gone?"

"Just my mom," I say with a shrug. "Want to come in?"

I hold out a hand, and she grabs on and scrambles through the window, dropping into my room and wiping her hands on her jeans after holding onto the grimy windowsill. "I've never been in your room before," she says.

SELENA

I realize she's right. We've lived next door to each other for years, and I consider her a friend, even if we don't share secrets. We don't have to. She understands me because we're the same somehow, even if she's quiet and shy and I'm loud and prone to getting picked up by the cops. We never judge each other for our differences. I don't think she's weak because I know better, even if I'd do things differently. I don't know her life, but I know she has her reasons, just like I have mine.

And she has her reasons for never having invited me in, I'm sure. She's come into my house before, but not my bedroom. That's a boundary she's always respected. Now, I don't feel protective of my room. It doesn't feel like mine, the only thing I have in the world. It's just a place to sleep now. It doesn't belong to me any more than I belong to it.

"Need help?" Blue asks after an awkward silence.

"Sure," I say. "Want to help me put the bed back together?"

After the bed's back in order, we make quick work of folding the clothes and shoving the notebooks and random school crap under the bed or in the trash. I tell her about my mom while we work. Somehow, it's easier to talk to her now. I don't know if it's because she's on my turf, or because I don't belong in her world anymore, or because I've gotten used to talking now that I have friends and have let people get close.

When we're done, we sit on my twin bed with our backs to the wall, smoke a cigarette, and talk about the Brody Villines poster we found in my closet, crumpled and crushed, and how we used to love his music, and about living at Royal's, and school. Then she tells me Olive is at a friend's house, and I offer to take Blue to pick her up. As soon as we turn onto Mill Street afterwards, I spot Royal's Rover in my driveway.

I wave to old Mr. Thomas across the street and pull up along the side of the road.

"Is there somewhere I can find you next time?" Blue asks. "If he takes you home again…"

I give her his address and ask her to call the cops if she sees Bobby Dale around my house. Then she and Olive cross the lawn to their house, and I walk up beside

SELENA

Royal's car. It's empty. I find him lying on my bed, his ankles crossed, his arm propped under his head on my pillow.

"Making yourself at home?" I ask, dropping my keys on the dresser and pulling my gun out of my skirt to set it beside them.

"Your home is my home," he says.

"I think you said the opposite."

"If you're staying here, I'm staying here."

I roll my eyes. "Right. Royal Dolce living on Mill Street."

"I'd live under a bridge if that's where you were living. Now shut up and get over here and sit on my face."

"You're actually going to stay here?" I ask, staring at him.

"What about it?"

"Royal," I say, leaning back on the edge of the dresser and crossing my arms over my chest. "In case you hadn't noticed, this place is a hovel."

"Noticed, didn't care," he says. "You can come home, or you can accept that I'm going to be here until you do."

"Did Baron tell you why I left?" I ask carefully.

Royal doesn't do well with betrayal. I know that for fucking sure. And even though he's not acting pissed, and he's not one for faking it, I have to make sure. I'm not sure he trusts Baron any more than he trusts me, but I'm not risking anything.

"No," he says, sitting up and swinging his legs off the bed, a frown darkening his expression. "He wasn't home. Why? What'd he do?"

I swallow and grip the edge of the dresser beside my hips. "Nothing. He just talked shit. Your dad put a gun to my head, though."

Royal stares at me a second and then drops his head into his hands. "Fuck," he mutters. "I should never have brought you into that house."

I cross the room and sink onto the bed beside him. "Don't kill me for this, but I think we need to do something about him."

SELENA

"Yeah," Royal says. "You're right. Of course you're right. Fuck."

"What are you going to do?" I ask.

"I don't know," he says. "We'll figure it out over the break. Don't worry about it, Jailbird. I'll take care of it."

"I'll miss you," I say, stroking a little curl behind his ear. They're all going home to visit their mom, and I'm not ready to take that step. Plus, I told Royal I wanted to go to Cedar Crest to visit my mom. By the time he knows I'm lying, he'll already be in New York.

"Want to show me how much?" he asks, wrapping his arms around me and pushing me back on the bed, with my head toward the foot. He rubs his nose slowly back and forth against mine, smiling down at me. "Or maybe I should show you how much I'll miss you."

"Yes, please," I say, smiling back and linking my arms around his neck.

"Mmm," he murmurs, rocking his hips slowly against mine. "You're a thirsty bitch, you know that?"

"I do know that," I say. "Now quench my thirst."

He presses his lips to mine, slowly at first. I wrap my legs around him, savoring his intake of breath, savoring the way his body feels on mine, so unstoppable and yet so safe. I know it's not safe, that I only feel that way because he won't hurt me, but that's okay. It's safe for me now. Safe to give in, to let someone else take control for a while, to let myself love him.

I open my lips, inviting him in, inviting him deeper into me, deepening the kiss.

His mouth takes control, his tongue stroking mine in a slow, sensual rhythm that makes me squeeze my knees around his hips and squirm under him. Coils of pleasure thread through my body, sending warm tingles from the top of my head all the way to my toes. I grind against him until I think I'm going to cum just from kissing him and the contact of our hips. At last, I pull my mouth away.

"More," I say, tugging at his tie.

He chuckles and watches me loosen the fabric and pull it over his head. Then he kisses me again. "What's the rush?" he asks, skimming his lips over my cheek to

SELENA

my ear. "I'm going to take my time with you tonight, savor my little Cherry Pie."

He slides a hand up the outside of my thigh as his soft lips tease my earlobe. He draws it between his teeth, biting down gently and tracing the rim with his tongue. At the same time, he palms my ass, pulling me firmly against him, my wet center pressed tight to the iron ridge in his pants. I swear I see stars I'm so hot.

"I can't wait all night," I say through panting breaths. "I need you inside me."

"We'll get there," he murmurs against my ear, his lips brushing the sensitive skin. "We've got time."

We've got time.

I let the words sink in slowly, and I force myself to relax even though I'm so frustrated I want to scream. I want him pounding me hard and rough, breaking my bed and my back at the same time. I'm used to our frantic, angry collisions, the way we crash together like two hurricanes meeting, leaving devastation in their wake.

I'm not used to the slow build, the tease, the wait. Royal doesn't wait. He takes what he wants when he wants it. He gets me just warmed up enough that I can take him, and then he forces me to take every inch, pounding me like he hates me. And I fucking love it. It fits us.

But maybe he's right. Maybe we have time now, the luxury of knowing this isn't going to end. The luxury of exploring each other, of not rushing through each moment, knowing it could be our last. I treasured every night with him, knowing they were always numbered.

Now, they aren't. We don't have to rush to cum so we can start over, fuck one more time before we have to leave each other, knowing it might be the last time. Now we know it won't be the last. There will be a million more moments, a thousand more nights to savor each other. Nights to let him make his agonizing way down my neck while his huge hands massage my body, possessing me, cradling me, winding me tighter until I think I'll explode. I don't know what to do with myself, how to contain the sensations rolling through my body, my heart, my soul. Girls like me don't get fucked like this.

No one's ever treasured me before.

SELENA

Somewhere I hear a knocking sound, but I'm too far gone, too lost in bliss, to even register it. Not until it comes again, loud and insistent.

"Who the fuck is at the door?" Royal asks, lifting his head from where he's been kissing my collarbone.

"I don't know," I say, shaking my head.

"If it's one of your fanboys, sniffing around here like you're a dog in heat, I swear I'm going to fucking end him," Royal says as the pounding continues, this time accompanied by muffled shouting.

"Just leave it," I say, grabbing his hand. "It doesn't matter. They'll go away if you don't open the door."

He scowls at me, suspicion clouding his eyes that a moment ago were so full of wanting, of *me*.

Now I'm the one who wants to kill whoever's interrupting.

Royal swings his legs off the bed and stands, grabbing my gun and tucking it into the back of his pants. Then he turns back. "Stay here," he says, his eyes softening as he leans down to kiss me. "I'll be right back. Don't move a muscle. I want to imagine you lying here all wet and ready for me to devour when I get back."

"Then hurry," I whisper, grabbing the front of his shirt and kissing him hard.

"And don't you dare touch yourself, my dirty little whore," he says, gripping my hand and staring down at me, his dominating command pinning me flat. "Your cum is mine tonight, *bella mia*. I'm going to drink every drop, so don't even think about wasting it while I'm gone. If I come back and you've moved, you won't get fucked until I get back from New York. Got it?"

I nod, and he kisses me quickly before standing and leaving the room.

I squeeze my knees together, cursing his bossy ass. I hear the door open and close, and then the muffled shouting of the guy outside. There's a short silence, and then an engine starts up.

Royal better have fucking sent him away, because I'm not lying here all night waiting for him to come back. I wait about five minutes before I yell for him. Then a sick feeling grips me. What if the guy had a gun, too? What if he shot Royal?

I lurch up from the bed and run to the front door. There's no sign of Royal outside, which is a relief, since part of me expected to see his body lying there. Still, they could have dragged him away, thrown him in their truck…

His car is still parked outside.

I run back to my room and call him, my heart hammering.

"Are you where I left you?" he asks without bothering to say hello.

"Yes," I say, sinking back onto the bed.

"Good," he says. "This will take a few minutes, but I'll be back as soon as I can. Keep my dessert warm."

He hangs up before I can say anything. Well, at least I know the asshole's okay. I imagine him sitting in the car with whoever came knocking, saying those words to me, and I squeeze my knees together. I'm so aroused it fucking hurts. If guys get blue balls, I've got blue clit.

I go check the front door to make sure it's locked, then turn off the light and crawl into bed to wait.

I wake to the sensation of my skirt being pushed up.

"Royal?" I mumble in the dark. I didn't mean to fall asleep, and I don't know how long I've been sleeping. My mind is groggy and slow. His fingers hook into my panties, pulling them down my thighs. He tosses them aside and pushes my knees open, spreading my lips with his fingers and blowing gently on my warm flesh. I shiver, and he chuckles and leans in, licking my clit with soft little strokes.

I moan sleepily and let my knees fall open, letting him have me. I can hear the wet sounds of his tongue lapping at me, coaxing me higher, until I'm gasping for breath. He slides a finger into me, pushing against just the right spot as his tongue slows, languidly stroking me from my entrance to my clit. When he pumps his fingers, I can hear how wet I am, the only sound in the darkness. He moans, sucking gently at my clit, and I bury my hands in his hair, his name falling from my lips as I rush over the edge.

SELENA

He moans and licks me a few more times until the pulses going through me subside. Then he slides his finger out and collapses beside me, pulling me into his arms.

"Where'd you go?" I ask, snuggling into his chest.

"I had some business to take care of before I leave for New York," he says.

"What kind of business?"

"The kind that makes sure you'll be safe staying here since you can't be at my house with my father while I'm gone."

"What time is it?" I ask, throwing my leg over his hip. "Do we have time for more?"

"It's almost morning," he says, sliding his hand over my ass, his fingers moving down my crack before finding my slippery opening. "I have to get to the airport, but I can water this thirsty little cunt one more time before I go."

I moan and rock against him. "Turn on the light," I say.

I want to see my beautiful man while he fucks me, to see my own face staring back at me from the tattoo that says he loves me more than words ever could. He switches on the lamp before rolling back, flipping me onto my back and sliding on top of me. His face is bruised, and I see traces of blood on his split lip and inside his nose, and I know he fought. He's wearing only an undershirt instead of the dress shirt he wore before he left, and there are flecks of blood on that, too.

I don't ask questions. I know I'm fucking a dangerous man, that I'm letting him inside my body and soul. But it's too late for me. He's already a part of me, the part that beats in my chest for him, that swells like a wave in the ocean he delivered to me on that beach, that fills me with a warmth that makes tears wet my lashes.

As he moves inside me, our eyes locked together as he claims me one powerful motion at a time, I think maybe this will be the night I can tell him. That maybe he'll say it.

But neither of us do.

Maybe we're not the type.

SELENA

Words are cheap, anyway.

I love him just as he is, no matter what he's done. I know he's done it to protect me. Like the tattoos, that says he loves me more than any words. His love is in every caress, every kiss, every touch, every rough thrust that makes me see stars and leaves me more satisfied than a girl like me has a right to be. It's in the leather seats of the fancy car that he could have left in his name, but he put it in mine, so it belongs solely to me. It's in the bruises on his knuckles and the blood on his lips, the ink on his skin, the fullness of his eyes when he cums without me having to bring him back to me.

He's already here, completely present, in this moment with me when nothing else matters but our names on each other's lips and our hearts beating out the rhythm of this crazy storm between us, and the sweat on our skin that combines to make the smell of us as we lay pressed together so tightly I don't know where he ends and I begin.

Love isn't found in words. It's found in us.

nineteen

Preston Darling

"Hey, cutie pie," says the middle-aged waitress who also happens to own the downtime diner I just walked into. "I saved your regular booth."

"Thanks, Scar," I say. "You're a lifesaver."

Scarlet's toughness is the stuff of legends, as is the scar that runs diagonally across her face and down her neck. No one knows how she really got it, but kids around town make up stories of its origin—she was slashed with a machete and left for dead when she cheated on her boyfriend with a member of the rival gang, her dad punished her for running with Crossbones boys by marking her face so none of them would want her, she stood up to the Disciples leader and got a taste of his switchblade. The only thing that anyone agrees on is that it's gang-related, but that may be rooted more in the fact that her partner is a gang leader than any truth.

"Don't I know it," she says, giving me a two-finger salute. "Two of a kind, you and me. Too bad you're not into cougars."

"And you're not single," I point out.

"Pssh, aren't all the kids poly these days anyway?"

"Somehow I don't see your boyfriend sharing," I say, shaking my head. "Or I'd be all over that. If I'd had a woman like you, I wouldn't be so fuck-ugly right now."

"Ugly is as ugly does," she says, waving a laminated menu toward the booth tucked away in the corner. "Go on back, sugar."

I slide into the booth, my back to the rest of the room. Scarlet's not a family friend, though she's my parents' age. She went to Faulkner High, and my parents didn't associate with girls like her. But we have an easy kinship, for obvious reasons, and the Dolces would never set foot in the greasy spoon diner she owns. So, it's a safe space for Darlings, for the time being at least.

If the Dolces find out we frequent the place, they'll send thugs to beat up the workers, since even they probably wouldn't fuck with Scar outright. She wouldn't back down from a direct threat, but she'd do it to save any of her workers or their families. So, that's where Mr. Dolce will hit her, knowing it's her vulnerability. That, or he'll trash the place, which is her livelihood. Then she'll pay the tax to keep the thugs out of her establishment, even though the same thugs will "protect" it. If she slips up and lets a Darling through the door, the protection will magically disappear for a night, and the place will go up in flames.

Better to stay home and keep our heads down than to endanger the town we still love. Scar might not have been my parents' type of friend, but she's mine. Anyone in this town who hasn't been corrupted is worthy of the utmost respect.

"Am I late or are you early?" asks a voice behind me.

I stand to shake hands with the man I'm here to meet. "Father," I say with a nod.

SELENA

"Mr. Darling," he says, giving me a quick shake before taking his seat opposite me in the booth. He's wearing his collar, but otherwise looks like a regular, built guy in a sweater and glasses. "I appreciate you meeting me out. I know you like your privacy."

"I'm more worried about risking Scarlet than myself," I assure him. "And you don't have to pay your students personal visits."

"Are you ready for finals?" he asks, flipping over his menu.

Scarlet appears beside us, a menu pad in one hand and a coffee pot in the other. "The usual?" she asks, pouring us both coffee.

"You have avocado toast yet?" I ask.

"The usual for you, then," she says, jotting down a note and popping her gum. "Father?"

"You shouldn't have a suggestion box if you're not taking suggestions," I say, laying my arm along the top of the booth and smiling up at her with all the innocence I can muster, little as it is.

She glowers at me, chomping on her gum like she chews out kids who come in to stare at her and don't order. "If I added your damn hipster toast, I'd have to change all the menus," she says.

"You could write it on the specials board," I say, giving her my most winning smile, which isn't saying much anymore.

"And you could shove it up your ass," she says. "Forgive me, Father."

Father Dante shakes his head and hands her the menu. "I'll take the number five, please."

She gathers the menus, fixing me in her most belligerent gaze before she stomps off.

"Thanks, doll," I call after her.

"You getting out at all?" Father asks when she's gone.

"Nah," I say, leaning back and removing my mask. I set it on the table within easy reach. Father Dante and Scar have seen me without it, but if someone else comes in, I'll replace it. I've worn it so long it's become part of my face. I'd rather not have my naked ugliness exposed for the world to see and mock.

SELENA

"It's not healthy," Father Dante says. "You should come to a service."

I laugh and pick up my coffee. "My family would disown me."

Southern Baptist or dead—those are the choices for a Darling. It's one thing to take classes at Thorncrown. I'm not an artist, and the only other school in town is the liberal arts college. There's a longstanding tradition that's created a pipeline from Willow Heights to Thorncrown, right down to the underground connection. The college is small, but there are enough Midnight Swans alumni to make it a reasonable choice for an undergrad degree. Then they use their connections to funnel students into top tier grad schools like Georgetown and Harvard. My family doesn't mind me taking online classes at a Catholic school that can get me places, but they'd excommunicate me if I converted.

"Then we'll keep having these chats in person," Father Dante says. "Otherwise I fear you'll turn to Dracula, all alone in that castle with the old man."

"You're confusing the vampire with Jane Eyre," I say. "And I assure you, *leader,* I will not marry him."

He raises a brow and sips his coffee. The guy's only ten years older than me, and I'm not Catholic, so I can be a smartass dick without guilt. "You haven't seen anyone else this month?"

"Oh, no," I say. "I'm a regular socialite, Father. I saw Harper just a few weeks ago, Sully's back, and Magnolia's doing her online schooling there, too, so I've got a pain in the ass kid underfoot all day. I guess I am Jane Eyre."

"Better than last time," he says, dabbing his neat goatee with a napkin.

"You can't grade me on my social life," I say. "Besides, I talk to Lindsey online almost every day. Mabel, Colt, and the uncles check in weekly to see whether me or the old man will kick the bucket first. That's like ten people. My social calendar's hoppin,' bro."

He doesn't even crack a smile. "Have you talked to your father?"

"Why would I do that?" I ask. "I've got you, Father."

He sighs. "Is that enough? Those connections?"

SELENA

Scar comes back with our plates, setting them in front of us and then hurrying off to greet new customers. I know she'll seat them far from us, but it's Saturday morning, so I have to eat fast if I want to keep the mask off until I'm done.

"What about you?" I ask. "You ever get lonely, old man? It must suck knowing you'll never be with a woman."

"No," he says, opening a creamer canister and pouring the drop of cream into his coffee. "I'm a man of faith. If I feel alone, I only have to pray to remind myself that He is always with me."

"Sounds pretty fucking lonely to me," I say, forking tepid hashbrowns into my mouth.

I'm an expert in that field, so I should know. If Thorncrown gave degrees in loneliness, I'd have a fucking doctorate.

Probably why I fell for the girl whose face lights up my screen just then. I reject the call and finish breakfast, making small talk with the priest about classes and the holidays, then replace my mask and tuck a hundred into the folder for a tip. Scarlet deserves more, but the one time I tried, she smacked the back of my head with a menu and told me if I wanted to donate to charity, go down to the Salvation Army. Apparently one bill is a tip, two is charity. I make sure to always have a hundred when I come in.

We step out into a rainy, grey November morning. Cold, wet wind almost rips the door out of my hand and back into my face. Couldn't make me uglier than I am, but that's a mess I don't want to clean up.

A faded red pickup pulls up, the window rolling down as it comes to a stop. A blond guy with neck tats, an unhinged smile, and a face so pretty it makes me want to fucking kill him leans out the window.

There's the fucking charity case, one of Father Dante's delinquents.

"Ready, *Papi?*" he asks.

"Be there in a minute, Heath," the Father says.

He steps in, and I freeze, standing like a statue while he wraps his arms around me. "Have a nice holiday," he

SELENA

says, patting my back without breaking the embrace. "We'll meet again next month. I'm proud of you, son."

I stare at the grey sky behind him, remembering the last time I hugged a man. Men in my family don't hug—according to my actual father, only women and gays hug.

I hugged Devlin goodbye.

The day I let that slip is the last time my father hit me, while I lay in a bed at Faulkner Memorial with my head in a bandage after they'd told me they couldn't save my eye. That's when he told them not to bother fixing the rest of my face. I wasn't worth it. I'd never have told him if I wasn't drugged up as I tried to recount the last moments I'd seen my cousin so they might find him. Lot of good that did.

Heath lays on the horn, and Father Dante steps back and pats my cheek. "There's a whole world full of fascinating people out there," he says. "Don't limit yourself to family."

I raise a hand and wave to his ride. "Hey, Heath," I call.

"What are you supposed to be, anyway?" Heath asks. "A clown or some shit?"

"Just another charity chase," I say, then turn and give the Father a smug smile. "There. I talked to a stranger. So I'm good until our next chat."

"Take care of yourself, Preston," Father Dante says, then pulls his coat around him and hurries around the truck.

I climb into Grandpa's Aston Martin and dial Harper. "Hey, Miss A," I say when she answers. "Royal know you're calling me, or am I about to get jumped?"

"Royal knows we're friends, and he's on a plane to New York right now," she says. "I need to talk to you, though."

"Okay."

"Can I come over or something?"

"I'm at Scar's diner," I say. "But I'm just leaving."

"The Downtown Diner?"

"Yeah. But I've got an appointment now."

"Okay," she says. "I guess we can do it over the phone."

SELENA

"Sure," I say, shifting into gear and gunning the engine as I turn out of the parking lot. "Unless you want to get a tattoo with me."

"You going to Mav's?"

"The only tattoo shop in Faulkner."

"I'll be there in ten," she says.

The line goes dead, and I toss my phone and pull up to the seedy little tattoo parlor. Of course Harper's well acquainted with the guys who run this place. Maverick and his brother are fucking legendary for the amount of pussy they pull in, and Harper's covered in tats.

I wait in the car until her Escalade pulls up. I'm glad she's got a car, but I fucking hate that Royal put her in it. The bitter acid of jealousy eats away at me every time I see it, every time I see her. But I can't seem to cut the ties that grew between us when she was with me. She's a weed that was felled by a Dolce scythe, and though she was supposed to die as she lay on the ground, she somehow regrew roots from the barest edge of her stem. As I watered her, those roots grew straight down through the barren soil of my life until they met my own roots.

She hugs me hard, clinging to me like she always does, like I'm something worth missing, something worth holding onto. We're tangled together in some way, holding on with something far below than the surface even though we both know we should cut our losses and walk away. She's Royal's, and therefore dangerous to me.

I'm dangerous to her for the same reason.

If we were smart, we'd forget those six months and pretend they meant nothing, pretend we didn't save each other night by night until enough heat built to thaw the winter that lived on inside us both all through summer.

"Want to go inside?" I ask, rubbing her arms. "It's cold out here, and you're not wearing a jacket."

She nods against my chest, not releasing me for another few seconds. I want to indulge in the same impulse, but I won't let myself. Some ugly part inside of me clings to her, though, those roots refusing to be torn from hers. We survived something together. The seeds of life in that barren soil cracked open their shells and let us both feel again, and that means something, even if it's not the same kind of something I had before.

SELENA

But Dolly left.

Harper's here.

At last, she steps back, and I hold the door of the shop for her. We step inside, where Mad Dog, Maverick, and a couple Crossbones members lounge on the couches. They all stop talking and just stare at us when we walk in. This is why I don't go out in public. At least when I'm at home, I'm just myself. I don't have to remember every second of every fucking day that I'm a freak, a grotesque beast that makes even the toughest gangsters lose the ability to speak.

"I have an appointment," I say stiffly.

"What about you?" Maverick asks, jerking his chin at Harper. "Need some more ink, little mama?"

"I'm just here to hold his hand," she says, but she's staring at the designs on the walls with longing in her eyes.

"Yeah, her too," I say. "Whatever she wants."

"You don't have to—"

"I know," I say. "Just get something."

She nods and turns to Mad Dog. "Can you do mine?"

A couple of the guys laugh and punch Maverick's shoulders. "What are you talking about?" he asks. "I gave you some of my best stuff."

"Yeah, turns out your best stuff wasn't that good," she says.

I expect the guys to laugh again, but they fall silent, just watching what their newest member will do.

"Not how I remember it, *hyna*," he says, then nods to his brother. "This one's the reason I'm ambidextrous. She likes it when you put a finger in her while you're working. The buzz of the machine and the pain gets her off."

"And that's why I wanted your brother to do mine," she says, batting her lashes at Maverick. "I'm with someone now, and I'm not looking to cheat. I don't know if I could resist if your hands were on me."

Now the guys are laughing. I marvel at Harper's easy way with these thugs. She's not even nervous when alone in a room with five gangsters. I'm fucking nervous around them, and I'm not a woman.

SELENA

"Come on," Mad Dog says, opening one of the curtains. "We got both machines ready."

I take the other seat, and Maverick talks to the guys for another minute before coming back. Their gangster friends leave, and then it's just the four of us.

"Can you close the curtain between us?" I ask.

Maverick pulls them closed around our chairs.

Harper laughs. "I've seen you naked, Preston. What's the big deal?"

"What are you getting?" I ask.

"I don't know," she says. "Maybe… A sunflower."

"That'd be cool."

"I can do that today," Mad Dog says. "Come back in a few weeks and we'll start filling in the color."

I lay back, and Maverick picks up the tattoo gun and shakes his head. "You're a brave motherfucker."

"What are you getting?" Harper asks.

"Just a name," I answer.

It doesn't matter if Dolly left. She's on my skin, in my soul, and she'll never be gone. I might as well stop fighting it.

For a few months, I thought Harper could be everything she wasn't. Harper's here. She's not like Dolly.

Dolly would never be happy with a hideous beast. She deserves a prince, someone as flawless as she is. If she wanted me, she'd still be here. I thought, for a minute, that I could catch her. But she wanted fame, and that comes with her pick of men, all those tattooed rock stars with perfect faces that she's probably fucking on the road. I could never compete with that, could never get a Dolly Beckett.

I could get Harper, though, so I did. I took her, at first just to piss Royal off, but then because I wanted her. She didn't care that I was ugly. She made me feel useful, even human again. I wasn't just the beast inside his castle, eaten from the inside out by impotent rage at his fate. I had purpose with Harper. I could fix her, show her that I could help, that what's left of me could be worthy of what was left of her.

But she left, too. She found the rest of herself, the pieces Royal had kept, and she put herself back together.

SELENA

She's whole again. I'm still only half a man, a shell of who I was.

I should let her go, the way I should let go of Dolly. But I can't seem to release either of them.

"What'd you want to talk about?" I ask the curtain.

"You said you're sure your cousin is still alive," she says. "Why?"

I close my eyes, burrowing down into the pain of the needle piercing my skin over and over. "He said goodbye to us," I say. "He took money from his trust fund. Some guy sold them a car for cash outside a liquor store."

"Zephyr's dad," she says, sounding excited.

"When Mr. Dolce offered a reward, the guy told him, but they never found them, so he wouldn't pay up. There were some others like him, and they were going to try to sue. My uncle paid off everyone who was making a stink about it so they'd drop the suit."

"Why?" she asks incredulously. "Didn't you want to find him, too?"

"No," I say. "We wanted him to be happy, and the sooner Mr. Dolce stopped looking, the safer they'd be.

So we paid off everyone who was going to keep pushing it, and they took their money and shut up."

"You have no idea where they are?"

"I know where they are," I admit.

"How?"

"My… friend," I say. "She went out to California about six months after that, when she graduated. She was trying to land a record deal, and it wasn't going so well. And then suddenly she got a call from Nyso. When she was recording one day, she swears she saw Devlin from the elevator. She's sure that's why the record company called. He put in a word or put her demo in front of someone there."

"Do you think you could find him?" she asks.

"Probably," I say. "But I won't."

"Why?" she asks, sounding more perplexed.

I shake my head, even though she can't see me. "Are you fucking serious? Look at me. Look at my family. You think they'll let Devlin live a single minute once they find him? He's my cousin, and I want him to be happy, even if it means I never see him again."

SELENA

"Fine," she says. "But Crystal's not your cousin, and if we want this town to survive, we need to find her."

"They'll follow you and find Devlin."

"They're in New York right now," she points out.

"You think they don't have trackers on your phone? They'll know where you are."

"You're paranoid."

"You're naïve," I say. "I guarantee that Royal knows exactly where you are at this very moment."

"They deserve to know she's alive," she says.

"They deserve a firing squad."

Harper sighs. "If you want them to leave your family alone, we need to find Crystal. It's great that Devlin's happy, but shouldn't the rest of your family get that chance? You told me to find my sun. I want that for you, too, Preston. For everyone in your family to be free, not just Devlin. Magnolia's fourteen. She shouldn't have to hide away in fear for her life."

"Then why don't you try calling off your boyfriend?"

"You're really going to let your hatred for Royal ruin this town when you can stop it?" she asks. "I thought you knew when it was time to put your pride aside."

"I don't think you realize the extent of what he's done," I say, bitterness sharpening my words. "You might forgive him, but I loathe him to the fucking depths of my being, and that will never change."

"None of us can change the past," she says. "But maybe we can make the future better for all of us. Not just Royal, but your family, too."

"Why should I help him?" I ask. "He'd gladly watch me die. In fact, he'd be the one holding the knife that made it happen."

"But you know who you love more than you hate Royal?" she asks.

I grind my teeth and glare at the side of Maverick's face. He's deep in concentration, seemingly unaware of our conversation. "My family," I mutter at last.

"This is the only way you're going to save your family, Preston."

SELENA

"There might be another way," I say. "You don't even know that this will save them. It might just get Devlin killed, too."

"And if we don't try, we'll never know," she points out. "Maybe you're helping your cousin, or maybe you're holding onto this because you want the Dolces to hurt for all they've done to you. I get it, but holding onto petty revenges never helped them, and it won't help you. In the end, you're just like him—you're only destroying yourself."

I clench my teeth together and glare up at the ceiling, the pain of the needle drilling into me. I never expected the girl who lay there as passive as a doll while I fucked her for six months to be the person who finally convinced my stubborn ass to do something about Devlin. I wouldn't do it if she wasn't right, but unfortunately, she is.

"Fine," I grit out at last.

"Good," she says. "Then let's bring Crystal home."

twenty

Harper Apple

"This is going to get us both killed," Preston says, lifting my suitcase into the bed of his truck. It would make more sense to take my car, but his terms included leaving my phone and car at my house, since he doesn't believe Royal won't track me. He even insisted on giving me one of his suitcases, in case Royal somehow bugged the ones he bought for me.

"Maybe," I admit. "But it'll save a lot of other lives."

Preston hesitates, and I think he's going to say something, but he climbs into the truck without a word. I climb into the passenger seat and buckle in, then flash him a grin. "Let's do this."

"You're not scared?"

SELENA

I shrug. "Royal may not trust me, but I love him, and I want to do this for him. And for you. There's literally not one person I care about who won't be positively affected by this."

"You think he's going to trust you once he finds out you're with me?" he asks, pulling away from the curb and starting down Mill, lined with decrepit little houses until we reach the corner, where an old, abandoned two-story house sits, looking out of place. Its fancy trellises are gauzy with cobwebs, and the white paint is dingy with pollen and mold. The neighborhood kids say it's haunted, and as we turn the corner, I swear I see a shadow moving inside.

I shiver and turn back to Preston. "Royal will definitely be pissed at first," I admit. "But it's what he needs. He forgave me, but it's not enough. Just like I could choose to forgive him, but I couldn't have gotten back together with him without all the other stuff. He didn't ask forgiveness. He proved he loves me and knows what I need. Now it's my turn."

"And what happens the next time you piss him off?" Preston asks. "You think he won't do the exact same thing?"

"No," I say, shaking my head. "He wouldn't."

I know that now. I understand Royal, understand the monster that lives inside him. It's not his enemy. It's his protector. Once, it was my enemy, but now… Things have shifted. We're on equal footing now. I am not his plaything. I am his soul. His darkness swallowed me, and I am a part of him. Our broken pieces have been tossed together until there's no way to tell them apart, until we're both part of the same whole. And that pile of broken pieces is what the monster protects. It will protect me as it protects Royal. It won't turn against me, because that would hurt Royal, and the monster is a part of him—the only part that won't hurt him.

"What if I'm not there to find you?" Preston asks quietly.

"Then I'll find myself."

We pass Blue's old Cutlass heading back toward her house, and a lightness expands inside me. I wish I could take her with me, but of course she'd never leave Olive. But I'm free to leave this town now. I have friends, the privilege to come and go, and a car. I'm going on a trip, all the way to California. I've dreamed of this since I hopped a train with Blue the summer I moved next door. It feels so glamorous and daring.

I roll down the window even though it's cold out, letting the wind whip through my hair. The song by Dixie's cousin comes on, and I turn it up, thinking it's a good send-off.

Preston turns onto the ramp for the highway, rolling up my window from the control on his door and jabbing the button to turn the radio off. "Turn that shit off," he snaps.

"What, we can't have fun?" I ask. "This'll be the second time I've ever been out of Arkansas."

"It's a straight shot on I-40 all the way," he says. "Twenty-four hours drive. If we drive straight through, we should get there by early afternoon tomorrow."

"Not quite how I pictured a cross-country road trip, but okay," I say, rolling my eyes. "I can help drive. And if you want to stop somewhere, we can sleep in the car if you don't want to get a hotel."

"Why wouldn't we get a hotel?"

"I don't know," I say. "They're expensive?"

He chuckles and shakes his head. "I can afford a hotel, Harper."

"Okay," I say with a shrug. "Just thought I'd offer. I mean, I don't have money for a room, but I can totally sleep in the car if you want to get a room for yourself."

"You really think I'd let you sleep in my truck, in a parking lot, by yourself, while I'm in a hotel room?"

"Probably not," I admit. "But I wouldn't blame you. I basically bullied you into giving up your Thanksgiving break to drive me to California in your car, using your gas money, to put your cousin in danger, for my boyfriend."

"Yeah, you can sleep in the truck," he says, sliding off his mask and setting it on the console.

I laugh and turn the radio back on. "You can't have a road trip without music. It's illegal."

"It's fine," he says. "Just not that song."

"Not a Dolly fan?"

He scowls. "No."

"Oh yeah, Dixie said she went to Willow Heights," I say, putting the pieces together as I go. "She's only a few years older than us. You must have been in school at the same time. Did you know her?"

He glances sideways, his lips tightening. "Yeah, I knew her."

"I take it you didn't like her?"

"She dated my cousin."

"Devlin?" I ask, since I figure Colt would have said something if he'd dated someone who's low-key famous, and Sullivan would have been too young.

Preston just nods, staring straight ahead.

"Kinda cool that someone from Faulkner is on the radio, though," I say, messing with the controls.

He hands me his phone. "Just find a playlist on here. My pin is 3655."

"Can I make a road trip playlist?" I ask, accepting his phone and punching in the code.

"Just don't put that song on it."

"Wow, you *really* didn't like that girl," I say.

He doesn't say anything.

"Want to talk about it?" I ask.

"No," he says, glancing at me and then back to the road.

"I mean, she told you where your cousin is. That has to count for something, even if she… Broke his heart? Cheated on him?"

He doesn't answer.

"Ooh, with who?" I ask. "Colt? You? Did she choose him over you?"

"You're annoying when you're happy."

"Was it a Dolce?" I ask. "Did she cheat on him with Royal? Is that why you hate him most?"

"She didn't cheat on Devlin," he says. "And I hate Royal most because he's the one who did the most damage, and all because he's pissed that a plan *he* cooked up with their dad to ruin us went wrong."

"Your family tortured, beat, and raped him," I say incredulously. "Are you really blaming that on him?"

SELENA

"No," he grumbles, scowling at the road. "But I didn't do any of that, and he still blames me for it. You don't seem to care about that."

"I told him it wasn't you," I say, reaching over to touch his arm. "I know you're not the person he thinks you are. If I agreed with him, I wouldn't be here right now."

He lets out a little snort of breath and doesn't answer.

"So," I say, turning back to his phone. "What should I put on the playlist?"

*

We drive the rest of the day, listening to music and talking. At around midnight, I'm the one who caves and asks if we can stop for the night. I'm not used to sitting still for so long, and I'm going stir-crazy from being in the car all day. When people talk about road trips, they always sound fun, but I didn't factor in the amount of time spent getting there.

Preston finds an all-night boxing gym, and we go there to work off our energy and annoyance with each other after spending twelve hours straight in a car together.

"You're not too bad," I say after we've been at it for an hour and the owner comes to ask if we want to pay more or get out.

"You sound surprised," Preston says, undoing his gloves. I can tell he was pulling his punches, and even though he's got a serious disadvantage since he has no peripheral vision at all on his blind side, he held his own against me.

"I am," I say. "You ever fight at Slaughterpen?"

He snorts and holds apart the ropes for me to climb through. He hops down after me, and I find myself admiring him the way I sometimes do. He's so sophisticated, so thin compared to Royal's thuggish bulk, that sometimes I forget he's an athlete, too.

"What?" he asks, straightening.

"Nothing," I say, jerking my gaze away.

SELENA

"The Dolces own that place," he says, and it takes me a second to get my head on straight. I don't know what the fuck is wrong with me. I don't like Preston in that way, but his body is so familiar and inviting, and when it's all glistening with sweat, his shirt clinging to him, he looks good enough to lick.

Back at the hotel, he showers first, and I log into my *OnlyWords* account to text Royal after making sure the location is turned off. I don't want to deceive Royal, and I know he'll see this as a betrayal even though I would never cheat on him. I wish I could tell him, but after agonizing about this idea for the past few weeks, I came to the conclusion that I can't. There's no way I could give him the kind of hope I have. Because if it all comes to nothing, it would break him in a way nothing else has.

I know what a cruel tormentor hope can be. I can't put him through that, especially when my goal is to do the opposite—to heal him, to give him the one thing he needs most, the way he gave me Syracuse. But if Preston is wrong, if they're not alive or we can't find them, and I made Royal hope again, it will kill him. So, I have to find out for myself before I risk losing him to the darkness altogether.

When I step out of the bathroom after my own shower a few minutes later, a weird wave of *déjà vu* sweeps over me. How many nights did we shower separately, and I'd step out of the bathroom in a towel, and Preston would tell me to get on the bed on all fours, call me his good girl as he slid his cock into me from behind?

Maybe he's thinking the same thing, because he sits up from his bed and smiles when he sees me. "Look at us," he says. "Just the two of us, like it always was."

"Yeah," I say, glancing back and forth between the two queen beds. At least he didn't shamelessly get a room with one bed and pretend it's all the hotel had available. Maybe my lecture about consent that night on the bridge hit home.

"What do you say?" he asks, pulling back the blankets. "One more for old time's sake?"

SELENA

I roll my eyes, forcing a laugh. "First of all, you're shameless. Second, what happened to being all worried Royal would kill me?"

"I thought you said Royal didn't get to tell you what to do anymore."

"Doesn't mean he won't try."

"He doesn't have to know."

"Preston…" I sink down on the edge of his bed. "I love Royal. Maybe I love you, too, but it's in a completely different way. And I don't think you love me that way, either.

"Who said anything about love?" he asks, giving the corner of my towel a little tug.

"I did," I say, taking his hand. "I'm not what you want, anyway."

He turns his hand over, so his palm is facing up, and links his fingers through mine. "You could be what I want."

"Want me to tell you what a very wise man once told me?"

He gives me a suspicious look. "Probably not."

I squeeze his hand, my heart aching for him the way it always does when I think of how good we should be together. "He told me to find my sun," I say. "Maybe it's time you found yours."

Preston looks away, but not before I see the grimace on his face. "I don't think my sun would want to be found. Not by me."

"I bet you're wrong."

"I couldn't ask her for that," he says quietly.

"For what?" I ask. "To love you?"

"To live with this," he says, gesturing to his face.

"She won't care," I say. "Not if she loves you."

He glares at me, retracting his hand. "We both know that's a lie."

"I'm not going to pretend looks don't matter," I say. "It's part of the attraction, sure. I'm just like any other girl. A hot guy gets me going. I love the way Royal looks. But it's not the reason I love him."

"But you love the way he looks."

"True," I admit. "But I wouldn't love him any less if he didn't look like that."

"Would he still ask you to love him, though?" Preston asks. "If he looked like a monster, would he want you to be stuck with that for the rest of your life?"

"Yes," I say without hesitation.

"Then he's a selfish bastard."

"True," I say. "But I love him just the same. And for what it's worth, I think you're beautiful. If she's your sun, she won't care how you look, either. She'll love you just the same."

"If I love her, I couldn't ask her to," he says.

"Then maybe she's not your sun," I say. "But there's someone out there who will be. You should find her. Find your sun. That person who shines just for you."

"I don't know," he says. "I did something pretty bad to her."

I can't help but laugh.

He gives me a look. "You think that's funny?"

"If I can forgive Royal for what he did, I'm sure she can forgive you for whatever you did to her."

"She deserves a happily ever after with the perfect Prince Charming," he says. "All I can give her is the Beast."

"Not every girl wants the perfect Prince Charming," I say, standing and snagging Royal's T-shirt from my suitcase. "Some girls prefer the Beast."

SELENA

twenty-one

Devlin Darling

I straighten from bending over the crib and move slowly backwards, waiting for the wail of ten thousand banshees to erupt from my little princess. I have to walk her to sleep, then lay her down while hovering over her, keeping her pressed to my chest where she can feel my heartbeat. Then by increments I let go, moving slowly up from her until only my hands cradle her. Getting the hands out and her covered is the hard part, but sometimes, she waits until she's all tucked in and snug and I think I'm in the clear before she wakes the neighborhood.

Just as I back into the hall, a knock comes at the front door. I wince, my first thought that it'll wake the baby.

The next thought is far more terrifying.

Every muscle in my body tenses, and I freeze, listening for a sound past the drumming of my heartbeat in my ears. We don't like people knocking on our door.

Crystal steps out of our bedroom, her eyes wide. "Did you hear that?"

I nod, my jaw tight.

"Should we answer?" she asks.

We have a plan in place for this, though hardly anyone knocks on doors anymore. Sometimes, though, it's the termite inspectors or landlord or someone else important. Crystal never opens the door when I'm not home. If I'm home, and it's daytime, we can open the door. We have a code phrase in case it's someone suspicious.

But it's already past dark, and no one should be knocking right now. Especially not someone persistent enough to knock again, this time harder than the first time. My heart picks up speed.

I shake my head at Crystal, edging down the hallway toward the safe. We keep it near the front door, and there's a reason for that. I crouch and quickly put in the combination.

"Give me the pistol," she whispers.

I quickly load it and hand it to her. She holds it pointed at the floor and takes off the safety. She'd never even held a gun before we moved here, but then, there was a lot of things her family never let her do, like driving a car and falling in love. Now, she's as good a shot as I am, and I grew up in Arkansas. I learned to shoot before I learned to throw a football.

The knock comes again, this time at the back door. A quiet little wail comes from the crib down the hall, and I want to shoot the bastard just for waking the baby. She's just getting started. Pretty soon, the neighbors will take care of this asshole for me.

"Watch the nursery," I tell Crystal while I quickly load my own weapon. I close the safe and turn to the back door.

"I know you're in there," calls a deep voice from the back door. "Open the door, Devlin."

My whole body freezes. Crystal's eyes go wide, and she shakes her head. "I'm coming with you," she says. "I've got your back."

I've played this scene in my head a thousand times over the past three years. Some part of me always knew it was coming. We have every scenario planned, from what happens if one of us dies, to both of us, to if we kill whoever comes. But it never felt entirely real until this moment.

I grab Crystal, pulling her in and kissing her hard on the mouth, knowing it could be the last time.

"No," I say, letting her go at last, when someone pounds on the front door again. "They won't hurt you if you let them take me. Go into the nursery and don't use the gun unless they try to hurt one of you."

"Devlin Darling and Crystal Dolce, get your asses out here," the voice outside booms again. They've just blown our cover, that's for damn sure. Even if the neighbors think they're at the wrong house, we can't risk it. If we make it out alive, we'll have to move to a new state, change our names again, start all over.

SELENA

The high-pitched wails have risen in volume, but they're only halfway to maximum. Whoever's at the door must hear them, though. They know we wouldn't leave a baby alone. And it's not some random person here to sell something. They know who we are.

They found us.

We had three good years though. In truth, it's three years longer than I expected, than I had any right to ask for. But it's a hundred years less than I wanted.

I kiss Crystal one more time. I can feel her shaking as she holds onto me, and I want to shoot through the door and kill them all just for scaring my girl that way.

Instead, I gently tug her arms from around my neck and press my lips to her forehead. "Take good care of yourself."

I move to the door, edging along the wall and then pushing aside the edge of the curtain over the small window at the top. There's a girl standing on the porch, one I've never seen before. Whoever was yelling must have gone around the back again. I don't know how many they brought, though.

"Who is it?" Crystal whispers.

Of course she didn't do what I fucking told her to. She's at my back, her gun drawn, ready to go down in a blaze of glory with me. By now I should know better than to think she'd do anything less.

"I don't know," I tell her.

A sharp whistle sounds outside, and I disengage the locks except for the chain, easing the door open.

"We're armed," I say, pushing the muzzle of the gun through the crack so she can see I'm not bullshitting. "What do you want? Name the amount he's paying, and we'll double it."

We thought they stopped looking, but maybe not. Maybe they've had bounty hunters and private investigators crawling the country all this time. But those people work for a living, and if I can pay to shut them up, I'll do that before I kill them.

"What?" the girl demands. "I'm not here for money."

I hear another set of footsteps on the porch, soft and quick and familiar.

SELENA

"Devlin, what the fuck," comes a voice from the past, one I recognize all too well now that he's not yelling.

I don't even think about how stupid the next thing I do is. I just undo the chain lock and pull open the door. Preston steps past the girl and yanks me into his arms, squeezing me so hard I can't breathe.

"Guess it's the right house after all," says the girl behind him. "You must be Crystal."

"Who are you?" Crystal asks. "Why are you here?"

"I'm Royal's girlfriend," the stranger says. "He needs you to come home now."

twenty-two

Royal Dolce

"I'm going to take care of Dad."

All three of my brothers turn to me. I pick up my beer from the wooden ledge that runs along one wall of the game room and take a drink.

"Take care of him?" King asks, his accent stronger now that he's been back in New York for a few years, hanging with the old men on the Valenti side. He sounds like a regular gangster. He rests the end of his pool stick on the floor and narrows his eyes at me, waiting for a response.

"Yeah," I say, sliding off the stool to take my shot. I settle a ball gently in the side pocket.

"Take care of him how?" Duke asks, swaying on his feet.

SELENA

"How do you think?" I ask, losing focus in my annoyance. I miss my third shot and give his shoulder a little shove. "Line up your shot."

Duke stumbles to the table and sways as he surveys his options. "Are we solids?"

He's well on his way to following in Ma's footsteps. She barely made it through the parade. Now she's happily tuned out, numbed by enough booze and pills to make sure she doesn't even dream. I wonder what she'd dream about if she could. Probably a life where she doesn't even have to see us on holidays. Dad wanted heirs, and she did her duty and gave him five. We're his problem now—and he's ours.

"You're going to kill Dad?" Baron asks, not moving from his barstool. "I don't think that's the best answer."

"I wasn't asking your permission," I snap.

King watches me thoughtfully, chalking the end of his cue. "What did he do?"

"You know what he did," I grit out, glaring back at him. Besides Dad himself, King's the only one who knows the full truth—or he was before I told Harper.

He nods and follows Duke's missed shot with one of his own. After sinking it, he circles the table to line up the next one.

"Because he touched Harper?" Baron asks, picking up his sucker. "That's not really fair. Everyone's fucked Harper, and Dad's always part of our Darling revenges."

"She's not a Darling," I growl at him.

"Is that why?" King asks, stepping back after setting me up for a great shot, if Baron doesn't fuck the table up too bad for once. There's no chance of that. Baron will clean the rest of the table in one turn, like he always does. That's why he goes last.

"It's on the list of reasons," I admit.

"He's not the one who told her about the Hockington," Duke says.

"What?" King asks, his voice low and sharp.

"Shut up," I tell my youngest brother, turning my glare on him.

He's too drunk to notice. "Dad's clients that needed a little push," Duke says. "He sent Royal to wine and dine them at the best hotel in Faulkner."

SELENA

King turns to me, his Adam's apple moving up and down as he swallows. I want to beat Duke's ass for that, but he assumes we tell each other everything. After all, we all knew that was King's job when he was around. Why wouldn't they all know I took over? Even though they didn't know about me until Harper told Mr. D, Duke wouldn't think of that right now. He's too wasted.

"You've been going to the Hockington?" King asks me quietly.

"What about it?" I ask, not dropping his gaze. "You did it."

"Dad promised he wouldn't make any of you do it after I was gone."

We stare at each other for a minute. Then I shrug and stand when Baron finishes mopping the table. "Somebody had to do it," I say. "Dad wasn't going to. He's married. It's adultery."

"Unless she's underage," Duke says, cracking up. "Then it doesn't count."

King glances at him and then back to me. "He shouldn't have asked you."

"Yeah, well, he did," I say, starting to rack the balls for another game. "And I wasn't going to let the twins do it. They're fucked up enough already."

"Hey," Duke slurs, fishing a few balls from the corner pocket and rolling them to me. "I would've fucked them if you didn't want to. You can learn a lot from a cougar."

"They've got the moves," Baron agrees when Duke throws his arm around his twin.

Only King is watching me with that quiet intensity. He knows what it's like. He knows why it matters.

"I killed our cousin," he says after a minute. "It's how I got my bones."

"What about it?"

I'm being a belligerent ass. I know he's telling me something he loses sleep over, but I'm too pissed at my brothers for telling him. Now he's looking at me like I'm someone to be pitied, like I'm an abused puppy or some shit.

"I'll do it," he says. "You shouldn't have that on you, Royal. You've done enough."

SELENA

I straighten, staring across the pool table at him. "You're going to kill Dad?"

"Yeah," he says, raising his chin and staring back at me with hooded eyes. "I'm the oldest. It's my job to protect you."

"You're a Valenti now."

"We all have Valenti blood, and we all have Dolce blood," he says. "I'm one of Al's men, but I'm my own man, too. If I tell him I have a job to do, he'll tell me to take care of it."

"To take care of us," Duke says quietly, swinging his beer up to his lips and taking a swig. Baron stands soberly beside him, their arms still over each other's shoulders.

"A man has a right to protect his family," I mutter, the thing I say to the twins that King and Dad have said to me. Our defense for everything we've done.

"You're really going to kill Dad for asking you to fuck a few clients to help close a deal?" Baron asks, tossing his sucker stem in the goblet with the others. He'd never let anyone know, but he's the closest to our parents, the one most devastated by their split, by both of their actions since. I always hated Dad, always saw what he was about. If there's one place where Baron has blinders, where he's not detached and analytical, it's about our parents.

"If you'd like to get a list of his crimes together to read him before his execution, it'll be real fucking long," I say. "But knock yourself out."

I return my stick to the rack and walk out because I'm fucking done with that conversation. I don't need King's help. I don't need anyone's help. I respect them—even the twins—enough that I recognize they deserve to know. That's all. They're fucked up enough already. I know the reasons, understand them, and I give them a pass more often than I should. But I've already made them kill a man. They just turned eighteen. It's time to let them grow up, and that means they get the burden of the truth, just like the rest of us.

I stop outside the door that used to belong to my own twin. After a moment, I turn the knob and push it open. For a fraction of a second, my brain skips, like it always does, and it's like she's there on the bed, half buried in a mountain of pillows and fluffy blankets, with a bowl of ice cream and her laptop on her knees.

Then I blink, and it's just the guest room that Ma had converted after Crystal died, when we knew she wasn't coming back. She didn't come to the funeral, but the next time we visited, Ma had called in a decorator to redo the room completely, as if she couldn't bear to leave even a trace of her daughter's memory alive.

I hear footsteps behind me, but I don't turn. I will my brother to keep walking, to let me have a moment here, trying to find that fleeting memory one more time, so she'll be alive for one more moment, if only in my head.

"Royal."

I turn and glare at King. "What?"

"I'm sorry."

We stand there in the hall, the words hanging between us like something dark and ugly, a different kind of monster. The men in our family don't apologize.

I shrug. "You didn't do shit."

"I should have known he'd do the same to you," King says quietly.

King doesn't lose his temper like I do. Even when he'd jump into a fight to have my back, he did it in a more calculated way, like Baron. But unlike Baron, there's rage simmering beneath his cool surface when he looks at me now.

"It's just fucking," I say. "It doesn't matter."

"It fucks with your head," he says.

We've never talked about this. We all knew King did it for Dad. He was the one sent to seduce the women because he's the perfect candidate. He's smooth and charming when he needs to be, detached when he's finished a job. He's not a loose cannon like Duke or a sadist like Baron or a ticking time bomb like me. Dad loves to remind me how much better at it King always was.

But maybe he's the perfect man for the job because he was groomed to fill the role, trained to do a job until he did it flawlessly.

"You seem to be doing okay," I say finally. "You have a wife and a son."

"You're doing better, too," he says. "You have Harper."

We stand for a minute in silence. "Yeah," I say at last, turning to close Crystal's door. "Until I kill her, too."

"Why would you do that?"

I shrug. "Probably by accident. I do that to girls."

"You didn't kill Crystal."

We never say her name. It's the unspoken truth in every room I walk into, the weight of my presence at every family dinner. I'm the reason she's not here. I'm the reason Ma doesn't have a daughter and had to erase the evidence from the room.

King's watching me intently, but this time, I can't meet his gaze. I just shake my head, glaring at the end of the hall. I only speak of her to Harper.

"You're the only one who believes that," King says at last.

"Don't treat me like a fucking child," I snap. "Everyone knows I did."

"No one thinks it's your fault except you."

"It doesn't matter what anyone thinks," I say. "If I held her under water and drowned her when no one else was there to see it, I still killed her."

"But you didn't do that."

"I might as well have."

"But you didn't."

"I did the equivalent."

"You didn't."

I stare him down, pulling myself to my full height so I'm looking down at him. He doesn't even blink.

"I told her she was dead to me," I say slowly. "And now she is."

"I got myself shot," he says. "I was the one in charge of protecting her, and I didn't. I didn't get her back in the car before we left."

I just blink at him, probably looking as stupid as his words sound. "I left her there," I point out.

"I let you leave her there."

"I told her she wasn't a Dolce anymore."

"I sat in the car like a pussy and didn't protect any of you."

SELENA

"You had a bullet in you."

"I let one little bullet stop me."

For another minute, we stand there in the hall, facing each other, not speaking.

Finally, I break the silence. "You think it's *your* fault?"

"I think Crystal chose herself for the first and only time in her life," he says. "I regret a lot of things, but one of the things I regret most is knowing she didn't get to do it again."

"She died for it," I point out.

"I blame myself for forcing her to make that choice more than I do for what happened to her that night," he says quietly.

I don't have an answer for that.

"I know you think you have to watch out for our brothers," he says. "And I'm partially to blame for that. But sometimes, you come before even family."

"That's why you wanted to work for Uncle Al," I say. "Even though I would have been better at it."

"No," he says. "That's the opposite. I wouldn't ask anyone to do what I do. Killing someone… It does something to you."

"I know."

We regard each other carefully.

"You didn't kill Crystal," he says again.

"I'm not talking about her."

King steps across the hall and drags me into his arms. There are a lot of things the men in our family don't do, but showing affection isn't one of them. "We'll get Dad," he says, holding me around the neck with one arm and gripping my other hand tight in his, pressing our clenched fists between our chests like a promise. "I'll fly back with you, and I'll take care of it."

"No." I grip his hand just as tightly, pounding him on the back once and then just holding on. I can't remember the last time I hugged him when it wasn't an obligation. But somehow, this thing that's been between us all these years is melting away now that we've shone a light on it, given it a name.

Guilt.

SELENA

"It's family business," I say, releasing him at last. "We'll take care of it together."

twenty-three

Harper Apple

"I got something for you," Preston says, handing me his phone.

"Your phone?" I ask. I've been texting Royal on it all week, since my own phone is at my house. I feel worse the longer the lie continues, but I don't want to explain over a text where I am. I know he'll be pissed, and I'll deal with it when I get home. Crystal insisted she wants to tell them herself, so I backed off and agreed not to tell anyone we'd found them. It's their family shit. I'm just the messenger.

Right now, I don't want to think about what happens to the messenger. I want to sit on the pier and watch the sun setting over the water, the colors breathtakingly beautiful over the rippling water and the stones jutting up

SELENA

from the sand. I thought California would be warm, and I might get to swim in the ocean, but we're both in sweaters.

"A plane ticket," he says. "You can ride with Devlin and them if you want, but I thought you'd be more comfortable…"

"Without a screaming heathen in the car with me?"

He cracks a little smile. "I haven't been around a baby in a while, but she seems extra loud."

"She's pretty extra," I agree. "But I don't know anything about babies, either."

We sit in silence for a minute, and then Preston takes my hand. "It's just one ticket, Harper. Are you okay flying alone?"

"I'll be fine," I say. "But why am I not going home with you? Because your truck will be so loaded down with their stuff?"

"No. They'll ship anything they can't take in their car."

I swallow hard, not wanting to accept what he's saying. Suddenly, my throat is tight, and I think I might break down again. Every time I think I've moved past that stage, something comes up and knocks me on my ass again.

"You're not coming home," I whisper, staring at his long, elegant fingers linked through mine.

"No."

We sit in silence for a moment, watching the glowing orange sun sink to the horizon.

"You found what you came for," he says quietly. "I didn't."

"What about fighting to the end?" I ask, trying not to sound as fucking desperate as I feel. "Never giving up on your town?"

"Believe it or not, I used to be the one who wanted to get out most," he says.

"Really?" I ask, pulling back. "More than Colt?"

"More than Colt or Devlin or anyone," he says. "Staying became my responsibility at some point, but that doesn't mean I stopped wanting to leave. It just means I couldn't. I had to protect my family."

"And what about them?" I ask. "Your sister and... And Magnolia?"

"Lindsey graduated," he says. "She's away at school except for holidays."

I sniffle, blinking back tears. "And Magnolia?"

Preston squeezes my hand again. "I did the best I could for three years, even if it wasn't much. It's Devlin's turn now."

"What am I going to do without you?" I ask quietly, letting myself be selfish at last, ask the question I really want answered.

"The same thing you've always done. Kick ass and take names."

"But how can I do that without you?" I ask. I bite back the urge to remind him what he said before—what if Royal turns on me again? What if finding his sister is not what he needs? What if seeing that she's happy and flourishing with a family while he's been devastated beyond repair for years is the last straw, the thing that finally breaks him completely?

Preston is my safety net, my safe space, my solace and quiet, just as Royal is my thrill of danger, my tempest, my chaos and passion. I need them both for different reasons. Royal brings me back, and Preston lets me retreat when it's too much. He tended me when I was too broken to take care of even myself, and he never made it feel like charity. He gave me so much and asked nothing in return. Not just clothes and jewelry, but a place to hide from the monsters that lurked in our town. He took me to the place where I was attacked and helped me let go, even knowing it would make me closer to Royal.

I know that he loves me in the ways he's able, just as I love him. He loves me enough to let me go, knowing Royal is my sun.

And I love him enough to do the same.

I lean my head on his shoulder, and we watch in silence as the barest sliver of sun lingers on the horizon for just one more moment, and then it slips away and is gone.

"I love you," I say. "Maybe not in the way either of us want, but I do."

SELENA

"I do too," he says, sliding an arm around my back. "But you never needed me, Harper. What you need has always been right there inside you."

"I'm my own sun."

He kisses the top of my head. "It's time I followed mine."

We sit there for a few more minutes, our arms around each other in the cold, dampness of evening, watching the streaks of color light up the sky and dance across the rippling surface of the sea. I smile out over the water, hardly able to comprehend my gratitude. Last year, I'd never left Arkansas. I was stuck and poor and desperate. Now, I've been all the way from one coast to the other, with two very different, very damaged men. Men who dragged me to the depths of hell and helped me crawl back out, dragging my broken, damaged soul behind me like a mangled limb.

"You know who told me I should do this?" Preston asks, giving me a little squeeze. "A very wise woman."

"God, I fucking hate you," I say, laughing and wiping my eyes.

"Don't give yourself too much credit," he says. "I talked to Devlin for a long time, too. I think I'll find her, and this time, I know how to keep her."

"How's that?"

He shrugs. "I just won't let her go."

"That's not really how that works."

"It worked for Royal," he says. "Seeing y'all… If he can love you enough to make you forgive him, anything's possible. Maybe she can forgive me, too."

"If she won't, you come get me, and I'll kick her ass," I say.

He laughs quietly. "Deal. And don't worry, I'll be home soon."

"Good," I say. "Because if you don't come home, I'll come get you and kick *your* ass."

"I'd expect nothing less," he says.

As the last colors in the sky turn to streaks of purple and bruise-blue, Preston stands and holds out a hand. I take it and let him pull me up. Then I throw my arms around him, holding on for one more minute.

SELENA

"And Harper," he says. "If I don't come back for a while... You can visit me here, you know. The world doesn't cease to exist at the Faulkner city limits. You should get out of that town, too."

"I am," I say. "I'm going to Syracuse next year."

There's a silence while those words sink in for both of us. I don't think I'd really let myself decide, let myself believe it was real, until this moment. But I'd be beyond stupid to turn that opportunity down. This isn't like when I turned down Preston's offer to include me in the Darling fortune if I was one of them. They didn't give a shit about me, even when my mother begged for help as a homeless sixteen-year-old mom after two men from that family had their fun with her.

Royal's always given a fuck about me, even when I hated it and long before I understood it. Royal loves me and wants to take care of me. There's no reason to say no to that except stubborn pride, and I'm done trying to do it all on my own. Royal is part of my life now, and letting him in and needing him the way he needs me doesn't make me weak. Admitting I'm not bulletproof, that I need help, takes a hell of a lot more humbling and strength than pushing everyone away. Being strong enough to be let down my guard and be vulnerable even after I've been hurt, to let people in even knowing some of them will hurt me again, and to forgive them when they do, is the hardest thing I'll ever do.

Walking away from Faulkner is easy in comparison.

When Preston turns on the truck, the song by Dolly Beckett is playing again. I reach to turn it off, but he catches my hand.

"Leave it."

"It's her, isn't it?" I ask. "She's your sun."

"Maybe," he admits. "Someday.'

We ride back and park in front of the little yellow house on a quiet, residential street. It's no bigger than my house, but the similarities end there. While my house is a drab, decrepit ranch-style brick house, theirs is bright and airy, and even though it's pretty old, it's been kept up, so it's more vintage than shabby and depressing. We have tiny windows, half of them fitted with AC units trailing condensation stains, while this one has white shutters and curtains and little flower boxes. The house is cute, but it's nothing like the fancy Darling houses in Faulkner.

We spent most of Sunday driving, and the entirety of Monday running around trying to get information. Preston spent hours combing through pictures of the people who work at Nyso Records and finally found the guy Dolly mentioned. Then it took a hell of a good sob story and a healthy sum of cash to get an address. Once we found them, it took a couple more days of filling them in on everything that's happened since they left and convincing them to come back even though it's not safe yet.

But I know it'll all be worth it—for all of us.

Either that, or the biggest mistake any of us have ever made.

twenty-four

Crystal Darling

What do you do when your whole world shifts in a moment? When the past catches up, and suddenly it's your present? Your life is uprooted, overturned, packed in the back of a Honda. And then you have to decide if you'll run again, the way you always did, or go crawling back.
Last time we ran.
This time we crawl.

"If there's one thing I've learned over the past few years, it's that I don't need much to be happy," Devlin says, depositing a key fob into my hand. "But damn it feels good to spend money again."

"Are you saying love isn't all you need?" I tease, smiling up at him. We're outside a Mercedes dealership, having just made our first major purchase since my wedding ring.

SELENA

"Sugar, your love is more than all I need." His hands fall on my hips, and he backs me against the car, kissing me hard and deep right there on the car lot. My thighs open for him, and he rocks against me just once, enough for me to feel that he's hard. My breath comes quick as his hand wraps gently around my throat.

"Any questions?" he asks, his hips keeping me pinned, his eyes shimmering with lust as they bore into mine.

"No questions," I whisper, my thighs trembling and wetness blooming between. My body still responds to his touch the way it did when we met, before he or I knew how much I liked his hand around my throat.

"There better not be," he says, slowly drawing back. "Or I'll bend you over and prove it right here and now, for all the world to see, Crystal Darling."

The name makes me weak, and I close my eyes and draw a shuddering breath. I didn't know how much I wanted my own name—the one that belongs to me and the one that tells the world I belong to him—until I had it.

"Call me that again, and I might let you," I say.

"Patience, Sugar," he says, his lips skimming over mine. "I'll show you later."

He circles the van and opens the door for me, and I climb in, resisting the urge to slide a hand between my thighs and relieve the ache his touch puts in me.

"Ready?" Devlin asks, swinging into his seat.

"I'm ready," I say, smiling at him even as my heart is somersaulting. I'm not sure if I'm more nervous, excited, or terrified. Last time I saw Faulkner, it was in the rearview of a car that barely made it across the state line before it crapped out on us. Last time, I was disowned and disgraced and desperate, a girl with no options. Now I'm a woman, a wife, a mother.

I won't have to wonder for long how my family has changed, either. We're thirty minutes from Faulkner city limits, having just transferred everything into our new car. We already went to the courthouse to fill out the application to change our names. It's over.

We're almost home.

"Do you think they'll be happy?" I ask. "Or mad?"

SELENA

Devlin reaches over to take my hand and squeeze it. "They'll be happy," he promises. "When I saw Preston, I didn't care about him finding us or yelling our names down the street. I was just so fucking happy to see him."

I glance in the back to make sure the kids are sleeping and didn't hear his potty mouth. Devlin grins when he catches me. "You're going to be fine, Sugar," he promises. "We're all going to be fine."

twenty-five

Royal Dolce

"Did you see your mom for Thanksgiving?" I ask Harper as we turn into my neighborhood.

"Do you already know the answer to that?" she asks.

"I know you didn't take your phone with you."

"You asshole," she says. "Preston was right."

"Preston?" I grit out, pulling into our driveway. I ignore the eyesore of charred rubble next door the way I always do. Someone needs to take care of that, though. If they leave it there much longer, they're going to find Preston Darling's body mummified in the ashes when they come to take it away.

"Yeah," she says. "He told me to leave my phone at home because you'd be tracking it."

"You spent Thanksgiving with the Darlings?"

SELENA

"With Preston," she says, reaching over to put her hand on my thigh.

I shove it away, shutting off the engine and turning to her. "Did you fuck him?"

"What is wrong with you, Royal?" she demands. "I'm not going to fuck your enemy."

"Why would I believe you?" I ask, staring at her, that cold pit opening in my chest like it does every time I'm reminded that I can keep her forever, but I can't make her loyal, can't make her want to be with me the way I want her.

"Because I'm not lying," she says just as flatly, refusing to drop my gaze.

"But you have no problem telling me you're spending Thanksgiving with your ma, and then going to his house instead, when I'm out of state and you know I can't do shit about it."

"You can be pissed," she says. "But I didn't fuck him or anyone, and I'm not going to. Ever. You're it for me Royal. Don't you get that?"

I climb out of the car and slam the door. The day is cool but clammy with humidity, which made the chill stick to our skin at the river. "You need to go home."

"Okay," Harper says, climbing out and coming around the car. "That's fair. But it's fair for me to be pissed that you're tracking my phone, too. How long have you been following me around?"

"I wasn't following you," I snap. "I needed to know where you were because you were a danger to yourself." All the peace from the river is gone, even though we spent the afternoon there. It just takes five minutes to ruin it all.

"When did you put a tracker on my phone?" she insists.

"When I pulled you out of Preston's truck."

I can see her calculating how long it's been since the day she tried suicide. Realizing that's why I texted her when she went to the quarry after that. I already knew where she was, I just had to know she was safe. That's how I knew she'd gone back to Faulkner High, too, and

SELENA

why I tracked her down there. She doesn't belong there. She's a Willow Heights girl now.

She turns and walks out of the open garage to the Escalade parked in the grass off the side of the drive. I follow her because I can't fucking let her walk away. "Are you going back to him now?"

"Royal," she says, sounding pissed. "I'm not fucking Preston. And maybe I'd explain things if you didn't fly off the handle like this at the slightest mention of him."

"You can see where I'd get that idea," I say. "Seeing how many times you've fucked him before."

"When I wasn't with you," she growls.

"Are you with me?"

She stares at me, then swallows. "Yes," she says. "Aren't you with me?"

"I wasn't the one fucking someone else all summer."

"You fucked Lo."

"Once," I grit out. "And it was before anything happened with you."

She takes a deep breath, squeezing her hands into fists. "I went on a road trip with Preston over the break.

I'm telling you this, even though I know you'll be pissed, because I don't want secrets between us. But I would never cheat on you. I had my reasons, and you'll have to trust me on that. Nothing happened between us. We're friends, and that's all."

Something shifts inside me, but all I feel is a raw sensation, like two boulders grinding together where my heart should be. I reach for the dark shadow inside me, the monster who keeps me from doing something worse than what I've already done. I shake my head in disbelief. "And I'm supposed to take your word for that?"

"Yes."

"Get off my property," I say, my voice matching the cold blankness that's taking over my body. I'm not even surprised at her betrayal. I've expected it all along.

"Can you give me the benefit of the doubt?" she asks. "Just this once, can you stop being such an impossible dick and trust that I'm not out to hurt you?"

"I have no reason to trust anything you say," I answer. "It's always been a lie. You've always been a lie. Why would this be any different?"

SELENA

"Because I fucking love you."

We stare at each other a long moment, the dense, cold air around us going still while we absorb what she said.

Then I shake my head. "You don't know the meaning of that word any more than I do. Now go home."

"Fine," she says. "Then I hate you. We both understand that one, don't we?"

Before I can answer, a van turns into the driveway. Probably one of Dad's or Baron's connections. Harper swallows and steps back toward her car, this look in her eyes I haven't seen in a long time—fear and trepidation mingling together. It makes a knot of dread fall into my stomach like a lead weight.

"You can get around them," I say, jerking my chin at the Escalade. "Go. I'm sure you have a few Darlings left to fuck on your rotation."

"Fuck you, Royal," she says. "I didn't have to tell you."

"Yeah, and you probably shouldn't have."

The van stops on the gravel drive, and the passenger door swings open.

"Royal…" Harper starts.

I barely hear her. I'm staring at the girl who just climbed down from the passenger seat. Her hair is light brown, almost blonde, but she looks just like…

Like…

I shake my head. A guy with dark hair climbs out of the driver's seat. I barely see him, either. I can't stop looking at the ghost standing in my driveway, floating toward me. She slips her hand into his, like it can keep her from floating off into the grey sky, a circus balloon that disappears into the endless blue, burned up in the atmosphere without leaving a single trace that it ever existed.

Time stops. Then she's a few paces off, just staring back at me.

"Royal," she says. "You're… Huge."

"You're alive."

She takes a tentative step toward me, and the monster inside me rises toward the surface. He was there to catch

SELENA

the pieces of me that crumbled away when she was gone, when she wasn't the glue that held together whatever pieces of sanity we shared. Without her, they fell endlessly until there was nothing left of the boy she knew. Little Royal is gone. There's only me now, me and the monster that is still here, still collecting the pieces to hold for me when I can't.

And now they've all escaped his clutches, an avalanche of who I was rushing to bury me alive.

I turn to the garage, but my car is inside, blocked by the huge van in the driveway. I keep turning, until I've almost made a full circle and I'm facing Harper. "Give me your keys."

Without a word, she hands me her keys. I climb into the Escalade, back it down the side of the driveway until I'm past the van, all the way to the road. Then I turn onto it and drive away, away from my house and the girl I tried to kill and the girl I didn't mean to kill. I won't think about them, about the girl who said she loved me when that's impossible, as impossible as the dead girl in my driveway, the specter of my life's deepest regret, my darkest shame, my unforgivable sin.

I press down on the gas pedal until everything is a grey blur of dead trees and blank sky on either side of me, as if I can drive fast enough to turn back time, as if I can break through a barrier in time, in reality, and find myself on the bank of that river three years ago, when I lost her the first time. Then it might all make sense.

As I fly around a corner and shoot forward, the tires eating up the pavement, I think about what King said just a few days ago. That his biggest regret was not letting Crystal choose herself. Not letting her choose Devlin.

But she did choose him. She chose him, and she left, because she knew what would happen if she didn't.

We'd kill him.

We would have killed him, not for any of us, but for Dad. He's the one who hated the Darlings. He's the one who set all this in motion.

That's where it all started.

And that's where it ends.

SELENA

twenty-six

Crystal Darling

"What just happened?" I ask, my voice shaking as I try to wrap my head around the fact that my brother, my twin, still hates me. Even after three years, he hasn't forgiven me for choosing Devlin. He wouldn't let me touch him. He turned away when I went to hug him, to make amends in some way. I've pictured this moment a thousand times, ten thousand, but I never imagined it would hurt so much.

Sometimes, I even let myself picture him happy. Like Devlin when he saw Preston, I pictured Royal being so relieved to have me back that he forgot all that. He'd pick me up and spin me around, and we'd laugh and cry and hold onto each other for so long, both of us apologizing and saying how stupid we were.

Instead, I get this.

This stranger, a girl who tracked me halfway across the country to tell me Royal needed me, when it's perfectly clear that he doesn't.

"What just happened is called consequences," Harper says in her usual slightly confrontational tone. "While you went off to live your fairytale life, Royal's turned into a fucking monster who's been terrorizing this town. We told you that already."

"But… I didn't think he'd still hate me," I admit quietly.

"He doesn't know how to love," Harper says. "But he loves you in his fucked up way. That's why he did all this—because the Darlings took you from him."

Devlin slides his arm around my waist, drawing me against him. "Give him some space. I'm sure he'll come around."

"That actually went better than I expected," Harper says. "Since you're both still alive."

A quiet squall sounds in the back seat of the van, and I turn, grateful to have something to keep me occupied

SELENA

and ground me in the present moment. This is familiar. It needs to be done now. There's no time for panicking. Take care of the kids. They come first. They need me.

I can worry about about Royal later.

"Believe it or not, the rest of your brothers are worse," Harper says. "But less likely to murder you, so there's that."

"Royal?" calls a voice from somewhere in the back of the garage.

Harper goes to talk to my brother, though I can't tell which one from here, with the echo of the garage and the fussing in the van. I take a second to breathe, trying to steady myself. Royal used to do that, to be my anchor.

Now, I have Devlin and our kids. It's not the same, but I've learned to fill the gaps, to be my own anchor when I have to.

I set our daughter in his arms, and he holds her up on his shoulder, pulling me in. "You okay?"

"As okay as I can be," I say, taking a shaky breath. "Was this a terrible idea?"

"No," he says firmly. "You heard what Preston said back home. We had to do something."

"You're right," I say, reassured by his certainty.

It's too late now, anyway. It was too late from the moment Harper knocked on our door. Even if we disappeared again, they'd never stop looking this time. They know we're alive.

I turn and find myself facing my oldest brother across a stretch of white gravel in the drive.

"It's really you," he says, not moving toward me.

I swallow, gripping the baby in my arms. A woman emerges from the garage, struggling to push a stroller over the gravel. King takes it and they move forward until they're only a few paces from us. I look back and forth between this stranger and my brother, my protector, who said love wasn't for people like us.

"You had a kid," King says, staring at me.

"You fell in love," I say.

"Yeah, I did," he says, his face serious as he pulls the dark-haired girl against his side. "This is Eliza. My wife."

SELENA

"Nice to meet you," she says, a heavy New York accent coloring her words. "We've got a kid, too. How old's yours? I bet they'd like to meet their cousin."

A sister-in-law. Cousins. It's more than I could have dreamed of. A family—a whole huge family again, not just the one Devlin and I are making for ourselves, but the Dolces and the Darlings. They're all family now.

My eyes mist over as I stare at King, my brother who brought me ice cream and tried so hard to keep everyone happy, sometimes at the expense of his own happiness.

He's found his happiness, just as I've found mine. I missed his wedding, just as he missed mine.

I've missed so much.

Eliza bends to undo the straps in the stroller before lifting a perfect little black-haired boy from the seat.

"This is our son," King says, his chest swelling with pride as he takes the baby into his arms. "Bishop."

"Knight," I say, pulling my oldest son forward from where he's hiding behind my legs.

My eyes meet King's, and a smile of understanding spreads across both our faces. He hands his baby to

Eliza, and I hand mine to Devlin. Then King steps forward and grabs me up in a bear hug, squeezing me so hard it hurts. It's the kind of hurt that heals, though, and when tears start flowing down my cheeks, they feel cleansing for once, as if they're purging me of the pain of being away for so long, the pain of my family's rejection.

"You didn't have to leave," King says, his voice choked, his hand cradling the back of my head and pressing my face into his chest. He buries his face in my hair and holds me, and neither of us move for a long time.

"I did," I say, my voice muffled in his shirt. "I had to leave, or Daddy would have killed the father of my children."

"Holy fucking shit," says a voice behind King.

He releases me at last, and I step back to see my two little brothers standing with Harper. They're not so little anymore, though they never really were.

"You're blonde," Duke says, gaping at me. "And you have kids. You're like, a whole adult now."

SELENA

"And your penis is on the internet," I say, laughing through my tears. I can't say much about how he looks—he's the same guy but bigger, and his hair is hidden under a black beanie, so I can't even comment on the length.

"Who's this little dude?" he asks, stepping around King and crouching in front of Knight.

"That's our first son," I say as Knight buries his face in my leg, clinging onto me when faced with this stranger.

I turn to take one of the twins from Devlin. "This is Prince, our second, and Diamond, our daughter."

"Diamond?" Duke asks, standing and peering at our devil child. "She doesn't look a stripper at all."

"Duke," I scold, smacking his arm.

"What?" he says. "You know damn well that girl has no other career path in her future with a name like that."

And then we're laughing, and hugging, and he's picking me up off the ground, and it's just like I imagined, so I'm crying harder. Prince starts struggling and fussing in my arms, and I have to pull myself away from Duke and make sure the baby's okay.

At last, I look up at Baron, feeling suddenly shy. Always the observer, he's standing with his hands in his pockets, watching me from behind his glasses with guarded interest. I see that he and Duke have kept their individuality apparent instead of reverting to their New York look, where sometimes even I had trouble telling them apart. Baron's hair is combed back, and he's wearing glasses, a button shirt and dress pants, while Duke is in jeans and a hoodie.

"Does Dad know you're here?" he asks.

"No," I say, shaking my head. "Is he home?"

"No."

Of course he's at work, even though it's evening. A damp, bracing wind blows brown leaves across the back yard where I remember walking with my *nonna*. I glance again at the burned rubble next door, the only thing that remains of Devlin's beautiful house. Even though Preston said his family is safe, my heart still aches at the absence of the house next door, where Devlin stood on the balcony watching me. The tree in the backyard where he threw his football is still there, though the tire swing is

SELENA

gone. A ghost of memory shimmers up my arms, making the hair stand up.

"Will Devlin be safe here?" I ask.

"Probably not," Baron says. "You ditched us for three years. You think you can just show up and Royal's suddenly going to be fine with him?"

"You mean *you're* not fine with him," I say, looking at my younger brother. He looks exactly the same, and yet, he also looks like a complete stranger. He's bigger, like Royal, but it's more than that. There's something guarded in his eyes, not just watchful. But then, there's a big difference between fifteen and eighteen.

"You're right," Baron says. "I'm not."

"Baron…" I say, giving him a pleading look. "I had to leave. I was having a baby. You would have killed him."

"And we would have taken care of you," he says. "You and the kid both."

I shake my head, drawing an unsteady breath. "I had no way of knowing if that would happen, if Daddy or the Darlings would let it."

He sizes me up for a second the way I've been doing to them. I guess there's a big difference between sixteen and nineteen, too. I've changed as much as they have.

"No," he says quietly. "You're just like Ma. You don't give a shit about anyone but yourself."

He turns and starts back toward the house, leaving me standing there stunned, crying into Prince's hair. But King grabs Baron's arm as he passes, stopping him. He murmurs something to our little brother, and Baron turns back to face us. His expression is cool now, his eyes flat and emotionless. He takes a Dolce Sucks pop from his pocket and starts to unwrap it as he stands there beside King under the stormy sky.

"Where's Royal?" our older brother asks.

"He took my car and left," Harper says.

"You let him leave?" King asks, wheeling on her.

"Do you think I could have stopped him?" she asks, not flinching at the sharp tone in his voice. I wonder how long she's been part of this family, if she's helped Royal through his loss the way Devlin helped me. I can't tell much about her besides that she's abrasive and doesn't like me, but no one seems uncomfortable with her presence in a family moment.

King curses quietly. "We need to find him right now, before he does something stupid."

"Like what?" I ask.

King ignores me, speaking instead to Harper. "You should have told me he left right away."

"I thought he went somewhere to calm down," she says. "You don't think he'd…"

"What?" I ask. "What's wrong with Royal?"

"You," Harper snaps. "You're what's wrong with him. Now we have to find him and make it right. You in?"

"Of course I'm in," I snap back at her. "He's my twin. If I upset him, then I'm the one who needs to make it right."

"Right answer," she says, taking out her phone. "Let's go."

twenty-seven

Harper Apple

King turns to me. "You know him best. Where would he go?"

"The bridge," I say instantly, though I'll come back to his other comment later to treasure it the way it deserves. I know Royal better than even his family, enough that King asked me and not the twins.

No one asks what bridge or questions my answer, either.

King turns to his wife. "Eliza, take Bishop inside," he says. "Crys, take the kids in, too. We have a nanny if you want to come with us."

"My car's biggest," Duke says.

"I'll move the van," Devlin says, handing a baby to Crystal, who already has her arms full with one. I can't

SELENA

even comprehend having that many small children at once. It makes me feel itchy just thinking about it.

"Baron," I say, turning to my least favorite Dolce boy. "Do you have a tracker on Royal's phone?"

He just looks at me coolly, and for a second, I think he's not going to answer. But then he nods and pulls out his phone, tucking his sucker into his cheek as he frowns down at his phone. I would have called Preston for his car whereabouts if Royal was in his car.

"It's here," Baron says after a second.

I curse under my breath, remembering Royal dropping it in the console when I climbed in his lap earlier, when we were parked beside the bridge having our reunion after a week apart.

My heart twists at the memory of what came next. If something happens to him, and the last thing we did was fight…

Duke pulls out of the garage in the big Hummer, and a flash of panic bolts through me. The last time I was in that car was the night they took me to the swamp.

But I've dealt with that, enough that I can swallow down the adrenaline and stagger to the car through the wave of dizziness. I'm grateful that they're all too focused on Royal to notice. I breathe through it for a minute as we all pile into the three rows of seats and get situated.

Then Duke guns the engine, and we take off.

After what feels like ten minutes, I look at the clock on the dash and see it's only been one. I remember another ride in this Hummer, how panicked and desperate I felt when the Dolce boys laid out the plan to go after Lindsey or Magnolia when Royal's car was bombed. I had no one to call, no contact except for our home computer and the *OnlyWords* app.

Now I have friends.

Ironically, the person who can help me now is the person I was trying to help then.

I pull out my phone and dial.

"Hey, boomer," comes a snotty, Southern voice on the other end. "I can't believe you're calling me. God, does anyone under fifty even do that anymore?"

"Do you have your license?" I ask.

SELENA

"No," Magnolia says. "Why?"

"Shit," I say. "Is there anyone there who can drive down to the bridge real quick?"

"I said I didn't have my license," she says. "I didn't say I can't drive. Me and Sully take the old crustacean's cars out all the time. He calls it joyriding. How cringey is that?"

"Can you go down to the bridge?" I ask. "Call me back if my car is there. Royal has it. *Do not* engage with him. I don't know what he'll do. And don't shoot him."

"On it," she says. "What's happening, though?"

"I've gotta go," I say. "Call me back."

I hang up, another idea having formed. I call Gloria next.

"Know anywhere Royal might go when he's upset?" I ask. "When he's being reckless?"

"There's a strip where we race sometimes," she says. "But there's way too much traffic right now. Why?"

"Can you go down there and make sure he's not there?" I ask. "He's in my car. Call me if he's there."

I hang up and hit Colt's number. "Hey, Dynamo," I say, already on a role. "Have you heard from Royal?"

"A couple days ago," he says. "When he booked his fights for December."

"Call me if he gets in touch with you about Slaughterpen," I say. "And can you do me a huge favor and run down and make sure he's not there?"

Colt sighs. "You're a pain in my ass, Appleteeny."

"Ditto," I say. "But somehow, I still tolerate you."

"It's the hope that you'll get a shot at this super mega fine dick one day," he says. "It's kitty catnip. Just ask Dixie."

"Seriously, thank you," I say. "You can have my cut next time I fight."

He laughs. "So… Never?"

"Book me in next weekend," I say. "Thanks, Colt. I gotta go."

"Anything for you, Teeny."

I hit end on the call and look at the clock. We're almost at the bridge. Just a few more minutes. My hands are shaking. What if he jumped? It's later in the year and

SELENA

colder than when he jumped with me, and it was cold as fuck that day. Will he be able to swim before hypothermia has his seizing up? Would he even try?

I remember his arms around me like a vice as he let out his breath, sinking into the depths of the water with me.

It's dark. It doesn't hurt anymore.

I hit call on my phone again, think of what Colt said.

"Hey, girl," Dixie's voice answers on the other end, sounding bubbly as always. "I thought you were still mad at me about the video."

"I need help," I say. "Royal's in my car, and he might be in danger, I don't know. Can you go by the school and just call me if my car is there?"

She's quiet a few seconds. "If you want to be friends again, you know I like everyone," she says. "If you don't want to be friends but you have tea, or even if you just want *me* to spill, that's fine. But don't call me asking for help with Royal."

"Dixie," I say. "It's important."

"Where were you when Colt was in the hospital?" she asks. "Was that not important?"

"Got it," I say. "You're right, we're not friends. And by the way, Colt didn't hesitate to help. Sit with that for a while."

I hang up just as Duke speeds toward the one-lane wooden bridge, the beams arching over it having recently received a new coat of white paint. They glow like ghostly arms reaching up into the low, stormy twilight sky. Headlights wash over the planks, nearly blinding us as a car shoots onto the bridge from the other side.

"Motherfucker," Duke yells, jerking the wheel. The huge vehicle seems to move in slow motion, lumbering off the road just as a zippy, little blue Miata skids to a stop beside us in a cloud of exhaust and burnt rubber fumes. Magnolia waves, her curls in a crazy tangle around her smiling face.

I roll down the window. "No sign on the other side?"

"Nope," she says. "What's going on?"

"I'm not sure," I say. "Thanks for checking."

"I'll come with," she says. "This is exciting."

SELENA

"You don't have a license."

"Okay, *Mom*," she says, rolling her eyes. "But just a fair warning, if anyone touches me, I have a gun, a knife, pepper spray, *and* a taser on me. Oh, and I guess I don't need these anymore."

She pulls my brass knuckles off her hand and tosses them to me. I catch them through the open window and slide them on, the warm metal settling into place and calming me like a security blanket.

"Thanks," I say, flexing my fingers.

"Oh, and Grandpa Darling left his cigar cutter in here, so if any of these boys tries anything, they gonna get their dicks cut." She sings the last few words, looking ferocious with anticipation at the prospect.

"Let me drive," King says as a few fat raindrops sprinkle onto the windshield.

"No way," Duke says. "I'm not getting out right now. You heard that bitch. She's crazy. Harper, tell her to go home and play with her dolls, or call her therapist or something. We don't need her help."

"Where else would he go?" I ask, turning to look at all his siblings around me.

"School, obviously," Baron says. "Or…"

"The swamp," I say, swallowing hard. Those are his remembering places, though I doubt he's at the swamp, since that has nothing to do with Crystal. Still, I've made assumptions that led me down the wrong road one too many times.

"I want to go by one other place first," King says. "Dad's work."

"Why?" Baron asks.

"Just a hunch," King says.

I watch Crystal while Duke drives over the bridge to turn around. She's clinging to Devlin's hand, her face white and tense. Good. She should never have left Royal the way she did. I know I'm being a bitch, but I'm glad this is hard for her.

When we're back on the road and heading out, I open the *OnlyWords* app.

SELENA

BadApple: Hey I kno this is awkward but can u do me a favor? I need someone 2 check the school n c if my car is there. Royal took off in it. Think he might be at the Swans.
GideonD17: sure np
BadApple: txt me asap?
GideonD17: everything ok?
BadApple: idk tbh. Prob not. Plz check now?
GideonD17: heading there rn.
BadApple: thank u so much

I scroll through my contacts for a minute, searching for anyone else I can employ to help. I'm already so grateful I could cry after talking to Gideon. So this is what having friends in an emergency is like. I'm pissed at myself for cutting myself off from that for so long. Now, when I need people, they're here for me. Even when I'm asking them to check up on their enemy or their competition, even when it's a guy who asked me out and then got blown off at the last minute. He didn't hesitate to help even though that must have hurt his pride, and even though I'm asking him to help find the guy who I showed up with after cancelling on him.

But I'm out of friends. The few other people I know—Quinn, Susanna, and Josie—are Dixie's friends.

I do have someone else, though. People who swore an oath to have my back, and to have Royal's back. I open the Midnight Swans group chat where we plan our meetings.

BadApple: Swans, I need ur help. Royal might need it 2. If I drop u a pin to a place north of town, b4 the quarry, can u go check for Royal?
BadApple: He's in my car. Just need u 2 txt if he's there.
TheBlackRose: I got u
BadApple: thx
TheBlackRose: anything 4 a Swan
ThatCreepCotton: I'll back u up
TheBlackRose: sounds good
ThatCreepCotton: drop the pin, A. We'll take it from here.
BadApple: kk thx

SELENA

I drop the pin and take a breath, trying to calm my racing heart. It's terrifying to let someone else take over, especially when I'm giving up control of something that has to do with Royal. But even my crazy love can't put me in five places at once, so if I can send someone else where he is, and they can keep him under control until I get there, that's better than leaving him alone with himself.

"Does Colt know we're okay?" Devlin asks.

I shake my head. "He thinks you're dead, and he'll probably be pissed, but not like Royal."

"No one's like Royal," Baron says.

"Oh, also, his entire hand and arm are burned, and he's missing a finger, thanks to your brothers," I say to Crystal.

"Not his *entire* arm," Duke says.

Crystal looks like she might puke. She hasn't even begun to realize the magnitude of what her leaving did to this family, and I'm not the person who's going to sugarcoat it. I don't hate her, but I'm not going to let her off the hook for everything she caused just because she fell in love. I understand the temptation, but I would never abandon my family to run off and live in blissful ignorance with Royal. And my family fucking sucks.

Not that hers doesn't. Besides Royal, I could leave the whole lot of them. There's a reason I didn't want to join them for Thanksgiving. I try to imagine a future with Royal, sitting around the dinner table with him, his two brothers who raped me, his sister who broke him in ways he will never heal from, his cold-fish mafia brother, his mother who abandoned him, and his father who pimped him out to land business deals.

Yeah, that's going to be pleasant.

Maybe we can invite my lovely mother along for extra fun.

"He's not here," King says as we pull up to an office building with an empty parking lot.

"He's not at the Slaughterpen or the stretch where Lo says he drag races, either," I say, checking my phone as texts start coming through. "I'm asking them if they have any other ideas."

SELENA

I send Colt and Lo messages and include the fact that Magnolia is tailing us, since I told Colt I'd let him know if I involved her in anything.

"Dad's not here, either," Duke points out, adjusting his beanie and looking over at King, who's in the passenger seat.

The oldest Dolce boy rakes his hand through his hair. "We had a conversation in New York," he says. "I bet you anything he's with Dad."

"Baron?" I ask. "You know your dad best. Where would he go?"

"He probably went home," Baron says, taking out his phone and texting, his fingers flying across the screen.

I want to ask if he'd hurt Royal, but there's no point. He's been hurting Royal for years, and he doesn't give a single fuck.

Another text comes through, and I flash the screen at them. "He's not at school."

We sit in silence for a few seconds.

Seeing Gideon's name on the screen snaps something into place, though, and I'm suddenly sure I know where they went.

"The mall," I say. "He's at the mall."

Duke spins the wheel and slams on the gas, and we skid into a turn on the damp pavement and then barrel out of the parking lot. I shoot a group message to the others to tell them what's been cleared and where we're going next.

"Why would he be at the mall?" Crystal asks.

"It's not the mall anymore," I say. "It went out of business."

"Crystal's right," Baron says. "Dad didn't get the land deal. Why would he go there?"

"Because he told me something illegal was going on there," I say. "And I'm guessing it's not the Delacroixs doing it. Which means if he said he was at work, and he's not here, he's probably doing some shady shit up there to set them up."

"Royal wouldn't know that," Baron says.

"Right," I say. "Only you'd know that."

SELENA

"He's probably at the swamp," Baron says with a shrug. "But we can waste time finding Dad first if you want."

"Whose side are you on?" I ask. "Royal's, or your dad's?"

"I'm on my family's side," Baron says, leveling me with that measured stare. "Always."

"If you're not on Royal's side, then why are you here?" I ask.

"They're my family," he says coolly. "Why are *you* here?"

If I thought it would work, I'd reach across him and open the door and push him out of the moving vehicle. But I'll have to deal with his ass later.

"The mall is on the way out of town," King says. "We'll swing by just in case. It'll only take a minute."

"Whatever you think is best," Baron says, tapping away at his phone again, moving the sucker stem from one side of his mouth to the other with his tongue as he texts.

"I don't know why he'd bother setting up the Delacroixs," Duke says. "We could just burn this motherfucker to the ground!"

He pulls up at the mall, which is set up in three wings coming off the center, where the food court was located when the mall was running. The security lights are still on in the parking lot, but the interior is completely dark, which sends an eerie shiver through me. The mall is a place that should always be lit up, full of people high off the purchases in their swollen shopping bags, fussy children with food on their faces, overwhelmed parents, lovers tossing pennies in the fountain, and teenagers shoplifting cheap jewelry in their fountain drinks—another trick Lauren taught me during our brief fling.

A pair or headlights sweeps over us, and I jump, turning that way with my heart in my throat. The vehicle roars toward us, the headlights blinding, and for a second, I'm sure it's going to barrel straight into us. A scream lodges in my throat, and then the vehicle turns, skidding to a stop beside us, and I see that it's Colt's truck, not my SUV. Gloria's Mustang pulls up next to him. With Magnolia still trailing us, we're gathering a regular parade.

Colt rolls down the window. "I went around the east wing," he says. "No cars."

"See?" Baron says.

"Let's just check the last lot," I say, nodding to the last wing of the mall. "We're already here."

I don't add the rest of my thought—that I don't trust Baron for one second.

Duke glances in the back seat at us.

"She's right," King says. "Might as well."

Baron looks annoyed, but he doesn't say anything. He rolls down the window and tosses his sucker stem, then keeps his face turned away. I wonder what the psycho knows, why he doesn't want us here. It only convinces me that my hunch was right.

"Who's armed?" King asks as Duke shifts into gear and starts for the last wing of the mall. "We don't know what we're walking into."

I silently curse myself when I remember dropping my gun with Royal's phone when we were frantically shedding our clothes, ready to fuck.

"I've got a knife," I say. "And knuckles."

"Magnolia's armed as fuck," Duke says, shaking his head.

"I have a gun," Devlin says.

"What?" Crystal asks. "Why?"

"Because your family wants to kill me?"

"You took care of our sister and her children for the last three years," King says. "We don't want to kill you."

"Thanks," Devlin says quietly.

No one speaks as we pull around the end of the building. I can't help but think Devlin's got some balls to get in a car with the Dolce boys right now, not knowing what they're planning beyond finding Royal. There's no way Colt or Preston would do that. It's a testament to his love for Crystal, that's for sure. I grudgingly admire him for it, even though I'm as angry at him as I am her.

We pull around the corner of the building to see the last wedge-shaped parking lot. Two cars sit side by side at

SELENA

center of the lot, near the entrance to the food court—Mr. Dolce's Porsche, and my Escalade.

I swallow hard, my heart thundering in my chest. If he hurts Royal…

I won't even think about it. I won't let myself.

Duke floors it, and we fly across the lot, jumping several curbs. The Hummer bumps over them, nearly jarring us off the seats, but he doesn't slow until he skids to a stop beside my car.

"I'm armed," King says. "Liza? Baron? Duke? Crys?"

"I grabbed a gun on the way out," Eliza says. "I'll stick with you."

"I just brought my fists," Duke says, shutting off the engine and punching his fist into the palm of his other hand. "Let's do this."

We all spill out of the car, joining those from the other cars.

"I think you're going to have to pick a side now," I say to Baron. "Otherwise, how do we know you're not going to shoot Royal to protect your dad?"

"I'm his brother," he growls. "In case you forgot, I'm the one who was protecting him when you stuck a fucking knife in his back. So if anyone's loyalties are in question, they're yours."

"I love Royal," I say flatly. "I would never hurt him."

"Then we're in agreement," he says.

I narrow my eyes at him. "Except you also want to protect your dad," I say. "Don't you? You said you and he have your own thing going."

He meets my eyes with a cool gaze from behind his glasses. "I had something he wanted," he says quietly. "We had our thing going until he got what he was after."

We stand there staring each other down, and I wish like hell I could read him better. If he's hurt, he hides it as well as all the Dolce boys. I shouldn't be surprised to hear him admit their dad was just using him. It's not like any of his children are immune. Royal's the oldest, so he tried to protect the twins, but he's not special in Mr. Dolce's eyes. He'd use them all if he could get something out of it.

"What was he after?" I ask.

"The recipe."

I don't have to ask what he means. It's the recipe for Lady Alice, the Alice in Wonderland drug that my mom and everyone else in Faulkner is doing. And now Mr. Dolce has the recipe. It only confirms my earlier suspicions that he's the head of it all, and he needs to be dealt with once and for all. As soon as we get Royal back, we need to get rid of their father, maybe get him thrown in prison for dealing drugs.

"Then let's get it back," I say to Baron.

He gives me the slightest nod, some unspoken agreement between us that for tonight, at least, we're on the same team.

Crystal and Devlin have come around the car, but Colt was too busy arguing with Gloria to notice. Suddenly, he stops mid-sentence and just gapes.

Devlin grabs him like he did Preston, and they hold onto each other while the rest of us stand there awkwardly, looking at the dark clouds gathering overhead and trying not to intrude on a moment that is obviously not ours to witness. It makes my chest ache deep down, and not because I'm wishing I had a family, the way I used to when I saw Royal and the twins. Now, my heart hurts for him, because I don't think the twins are capable of the kind of love the Darling men seem to have for each other.

The sound of an engine approaching interrupts the awkwardness, and we all let out a quiet sigh of relief. Colt and Devlin pull apart, but then they just stand there, their hands gripping the side of each other's necks, staring at each other from arm's length like they're locked in some silent communication that the rest of us aren't privy to.

We turn away from them to watch another car roll up. Gideon and his brother, the librarian, hop down from an SUV.

"You brought a teacher?" Duke asks, pulling off his beanie and ruffling his hair. "What the fuck, man. Could you be any more lame?"

"It's our property," Mr. Delacroix says. "We own this place. Which means technically you're all trespassing."

"Do we have a problem here?" King asks.

SELENA

There's something so commanding in his voice, so cold, that even though he's no bigger than his brothers, even they fall silent and look to him.

Mr. Delacroix swallows so hard I can see his Adam's apple move up and down. "No," he says. "We're just here to protect our property."

"Good," King says. "Do you have guns?"

"I have a concealed carry permit," Mr. Delacroix says. "I've got a handgun and a couple hunting rifles in the back."

"Get them," King says.

"Are we in danger?" Mr. Delacroix asks, frowning and shifting closer to his little brother.

"I think it's safe to assume Royal came to confront our father—Tony Dolce, if you're not familiar. What he's doing here, I don't know. So, take necessary precautions or stay out here."

Mr. Delacroix goes to get the guns, and King turns to the rest of us. "There are twelve of us, so that means we split into three teams of four and fan out. Darlings, take the northwest corridor. You've got two guns. Dolces will take the east wing—we've got two guns as well. Delacroixs, take Gloria and Harper with you to check the southwest wing. We're going to get Royal back just fine. No casualties today."

He nods at me, and then turns to take his group toward the doors.

Mr. Delacroix holds out one of the rifles toward me and Lo.

"Know how to shoot?" I ask Gloria.

She snorts. "Please. You're not the only girl who grew up in the South."

"Take it," I say, holding up both hands. "I'm better with my fists, anyway."

We cross the lot under the low, churning clouds and cluster around the doors to the food court while Mr. Delacroix unlocks it. Lightning flickers in the clouds, but inside the mall is pitch dark.

"Can I go with Harper's group?" Colt asks. "My money's on her in any fight."

"You can have my gun," Magnolia says. "As long as you let me use the cigar cutter once you shoot him."

SELENA

Duke scoots away from her, pulling his beanie down over his ears and scowling at her.

"Stay with your group," King says.

He steps inside first, insisting on checking it out before giving us the all-clear a few minutes later. Adrenaline pumps through me as I step through the doors into the darkness within. I turn on my phone's flashlight and cast the beam around the huge room when I see others doing the same. The food court is empty, the tables and chairs gone and all the booths around the edges boarded up and empty. I slide along one side, past the stir-fry place that Lauren liked and the sandwich place that gave us free refills on drinks if we flirted enough. There's the stall that sold pizza by the slice and still smells like it even though it's closed, and the smoothie station where I went with Gloria last year.

Then we step into a long, dark corridor. Our lights reflect off the glass fronts of the stores, casting eerie shadows and making me squint when they hit my eyes.

"This is creepy as hell," Gloria whispers beside me, carrying the rifle over her shoulder like a hunter. Our footsteps and whispers echo down the corridor and off the ceiling. I can hear footsteps from far off, too, but I can't tell where they're coming from. A long rumble of thunder builds outside, the kind that sounds like something ominous is approaching.

"We'll check the left side," I say to the Delacroixs. "You check the stores on the right. Anyone who finds anything, whistle, and we'll come to you."

"Should we call for Royal?" Gloria asks. "Or be quiet?"

"They'll see us coming," I point out.

Gloria calls out, her voice echoing through the silence, sounding small and shrill. She giggles nervously. "You do it."

About halfway down our corridor, there's a short side hallway that used to have massage chairs and then a circle of benches in front of a restaurant on one side, a hair salon next to it, and a four-screen movie theater that always smelled like piss from all the parents bringing their kids for matinees.

SELENA

"What if they pass the end of the hall while we're down this way?" Gideon asks, shining his light down the side hallway and then straight ahead again. Footsteps sound in the hall behind us, and I spin around. A light shines straight in my eyes, blinding me to the figure beyond.

"King sent us to check out the movie theater and restaurant area," Baron says, not lowering his light until he's so close I could practically knock it out of his hand.

"Why?" I ask.

Despite our earlier truce, I trust Baron about as much as I like him.

He shrugs. "Call and ask him. He probably forgot about that part of the mall. He only lived in this town for a year."

King doesn't strike me as the kind of guy who forgets anything—ever. Baron also knows damn well that I don't have his number. For all I know, he shot King and Eliza to give them the slip. I wouldn't put anything past him.

Or maybe he's telling the truth, but I've been burned too many times to believe a word he says.

"There's more area to cover on this wing," Duke points out. "We can sweep it and then go back."

He and Baron start down the short hallway.

"I'm going with them," I say. "Something feels off."

"Are you sure?" Gideon asks, frowning at me. "Want me to come?"

"No," I say. "I just want to make sure Baron's not up to his usual shady shit."

"I'll come with," Gloria says.

"We'll keep going," Mr. Delacroix says. "Be careful. Whistle if you need us."

I turn and hurry down the hallway. Duke and Baron have disappeared by the time my light hits the end of the corridor, which only convinces me further. They're up to something.

We're halfway to the end when a sound echoes from somewhere in the movie theater, ahead and to our left—a distinctly female scream.

SELENA

twenty-eight

Harper Apple

"What was that?" Gloria asks, her eyes going wide. She lifts the rifle back to her shoulder and holds it up, making her way slowly.

"Cover my back," I say as another scream echoes from the pitch dark entrance of the movie theater. "Don't shoot me."

"Where'd the twins go?" she asks, her voice high with fear.

"If I had to guess, the screams will lead us to them," I mutter darkly, hurrying to the entrance before hesitating. Both glass doors are propped open, but I can't see anything but a gaping maw of darkness within. I turn my light up and shine it into the red-carpeted entrance. The ticket counter and concession stand lies ahead, with two small screening rooms and one restroom on either side.

The echo of the last scream dies away, and there's silence all around us. My heart is beating so loud I hardly hear Gloria come up behind me.

"Who was that?" she asks, her breathing shallow.

Fuck. My mind races through the possibilities. Eliza, Crystal, or Magnolia.

Eliza could have come to track down the twins, and whatever they're hiding is worth killing for, so they shot her or otherwise put her out of commission. If Crystal came down here for whatever reason, the twins or Royal might have been pissed enough to kill her. And then there's Magnolia…

There's a soft clicking and a familiar whirr, and then the sound of a girl crying coming from one of the rooms to the left.

"Cover," I say, starting that way, my heart hammering as the cold light of my phone falls on the handle of the theater door. I throw it open and jump to one side, flattening my back to the wall in case anyone's waiting. Nothing happens except the sniffling and crying is louder now—too loud.

SELENA

I turn and step into the theater. The sound isn't coming from a person, at least not one in the room. It's coming from the sound booth overhead. Something that looks suspiciously like porn is playing on the screen.

"Welcome to the den of iniquity," Duke says, kicking his feet up on the back of a seat. "I've got beer and weed and a couple Pearl Ladies."

"What the fuck, Duke," I snap. "We're supposed to be looking for Royal. Where's Baron?"

"He's in the booth," Duke says, pointing up at the projection booth. "He's the pro."

"What is this?" Gloria asks, lowering the gun and gaping at the screen. "Is this…?"

The scene has changed from the shot that was so close up it was almost impossible to tell what was happening to a shot of… *Me*.

I swallow the bile in my throat, swaying on my feet. My fingers close around the back of one of the seats, and I stare at the screen and what is very obviously my tattoos.

"It's the highlight reel," Duke says, throwing his head back and taking a long draught of his beer. "Faulkner's favorite porn stars, if you will."

"Where did you get this?" I ask.

"Baron paid for it and screen recorded it," he says, setting his empty on the floor and belching. "It's totally worth it. Preston gives you a big old cream pie in the ass in a minute."

"Turn it off," I snap, squeezing my eyes closed.

"Was that Harper screaming?" Gloria asks, her voice faint.

"Nah," Duke says. "But that'll come back around in a second. Baron did a good job editing the clips together, but it's only like ten minutes. Don't worry, you're on here, too, Lo."

"Turn it off," I say again, louder this time.

"Oh, I can't," he says, flicking on a lighter. The flame dances around the end of the blunt he's holding. "I don't know how to work the projector. Plus, we'd have to go up to the booth, and I need a minute to chill. Here, come sit down. I'll smoke you out. I might even eat you out if you suck my dick first."

"Fuck this," I say. "I'm leaving."

I turn just in time to see the door swing closed behind me. I leap at it, crashing my shoulder against the surface, but it's unforgiving and solid. I hear a click outside, and I know that bastard just locked us in.

"Let us out," I demand, banging my fists on the door.

"Just sit down and watch," Duke says. "Ten minutes isn't that long. Just long enough for me to smoke a blunt, bust a nut, and maybe finish a beer or two."

"Why are you doing this?" Gloria asks, her voice shaking.

"Look, he's fucking her ass now," Duke says, a cloud of smoke billowing from his mouth. "Hold on, it's so good when his cum runs out and he goes from ass to cunt."

"Let me the fuck out," I say, stomping up the aisle to where Duke is sitting, halfway to the screen.

"Come on, baby, don't you want to see what we have on you?" he asks, grabbing my hand and pulling me down on his lap. His iron arm wraps around me, holding me around the middle, and he pushes his erection up against me. It's almost exactly how Mr. Dolce held me, and my skin crawls just as much this time as it did then.

Duke grips me with one arm and puffs on the blunt for a few seconds.

"What do you want?" I ask. I can get away from him when I need to, but cooperating for a minute can get me answers.

"Feel how hard I get watching him take that ass," he says. "You know, I never got to do that. Only Baron got anal. Want to fix that tonight?"

He offers me the blunt, but I push his hand away. I want to be clear right now, as tempting as taking the edge off is. My muscles are shaking, a sick feeling churning in my stomach. I don't want to go back there, don't want to slip into the horrors of my trauma.

"I can't figure you out," I say, swallowing past the trembling in my throat.

"So stop trying," he says. "No one else ever has, and you won't be the first."

SELENA

"Are you in on whatever Baron's doing, helping him keep us from finding Royal?" I press. "Why would you do that? Royal fucking loves y'all. He's sacrificed himself for you."

"We're just having a little fun with you," he says. "Look, this is the best part."

I try not to be sick watching the last few seconds. I like porn as much as the next girl, but this isn't porn. It's me. At the time, I knew what Preston was doing, but it didn't feel real. I just lay there with my head in the pillow, too numb to care. Now, seeing him fucking me when I was basically comatose, makes me want to hunt him down and rip his fucking throat out—especially because he sent those videos to these assholes.

There I was being so thankful for what he bought me, and he was probably using the money from these clips to do it. He really did make me a whore. I didn't even want those clothes, and I sure as fuck wouldn't have traded them for this. If he made me a whore, he did it without my permission. I want to forget the nightmare of those months, but it keeps coming back.

The clip ends with a mutter of "good girl," from Preston.

Duke groans and squeezes me tighter. "See, I always knew you were nasty as fuck, but Royal wouldn't tell us shit. Preston did, though. I was right about you all along. I get you, Harper Apple. And you're the only one who really gets me."

I laugh at that. "Sorry, you're wrong. I don't get you at all. I don't know if you're stupid, or if you know Baron's pushing you aside, but you're just pretending that's not what's happening because it hurts too much for you to admit it. You're just a distraction like the rest of us. Do you even know what he's doing out there?"

The video changes to a girl lying tied to a bed, lifting her head while a guy stands over her, his back to the camera. It's grainy, like a security camera took it. I don't stick around to see if this is where the screaming came from. I stomp on Duke's foot, and when his grip loosens, I slam his elbow down on the arm of the seat. He curses and releases me, and I twist from his grip and back to my feet.

SELENA

"I'm going out the emergency exit," I say. "Gloria?"

She swallows hard, her face pale in the light from the screen. "What if you get locked out?"

I don't know if Mr. Delacroix locked the doors behind us, but I know they're glass. I'll find a way back in.

"I'll come around and get you out," I say. "Will you be okay here?"

"She'll be fine," Duke says. "She just wants to know if what we have on her is as nasty as Preston nutting in your ass and sticking it back in your pussy. Truffle butter, baby!"

Gloria nods mutely, her eyes wide as she stares at the screen behind me. I don't know if that's her, since I didn't look too closely. I won't, either, because if it is her, I'll let her keep whatever dignity remains. It's what poor girls do.

"Remember what I said to you before?" I ask Duke. "About you fucking with girls and hurting them? That means Gloria, too. *Especially* Gloria."

He nods, staring at the screen with a glazed expression. I'm not into snuff films or whatever sick shit Baron put on there, so I avoid looking and hurry to the exit door. I slam my shoulder against the bar, half expecting it to be blocked from the outside, but it swings open into the cold night.

I glance back once and see Gloria taking the blunt from Duke with shaking fingers. No matter how much I like figuring people out, I don't know if I'll ever know what's going on with either of them.

I let the door swing closed behind me, then jog around toward the doors we came in. The wind whistles through the empty branches of the trees in the parking lot, and I pull my hoodie close around me and glance over my shoulder, my heart lurching in my chest. I'm sure I'll see Baron coming after me.

But the lot is empty when I sweep my eyes over it.

I reach the food court doors and stop, taking a few breaths before trying the door.

Locked. I curse, then look around, grab a rock, and smash the glass. It falls in sparkling, tinkling fragments around me. I kick out the rest of it and duck under the center bar in the door, then race across the food court again, my heart pounding. If Baron doesn't know I got out, I can sneak up behind him, but I can't count on that. Duke might have texted him.

I tiptoe down the wide corridor, the hair standing up on the back of my neck at the thought of being so exposed. If Baron steps out, I'm the only target in the hall.

I duck around the corner to the small hallway, flattening myself against the wall and catching my breath for a second. I'm about to go on when I hear a low whistle. I turn back toward the main hall, my heart hammering.

Did they find Royal?

"Gideon?" I whisper as loud as I can. It echoes down the empty corridor. Somewhere, I hear a distant rattling sound, almost like a rain stick. I tense, listening to the sound go on for a full thirty seconds, my skin crawling from head to toe.

What the fuck was that?

Another low whistle sounds, and I whip back around. In the flickering lightning coming from the exit between the movie theater and restaurant, the silhouette of a man stands motionless.

"Royal?" I ask, fumbling to get my phone out.

Another whistle sounds, this one from behind me. I whip around, and when I turn back, the figure in the hallway is gone. The hair on the back of my neck prickles as I creep down the hall. Another whistle comes, this one from the left, in the movie theater. The darkness within is dense and oppressive, like it's waiting for me.

I take a breath and try to calm my racing heart and spiraling thoughts. The darkness won't hurt me, but whoever's hiding in it might. They keep leading me that way, which means they're trying to keep me from going right. I thumb my flashlight back on and turn to the right, where the restaurant sits dark and silent. I sweep my light to the door and almost scream.

Duke is standing there, his hands in the front pocket of his hoodie.

"Duke," I say. "What the fuck?"

SELENA

He shoots me a sloppy grin. "Just having a little fun with you."

"You're the one whistling?"

"I'm a man of many talents."

"What are you doing here? Where's Lo?"

"She's not with you?" he asks. "She went out the side door to go find you."

"How'd you get out?"

"Baron let me out," he says. "We checked the restaurant, and then he went back to report to King."

"Why didn't you go?" I ask, narrowing my eyes.

"I figured you wouldn't believe us," he says with a shrug. "So let's check it out and then get back to the others."

He pushes open the door of the restaurant, and we step inside. The place still smells like spaghetti and barf from all the kids who ate too much at the pasta buffet, but the tables and chairs are gone, leaving only the booths along the edges.

"See?" Duke says. "Empty. Let's go back. I need another beer."

My heart sinks. He's right. They aren't here. There's nothing here. I do a loop around the tiny restaurant and then sigh. "Okay."

He holds open the glass door, and I step in front of him, casting my flashlight beam back one more time. It hits a shape under one of the booth tables, and I stop in my tracks, my pulse racing.

"What's that?" I ask, backtracking.

"What?" Duke asks.

I hurry back to the booth and reach under, pulling out a black duffle bag. There's a briefcase behind it.

"That's Dad's," he says, sounding puzzled.

"Why would he leave it here?" I ask, a chill running down my spine.

"Don't open it," Duke says sharply.

"You think it's a bomb? He's going to… Blow up the mall?"

"I don't know," he admits.

"We have to find Royal," I say, standing. My eyes fall on a brown plastic swinging door on the far side of the room, near the bathroom. "Shit."

SELENA

"What?"

"We didn't check the kitchen."

I take a step, and the next second, I'm yanked to a stop by the hair. His arm wraps around my throat this time, lifting me off my feet.

"You just don't know when to quit, do you?" he growls into my ear, so close I can smell aftershave and cough drops as he breathes on my neck. Something snags at my mind, but he tightens his grip, fisting his fingers in my hair and cutting off my airway with his forearm, and then I'm too focused on trying to stay conscious to think of anything else. I grab his arm, turning my head a bit and digging my chin into the inside of his elbow to keep a little air flowing into my lungs. God, his muscles feel like iron. He crushes the side of my neck, and blackness splotches my vision.

"This is Dolce business," he snaps, dragging me backwards toward the door. "Why the fuck are you still working with the Darlings when you're not one of them? And this isn't even Darling business—it's between us and the Delacroixs. The rest of you need to see yourselves the fuck out. Especially you. You just can't stop fucking shit up, can you?"

This asshole had me fooled, if not into thinking he was a nice guy, at least into thinking he was harmless. But he's as bad as Baron—worse, really. At least with Baron, you know what you're getting. He doesn't pretend to be a drunken clown and then turn around and cheer his brother on as he tortures me. He makes no apologies for who he is and no attempts to hide his psychotic tendencies.

I grind my heels into the floor, scrambling to push myself upwards, desperate to get the pressure off my neck before I black out completely.

"Royal doesn't want you here," he says, jerking me off my feet just as I almost get my boots planted hard enough to relieve the pressure on my neck. "That's why you haven't found him. He's working with Dad, and it's none of your fucking business, because you're not a Dolce and you never will be. Why do you think he wouldn't introduce you to our mother? As soon as he gets bored of fucking you, he'll realize what a mistake you are."

He drags me out through the restaurant doors into the corridor. I manage to twist around and throw my elbow into his groin—hard. He curses savagely, but he doesn't let me go. He grips me tighter, cutting off all my air this time. His hot breath comes quicker in my ear, as if to emphasize how much oxygen he's still getting.

"You bitch," he snarls. "I should have killed you in the swamp that night. We shouldn't have stopped at succeeding where the Darlings failed. I should have seen it through. Ever since the first time, I've wanted to see someone die again—up close and personal this time."

My fingers start going numb, and I know I'm about to pass out. I pull my foot up, yank my knife out of my boot, and use all the strength left in me to slash across his thigh. Hot blood gushes over my hand, and this time, he lets me go, throwing me to the floor. My hands and knees hit the linoleum tiles, and I want to stay there, breathing until my eyes see more than black, but if I take the time to recover, he might recover, too. I don't know how badly I cut him. So I force myself to roll away, though I'm blind in the dark. I grip my knife and come up onto my feet, staggering as my brain replenishes with oxygen. I take a few deep breaths to get the feeling back in my fingers and my brain thinking straight.

I can see him kneeling, gripping his thigh where I cut him. He peels off his hoodie and wraps it around his leg, cursing and gasping with pain. A shock of horror grips me. Did I kill him?

Then he lurches to his feet. Guess I didn't hit a major artery. I should be relieved, but now that he's lumbering toward me out of the dark like some Frankenstein monster, I'm sorry I didn't finish him off.

"You fucking whore," he rages. "You're going to pay for that. We told you that you'd never get away with releasing that video of me, that you'd pay for it. It's time to pay up, bitch."

I circle to keep him in front of me, stepping back when he lunges for me. "I don't think so," I say. "You're injured, and I'm not. Stay back, or you'll end up in even worse shape."

SELENA

"I guess I'll get to see you die after all," he says. "Tonight's as good a day as any. And it's way past time you were out of our lives. You were supposed to disappear the day I put that bomb in Royal's engine."

"You did that?" I ask, gaping with shock. "Why? He could have been hurt."

"You think I don't know my way around an explosive? If I wanted to watch his car go up in a fireball, I'd have made it happen, sweetheart. I just needed to remind him where you stood—that you were a Darling—so he'd get his head out of his ass and let us get rid of you once and for all. The swamp was supposed to do it, too, but you're too stupid to stay away even after that."

"Or maybe you're too stupid to accept that Royal and I love each other," I say, bending to slide my knife into my boot. "That triumphs over everything—even what you did to me. You and your psycho twin would understand that if you were capable of loving anyone but yourselves."

"Oh, we loved someone," he says, backing me into the alcove at the front doors of the restaurant. "And you know what happened to her? We let her go, because she was a Darling, and we're Dolces. You're too naïve to realize it, but Royal will do the same to you. Family always comes first. Always."

"Yeah, well, not for me," I say, bracing my back against the glass and planting my feet wide, letting him come up on me. "Our love comes first."

He makes a grab for me, and I swing with my left hand. He's ready, though, and he blocks the blow. Before he can recover, I twist my hips, using all the power in my body to drive my right fist up. The brass knuckles cradle my hand in their protective embrace as they slam into his jaw with an uppercut that's truly a thing of beauty.

"Sucker," I mutter as he crumples to the floor, his head smacking the tiles with a sickening thud. "By now you should know I'm right-handed."

Leaving his body, I turn and duck back into the restaurant, heading straight for the kitchen door.

SELENA

twenty-nine

Royal Dolce

The door bursts open, and I look up, but it's not Baron coming back to help.

It's Harper.

Dad wheels around, his gun in his hand before I can even reach for mine. He levels it at Harper, and a red-hot brand sears into my cold soul. If I were close enough to reach him, I'd shove the gun down his throat and splatter his brains on the wall, but I'm halfway across the fucking room while he holds a gun on her.

"Royal," she says, her shoulders sinking. "Thank fuck. Are you okay?"

"I'm fine," I snap. "You shouldn't be here."

Dad gestures at her with the gun. "Baron was supposed to get rid of you."

"Yeah, in case your sons haven't told you, I'm not so good at taking orders," she says, seemingly oblivious to the gun pointed her way. "That includes being told to fuck off."

"This doesn't concern you," he says.

She glances around at the metal equipment and the open boxes on the floor. "It concerns Royal, so it concerns me," she says. "So, what are we doing?"

"Get out," I say flatly.

She strolls over and kicks a box lightly with her toe. "Candy?"

Dad turns, following her path with the barrel of the gun. "You heard my son," he says. "We don't have time for your interruptions."

I watch Harper's gaze move back to the equipment that stretches across the room, to the chute above the long stainless-steel table where I'm packaging the product, and finally lifting to me.

"Why are you doing this?" she asks, and I can read the disappointment all over her face.

SELENA

"It pays better than candy," Dad says, picking up an iridescent, pale blue bead from the table. "Do you know how many Dolce Drops I have to sell to make the same profit as one of these little pearls?"

"I wasn't talking to you," she says, her gaze never wavering from me.

I seal a bag and toss it into the box of candy, staring back at her without flinching. "You wanted to be part of my life," I say flatly. "I tried to keep you out of the shady side of Dolce Sweets, but if you're going to put yourself in the middle of it, here it is. Welcome to the fucking family."

I slide my hands over the hundreds of blue pearls on the table, making sure they're only one layer deep where I'm working.

"You want to put her to work?" Dad asks. "She's seen too much already."

"Fuck no," Harper says. "I'm not doing this shit. This is what fucked up my mom."

"It's either get to work or you don't walk out of here," Dad says, raising the gun again. "We're on a tight deadline here, thanks to you sticking your nose where it don't belong."

Harper just shakes her head slowly back and forth, staring at me with a look that slices me wide open. "I can believe Baron's responsible, but you, Royal? Why are you doing this? You're putting all this on the streets?"

"Somebody's going to do it," I say. "If it's not us, it's the Disciples or the Crossbones."

"You don't have to obey your father."

"Family business, sweetheart," I say, shaking the hoop on the surface of the table to kick out any extras. It's designed to fit exactly one hundred pearls when they're one layer thick. I slide it into a bag, depositing the pearls, then start over.

Harper swallows and looks back and forth between me and Dad. "What does he have on you?" she asks. "Is this the trade-off for not working at the Hockington?"

"Shut your mouth and move your hands," Dad says, shoving a roll of tape into her hands. "Those boxes are ready to go. Get 'em packed tight."

SELENA

I toss another bag into the box at my feet and kick it her way. "Add that one."

"This is fucked up," she says, shaking her head and staring at the stainless-steel tubes and chambers around the room, Baron's own design, an intricate system worthy of Rube Goldberg. Usually, we're not the ones packing our own product, but then, usually the mall's owner isn't hunting the halls of the abandoned mall, looking for us.

I glare at her, willing her to obey. She doesn't know how dangerous my father is, but I do. He waves the gun at her, but she doesn't move until he takes the safety off. Then she grabs the tape and runs a strip along the top of the first box.

"So, this is your drug empire," she says. "Is this the real reason you wanted the mall? Was the casino even real?"

"It was going to be," I say, not wanting her to think I'm a lying sack of shit. At least not more than she already does.

"This is more profitable, though," Dad says, finally getting back to work. He circles the table to keep Harper in front of him, so he can watch her, and I can watch his back. "No expenses or permits needed, either."

"Yeah, well, the Delacroixs are about to find you," she says. "And then your little operation will be done."

She's silenced when I tilt the pan to let another batch roll down the chute, the sound drowning out any chance at conversation as the beads rush over the metal and onto the surface of the table.

"If the Delacroixs come this way, we'll get rid of them," Dad says. "That's why I have a gun here."

He pats the Glock on the table beside him and then goes back to packing.

Harper's eyes go wide, and she increases her pace, quickly running three lines of tape over the boxes before pushing them against the wall. "You're going to kill them?" she asks.

"The blood will be on your hands," he says. "You brought them here."

"They won't come down here," I assure Harper, seeing the stricken look on her face.

"If I don't come back they will."

SELENA

"I'll text them," I say, pulling out my phone.

Her eyes narrow. "You have your phone?"

"Yeah," I say. "Why wouldn't I?"

She closes her eyes for a second. "Of course he was lying."

Dad's phone chimes, and he looks at it and then nods to me. "Colin's here. Go open the door for him."

I glance from him to Harper.

"Go," Dad barks.

"I'm taking her with me," I say, grabbing Harper's arm.

Dad snatches up his gun. "She's not going anywhere. You'll let her leave."

"I won't," I say, glaring back at him.

He lowers the gun toward her legs. "I'll take her kneecap to make sure she can't run. Then you can take her with you."

"Don't fucking point a gun at her," I grit out. I slam out of the room and across the dining area, waiting for the sound of a gunshot. It doesn't come. He knows that would end the saving of his operation, and he's too greedy to chance it.

I shove open the outer doors to the mall, bracing it open against the gusting wind while six men file in. I lead them into the dining room and tell them to wait. When I step back into the kitchen, Harper's right where I left her, and Dad's still holding the gun. The bastard's too scared to put it down when she's in the room with him.

I can't help but be impressed. It takes a lot to intimidate Tony Dolce, and even if he'd never admit it, that's why he's not working right now. He knows our time here is limited, and if he'd give up five minutes of money to guard her, he's pissing himself with fear of what she'll do—or what I'll do if he fucks with her again.

When the packed boxes are gone, Colin sticks his head into the kitchen. "Got any more for me tonight?"

"Wait in the parking lot," I growl.

His eyes fall on Harper, and a predatory grin spreads over his face. "Well, fuck me," he says. "Why am I not surprised to find this little lassie running Alice? Or are you just picking up enough to keep you going through your new football team this week?"

He nods at the box next to Dad's table, and she fixes him with a withering glare. "I don't need your creepy sex drugs," she says. "Though you might want to dip into your supply. Duke says they keep you going all night. Now, I don't believe in miracles, but they might get you past the two-minute mark."

"If two minutes is all it takes to get mine, why waste time going longer?" he asks.

I wheel around and clock the dumb fuck right in the face. He stumbles back, grabbing his nose before the door swings closed in his face.

"Royal," Dad barks. "That's our connection."

"I told him to wait in the parking lot," I say, starting toward my table.

The door swings open, and I turn back, ready to continue the little dance Colin and I have been doing for years. The bastard's the only man in Faulkner who likes to fight more than I do.

But King's the one who steps through the door. Behind him, there's a whole army of random faces. I don't take the time to place them all. I dive for the Glock on the table beside Dad.

He grabs for it at the same moment. He's closer, and his fingers close around it before mine. My hand lands on top of his, and I grab his wrist.

We stare at each other for a second, and then I bring my other fist down on his hand as hard as I can.

Dad howls in pain.

Bones crunch under my fingers as I smash his hand between my fist and the metal table. His grip instinctively loosens, and I rip the gun free and bring it down on the back of his head.

He flops facedown on the table.

I grab the back of his neck and press the gun to his skull.

"Don't," King orders, his voice sharp and final.

I loosen my grip.

"What's going on?" he asks.

SELENA

"Exactly what it looks like," I say. "I'm getting rid of him, just like I told you."

"You don't need that on you," he says. "Let me do it."

"You're going to kill him?" Crystal asks.

Always Daddy's little girl.

"He's the reason we left Faulkner," Devlin says.

"Which is the reason for all of this," Harper says. "The reason your brothers are all fucked beyond repair, and the streets are running blue with this fucking Alice in Wonderland shit."

"He wouldn't pay anyone who tried to help find you," Colt says. "Our family paid them off so they'd stop looking because we hoped you were out there alive, and you'd live in peace if they stopped trying to find you. We knew he'd kill you both if he found you."

"You knew we were alive?" Crystal asks.

"No," Colt admits. "Preston never gave up, but I figured you would've come back if you were alive. But it doesn't change what your dad did. Our family is in ruins, and for what? Because our dads threw yours out of a party twenty-five years ago?"

"Or because Crystal and Devlin left," Harper says quietly. "Maybe he didn't want you found, either."

I stare at her, hating her for voicing the thought I've kept at bay since Crystal stepped out of that car. Everything we've done... I did it all for her.

But if she's alive, we didn't destroy the Darlings because they took our sister. It's all for Dad, to keep the Darlings from claiming a part of his business. He knows they have a legitimate claim, and the more profitable Dolce Sweets becomes, the more likely they'll come to collect. They came up with the first recipe, after all.

Of course it was about that. It's always business first.

The Darlings didn't kill my sister or even kidnap her. Dad's the one who would have sacrificed her that night, framing the Darlings for kidnapping her. If I hadn't stepped in, she's the one who would have endured what I did. I would never let him risk her, so I helped him set them up. I paid the price, but he didn't care. It made no

SELENA

difference to him which of his children he risked, as long as we got the job done.

When it all went wrong, and they found me before the cops, he helped me get revenge. But he never gave me what I needed.

Harper did. She's the one who found my sister, who brought her back to me.

And Crystal, she's happily wifed up with fucking Devlin Darling, popping out abominations that mix our blood with theirs. She looks perfectly happy about it, too.

They never hurt her.

We did.

And we hurt them, the family that didn't do more than fight back when we stepped on their turf. We annihilated them—killed and maimed and drove them to suicide and insane asylums.

It wasn't because of what their grandfather did, despite what Dad thinks. I could have survived what they did to me. I couldn't survive losing Crystal, too. That's what broke me. Dad knew that all along, knew how to use us to his advantage, twist us to fit his sick ambitions, to keep his empire running.

All Devlin did was make my sister fall in love with him. He didn't use her up and toss her the way I thought he would. I thought he was using her to get to us. But when we were a danger to her, he took her out of harm's way. He kept her safe—safe from us.

The Darlings aren't our enemy. They never were.

Dad is.

SELENA

thirty

Harper Apple

"What are you going to do to him?" Duke asks from the small crowd. Everyone from the parking lot is here, along with DeShaun and Cotton, who must have joined after their swamp expedition. They gape around at the impressive operation—basins and pans, popcorn kettles that must be from the movie theater across the hall, the long stainless-steel tables, catering pans, and other industrial kitchen supplies, all put to good use making drugs.

"We're going to decide together," King says. "All of us."

"We already decided," Royal says quietly. He's still standing behind his father, but he's lowered the gun.

"Not everyone was there then," King says.

"This isn't about everyone," Royal says. "He fucking touched my girl."

"I think Duke needs to be on that side of the table with him," I say. "He's obviously on your dad's side."

"What?" Duke protests. "What did I do?"

"Um, you just tried to kill me?"

"What?" Royal growls.

"I did not," Duke says, pushing past Gloria and Colt.

"You said tonight was as good a time to get rid of me as—"

I break off, my gaze moving from his unmarked jaw to his hoodie, which he's wearing, to his leg, which has no blood on it.

"Ohhh," he says slowly, nodding.

"Baron," Crystal says, glancing around.

"Right," I say, feeling stupid. I almost forget they're identical because I know them so well, it's easy to tell them apart. I should have fucking known. From the moment he grabbed me, when he didn't smell like beer and weed, something went off in my brain, but I was too busy fighting for my life to register it. It should have

SELENA

taken more than a change of clothes and losing the glasses for him to fool me.

Guess I'm the sucker.

"Where is he, anyway?" Duke asks.

"I knocked him out in the hall," I say.

"Well, he's not there now," Mr. Delacroix says.

"Then we probably need to get out of here," I say. "This is his operation. He's going to be pissed that we all busted in on it."

"If he hasn't already notified the cops," Colt says. "To tell them the Delacroixs are cooking with the Pearl Lady down here."

"But it wasn't us," Gideon says.

"It's on our property," Mr. Delacroix says. "If it's our word against the Dolces, you know what the judge will rule."

"Because the judges are all bought off," I say, nodding.

"We should get out of here," Mr. Delacroix says.

"What about all this?" King asks, nodding at the drugs on the table. "Want a cut?"

"No," Mr. Delacroix says. "That's dirty money."

I remember Preston calling it blood money. I guess he got his principles from the Delacroix side of the family.

"The cops will confiscate it," Duke says, crossing his arms and surveying the room. "All Baron's hard work."

"He has the plans for the design," Royal says. "And the recipe. It's in a briefcase in the dining area."

"I'll grab it on the way out," Duke says.

"Or," I say. "We can burn it all before the cops get here."

They stare at me for a second.

"You know how much money is in this room?" Duke asks.

"Don't care," I say. I once thought money was everything, but now I know better. I'd rather have none than use the Dolce's dirty money. I've already benefited enough from it. It's not just blood money. It's a whole fucking operation, a huge kitchen full of equipment for mixing and cooking the shit. It's an entire blood empire that started with Baron's experiment to find a drug that would help Duke keep it up when he was drunk so he and Baron could double-team girls. Now, it's boxes of candy with bags of drugs nestled underneath, shipping all over the country.

I've seen what that shit did to my mom. I think of all the other parents and kids who will be lost to it, and I have zero interest in contributing to their end.

"Someone's going to control the drug scene," Duke says. "Might as well make some money."

"You sound exactly like him," I say, nodding to their dad.

"She's right," Royal says. "Let's get rid of all of it."

"It'll go up like a meth lab when the heat hits the tanks," Duke says, his eyes glazing over with a look that can only be described as pure lust.

"Then let's get out of here before that happens," I say.

"I'll light the match," Duke says, heading for a stainless steal drum at the far end of the room.

"What about him?" I ask, nodding at Mr. Dolce.

Our attention turns to his limp body for a minute, a silence in which we all come to our own conclusions.

Then Duke lights the match. He holds it, swaying slightly on his feet as he stares at it. Then, he drops it into the basin.

I gulp as a flare of flames shoots up. Duke stands there, transfixed as he gazes at the dancing flames. When I stepped into the kitchen, the smell was like the taste of cocaine—bitter and chemical and harsh. Now, the burning smell is even worse. I cover my mouth and nose with my sleeve.

"Duke," King barks. "Come on."

"Huh?" Duke says, tearing his eyes away.

Royal strides over and grabs him, dragging him over to us and herding us toward the door. "Let's go."

"Your dad?" I remind him.

He glances back, then shakes his head, his lips tight. "Leave him."

I open my mouth to protest, to tell them we have all this evidence, that we could put him in prison for life. But I'm not naïve enough to believe it. He's paid off

SELENA

everyone, and he has enough money to get out of this. There's no other way to get rid of him permanently and make sure he never comes back.

A wrecking ball is not the only way to destroy a house—but sometimes it's the best way.

Everyone pauses for a second, the room silent except for a rumble of thunder outside and the crackle of the flames.

Then, one by one, we file out of the kitchen.

Crystal hesitates in the door, the last person to leave. She looks back for another long moment and then turns, letting the door fall closed behind her. We stare at each other for a second, and I think maybe she's not so bad after all. At least, I'll give her a chance to prove herself.

Royal slips an arm around my shoulders as we walk out of the restaurant, then out of the mall into the cold night. The fog from all our breath rises, disappearing into the blackness overhead. Tiny, sharp raindrops bounce off our shoulders, but despite the ugly weather, a sense of peace settles over me.

"Who are all these people?" Royal asks, nodding to the small crowd.

"They're… My friends," I say. "We were all looking for you. We were scared you'd hurt yourself or that your dad would."

Royal frowns down at me. "Why?"

"Because they're your friends, too," I say.

"I don't even know half these people," he says. "And the ones I do…"

"You hurt," I finish. "When you were working for your dad."

"Not just then," he says quietly.

"Well, I think they understand," I say. "Or at least they're willing to give you another chance."

We climb into my car and sit there as the others climb into theirs. I don't know where Baron went, but he must be on foot or still in the mall. I decide I'm okay with that. If he gets blown up, he deserves it.

"I didn't want you involved in that," he says quietly. "This part of my life isn't pretty, Harper."

SELENA

"Shocking as this may be, I don't expect everything in life to be pretty," I say with a little grin.

"You're okay with what we just did?"

I nod, and we sit in silence for a minute. I'm zero percent interested in being a murderer, but some people don't deserve forgiveness.

"What did he have on you?" I ask at last. "Why were you still helping your dad after everything he did to you, and your brothers, and your sister?"

"You brought my sister back," he says, staring at the mall as the Delacroixs pull away in their car. Royal pulls my car around, but he doesn't follow the others from the lot. He stops in front of the restaurant and stares out the windshield where icy pellets are melting down the glass.

"Are you mad?" I ask.

"No."

We sit in silence, the roar of the heater the only sound in the night.

"Want me to do the same?" he asks.

"I have a sister?"

"Yeah," he says. "A half-sister, anyway. I've only found her so far. And your dad. You have a dad."

I wonder if he's regretting it, that we left his dad in there. He won't have a dad anymore after tonight.

"No," I say at last. "He didn't want to know me, and I don't want to know him. Whatever I am, it has nothing to do with him. He can't take credit or blame. Just like I didn't want to know if I was a Darling. I only did it for Preston. I didn't want their money or anything from them if they didn't bother with me all my life."

"You don't even want to meet him?"

"No," I say. "If I ever change my mind, I know where to find him. In prison."

"Okay."

We sit there a few more minutes, until the first explosion sounds inside the restaurant. It's muffled and unimpressive. I glance at Royal, but he's staring straight ahead, expressionless.

"Are you afraid your brother's in there?" I ask, laying a hand on his knee.

SELENA

"No," he says, placing his hand over mine. "He's long gone."

"Are you upset about that?" I ask carefully.

"I'm sorry I didn't protect you from him," he says, turning my hand over and lacing our fingers. "I should have done something about him sooner. I lost my sister, and I didn't want to lose a brother, too. But the truth is, I lost him a long time ago."

"He said he's the one who blew up your car."

"I know," Royal admits. "I suspected as much when the report came back. It was an explosive he and Duke are particularly fond of. I didn't know why, though. I told myself it was a coincidence that Preston was using it, too. But when he said he didn't do it…"

"Baron was trying to get rid of me. I guess he got tired of waiting for you to dump me and was trying to stir shit up so you'd remember I was a Darling."

Royal grips the wheel with one hand, his jaw tense. "When you said he tried to kill you tonight…" He shakes his head. "If I saw him right now, I'd put back in there beside Dad."

There's a minute of silence, and then a series of explosions that become progressively more violent, at first sending tremors through the ground and then rocking the car as the glass blows from the windows at the front of the restaurant and tiles rain down from the roof.

When it's over, my heart is hammering, but not loud enough to drown the sound of the fire eating the front of the building. At last, Royal pulls away from the restaurant, and we circle the mall in the other direction, leaving the blaze behind.

"You never answered my question," I say when we're on the road.

"What question?"

I smile at the town slipping by outside the window of the Escalade. I can't remember the last time he told me I couldn't ask questions. I'm in his life now, and not just in it, but part of it. I affect his life. I know all his secrets, and he knows mine.

"Why were you helping your dad?"

"The same reason I always do."

SELENA

"You went to confront him about Crystal," I say. "And he threatened to go after her?"

He adjusts his grip on the wheel. "I told him she was back, and he was the reason she left. He said he'd help me get rid of Devlin."

"And you said no to that?"

"It's what I've been doing for years," he says. "Getting revenge. But if she's back… There's no reason. Part of me wonders…"

I grip his hand tighter. "What?"

"If he stopped looking and had a funeral for her so we'd keep doing his bidding. He told us she wasn't coming back, and we couldn't do anything about it, so we should focus on what we could do."

"Which was destroy the Darlings."

"Yeah."

"Then why were you still helping him tonight?"

He glances at me. "He threatened someone else."

"Me?" I ask.

He doesn't say anything.

"Aww, but I thought you hated me."

"I do," he says, pulling his hand away and giving me a sour look.

"I hate you, too," I say, leaning over and kissing his cheek. "I'll hate you forever, until the day I die, Royal Dolce."

SELENA

thirty-one

Baron Dolce

A town is waiting for her king. They've never worshipped like they'll worship me. Her people don't know it yet, but their lives are about to change forever.

I can't just walk in and demand their obedience, though. I've learned from our mistakes in Faulkner. I'll earn it.

I glance at the boxes in the back seat. Nestled beneath the Dolce Crystals, five thousand nights with Lady Alice wait in each one, precious currency to start a new life.

They'll think I'm generous when I show up with a good time, free of charge. They've never had anything like this, never been to Wonderland.

One pill makes you larger.

The individuals will line up for more. The collective will be impressed at how their economy flourishes as the money flows in. By the time they realize they need it, need me, they'll be completely reliant on what I provide.

Money. Intelligence. Drugs.

They'll be nothing without me.

One hundred make you small.

I pat the briefcase in the passenger's seat. Everything I need is here. Even if I hadn't taken a single pearl, I'd be fine. But I have enough to get me started and keep me going while I get the equipment to start up a new operation. The first one was just an experiment. I've learned from that, too.

The past three years have been nothing but practice for this. People say high school is a joke, but they're not paying attention to the right things. I'm smart. I could say the same thing. I didn't learn anything in my classes that I couldn't learn on my own, that I will use in any career. But I learned.

Everything that goes on in a high school is just practice. The way people treat you inside and outside that

SELENA

school, the power dynamics of teachers and students, other students, parents, coaches. You learn how people see those in each of these categories, how they treat others, what they expect and how they react when expectations are or are not met. Once you master the art of observation, you know how to get what you want. What you can get away with. How far you can go.

There's so much to learn.

I've been watching, though. I'm prepared for the real world, for the rest of my life.

My only regret is Harper.

I underestimated her. She was supposed to be an easy target. An unwanted Darling, one we could take all the way. Mabel had too much power, even when she was powerless. She had a name, a reputation among the families, at the school.

Harper had nothing. She was the one.

As soon as I saw her blowing that teacher, I knew she'd be the one we could finally end. Not just leave them to suffer, the way Royal likes.

It wasn't enough.

Not because of anything she'd done, but because of what I hadn't.

I remember the first time I saw a man die. I remember my uncle holding him down in the water. I wondered what he felt in that moment—not the dying man, but my uncle. As he watched the life drain from the man's eyes, the realization sink into the man that his life was over, what did he feel?

He must have felt like a god.

That's what I wanted. Once, when I was fucking Mabel, I choked her until she passed out. I'm not some creep who likes his women unresponsive, like Cotton. But for a minute, I thought she was dead. I've never cum harder in my life.

I didn't quite dare kill her, though. I didn't want to.

Harper was a fresh start. She was no one. Someone who could disappear without anyone making a fuss. She was the perfect target.

The perfect victim.

I thought it would be harmless to have a little fun with her first. I didn't count on Royal falling for her.

SELENA

That's where everything can go wrong, the one variable that cannot be controlled for no matter how much you've studied, how many game tapes you've watched, how predictable people usually are. Once in a while, they catch feelings, and everything falls apart. Chaos ensues.

The shit she pulled this year was nothing. I could have dealt with it if she didn't have Royal's protection. Of course she couldn't topple our empire at Willow Heights. We played football, and football is god in Faulkner, so we were gods. But I want to be a god in a different way. I want to hold life in my hands.

It should have been her life. It shouldn't have happened the way it did. I kept trying to find ways to bring it back under control—blowing up Royal's engine so he'd remember he hated all Darlings, revealing the texts she'd sent me as Mr. D. But no matter what I did, he kept being pulled back into her orbit as if magnetized by her gravity.

I should have just killed her in the swamp. I didn't want to do it in front of the others, though. They might have interfered. And it was somehow private, something I wanted to keep all for myself. She was my find. My kill.

She was never supposed to be Royal's.

He wasn't supposed to want her, to claim her.

Not because I'm jealous, but because some things are just for me. I'm a selfish bastard like that.

It wasn't *her* that I wanted to keep, though.

It was her death.

Not even Duke could share that. I didn't want him to question my methods. I didn't want him or Dawson to look at me differently. I didn't want any witnesses, not even my brother. No one could know what I'd done, so I let them think I spared her.

But I went back for her.

Royal thinks he's the only one who went back, but I went back, too.

He couldn't find her. He was too out of it to pay attention to where we were going that night, but I was sharper than I'd ever been, more alive.

SELENA

I knew exactly where we left her. We'd found our way back in the dark with Dawson. It was easy in daylight.

I pictured what I'd do as I made my way to the tree. I didn't want to do it too quickly. I needed to pinpoint the moment life ended. Strangulation seemed the best option. That way, I'd have just enough time to feel the struggle, to feel her fighting and to earn the win, when my life triumphed over hers. I wanted to feel it end, to feel the power of a god in my hands as I took her life from her body. I wanted to see life turn to death, up close and personal, like my uncle had. She would be my first kill.

And I would become a god.

But she was gone.

I couldn't have predicted that. After all, I thought I, as Mr. D, was her only friend and confidant.

Trust a Darling to come along and fuck it all up. They've always been the destructive force, sowing chaos wherever they go. Since Dad was our age, that's their purpose. The masters of mayhem, the reapers of madness.

Devlin stole Crystal.

Mabel stole Duke.

And Preston stole Harper.

But I'll have more chances. It was never personal with Harper. She could have been anyone. There's a whole world full of people, and I'll use her survival as a lesson. I'll learn from those mistakes like I learn from all of them.

Don't fuck with someone once they are loved. Even after what she did, I couldn't turn the tide. Royal had caught feelings, and they didn't go away no matter what she or I did. So I gave her back, brought him to her at that party. That was my apology to him.

I don't owe her an apology. But maybe I owe her a debt of gratitude for all she taught me.

Next time, I'll make sure it's someone who won't be missed, someone that no one loves. An outcast, a loner, someone without friends or concerned family. And I won't involve anyone who can change that.

SELENA

I'll get it out of my system, just to see what it's like, and then I'll find Mabel. I won't kill her. I won't let her die. Like Royal, I'll pull her out of the river and force her to live, to endure. She is mine, just like Harper is his. If he gets to keep one, I can keep one, too. If Harper isn't a Darling, it doesn't make a difference. Not anymore. Crystal got to keep a Darling, and everyone forgave her.

So I'll go find Mabel, and I'll keep her forever, too.

Sparse, fat drops of rain splatter on the windshield as I turn a corner, the Tesla's headlights slicing the night. And there, like an answer to an unspoken prayer, is a hitchhiker.

She's walking along the side of the road, a backpack on her back, a beanie pulled down over her hair, only a jean jacket to keep out the cold.

I flash my headlights and then pull over ahead of her. I watch her in the red glow of the taillights. She's young, around my age. A runaway, from the looks of it. My heartbeat picks up speed as excitement churns in my belly. It's closer to home than I'd like, but I don't have to do it here. I can wait a few hours, maybe even cross the state line first.

I hit the button, and the window glides down when she reaches the car. She bends down and peers in, the tips of her shoulder-length blue hair catching the light. She looks familiar, though I can't place her right away.

"I didn't expect a car this nice to pull over," she says, sounding nervous.

"You can wait for a creepy old trucker if you're afraid to get in a car with a guy like me," I say, flashing her a grin.

Her cheeks turn pink, and I know there's no way she's walking away from this ride. Girls like her don't turn down hot rich guys.

I pick up the briefcase and move it to the space behind her seat. "Now or never, sweetheart," I say. "You're getting my leather wet."

"Okay," she says, opening the door and sliding in. She sets her bag between her feet and closes the door, and my excitement pulls tight like a knot inside me.

SELENA

I roll up the window and hit the accelerator, and the tires purr as we slide back onto the road. "You from around here?" I ask, watching her from the corner of my eye. She smells like cigarettes and sex.

"Faulkner."

"What part?"

"Mill Street," she says. "You from there?"

I knew she looked familiar, but that's when I realize where I've seen her. She's Harper's neighbor.

"Just passing through," I say.

"This is really nice," she says, touching the leather seat like she's never seen one before. "Thanks."

"I could use the company," I say. "Where you headed?"

She shrugs. "Away. West. Where are you going?"

"Away," I say, smirking at her.

"What's in the boxes?" she asks, glancing into the back seat.

"Candy," I say. "I'm making a delivery."

She looks as doubtful as she should, but she doesn't ask questions. Smart girl.

"You got a phone?" I ask.

"Yeah."

"Put it here," I say, patting the cup holder. "You're going to entertain me. Not sit on your phone while I do all the work."

She chews at the corner of her lip. "I won't get on my phone."

I raise a brow and tap the cup holder with one finger, keeping my eyes on her instead of the road until she slowly obeys, setting her phone in the holder.

"Good choice," I say, picking it up. I hit the button to roll down my window and throw it as far as it will go.

"What are you doing?" she cries, her eyes going wide with shock. "That's my phone!"

I grin at her and roll up the window. "Were you going to call for help?"

She gulps and stares at me like she's just realized her life is in my hands. My cock twitches in my jeans at the thought.

"You don't fool me, sweetheart," I say. "If you had someone, you wouldn't be hitchhiking in the rain in

SELENA

November. You might as well accept the truth now. There's no helping either of us."

thirty-two

Royal Dolce

"It's done," I say, sitting down in my usual spot in the family room. I just said goodbye to Harper, told her I have family shit to deal with tonight, and sent her home. I'm still not sure if I'm pissed at her for what she did, but I'll deal with that later. "The whole place went up. Now we just have to do damage control."

"It was an accident," King says, not missing a beat. "He must have fallen and hit his head while he was packing up the pills. The place went up with him still inside."

He speaks with such certainty I almost believe it. No wonder they were able to convince us Crystal was dead.

"Harper broke the glass on the door to the food court," I say.

SELENA

"Teenagers breaking in to cause mischief," Devlin says. "No evidence that it's related or that it happened the same night."

I stare across the square coffee table in the center of the room at him. Of course he has a story to cover it up. He's a professional liar.

For some reason, this asshole is sitting in on our meeting like he's a member of the family, even though Eliza's not here. She went to relieve the nanny, and Crystal went to check on their kids.

My mind fumbles the thought. *Three kids.*

Last time I saw my sister, *she* was a fucking kid.

They've made three whole human beings since I've seen them.

"Why are you here?" I ask, glaring at him with a mixture of rage and regret that has me even more fucked up than usual.

"I told him to join us," King says, levelling me with a cool stare.

Devlin's watching me, too. He's calm on the surface, but his posture is stiff, his shoulders squared as he meets my gaze without flinching. "If we're not welcome in this family, we'll leave."

No one moves as we sit staring each other down, his words settling into the empty spaces, places where Baron and my father and my sister should be.

They could run again. He has the money to disappear like they did before, and without Baron, we won't find them. We didn't even find them when we had Baron.

I've lost more tonight than I gained.

Add one sister, subtract a brother and a father.

Except I got more than a sister. If I want, I can have two nephews and a niece. I could even have a brother-in-law.

If I don't want that, no one is going to force me to accept them. They were happy living out in California, apparently, without any of us. They don't need us. The question is, do we need them?

"You're going to take my sister and run like a fucking pussy again?" I ask.

"That depends," Devlin says. "Your father's gone, and according to Preston, our grandfather and most of my uncles are... Diminished."

That's putting it literally, but I don't say as much. I don't know what that asshole told Devlin, and I won't give him more information than he has.

"It's up to us now," Devlin says. "Our generation is the one that has to go on from here."

"You're leaving it up to me?" I clarify.

Devlin gives the slightest nods. "My wife loves you," he says. "But you hurt her before. It won't happen again. If that means leaving this town, that's what we'll do."

"It doesn't have to be that extreme," I say grudgingly. "I'm not going to kill you."

"And Crystal?"

"She's my fucking twin," I snap. "I'm the one who should be worrying if someone will hurt her."

"You gave up that privilege when you disowned her," he says flatly. "It's my job to worry about whether staying in this house will leave her with three kids to raise on her own, and those kids without a father."

"I said I won't kill you," I growl, though I'm fucking tempted when he reminds me what I gave up, what I did. Anger roils inside me, and the monster flickers to life, offering me relief. But I won't hide from this, from my mistakes, not even when he offers to take the burden. I told her she was dead, and I have to take responsibility and live with the consequences, just like I have to live with what I did to the Darlings when I thought they'd killed her. I was wrong about that, which means all I did to avenge her was wrong.

But they're far from innocent, either.

"I'm glad you still care about her," Devlin says. "And that you're not after me anymore. But if it's too much for you to see her with me, there's another family in this town we belong to. If we're not welcome here, there's a place for us there."

I stare at the prick in disbelief.

Fuck. He's right.

The Darlings are family.

Which means *we're* family.

He's part of our family, and she's part of his.

SELENA

A Darling, a member of the family I've spent the past three years destroying, is sitting in a Dolce family meeting. And if I kick him out, I have to kick her out, too.

Because she's not just a Dolce. She's a Darling now, too.

As Devlin and I wait for the other to make a move, I play it out in my head. How much it would kill me to see her around here, with their Darling-Dolce babies reminding me every fucking day that they have joined these two families that cannot be reconciled. They have the blood of both our families running through their veins.

It's too late to stop it. Our families have already been tied together.

They always have been, for the past three years, even when I didn't know it. The family that killed Little Royal is now part of my own family. My twin married into the family that destroyed ours every bit as much as we destroyed theirs.

If I kick Devlin out now, he'll take her with him. I weigh whether that's the best option. I could keep going on the path I've trodden for three years, keep the hatred alive even after our father is dead, his drive for revenge dying with him. It would live on through me. I'd tear apart their family just like they tore apart ours. I'd forbid Duke from going to find Mabel when he graduates. It would never end.

I could disown all their kids because they carry a Darling name. Devlin could be a stranger I see at the gym and nod as I walk by. Crystal could be another woman waiting in line for concessions with her kids at the football games, even if she doesn't carry their blood. She carries the name.

But she's not the one who would hurt most from that. She's already proven she can live without us, that she's fine on her own. She flourished.

We're the ones who fell apart without her.

I look at King.

SELENA

He jerks his chin at me in a slight nod, his eyes hooded as he watches me. "It's your family now, Royal," he says quietly. "I don't live here."

I sit with that for a minute, the weight and responsibility falling officially onto my shoulders. He told me to watch out for the twins when he left for New York two and a half years ago, and I've been learning the business from Dad since I turned eighteen. But this is the first time it's been solely mine.

Dad's dead.

This is my family now, my business, my empire.

It's my choice whether to accept them or not. My brother is showing me the utmost respect, a gift of value beyond comprehension, by deferring to me. He's letting me make a choice that affects the whole family, showing that he trusts me with the responsibly of doing what's right even after all the wrongs I've committed. He's also telling me that he's my brother first and will have my back no matter what I decide.

And in return, I know I have to give him what he needs, too—what everyone needs. For three years, this wedge of guilt and blame has torn us apart. I won't add more to it, widening the distance between us just when we've made progress, taken steps across the gulf between us, slowly moving back toward each other.

At last, I give my brother a solemn nod, knowing the weight of my next words.

Then I turn to Devlin Darling, the man who took my twin away from me.

"You can stay."

His lips tighten, and he gives a quick nod to show he understands and accepts. "Then it's time to start talking about how to fix this town."

"I'm not interested in fixing this town," I say. "I'm leaving when Harper graduates. I have a business to run and a better school waiting. Duke is graduating and leaving, too. Crystal will be the only Dolce left in Faulkner by summer."

"And what about this town?" Devlin asks.

"It's yours," I say. "Take it."

SELENA

thirty-three

Harper Apple

"How does it feel having your sister home?" I ask, hopping up beside Royal in the open back of the Rover.

It's only been a day, but he seems to have calmed down at least enough to want to go to the river and fuck. We fogged up the windows inside, and now we're letting the car air out and having a smoke in the cold wetness of the winter afternoon.

"It's… okay," he says. "Different."

"You okay?" I ask, accepting the joint he hands to me.

"It's not really like having her back," he says. "She's not the same person."

"She's probably thinking the same about you," I say, taking his hand and linking my fingers with his.

"Yeah," he says, retrieving the joint with his free hand. "I guess so. It's been almost three years. She's not a kid anymore, the innocent little sister I have to protect. She's a wife now—a fucking mom."

"Maybe that was Crystal Dolce," I say. "And this is Crystal Darling."

"What about you?" he asks, turning to study my face. "Are you going to stop being a bad Apple one day and be a Dolce girl forever?"

"I don't know," I say lightly. "Maybe I'll keep my name. I kind of like it."

"The hell you will," he says, his grip on my hand tightening possessively. "I want the world to know you're mine. If I have to carve my name over every inch of your skin, I'll do it."

"Fine, I'll take the name," I say, laughing. "I was just fucking with you anyway. Although if I have your name, what do you have to prove you're mine?"

"Is this enough?" he asks, slowly unbuttoning his shirt with one hand, so he can keep holding mine in the other. I know what's there, but every time, it makes my heart flip again. I wait, my heartbeat thudding as he undoes each button with agonizing slowness until he reaches the bottom. He pulls his shirt open, and I gaze at his ink, my heart in my throat.

"I still can't believe you did this," I say, reaching out to run my fingertips over his chest.

"And you got a sunflower," he says. "What's that about?"

"Um," I say, taking the joint and getting a good toke to work up my courage. "So, Preston told me sunflowers always follow their sun. And I should follow mine."

"And I'm your sun?" he asks with a haughty little smirk.

"I figured you'd be mad," I say, sinking back in relief.

"Why?" he asks. "I still think you're more of a black cherry, but you make a cute sunflower, too. If that means you're chasing after me, it seems fitting."

"Hey," I protest. "You're the one who stalked me until I relented."

"Keep telling yourself that, Stalker Girl," he says. "You chased me around like a bitch in heat for half of last year. Not that I blame you."

"Ugh, you're infuriating," I say.

"Besides, why do I care what he said? I'm the one who carved my initials into your ass," he says, wrapping his arm around me and pulling me in so he can palm my left ass cheek in his huge hand.

He takes a long drag, then wraps his fingers around my chin, pulling it up so plant his mouth on mine. I open my lips, letting him fill my lungs with his breath and the smoke. We pass it back and forth a few times before I pull away and blow it out into the cold afternoon. The last rays of sunlight reflect on the wet surface of the road leading back toward town.

"Any word from Baron?" I ask.

"No," he says. "He fucked up and he knows it. I don't know that he'll be back."

"You don't seem worried."

SELENA

"He's alive," he says with a shrug. "He'll probably go find Mabel. Duke will track them down when he graduates."

"Baron's not going to graduate?"

"He has all the credits to graduate early," Royal says. "He only stayed for Duke."

"That's kind of sweet."

Royal snorts. "I don't think you're allowed to use that word to describe Baron."

"Okay, true," I say, taking the rest of the joint from him. "Anyway, I didn't know you'd be trading one sibling for another. But I'm glad you're not too upset about Baron."

"Yeah," he says, squeezing me against him.

We sit in silence for a minute. I curl into his side, seeking his warmth, and he holds me tight to his side. He finishes the joint and flicks the roach in the dead grass, then turns and pulls my chin up. He presses his lips softly to mine before pulling back. "Thank you."

I don't have to ask what he's thanking me for. My chest swells, and I wrap my arms around his neck and kiss him hard. "I hope it's what you needed," I say. "I hope it makes you happy."

"You make me happy, Harper Apple," he says, sliding his arms around me and twisting me around in the trunk. He pushes the seat flat and slides up it, keeping me pinned to him. Settling between my legs, he kisses me again, the deep, hungry kisses that make my head spin and curls of arousal lick at every inch of my skin. I wrap my legs around him, squeezing him with my knees.

Royal rests on his elbow and lifts up just enough to reach between us and shove my jeans down. He pulls his cock free of his pants and pushes up into me slow and deep. A wordless sound of pleasure escapes me at the sensation of his thick cock stretching me open again while I'm still wet with his cum from the last time. I squeeze my walls around him, gripping his shaft inside me and locking my gaze with his dark, smoldering one. He growls and leans down, pressing his lips to mine as he pumps into me in a slow, steady rhythm that drives me up the seat a few inches with each pass. I let my head fall back, digging my nails into his back as his lips ravish my neck, my collarbones.

"Royal," I gasp, feeling so good I don't know how it's possible, how I can contain this much feeling at once, the pleasure and pain and love that spiral inside me until I think I'll erupt.

"I know, *cuore mio*," he says, driving into me with hard, dominating thrusts. He grips my chin in his hand, forcing my gaze to his. "I know. Stay with me."

He doesn't let go until I cum. Then he leans down and kisses me, and the warmth of his own release deep inside me has me shuddering with pleasure all over again. He draws out, and I can feel his cum leaking out of me as he lowers himself onto me, resting his weight on his elbows and lying his head on my chest.

"Harper," he says, squeezing me.

"I know," I say, threading my fingers through his thick hair.

We lie there a long while before he rolls off me and pulls up his jeans. I lie there in a puddle of cum and bliss, not even attempting to move. He chuckles and pulls my jeans up, buttoning and zipping them. "Do I need to carry you to the front seat?" he asks, smirking down at me.

"Maybe," I say.

He quirks a brow.

I reach up and link my hands behind his neck, smiling up at him. "Yes, please."

He scoops me up and carries me to the front seat and buckles me in. "You're ridiculous, you know that?"

"You should take it as a compliment," I say, grabbing the front of his shirt and pulling him in for a kiss.

"You better stop, or I'll have to fuck you again."

I tighten my grip on his shirt and kiss him harder.

"You're really asking for it today," he says, smiling through our kiss. "You sure you can take it three times in one day?"

I pull back and smile up at him through my lashes. "Maybe… You could put it somewhere else this time?"

He groans and runs his hand up the back of my head, burying his hand in my hair and pressing my face to his chest. "What's gotten into you? You never ask for anal."

SELENA

"I'm just happy," I say, wrapping my arms around him and squeezing him against me. "And I'm happy that I could make you happy, too."

By the time we leave the river, evening has fallen. My ass, throat, and cervix all took a beating, but it's a good kind of sore. Royal turns on the headlights and drives across the bridge, the Rover lumbering along the wooden slats until we reach the far side, where he can turn around.

"You think you'll keep coming here?" I ask when we're back on the road. "I mean, this is where you came because of her, and now that she's home…"

"Now it's where I come with you," he says, reaching over and laying a possessive hand on my thigh. "It's not her place. It's *our* place."

"Are you mad at her?" I ask carefully.

He glances at me and then back to the road. "Of course I'm fucking mad," he says. "She was alive all that time. She let us believe she was dead for three fucking years."

"But you're not pissed at me for finding her?"

"I told you I wasn't," he says, squeezing my knee. "I'm glad she's back, even if I'm pissed. We're… Working through it. She's still my sister, even if I'm pissed at her. I don't hate her."

"That makes sense."

"How'd you find her, anyway?" he asks. "If Baron couldn't, I don't know how anyone could."

"It was shockingly easy," I say. "Considering Preston knew where Devlin worked. If you'd even stopped feuding with the Darlings, they probably would have told you."

He gives me a withering look, and I cringe.

"Sorry, that was bitchy. But basically, Dolly Beckett told him a while back, like a year or two. But since you were a dick to both of them, he convinced her not to tell y'all because he wanted y'all to leave them alone to live their best lives or something along those lines."

"I can't really blame her," Royal mutters.

"Dolly?"

"My sister," he says. "For wanting to leave this shit behind. I fucking hate her for it, but I respect it, too.

SELENA

She's brave. Not many people have the courage to say fuck everyone else, leave their whole whole life and everyone in it, and do whatever the fuck they want. I didn't."

"You were protecting your brothers," I say, reaching over and sliding my hand behind his neck, massaging it with my thumb while he drives. "You did the right thing. You're right to be pissed at her. I'm pissed at her, and I don't even know her. What they did might be brave, but it's also selfish."

We drive in silence for a minute. "You think you'd have done that?" he asks. "If you'd gotten pregnant, and you had the money..."

"What, run away?" I want to say I'd never do that, but if I'm honest, I have to think about it. "I don't know," I admit at last. "Probably. I wanted to get out of this town, and you were scary as fuck."

"Is that still what you want?" he asks.

"Yeah, for a while," I say. "But I think I'll actually miss this place. I don't think I ever really hated Faulkner.

I hated being trapped. Probably why I also don't want to have kids."

"You don't?" he asks, his brows lifting as he turns to look at me.

"Do you?"

He turns back to the road for a minute and then shakes his head. "No. I'd fuck them all up."

"And hey," I say. "If we ever change our minds in the future, at least we know we can't be worse than our parents."

"What about the other thing you said?" he asks. "You still think I'm scary?"

"Sometimes," I say. "But not to me."

He's quiet as we turn onto the road that leads to his neighborhood, the quiet, two-lane blacktop that winds through an area of skeletal winter trees. The road is still wet from last night's rain, and the yellow lines in the center glow out of the dark. I'm sure we're both thinking the same thing, about how we blew up his father just last night. I don't want to know how many people he's killed before that, but I'm not stupid enough to think he's

SELENA

harmless. I'm just secure enough to know that he won't let any harm come to me.

thirty-four

Duke Dolce

The house is veiled in darkness, like it was after Crystal died. Ghosts float through the halls. No one can see them but me. No one can see the shadow over us, either. They're lucky.

I fall back on my bed and scroll my phone, ignoring the presence hovering over me, like when you walk through an invisible spiderweb, and it sticks to your face.

I reach for the remote and flick the TV on, scrolling to *Local News with Jackie*. I'd bang that MILF in a heartbeat, but apparently she doesn't like younger dudes. Her husband is ancient.

She's standing in front of the mall, her dark hair blowing in her face and the wind trying to steal her voice from the microphone. "In the latest development from

SELENA

the explosion that happened last night at the recently-shuttered Faulkner Mall, a body has been recovered at the scene," she says, clutching her khaki coat around her. "Police have not yet released the identity of the victim, as this is an ongoing investigation."

I switch over to an internet browser and pull up something better—girl on girl action. I grab the lotion and a box of tissue and get to work, throwing an arm over my face at the last minute to block out the unseen eyes.

It's not my brother. He's alive.

He took the Tesla and got the hell out.

I know he's okay. I'd feel it if he wasn't.

Or maybe I wouldn't. Royal thought Crystal was dead all that time, and he's her twin. He said he couldn't feel that she was alive, which means I can't feel that Baron is.

But I know it, anyway. He's too smart to die.

It's Dad's body. He's the ghost haunting the halls of our house, back for revenge. Dad doesn't forgive. It's why we're in this town.

I get up and throw away the tissues and wash my hands. Then I shut off the TV and open the fridge. The worthless maid didn't restock my beer. Again.

I stomp downstairs, the emptiness hovering around me like another ghost. That's not Dad. It's Baron's absence.

I grab a sixpack and head outside to escape the hollowness inside. Dad's not here, but it's not like we spent any time together. It's the empty space of knowing he'll never be home again that fills me with heaviness. Baron's gone, but he'll be back. Royal is gone, off somewhere with Harper. Even she's better company than the ghosts.

I could call a chick from school, but it all got monotonous at some point. Even with Baron around to make things interesting by making them do some sick and twisted shit, there came a point where there was nothing new. One pussy was the same as the next, and there were no more things to try that weren't so extreme even I wouldn't cross that line.

SELENA

Besides, half the girls at school won't come crawling back when I call, thanks to Harper and Dixie. Not that it was a great loss—we'd already run through most of those girls, anyway. We didn't even want those bitches, so it's not like we cared if they cock-blocked us. There's plenty of other girls to fuck, but I'd rather go jerk off again than have one of them in here asking where Baron is and faking sympathy in hopes of sticking to me the way Harper stuck to Royal.

When I step outside, there's a kid sitting on the steps that curves around one side of the house, the side where I always sit. I take a seat there anyway. There are too many kids to keep track of anymore.

"Who are you?" I ask, opening a beer.

"Olive," she says. "Who are you?"

"Duke."

"That's your name?"

"No weirder than yours."

"Did you know a duke is the same thing as a prince?"

"I did not know that," I admit. "Are you sure?"

"Yep," she says.

"What are you doing here, Olive?" I ask.

"Waiting for my sister to come back."

I take a drink and wipe my mouth with the back of my hand. "Same."

"You're waiting for your sister?"

"Not anymore," I say. "Now I'm waiting for my brother."

"Oh."

We sit there for a while. I'm not sure what to do with a girl her size. She's way too old to bounce on my knee like a baby, and way too young to fuck. I don't get the point of children. They have no purpose.

I finish my beer and open a new one. "Want one?" I offer.

"Sure," she says.

"You ever had one?"

"Yeah," she says. "And I've smoked a cigarette."

"Hm," I say, handing her the beer. "So, when's your sister coming to get you?"

"I don't know," she says. "I spent the night with a friend last night, and Blue said to get off the bus and come to Harper's house and don't go home until she comes to get me."

"Oh," I say, relaxing against the railing and opening my own beer. "So, you're Harper's problem. She's not home yet. But I can take you to see my neighbors if you don't want to hang out with me."

She takes a little drink of the beer and makes a face, then tries to hide it when she sees me watching. "Why wouldn't I want to hang out with you? Are you a weirdo?"

"I don't know," I say. "Maybe. Probably."

"Oh," she says, leaning back on her backpack against the far railing. "You don't seem that weird to me."

"Maybe that means you're a weirdo, too," I say, grinning and bumping her beer with mine.

"I'm not a weirdo," she protests.

"How do you know?"

"Because I know me," she says. "And I'm not a weirdo."

"Maybe we can figure out if I'm a weirdo," I say. "How could you tell?"

"If you asked me to sit in your lap," she says promptly.

"Good call," I say. "But, like, if you want to hang out with a girl, there's one down the street who might know what to do with you. She's really cool. She's a cheerleader. Want to meet her?"

Olive wrinkles her nose. "My sister says cheerleaders are backstabbing bitches."

I nod. "That's fair. So, what are kids for, anyway?"

"What do you mean?"

"Like, what's the point of you existing?"

"Oh," she says, brightening. "Well, I like to dance, and ride my bike, and Hula hoop, and try on my sister's clothes when she's not home. But mostly, I like cars. I'm going to be a mechanic one day, and I'm going to drive a Bugatti."

That cracks me up. "You might want to look up the salary for that job before you take out a loan."

"What's the salary?"

"I don't know," I admit. "But in movies, mechanics are always poor."

SELENA

"Well, my backup plan is NASCAR."

"You'd really like my cheerleader friend," I say. "She races cars, *and* she knows how to fix them."

"Really?" Olive asks, her eyes going wide. "Is she poor?"

"She lives in my neighborhood, if you want to walk down the street and see."

"Okay," she says, hopping up. She staggers a little, and I can't help but laugh. Half a beer and she's already stumbling.

"You okay there?" I ask, reaching out to steady her.

She belches and then giggles. "I don't feel that good."

"A walk will help," I assure her. "Come on."

"Is this your house?" she asks, twisting around to look at it as we start down the walkway. She's still holding her half-empty bottle, and I've got a new one for the walk.

"Yup."

"You're, like, rich," she says. "What do you drive?"

"A Hummer."

"Can I see it?"

"Maybe when we get back."

"Okay," she says, taking another drink and wiping her mouth with the back of her hand like she saw me do. "So, how rich are you?"

"Medium-rich."

"How rich is that?"

"Private school rich, but not private jet rich."

"I'm going to be super rich."

"Okay, but just warning you, it's not that fun. I had super rich friends in New York, and I had it way better. I get everything I want and can do anything I want, but I don't have to have a bodyguard following me around."

"I want a bodyguard," she says, skipping along the sidewalk, her hair uncombed, her skinny ankles bare below too-short jeans.

"How about I'll be your bodyguard?" I offer.

"Really?" she asks, looking up at me suspiciously.

"Sure," I say, then give her a wink. "But just for today. I'm too rich to be a full-time bodyguard."

"How'd you get so rich, anyway?" she asks, jumping over another crack in the sidewalk.

SELENA

"My dad's the CEO and founder of Dolce Sweets. It's a candy business."

"You own a candy business?"

"Pretty much."

"So, you're basically like Willy Wonka."

"Sure," I say, laughing. "Or the Candyman."

"Wow." She slips her little hand into mine and clings on as she jumps over another line on the sidewalk. Her fingers are icy cold, and even though pretty much everyone thinks I'm the shit, I swear some fucking part of me dies that this scruffy little kid without a jacket thinks I'm so cool.

I'm actually disappointed when we get to Gloria's house. I'm not sure I've ever had fun hanging out with someone I couldn't fuck before. I'm pretty sure it says something about me, probably that I am a fucking weirdo, even if I know better than to ask a kid to sit on my lap.

Gloria seems as enamored with Olive as I am, and she takes her to the garage to poke around. I stand there for a minute finishing my beer, resenting Gloria and annoyed with Olive for being more interested in showing off that she can already check the engine oil than walking back home to see my Hummer.

But then I think of the fucking evil that infects everyone in my house, and I decide it would be shitty to take her back there and let it infect her, too. It's already in me. Whatever's wrong with me has taken root and won't let go. But it's not too late for her. So, I text Harper and tell her where to find Olive, and then I leave her under the hood of the Mustang with Gloria, and I walk home alone.

SELENA

thirty-five

Royal Dolce

I'm sitting on the balcony outside my room when the window slides open behind me. I don't turn. It's been ten days, but I'm still not ready for the conversation I know is coming. Each day we've avoided each other, finding reasons to stay busy and put it off. Right now, the house is too full of noise and chaos and people for private conversation, like its days of mourning are over and it's time to celebrate. Funny, since they're all here for the funeral.

"Help an old lady out, would you?" demands a grumpy voice from my room.

"Nonna," I say, jumping to my feet. I reach through the window and lift her out, squeezing my tiny grandmother until she lets out a few Italian curses. I laugh and set her down.

"Well, look at you," she says, patting my cheek, a mischievous grin making the corners of her eyes crinkle. "I hear you're in love. Can she cook?"

"Who the fuck said that?" I ask. "I don't know what that word means."

She laughs and flops down in one of my deck chairs, a chaise lounge looking out toward the burned rubble of Devlin's old house. "Make sure she can make the lasagna you like. I can give her your nonno's recipe. I pass it on to all my grandchildren when they get married."

"Did you give it to Crystal?" I ask sourly, taking the seat in the chaise beside hers.

"Of course I did," she says. "I have to make sure it's her kids' favorite, too."

"Harper's not really the cooking type," I mutter. "And we're not getting married."

She checks the windows behind us before pulling out her pack of cigarettes. "Give me a lighter, would you?"

"If you're smoking, I'm smoking," I say, pulling out the box where I keep my joints. I take one out, light up, and pass my grandmother the lighter.

SELENA

She lights one of her tiny Virginia Slims and lays back, closing her eyes while she inhales deeply and then exhales. "You know, your sister-in-law Eliza told me something her grandmother told her," she says after a sigh of satisfaction. "A woman can only be good in one room in the house. You pick the room."

"Nonna," I say slowly, dragging on the joint. "Do you know what TMI means?"

She laughs. "Your cousin told me that one last year. Apparently, young people don't appreciate the wisdom of their elders the way they once did."

"I really don't."

"Well, you know what a good cook your grandfather is," she says, puffing on her cigarette before giving me a wink. "That's not for nothing, so I think Eliza's right."

"Nonna," I groan. "I did not miss you."

"That's too bad," she says. "We thought we might stay through the holiday, since it's so close, and we're already down here."

"You too?" I ask. "King and Eliza are already staying a whole month."

"You should be grateful," she says. "Your brother knows what that word means that you don't. He could be giving up a big opportunity back home. A man in his position, you never know what can happen while you're gone for a month."

I grunt in response to that.

"It's not just for you," she says. "Your sister needs help with all those babies. A whole brood of them already."

"I noticed."

I hear footsteps further down the balcony, and I know she's out here, too. I can feel her, the way our blood is tied.

There's a pause, and then she pads toward us on bare feet. She's wearing a modest black dress I remember from before, even if it fits her differently. The first thing she said to me was that I was huge. She's not huge, but she's bigger, all her curves amplified and softened by motherhood. She looks out of place in the designer dress, like she no longer fits rich girl clothes after living in obscurity for three years.

SELENA

"Can I join?" she asks, her eyes guarded as she looks from me to our nonna.

"I'm just going in, in fact," Nonna says. "I'll leave you two to it."

"You can stay," I say. "I'll go in."

She struggles to sit up in the chaise, but when I reach out to help her, she slaps my hand away. "I haven't even gone grey yet," she scolds, hauling herself to her feet. "I'm certainly capable of getting out of a chair."

I hold up both hands in surrender, and she gives me one final, scathing look before climbing through my window and disappearing into the house.

I take a drag on my joint and stare at Crystal.

"You smoke pot?"

"Yeah," I say. "And you breed like a fucking rabbit. We're adults now. What about it?"

"Nothing," she says, smoothing her skirt under her as she sits, that ladylike gesture she probably got from Ma. It's funny how little things like that remain, even when she's so changed.

"I've been wanting to talk to you," she says, settling onto the edge of the seat, facing me.

I lounge back in my chair and cross my ankles. "About what?"

I've been an asshole so long I don't remember how to stop. It's who I am now. Maybe it always was.

She sits up straight and runs her hands along the tops of her thighs. "About moving out."

"What?" I ask, straightening.

"I have a family," she says. "We want a family home. I've got three kids. Diamond screams like a banshee half the time."

"It doesn't bother me," I grit out.

She shrugs, staring down at her knees. "This is your house. Devlin says you two made peace, but I know you feel this tension, too."

"Not because I don't want you here," I say quietly. "This is your house, too."

"Then why won't you even talk to me?" she asks, raising her dark gaze to mine. Her lashes are dark and thick even without makeup, her eyes like staring into a

SELENA

mirror. That's what we were, opposite images of each other. She was the good one, and somehow, she kept me good.

Until she didn't.

"There's been a lot going on," I say stiffly. "The funeral planning, the relatives arriving…"

There's been so much more than that, too. Talking to cops. Talking to the board of Dolce Sweets. Talking to lawyers and estate planners. Talking to Colin Finnegan, who admitted Baron convinced them to take him back here to get his car that night, took the six boxes of Lady Alice that we'd hauled out to Colin's vehicle, and took off into the night. Considering Baron's genius, he can make sure we never see him again if he wants, but at least he didn't make us think he died.

And I have a feeling he'll be back, at least for Duke. Not only that, but I have a pretty good idea that he won't go much further than the Mississippi River to the east.

"The relatives just started arriving yesterday," Crystal points out.

"King's been here since Thanksgiving."

"He's not a relative," she says, leveling me with a look. "He's our brother."

"Yeah," I say, busying myself with putting my paraphernalia away.

"What happened between you?" she asks.

"He convinced us to move on," I say. "Him and Dad. He said you were dead, that you were never coming back. I would have kept looking forever if not for him."

"He thought I was," she says, swallowing. "He was trying to help you. All of you. It's not like he was tricking you."

"You talked to him about it?"

"Yeah," she says. "I've talked to him and Duke both. I wished I'd gotten to talk to Daddy…"

"Well, he's dead," I say. "It was him or Devlin. He wouldn't have let him stay in his house like I have."

"See?" she says, her voice cracking. "You're the one who won't forgive me."

"Forgive you?" I ask, then shake my head. "You let us think you were dead, Crystal. Don't you get what that did to us? We searched for you for weeks. We gave up,

SELENA

accepted you were dead, and had a fucking funeral for you. We fucking *grieved* you. Do you know what that's like, to think your sibling, your twin, is fucking dead?"

"I know what it's like to grieve for a twin you lost," she says. "For a whole family. You think I didn't miss you, too?"

"Miss us?" I ask incredulously. "You think that's all it was? We avenged you, Crystal. We burned this town to the ground for you."

"And you think I didn't mourn for what I lost?" she asks, swiping angrily at a tear on her cheek. "You think it didn't kill me, too?"

"I think you're the one who made that choice," I say flatly. "We didn't."

"I didn't have a choice, either," she cries, tears streaking her cheeks now. "You and King and Daddy all said you'd kill Devlin."

"We'd never have hurt *you*."

She wipes both cheeks at once, her breaths hitching. "Killing Devlin would have hurt me. It would have killed me."

"Then what's the difference?"

"If you knew someone in this town was going to kill Harper, would you shrug it off and let it happen because she's not part of our family?" she asks. "Or would you take her across the world to protect her if you had to?"

I just stare at her.

Harper. Of course that's what it's like for Crystal. Harper isn't just mine to possess. She's a part of me, the replacement for my soul that was long ago destroyed. She may not know it, but she's already possessed me, owns every breath I take and every fucking murderous intent that arises when I think of someone touching her. I wouldn't just take her across the world. I'd set the world at her feet, bring her the fucking stars one by one.

"I'd kill them," I say quietly, remembering the body swinging at the bottom of the rope over the river and the one I dumped later, the night that redneck asshole came knocking on her door, thinking he'd take her as payment for her mom's addiction.

"Then how can you not understand?" she asks. "I'm sorry, Royal. It's not that I didn't think about you. I just couldn't let myself imagine what you were going through. It would have really killed me. So I had to think about what you said last, that I wasn't part of the family. I wasn't a Dolce anymore. And then we changed our names, and I told myself I was Devlin's family now, because if I wasn't yours, I didn't have to remember what I lost. But I never stopped being your sister, not even for a minute. So why are you acting like I'm a stranger?"

"I don't know," I admit. "Maybe we're both strangers."

"Don't say that," she cries, shaking her head. "I'm sorry for what I did, but I had to make an impossible choice. There was no right answer. They were both wrong. I could let you think I was dead, or I could let Devlin really be dead. How could I choose that?"

"You couldn't," I say. "And I'm sorry, too. I'm sorry I said that to you."

She sniffles and nods her head, wiping away the last of her tears. "I can't change what I did, but I hope you can understand what it's like to love someone so much you'd die to be with them."

"I do."

We stare at each other a long moment. "You love her, don't you?" she asks.

I don't know how to answer that. What I feel for Harper is so much more than that, more complex, deeper, and less trite. She knows me, and she still stays, even after I destroyed her. I didn't believe someone could care, could accept even the monster, but she proved me wrong until I had no choice but to believe. She has tamed even the monster inside me, so he no longer has to shoulder the burdens I couldn't carry alone. She helps me carry them now.

And I help her carry hers. Somehow, they're easier to bear than my own. I know her, too, know how to make her lose control when she needs it, even when it terrifies her. I accept all of her, even the ugly and conniving parts. I know who she is, and I don't separate the parts that don't serve me. Together, we're healing, stitching our brokenness together until scars cover the old wounds, sealing us together as one. I don't know how to describe that to my sister, a girl who knows love in such a pure and uncomplicated way. There's no simple four letter word that can begin to encompass all that Harper and I share.

"I tried to kill her," I say at last. "And she still brought you back. For me."

She nods. "She hates me, you know."

"She hates what you did to this town," I say. "She'll come around when you start making things right here."

"Will she?" Crystal asks, a shaky laugh escaping.

I shrug. "She wouldn't have found you if she didn't want you in my life."

She nods, raising her tear-stained face to meet my gaze, her eyes pleading. "Will you?"

"Eventually." I stare off at the skeletal lilac bushes between our lawn and the next.

"Please?" she says. "Just give me a chance. You wanted me to be alive, didn't you? And I am. I'm here, and I'm not dead. Don't act like I am."

"You were never dead to me, Crystal," I say. "Even when I believed you were dead."

"Then can we start over?" she asks, her dark eyes bloodshot but so full of hope it kills me to look at her.

I have to look away. "I don't think so," I say. "It doesn't work that way. But maybe we can start from here."

She nods, slipping off the edge of her chair and onto mine. "Thank you."

She lays her head on my chest and wraps her arms around me, scooting down beside me on the chair. For a second, I tense. But then I feel the forgotten shape of her against me, smell her same shampoo, and it's so familiar it aches down to the marrow in my bones. Her tears start again, dripping onto my shirt and soaking through to my skin. They burn into me like acid, like shame and sorrow, regret and relief.

Harper once said forgiveness was a process, and I agreed with what she said because it was more than I deserved, but I didn't really understand. I thought you could choose to forgive or not. But it's not that simple. It takes time, time to find the broken pieces and reassemble them, not into what was, but what is now.

SELENA

Even though Crystal and I have a long way to go to heal all that's broken between us, I don't add another fracture to our shattered family. We're already picking our way carefully over the wreckage just to reach each other. So I put an arm around her, and I let her stay. Pressing a hand to her back, I savor the solidness of her body, so heavy, yet so much lighter than her ghost. I close my eyes, take a deep breath, and feel her heart beating under my palm.

thirty-six

Harper Apple

"Damn," I say, slipping my hand into Royal's. "Is the entire town here?"

"Looks like it," he says, his lips tight. He doesn't pull his hand away like he used to, though. His fingers grip mine in a firm, possessive hold, and he pulls me into his side as we walk across the wet, brown grass of their enormous back lawn. They rented two hundred chairs, but there are at least twice that many people standing around the edges of the seating area, where every chair is filled.

I'm glad for the steady grip of Royal's arm as he leads me to my seat. It's not my imagination to think everyone's watching. They always do when Royal Dolce appears. And now that I'm on his arm, I'm in the spotlight, too. Not only that, but I know I'm being judged—by his family, his friends, this town. They're all weighing my appearance, my clothes, my expression, and deciding for themselves whether I'm good enough to grace his arm. And they're probably wondering if I'm here for the money.

I don't blame them. I'd be doing the same thing.

After all, I'm a girl like me, a girl from a trailer park, who landed a guy who just became the heir to a candy-and-drug empire. Apparently Alice wasn't the first illegal substance to pass through Dolce Sweets empire. I'm still coming to terms with how comfortable Royal is with that, with murder, with all the things that come with the territory for him and his world. It's not all champagne fountains and pillows made of money.

We make our way to our seat in the front row, with his family. A priest is standing on the grass in front of the small podium they have set up, looking somber and dignified and pretty fucking hot for a man of the cloth. Royal approaches and extends a hand.

"Father," he says, nodding to the man. "Thank you for being here."

"Of course," the priest says. "If there's anything else I can do…"

He pulls Royal in for a one-armed hug while clasping his other hand in a handshake.

"If you need the confessional," he murmurs to Royal, and I wonder how much this guy knows about the Dolce dealings. Does he know it was a murder, despite the police ruling it an accident?

Royal draws away and puts an arm around me. "Harper, this is Father Dante, from Thorncrown. Father, this is my girl, Harper Apple."

I know we're at a wake, but I have to fight the urge to smile like a fucking idiot or break into my I-just-won-tickets-on-the-radio dance. Somehow, being introduced to his priest feels more important than being introduced to his actual father ever did. So I school my face into something befitting a death in the family, and I shake hands with the priest before following Royal to our seats.

SELENA

Eliza pats my knee and smiles. "You look great in this," she says, gesturing to a black dress she helped me pick out in New York.

"You warm enough?" Royal asks, putting an arm around me. "This is going to take a while."

"I'm warm," I say, but I huddle into his side anyway.

The priest starts talking about Tony Dolce. I watch Royal, who's staring straight ahead with that hollow-eyed look. But I know now what it means, so I don't worry. He's not empty. His monster isn't the enemy. He's just protecting himself from whatever pain he feels, and the monster helps. If I feel guilty about my part in his father's death, I know it's so much worse for his own children.

An hour later, I understand what Royal meant. I've been to funerals, but never a Catholic one. There's standing and kneeling, prayers for the family, his parents, his children, and the community. Then people get up to take the podium and say nice things about Tony Dolce over his casket, which is thankfully closed, since he was basically incinerated. They're flying him back to New

York for the burial, but everyone in town wants to say goodbye first.

It seems like a bit of a farce, since we all know he was a sleazy scumbag. He's dead now, so you'd think they'd drop the charade, but then, it's the South. Someone's always watching. Judging. The spectacle must go on.

When it's finally over, there's still the visiting that has to happen, and everyone wants to come by and give their condolences to every member of the Dolce family. The wake is basically an all-day event. The Dolces have catered, so there's food, and everyone stands around talking. I spot the Roses and give DeShaun a wave. He jerks his chin in a little nod.

Royal's doing his zombie routine, greeting everyone and shaking their hands and accepting their sympathy with all the emotion of a robot. I know how exhausting he finds performing, but I also know he's traditional in a way, and he'd never skip the ceremony of it. It's his duty, and he'll stick it out to the bitter end.

SELENA

I break off during a lull and go to get us food. Colt and Gloria are standing with plates near the end of the line, so I step up behind them.

"I'm surprised you'd crawl out of your hole long enough to come to this," Gloria says to him, tossing her hair back.

"I'd make a joke about your hole, but seeing as how you just lost your sugar daddy, I'll be nice today," Colt says to her before turning to look me up and down. "Damn, Teeny."

"Yeah, why *are* you here?" I ask, glancing around. "Your families are enemies."

He throws an arm around my shoulders. "No, see, now that Devlin and Crystal came back and they're *married* and have kids and shit, the Dolces are part of the family. Like half the Darlings are here, pretending Royal and the demon twins didn't ruin our lives. It's nauseating, really."

Despite his words, he sounds cheerful, and he's smiling in that lazy way that makes it seem like he's just some dumb golden retriever and not someone who pays as much attention to his surroundings as Baron or Royal.

"Is Dixie here?" I ask, glancing around. I don't see her, but I do spot Magnolia and Gideon over near Cotton, Rylan, and Amber.

"She didn't come," Colt says. "But hey, I thought Lo was more your type. You know, if you ever need some meat in that sandwich…"

"We're at a funeral," I point out, glowering at him.

"True," he says. "But you said I could bring up the girl-on-girl stuff when Lo wasn't bawling about her slut status."

"Yeah, no more appropriate now than it was then."

"Too bad," he says, moving forward through the line. "But no, Dixie's not here. Not even to take a peek into the casket and make sure the vampire is really dead."

"I don't see why you're even with her," Gloria says. "She almost got your cousin murdered, and it's obvious to everyone that you're settling."

Colt laughs and shakes his head. "Should I shoot for a better girl… Maybe you?"

SELENA

"You wish," Gloria huffs, stepping forward to get food.

"Oh, right," Colt drawls. "You're no longer in the elite squad, which means you're no better than me. You got booted from the Dolce girl squad for being a slut, right? One too many notches on the ole bedpost, huh?"

"You're one to talk," she snaps. "You think you're so virtuous because you've only hooked up with one girl in the past three years, but everyone knows that's because it's all you can get. She's the only girl the Dolce boys don't want, so they let you have her. Pathetic much?"

"Now that you're in my league, I have more choices," he says. "And hey, next semester, you may be scum while I'm king. After all, there's only one D-bag at our school now, and if we're on good terms with the Dolces, Magnolia and Sullivan can come back to school. Which means the balance will finally be restored—the Darlings will be on top again."

"Like Willow Heights would ever let a troll sit on its throne," Gloria says. "You have to be hot and play football to be king."

"I don't know," Colt says. "My girl's already the rebel queen. Maybe the rebels will overthrow the whole monarchy, and I'll be their king. But don't worry, babe. I'd slum it with you a couple times."

"Gross," Gloria says, wrinkling her cute little nose and looking him up and down. "I'd never sink that low."

"When you change your mind," he drawls. "I'll throw you a pity fuck if you crawl for me the way you did for the Dolce boys, maybe eat Harper out while I hit it from the back."

"You're intolerable," Gloria huffs.

They continue bickering, but I stop listening and survey the crowd. Colt's right. The Darlings are here. And so are all the rest of the founding families, the mayor, and a judge I remember from some signs around town when he ran a few years back. I spot Colt's dad talking to Mr. Rose, and this sense of being off-balance settles over me, like everything is slightly askew.

I think we did it. We really ended the feud.

Mr. Dolce is gone, and the Darlings are now tied to the rest of the Dolces through Crystal and Devlin's marriage. Maybe Royal will never forgive the Darlings, but he'll forgive his sister. He'll move on, and that's all I can ask.

While I eat, I take out my phone and thumb it on.

Bad Apple: At Mr. Dolce's funeral. Think we might have fixed Faulkner.
SilverSwan: Good work, Miss A.
BadApple: u coming home? It's safe.
SilverSwan: soon

I'm busy getting a big head about what we've accomplished when my eyes spot movement over in the side yard. Olive is standing next to the lilacs, breaking off branches from the bare bushes. Preston's fresh in my mind, and his words come back to me.

"If I see a way I can help even one person, isn't it my job to at least try?"

He helped me, and it's time I pass it on. My chest tightens as I watch the diminutive figure—so alone and out of place, small and insignificant. I remember thinking that I didn't have space in my heart for an Olive. That was only a few months ago, but so much has changed. Now, I have an Olive. I have to make space for her in my life, whether I'm ready or not, because I'm all she has. I won't let her down, and I won't let Blue down after all she did for me.

Without me even noticing, Blue saved me in a hundred little ways. She didn't just give me cigarettes. She gave me a connection, companionship, a reminder of my roots. She let me be who I am, even when I didn't tell her. She was a safe space for me when I couldn't tell anyone else what had happened. She dragged me out of bed and told me I was too smart to drop out of school. When I doubted myself, she reminded me that I deserve a better life, to get out of this town, to accept Syracuse.

I'm only now coming to terms with the fact that it's real—I'm really getting out of here. I'm doing it. I'll be going to Syracuse next year. It's scary, but also a sense of ease and relief have come with the decision now that it's settled, the same way I felt when I accepted that I belong to Royal. I know I'll always have him, no matter where we go. I'll also have roots here.

If this is all Blue wants in return for helping me realize that, we're not nearly even.

I stand from the chair I took and cross the grass to her sister.

"Hey," I say. "Want some food?"

"Isn't it just for the rich people?" Olive asks.

"No," I say, holding out my plate. "Girls like us gotta eat, too."

She shakes her uncombed hair back and points to something on my plate. "What's that?"

"You know, I have no idea," I admit. "Rich people eat weird stuff."

She wrinkles her nose. "Does it taste good?"

"So good," I say, popping the little pastry into my mouth.

She takes one and nibbles at the edge of it. "Come on," I say. "We'll get you a plate. I've been meaning to get you and Eliza together to go shopping, too. Just the three of us. How about it?"

Olive looks doubtful. "What about Crystal?"

"Sure," I say. "She can come, too."

"And the babies?"

"They should probably stay with the nanny."

She follows me back toward the food line. "The mall is closed," she points out. "And I don't think these people would like Goodwill."

"We'll go to Little Rock. I said I'd take you for a ride in the Escalade, anyway," I remind her. "We can even take the girls to get burgers and eat at the quarry. I bet they've never been."

She's quiet, and I know exactly what she's thinking because no matter how good things are between the founding families, there's still the rest of us. Nothing's changed on our side of town. I might have left the trailer park, and Mill Street, and the life of poverty that trapped me here. Royal even gave me a credit card, and though I know it'll take me a long time before I stop feeling weird about using it, he promised he won't even monitor it. It's mine.

But everyone else is still here.

SELENA

Jolene is still in the trailer park. Zephyr's still on Mill Street with his alcoholic dad and his car up on blocks in the front yard. Maverick is still running with the Crosses because that's his only option. Blue is… I don't know where she is. Olive came to me with instructions that make it sound like she had a plan and wasn't murdered or taken off the street on her way home from school. She's going to Oregon to find their aunt, and then she'll be back for her sister. If keeping Olive safe is the only thing I can do for that side of Faulkner, I'm going to do the best damn babysitting job the world has ever known.

Because Blue may be gone, but Olive is still here, reminding me where I came from, that there are still girls like me. That I'm still a girl like me.

So I do what girls like us do, and I give her dignity, even if the price is a little white lie. It's what her sister and I always did, ignoring each other's bruises and never prying. I can honor her sister this way until she comes home. I know she wouldn't have asked me to watch Olive if she had anyone else, if she weren't desperate. She'd never leave Olive if she had a choice.

"Your sister left me some money," I say as we take two seats at the back of the sea of chairs. "So we could get you new clothes and stuff for school if you need it."

"How much?" Olive asks, looking at me suspiciously.

"A hundred dollars."

"Really?" Olive asks, her eyes going wide.

"Yep," I say, my chest squeezing.

"And she said she'd send more when she could."

"When did she say that?"

"She texted a while ago," I say.

"Where is she?"

"She didn't say," I tell her. "But she said she loves you, and she's coming back as soon as she can."

"I know," Olive says, biting into a shrimp and swinging her legs back and forth under the chair.

"Good," I say. "Then we'll go shopping over Christmas, and you can go back to school with new clothes."

"Is there enough for shoes, too?"

SELENA

"Definitely," I say, smiling sideways at her and nudging her shoulder. "And if there's not, we can always steal a little from these rich people."

She grins bigger than I've seen since I found her at Gloria's. "I won't tell," she whispers.

I spend the rest of the day trying to stay out of the way of the mourners, watch over Olive, and be there for Royal when I think he needs it. It's not exactly a big happy family I imagined, but Royal's relatives seem okay with me, and I'm even warming up to his sister a little. It's better than sitting around a dinner table with Mr. Dolce, my mother, and Baron, that's for damn sure. Maybe the happy family thing takes time and looks different than any of us expected, but I know it'll happen when the time is right. And if it doesn't, I still have the family I made—my friends, me, and Royal.

It's evening before everyone clears out, and by then, I'm ready to be out of the spotlight. Even when I'm not by Royal's side, I notice the attention I garner everywhere I go. I guess that's the price of landing the most coveted man in town.

When the place is mostly empty, I start to pick up plates. I've barely started when an arm snakes around me from behind. "What are you doing?" Royal asks, rubbing his chin against the top of my head.

"Party's over," I say.

"You're not the help."

"It's just a few plates."

He takes my hand and raises it over my head, turning me to face him and pulling my arm around his neck. His other hand rests on the small of my back, pulling my body flush against his. "They can take care of it," he says, bending to rest his forehead on mine. "Your job is to take care of me."

"Is that right?" I ask, smiling up at him.

"Damn right," he says. "Now, Cherry Pie, you want to show me how good you serve me?"

"Right now?" I ask, running my finger down the center line between the ridges of his abs and hooking it into his belt.

"Right now," he says.

SELENA

I start to sink to the ground, but he grabs me under the arms and hauls me up.

"You said right now," I say, batting my lashes at him.

He growls and grabs my hand, dragging me across the grass to the back door. He doesn't let go as we pass his father's office, which is now his office, and hurry up the stairs. Inside his room, he kicks the door closed and spins around, pinning me against the wall. The room is dark, and I can only make out the shape of him as he pushes his thigh between my legs, holding me in place. He spits into his palm before shoving his hand roughly up my dress.

His fingers are icy cold but slick as he pulls my underwear aside and slides them between my lips.

"Fuck," he groans. "You're so hot."

"You're fucking freezing," I say, my knees squeezing together.

"Shut up and open for me," he growls, grabbing my underwear and ripping them off my body. He tosses them and slides his hand between my thighs again, his long, wet fingers finding my entrance and sinking into me. I gasp with shock at the cold, and he grabs my hair and yanks my head back. "Your mouth, too."

"Fuck, I hate when you do that," I protest.

"Open your fucking mouth, my little slut," he says, pumping his icy fingers into my hot core until I'm trembling all over. "Or I'll open it for you."

I force my lips open, waiting with a mixture of revulsion and anticipation as he works his jaw back and forth, working up enough spit to lean forward and let it fall into my mouth in a wet blob. I almost gag, but he groans and rewards me by decreasing his pace, his thumb stroking expertly across my clit as his fingers move in slow circles inside me, hitting every wall and making my thighs quake helplessly.

"My little whore," he purrs against my lips. "You got so wet when I did that, it feels like I spit in your cunt instead of your mouth."

"I still hate it," I manage.

"But your cunt loves it," he says, sliding his fingers out and pushing them against my mouth. They're wet and smell like me, and a pulse of heat goes straight to my core. "Taste it."

I clamp my lips closed, and he chuckles and slides his fingers back and forth, coating my lips with my own wetness. He wrenches my head back, and I cry out in shock, my body bucking against his. He slides his fingers into my mouth before I can close it, pushing them so far back I gag, tears blurring my eyes from that and the stinging in my scalp.

"Suck on them," he demands.

I'm choking too hard to answer, and he pulls them back enough to let me take a couple breaths, pressing his fingers down on my tongue. I catch my breath and then close my lips, sucking on his fingers with tears trickling from the corners of my eyes.

He leans down to run his tongue along my temple, where my tears are dripping down, since my head is still pulled all the way back. Then he straightens and smiles down at me, sliding his fingers out. "That wasn't so hard, was it?"

"I fucking hate you," I snap.

"Your cunt says otherwise," he taunts, reaching down to unbuckle his belt. "But since your head needs a reminder of how much you fucking love me…"

He picks me up and slams me down onto him. His bare cock drives to the hilt inside my slick cunt, filling me so deep I think I'll faint from pain. The shock knocks the breath out of me, and I can't even protest as he lifts me and brings my hips down on his again, impaling me with every inch of his brutal length.

"Tell me how you really feel, Cherry Pie," he growls.

"I fucking hate you, and I'll hate you forever," I growl back, finally finding my voice past the pain of his roughness. "Until the day you die."

"You're a fucking liar."

"What are you going to do about it?"

"I'll tell you what I'm going to do," he says, turning and striding to the bed, still buried painfully deep inside me. He drops me on my back and then plows onto me, pinning me and driving his slick cock deep inside me again, forcing my clenched walls to stretch around him. "I'm going to fuck you so hard your soul leaves your body, and then I'm going to fill it with my cum. Then I'll ask you again, and you won't be able to remember your own name, let alone that you hate me."

"Oh, I'll remember."

"Challenge accepted," he says, driving into me so hard the blankets slide up the bed with me. "Now tell me which one is lying, your mouth or your cunt, or I'll give them both a reason to hate me."

"Neither is lying," I say, wrapping my legs around him and letting my head fall back, letting him pleasure me and punish me at the same time, knowing it's what he needs, and more than that, what I need. I don't need to cut myself to feel anymore. If I need pain, Royal gives it to me, and more than that. He fills me with his darkness, and I don't try to make it light any more than I try to make him gentle. I love him, all of him. The monster and the man, the darkness that dances with mine, the brokenness that cradles mine with perfect acceptance.

"Take all of it, my pretty little slut," he croons, gripping my chin and pumping into me so deep I can't help the cries that tear from my lips. When tears spring to my eyes, he doesn't slow. He slams into me even harder, fucking me so roughly I think I'll sob for mercy if he doesn't stop, and I'll scream with fury if he does. At last, he pushes up on his hands and grinds into me so deep that new tears pour from my eyes, and my walls clench around him in agony. He curses and reaches down, pinching my clit and making me cry out.

"Cum on my cock like my dirty plaything," he commands, rolling my clit between his thumb and finger.

I can't hold back. My cunt grips onto his shaft inside me, rhythmic waves of pleasure crashing over me as I cum, gasping his name helplessly. His cock throbs inside me, and then his own release spills into me, filling me with warmth and bliss until nothing else exists but us, and this, and the momentary sating of the need only we can fill in each other.

Afterwards, he lowers himself onto me, and I hold onto him, our hearts beating together, our sweat mingling on our damp skin. All I can think about is that this is it for me, he's it. He's my sun, my savior, my destruction. And I am his.

SELENA

He leans down, his lips brushing softly over mine. "I hate you too, Harper Apple," he whispers, stroking my hair back and kissing each of my eyelids with agonizing tenderness after the brutal pounding he just delivered. "Forever."

BLOOD EMPIRE

SELENA

The Ties That Bind

A father's love
Dropped like breadcrumbs
One for each time you obey
Never enough to fill the hunger
But enough to keep you following the trail.
A mother's love

> *Doled out with teaspoons*
> *One for each correct answer*
> *But retracted at the first error,*
> *The first perceived slight.*

A brother's love
Laid out before you like a meal
That you fail to notice is an illusion
Until they laugh as your fingers pass through
And you're left empty-handed.

> *A sister's love*
> *Dangled before you like the sweetest dessert*
> *But after a single bite*
> *You notice the strings*
> *That take it all away.*

A lover's love
When it finally appears
Is too dangerous to be trusted,
As foreign as a feast
Where every taste is toxic.
And if it's real
How could you be worthy of so much
When you've lived in starvation so long
And been told you have it all?

author's note:

This concludes Royal & Harper's story. There will not be more books about them. However, they will make appearances in future books set in this world, so keep a lookout for Easter eggs!

In addition, you can vote for additional short stories about them when you join my Patreon.
https://www.patreon.com/selenaauthor
When you become a *Midnight Swans* patron, you'll receive short stories and other goodies, from early access to audio files, signed paperbacks and hardbacks, bonus chapters, and swag.

If you have questions about any of the side characters, don't worry! You can find all the answers in their own books/series.

SELENA

Upcoming releases:

Preston Darling's story is a stand-alone coming this spring.

Preorder today:

http://books2read.com/deviantdeception

Baron & Duke's duet is coming soon as well. I do not have a release date yet, but I suggest joining my newsletter for updates:

https://landing.mailerlite.com/webforms/landing/q5z4y6

Completed stories:

Crystal & Devlin's story is a complete trilogy that starts here: http://books2read.com/bullyme

King & Eliza's story is a stand-alone that can be found here: http://books2read.com/mafiaprincess

Keep reading for a bonus epilogue from Preston, the next character to get a book in the Willow Heights world!

bonus epilogue

Preston Darling

As I sit in a gridlock of traffic, my impatience grows. I've already lost so much time. I let her go two and a half years ago, and once again after that. This time, my resolve is strong. I won't let her go.

It doesn't matter what she wants. She'll see it's the right thing once it's done.

I've realized a lot since she came home for Christmas, since she wanted to hang out like we were together and then disappear like it never happened, like I could move on from that.

I learned to spot the difference between love and doing what she said and trying to move on. I learned how to get the girl, what you'll do if you really love her, and it isn't letting her go.

Harper reminded me what love is—and what it's not.

No matter how many things I tried, no matter what I did to try to forget Dolly, to make Harper into someone I

SELENA

could love instead, it was never enough. Even when I fucked her without a condom to try to force intimacy, even though I cared about her in whatever fucked up way I'm able, she could never be Dolly.

The most she could be was Crystal for a few minutes while I came inside her. And even that wore off when I got to know her better than I ever knew Crystal. Crystal was a fantasy, a regret. Harper is real.

Real enough to teach me what it takes to win in this game. What love can overcome. What it's worth.

Not because she loved me, but because she loved Royal. And hell, even that asshole taught me a thing or two. She told me on the way to California all he did to get her back. I still think she's fucking crazy to forgive him, but I can't help having a grudging respect for him now that I know the lengths he went to for her.

I should have done the same for Dolly all along. I shouldn't have believed her, shouldn't have believed that bullshit about loving someone enough to let them go.

Fuck that.

Royal didn't let Harper go, and she never let him go. They fought for each other.

I'm going to fight for Dolly just as hard and even harder. I'm going to fight everyone including her, until she admits I am it for her. I'm endgame. I don't care if the beast is supposed to hide away in his castle waiting for his beauty to come stumbling in. This is not that story, and this beast is done sitting around waiting. This beast is coming for his beauty.

Now that I know what it takes, I realize the mistake I've made. It's not too late, even if *Your Celebrity Eyes* and the other bullshit tabloid content says she's been seen out with whatever famous person. She's not married.

But she will be. Once I get her, I'm not letting go.

I replay the conversation I had with Devlin before they left, when we talked about him disappearing. We left the girls and took the boys on a little trip to the beach.

"You knew I was alive all that time?" he asked as we walked along the shoreline.

"Not at first," I admitted. "You said goodbye to us, though. I thought you had something planned. And

Crystal sent that letter, which came out pretty soon after you left. When they found your car…" I switched the baby to my other arm. "At first I thought maybe suicide."

"You should've known better than that," he said, setting Knight down. It was funny, the way they named their kids like the Dolces, but also that he named his first son after our school mascot. I wondered whose idea that had been.

"It didn't seem right," I said. "But you'd lost your mind over Crystal. I wasn't sure what you'd do. But then when we found out you'd taken money out of your trust…"

"How'd you keep the Dolces from coming after us?" he asked.

I shrugged. "Just paid off anyone who was making a stink about you being alive."

"You weren't pissed?" he asked, squinting into the sun reflecting off the water to keep his son in his sights.

"Sometimes," I admitted. "But never pissed enough to put you in danger by contacting you. Those bastards are completely insane. You never know what they're tracking, when they're listening."

It was hard to explain to someone who wasn't there. I must've sounded like the crazy one to him. But he hadn't experienced it, and I wasn't sorry about that.

"I would have been pissed," he said, watching Knight standing at the water's edge, looking out for a wave. "If you were the reason they were coming after our family, I would have been pissed at you."

"There were easier people to blame," I said. "I was glad at least one Darling got out unscathed."

"I wouldn't have just left you to fight them alone if not for the baby," he said. "But all I'd have gotten if I stayed was killed. That wouldn't have helped anyone."

"No," I agreed. "You got out when you could. You had another family to think about—your own family."

"Yeah," he said, watching as Knight ran from a wave in that waddling way toddlers do, with his short little legs pumping as he crossed the sand.

I imagined what it would be like to have a kid relying on me, a helpless baby to protect as well as the woman I loved. I'd imagined myself in his shoes a thousand times—out of Faulkner, starting a new life where no one knew me, with Crystal Dolce on her knees for me every night. But now, it wasn't Crystal in my mind, her body laid out before me like a buffet, her glorious tits mine for the taking.

It was Dolly.

If I'd gotten her pregnant, our families would have lost their minds. And I'd have done the same as Devlin in a heartbeat. I couldn't be mad about it now.

"Do you think it would have been different?" I asked. "If you hadn't gotten her pregnant?"

"Probably," he admitted, taking Prince from me when he started fussing. "Everything changed the moment she had my kid inside her. That was what mattered—that baby, and even more than him, the woman carrying him. I can't explain it, man. It does something to you. You'll see when it happens to you."

Devlin propped Prince up on his shoulder, as natural with the kid as if he'd been doing it all his life. Two and a half years of being a dad, and he was a pro. He wasn't just older than me, he was a fucking adult. Married with three kids, a job, a wife. He'd given up Dolly for this. He'd given up Faulkner, too, and all the other Darlings, our entire family.

But Crystal gave it up, too. If she hadn't had a baby to think about, maybe her psychotic family would have convinced her to leave Devlin alone. If they couldn't convince her, they would have convinced him. They would have told him they'd hurt her, or even one of us, and he'd have left her alone. When a baby was in the picture, though…

Like he said, a baby changed everything.

In his mind and in hers. She'd left her whole life for him, too. She didn't worry about chasing her dreams or what she'd wanted before. Everything changed.

Everything has changed for me, too.

And now, it's going to change for Dolly.

She just doesn't know it yet.

And by the time she does, it'll be too late for her to walk away again.

SELENA

acknowledgements

Thank you so much to everyone who helped make this book possible! Special thanks to my patrons, who help keep me writing. Big shout-out and a thousand handfuls of heart-shaped confetti to Rowena, Joyce, Michelle, Heather, DesiRae, Shawna, Chelsea, Marisa, Jaclyn, Nicole, Terra, Ashley, Christina, Elizabeth, Kandace, Mindy, Tina, Shirley, April, Adriana, Iyesha, Lena, Audriana, Tatiana, Nicki, Janice, Tessa, Melanie, Nikki, Jennifer, Jessica, Brooke, Emily, Emma, Annalisse, Jennifer S, Alysia, Megan, Margaret, Tami, Crystal, Kelli, April H, Nikki T, Kat, Anne, Tasha, Melissa, Jennifer M, JG, Doe, Jasmine, Makayla, Rebecca, Carmen, Emma P, Amy H, and Lucy.

I cannot thank y'all enough for your support!

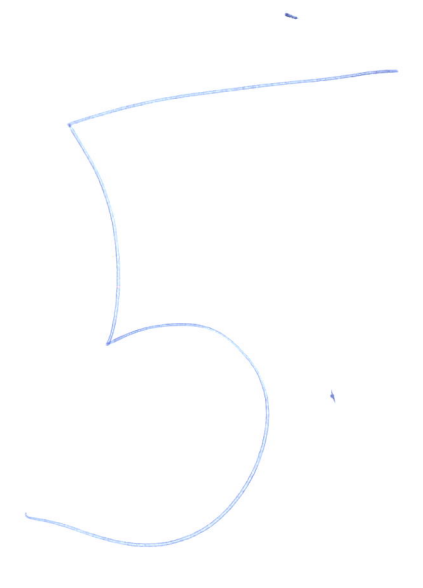

Printed in Great Britain
by Amazon